Ilsa Evans lives in a partially renovated house in the Dandenongs, east of Melbourne. She shares her home with her three children, two dogs, several fish, a multitude of sea-monkeys and a psychotic cat.

She is currently completing a PhD at Monash University on the long-term effects of domestic violence and writes fiction on the weekends. *Odd Socks* is her third novel.

www.ilsaevans.com

*Also by Ilsa Evans*

Spin Cycle
Drip Dry

# Odd Socks

## ILSA EVANS

MACMILLAN

Pan Macmillan Australia

*To my father,*
*Maurice Vivian Evans*
*(1927–1988)*
*I wish I could have told you . . .*

First published 2005 in Macmillan by Pan Macmillan Australia Pty Limited
St Martins Tower, 31 Market Street, Sydney

Reprinted 2005

National Library of Australia
cataloguing-in-publication data:

Evans, Ilsa.
Odd socks.

ISBN 1 40503646 X.

I. Title.

A823.4

Typeset in 13/16 pt Bembo by Post Pre-press Group
Printed in Australia by McPherson's Printing Group

The characters and events in this book are fictitious and any resemblance
to real persons, living or dead, is purely coincidental.

Papers used by Pan Macmillan Australia Pty Ltd are natural, recyclable products
made from wood grown in sustainable forests. The manufacturing processes
conform to the environmental regulations of the country of origin.

# Despite the efforts of the following:

Lately I have come to realise that books are written not so much *because* of the efforts of many, but *despite* the efforts of many. Therefore, here is my list of those people/animals/ inanimate objects despite whom this book was still written.

This book was written despite the fact that children expect three meals a day, preferably served in a brightly coloured box or wrapped in butcher paper. And despite the tendency of children to get sick every time you have (a) given them too many meals in brightly coloured boxes or wrapped in butcher paper; (b) a deadline; and/or (c) a particularly important meeting you were keen to attend without vomit on your lapel and a feverish child in tow.

This book was written despite the fact that all three of my particular offspring insist on using my computer despite ample evidence it loathes them. Thus, whenever I have carelessly left work up that hasn't yet been saved, the house echoes with phrases such as 'But I was *only* looking!'

This book was written despite the fact that these children, although very lovable, are all a tad faulty and therefore require regular visits to optometrists, speech therapists, podiatrists, dentists, ear, nose and throat guys, etc. And don't let's forget the mandatory activities! Tennis, karate, saxophone, swimming, pottery, chess . . .

This book was written despite phone calls from people I don't even know selling me things I don't even want and refusing to understand this is an invasion of privacy (you're all going on a list of companies I will never use!). And despite phone calls from people I *do* know, who, apart from all evidence to the contrary, remain convinced that I enjoy a chat.

This book was written despite bloody housework – and the bills to pay, washers to replace, walls to paint, bulbs to either change or plant (depending on the bulb) – and the myriad other incidentals that fill our days.

This book was written despite my inability to set mousetraps without endangering a digit or two, and the Band-Aids that make it very difficult to type efficiently.

This book was written despite ex-husbands. Full stop.

This book was written despite the fact that we own the stupidest dog in the world, who firmly believes that peeing on my bed is an expression of love. And despite the fact that we also have a cat against whom we should apply for an apprehended violence order. And despite the fact that some entrepreneurial possums have established a singles bar in the roof and it appears to be a thumping success.

This book was written despite the ongoing battle for 'me' time, and all the things, like tennis, champagne, good books, friends, family and the occasional convivial lunch, which lure me away from what I *should* be doing.

Despite you all, because of you all, about you all – here is the book.

# MONDAY

# MONDAY

## 0345 hrs

Rafter's serve comes whistling across at a severe angle into the forehand court, and I've got to perform a desperate lunge to reach it. Then, because I've been driven so far out, the most logical place to hit it seems to be past that Minogue female at the net. So I execute a *perfect* sideline that screams down the tramlines and raises chalk when it lands. She shuffles her feet and looks embarrassed. But stuff sportsmanship, that little blonde had it coming – I call it *really* bad cricket to try to distract your opposition by not wearing knickers.

'Game over,' announces the umpire solemnly. 'Newcombe and Diamond lead five games to love. Diamond to serve.'

'Fan-bloody-*tastick*, Terry!' Newk comes trotting over and slaps my raised hand with a grin. 'Sheer brilliance!'

I smile happily back while the cheering in the crowd turns into a methodical chant of my name: Terry, Terry, Terry. As the ball-boy bounces a couple towards me for my serve, the chanting gradually dies off – except for one persistent female fan, who is not so much chanting as *screaming* my name. Her noise

3

makes it impossible to concentrate, so I practise my serving motion and take a few seconds to admire Newk's posterior as he bends over at the net. Not too shabby at *all*. The umpire sternly asks for silence in the stands, but it makes no difference. Instead the incessant screeching just gets louder. And louder.

I sit up in bed with a jerk – or rather, I sit up rapidly but by myself as I've been divorced for years. Newk's butt recedes as I fight my way out of the cotton wool of sleep with just the piercing shrieks accompanying me every step of the way. And then I'm out, staring around my bedroom groggily while I try to remember where I am, when I am – and what the hell is making all that racket.

My first clue is the realisation that it is not my actual name being screamed, just 'Mum, *Mum*, **Muuum**!' over and over from downstairs. Which rules out the chances of it being a persistent fan who has followed me back from the land of Nod. And, as I'll bet very few burglars accompany their nefarious exploits with loud pleas for their maternal parent, it only leaves one candidate: my twenty-one year old daughter, Bronte. Who just happens to be eight and a half months pregnant.

'*Mum – help,* **help!!!**'

A sudden surge of panic catapults me out of bed and I gasp as the icy chill of the mid-July night slaps me vigorously, causing goose bumps to break out across the length and breadth of my naked body. As my breath puffs out into plumes of mist that hover in the air before me, I hurriedly pull on my white candlewick dressing-gown and look around for my slippers.

'*Mum, Mum, Mum, Muuuum!*'

'I'm coming!' I yell, forgetting about the slippers as I tie my dressing-gown cord securely and race out of the bedroom to attack the spiral staircase two steps at a time. 'I'm coming!'

Just past halfway down I realise light is flooding out from the lounge-room, so I hike up my dressing-gown and take the last four steps in a single jump before sprinting in that direction. As I approach, the screaming suddenly stops and is replaced by a low keening noise, almost primeval in intensity, that sends a frisson of fear vibrating up my spine. Then, arriving at the doorway out of breath, I take in the scene before me with one incredulous glance.

Because there, on my pale moss-coloured, low-pile lounge-room carpet and lying flat on her back, is my one and only daughter. Which is probably how she got *into* this mess in the first place, but that's neither here nor there at the moment. Especially since it looks suspiciously like the culmination might be in process. Dressed in a pastel pink and blue maternity tracksuit, her knees are bent and she is staring straight at the ceiling with her hands clasped across her very pregnant belly. The droning, guttural hum she is emitting ceases when she registers that I've arrived in the doorway and, raising her head, she looks at me out of puffy, reddened eyes while holding out one hand in a pleading gesture.

'Mum, *Mum*!' Bronte starts to cry piteously. 'Mum – oh god, oh *god.*'

'Bronte!' I break out of my trance and move rapidly across the lounge-room towards her, squatting to take her outstretched hand and holding it tight. 'Bronte! What's going on? And what on earth are you doing *here*?'

'I thought . . . I just thought I'd –' Bronte's face suddenly goes pale and her mouth opens in a stretched, silent scream as her back arches and her body grows tense. I grasp her hand firmly to show support but she immediately grips it back with such unbelievable tightness that it cuts off my blood supply. My face goes pale too.

After a minute or two, Bronte's body begins to relax a little.

At the same time, her mouth closes slightly and she begins to pant shallowly and rapidly. I wrest my hand away and shake it to get some circulation back.

'Bronte, we need to get you to the hospital,' I say, chewing my lip with concern – for her, for the baby, and for my pale moss-coloured, low-pile carpet.

'No, no. I can't go,' pants Bronte rhythmically as she claws at my arm, trying to regain my hand. 'And it's too late, anyway. And I can't get hold of Nick – I've tried and tried. And it's coming, Mum – it's coming *now*.'

'All the more reason to get in the car quickly. Come on!'

'Mum, it hurts – it *really* hurts,' Bronte sobs as she wipes her nose with one pastel-pink tracksuit sleeve. 'Make it *stop*!'

'They'll make it stop in the hospital.' I try to help her up but she resists with a considerable amount of strength for someone in the midst of labour. 'Come *on*, Bronte!'

'No! I just want it to stop! And I want Nick!'

'They'll give you nice drugs in hospital, you know.' I stop tugging her and try a little gentle persuasion. 'And the nice drugs'll be much better than Nick.'

Instead of answering, Bronte stiffens as yet another contraction begins to rack her body. And this time there's nothing silent about it as she lets out a wail that sends sharp chills through me. I lean forwards and hold her shoulders securely because I really don't know what else to do. As the contraction reaches its climax, she sits bolt upright and stares rigidly ahead whilst her breath whistles through her clenched teeth. Then the whistling gradually turns to panting as the pain starts to recede and she collapses back onto the floor, crying again.

'Come on now, Bronte.' I let go of her shoulders and, slipping my hands under her arms, try to pull her up off the floor. 'Come on, we have to get to the car!'

'Leave me alone!'

'Come *on*!' I give up trying to lift her and instead start dragging her backwards, an inch at a time. 'A tad of cooperation wouldn't go astray, you know!'

'I said leave me *alone*,' Bronte shrieks as she digs her heels in, 'or I'll have it in your freaking car!'

'What?' I let go of her quickly. 'You'll what?'

'Have it in your freaking car!' she repeats hysterically as she wraps her arms around her lower abdomen and groans. 'And I've changed my mind, anyway – I don't *want* to do this anymore! At all!'

'I'm calling an ambulance.' I get up without making even one sarcastic crack about how it's a bit late for regrets now, which just goes to show how worried I am. She can't possibly have the baby here – I don't know the first thing about what to do or how to do it. Because it's not like I was paying attention when Bronte herself was born – all I remember, between heady injections of potent painkillers, are my attempts to rally the medical staff with a rousing rendition of 'She'll be coming round the mountain when she comes'. And I can't even remember the words now. I pat Bronte on the shoulder reassuringly and head over to the phone by the armchair.

'Mum! Don't *leave* me!'

'I'm not. I'm ringing an ambulance,' I reply soothingly. Now that I'm taking decisive action and feel a little more in control, I realise how cold it is down here. I also register that for some time my bare toes have been sending regular little distress signals that have been washed away by the adrenalin. Accordingly, I lean across, flick the central heating thermostat to full, and then flop down next to the phone and try to cover my feet with my dressing-gown hem. I pick up the receiver and the doorbell rings. For a second I stare at the phone in astonishment because it's never made *that* sound before, and then the doorbell rings again and I grasp the fact there's actually somebody at the door. At four o'clock in the morning.

I put the phone down and hurry over to the front door instead, glancing quickly at Bronte, who appears to be mid-contraction again. While I try unsuccessfully to smooth my hair, I send up a brief prayer that it's someone useful. Like perhaps one of those multiskilled male doctors from *All Saints*, who are apparently capable of performing everything from a facelift to brain surgery. One measly baby would be chicken-feed. He'd probably deliver it with one hand while the two of us sit on the couch, having a glass of wine and a convivial little chat. After I do my hair, that is.

But it's not one of the good doctors and, in fact, it's not even close. It's my plumpish, thirty-something neighbour, Stephen, dressed in a pair of black satin pyjamas with black fluffy scuffs on his feet and a fluorescent green beanie on his head.

'*Teresa!*' Stephen grasps my hand, his normally ruddy complexion pale with concern. 'Are you okay, schnooks? I heard screaming! What on *earth* is happening?'

If the situation wasn't already so fraught, and if Bronte hadn't chosen that moment to begin crying again, I probably would have burst out laughing. Because, of all the people I know, Stephen is almost certainly the most useless in the current circumstances. Apart from the fact his intimate knowledge of females is non-existent, he's the first to admit that even ads for sanitary napkins make him feel faint. But beggars can't be choosers, so I reach out, grab his arm and drag him across the threshold, shutting the door firmly to cut off any escape route.

'I *need* you.' I lead him towards the lounge-room. 'Bronte's having the baby and you'll have to hold her hand while I ring an ambulance.'

'What!' Stephen grabs the doorframe with both hands, plants his fluffy feet firmly and starts shaking his head as soon as he spots Bronte lying on her back next to the couch. 'Oh, no. Oh, no. Anything but *that* – because I can't. I just can't!'

'Well, you have to.'

'Where's the father then?' Stephen looks at me accusingly, as if I've just buried him under the hydrangeas. Which, tempted as I have been over the past eight months, I haven't. It'd be far too messy.

'Don't know and don't much care.' I leave him in the doorway and head back to the phone, calling over my shoulder, 'Come on, Stephen, you don't need to deliver it! Just hold her bloody hand.'

'Mum!' Bronte hefts herself up onto one elbow and fastens me with a glittering eye. 'I want this to *stop* – NOW!'

'I *really* need you.' I look at him beseechingly as I pick up the receiver. 'Please?'

'Oh . . . all right! All right!' Stephen grimaces at me and then lets go of the doorframe and, flexing his fingers as if he is about to perform surgery, advances across the room towards Bronte. 'Now then –'

'Piss off!'

'Well! No need for language, love,' Stephen replies as he touches her shoulder gingerly with a fingertip. 'I know! What about an aspirin? *That* should help things.'

'I don't *want* a freaking aspirin!'

'How about two?'

I try to tune them out while I dial 000 – and get an engaged tone. I sit for a minute, tapping my fingers on the phone and staring at Bronte, who is clasping her stomach and groaning loudly while watching me over her shoulder. After taking his beanie off for a moment and running his fingers agitatedly through his dark hair, Stephen is now squatting down by Bronte's side and ineffectually patting her while pulling weird faces at me. I think he's trying to convey that he is out of his depth. But tough luck, so am I. I try 000 again and this time I get put straight through to a rather nasal female operator who asks me brusquely whether I want police, fire brigade or ambulance. I request the latter, give her my details, describe the situation and hang up. By this time, Bronte is in the midst of yet another contraction and Stephen has turned an ivory colour that looks positively sickly under his fluorescent beanie. I hurry back over to them just as the spasm starts to leave Bronte's body and she flops back, quivering.

'Are you all right?' I ask inanely as I kneel down next to her and grab her hand. 'Can I get you anything?'

'Just air,' says Stephen, standing up and putting his hand delicately to his forehead. 'I need some air.'

'Not you, dork! *Her!*'

'Towels!' states Stephen as he clicks his fingers emphatically. 'Towels! Hot water! That's what we need!'

'What for?' I query, mainly because I've always wanted to know.

'For – um, well . . .' His face falls. 'I'm not quite sure.'

'Exactly.' I turn back to Bronte. 'The ambulance'll be here soon. Just hang on.'

'I can't,' she wails, 'I just *can't!*'

'I know!' Stephen says happily. 'The hot water is for a cup of tea! *That's* what we all need – a nice, relaxing cup of tea!'

'Do you know what you can do with your freaking tea?' gasps Bronte, staring at Stephen with a look straight out of *The Twilight Zone*. 'You can –'

'And what are the towels for then, Einstein?' I interrupt quickly. 'A soothing facial, perhaps?'

'No! A *bath*. The towels are for a bath. We need to get her in a bath!'

'Actually,' I say, looking at my pristine carpet thoughtfully, 'perhaps we *could* move her somewhere more comfy till the ambulance arrives. What about it, Bronte?'

'I'm *not* moving,' pants Bronte in agitation. 'Mum – try Nick again! Please!'

'Okay then.' I squeeze her hand soothingly. 'I'll try him in a minute. But first I'll get those towels and pop them under you.'

'*That's* what they're for!' Stephen exclaims with a grin of relief. 'Of *course*!'

'Mum – god! God! God!' Bronte grabs my hand again and arches herself forwards in pain. 'GOODD!'

'Bronte, hang on. You're doing great, just hang in there.'

'Mum! Get it OUT! Get it *OUT*!'

'The ambulance will be here soon,' I say with a confidence I'm far from feeling, 'and then they'll get it out for you. And now I'll just grab those towels. Stephen, you're in charge.'

'Okay.' Stephen takes a deep breath, pushes his shoulders back and squats next to Bronte again. 'I know! You need to *breathe*, schnooks, just breathe. That's it.'

I leave the room as Schnooks replies with a few well-chosen obscenities. But by the time I return with an armful of towels, Stephen has her breathing rhythmically and relatively calmly. I'm impressed. I dump the towels on the floor and sit myself down near Bronte's head, taking hold of her hand again and stroking her forehead. It's starting to warm up down here, and my toes are feeling less like miniature Popsicles. We sit like that for a few minutes, in relative peace, until the next contraction hits. And this one's a doozy. Stephen and I look at each other in concern as Bronte's entire body goes stiff and, with her shoulders straining back, she leans forwards and emits a long, low grunt of pain.

'Remember to breathe, love!' Stephen urges as he pats her left leg. 'Just breathe!'

'But it's *coming* – NOW! It is, it is!' Bronte puffs rapidly and then, as the apex of pain passes, she clutches my dressing-gown sleeve frantically. 'It really is! Have a look – have a look!'

'Really?' I say doubtfully as I glance down at her tracksuit-encased legs. 'You're sure? Why don't I just ring the ambulance again and see what's keeping them?'

'HAVE A *LOOK*!'

'All right then. Hmm . . .' I gingerly take hold of the waistband of her tracksuit pants and begin to peel them slowly back over her extended belly. But before I can continue with my reluctant stripping, Bronte hefts herself up and, with one impatiently fluid movement, sheds herself not only of tracksuit pants, but knickers as well. And there she is, my daughter, clad only in a tracksuit top with her legs wide apart and knees up – and with more of her nether regions on display than I've seen for many a year.

'*Yech!*' says Stephen, as he stops patting her leg and goes pale once more.

'Now – *LOOK*!' Bronte demands hoarsely.

Accepting the inevitable, I crawl slowly down to where her legs are bent and spread. I *really* don't want to do this – I didn't think it was all that cute when she was a baby, let alone now, two decades later. I tuck my hair behind my ears and take a deep breath to steel myself. Then, grimacing, I lean over and unenthusiastically peek up between her legs.

'Oh, my lord!' shrieks Stephen, breathing down my neck. 'Oh, my dear sweet lord!'

'What is it?' Bronte asks in panic between pants. 'What's wrong? Tell me what's wrong!'

'Oh – nothing, nothing,' I answer quickly as I grab a knee and peer in for a closer look. I'm actually trying to work out exactly what I'm seeing here, because it's not nothing – not at all. There is definitely *something* happening down here and I'm pretty sure it's exactly the something I was hoping wouldn't be happening. At least, not until the ambulance got here.

'*Teresa!*' Stephen whispers loudly in my ear. 'Teresa! That's not *normal*, is it? Has she always had that? It looks like a growth, or is it a genital defect? Oh, my *lord*, it's revolting.'

'Will you *go* and hold her hand,' I hiss violently at him. 'Go on – shoo!'

'It's *not* nothing!' Bronte is staring down between her raised knees straight at Stephen, and has easily read his horrified expression. '*Mum!* What is it? What's wrong?'

'Absolutely nothing, schnooks,' replies Stephen, bobbing up with a cheerful look at Bronte before hunching back down and staring once more at the display with a disgusted grimace. 'Teresa! Is it a tumour? And how on *earth* is the poor little baby going to get past?'

'It's not a tumour, you dingbat!' I say as I try frantically to decide what to do next. 'It's the baby's *head*!'

'MUM!'

'It's fine, Bronte. I'm sure the baby's just fine.' I look at Bronte reassuringly, with a confident smile plastered on. 'You just concentrate on your breathing. In – two, three. Out – two, three.'

'There *is* something wrong! I *know* there's something wrong! I want *Nick*!' Bronte wails as she flops back down and starts to tense up once more. Her fists clench and drum on the carpet as another contraction begins its relentless climb. Then her back arches and she groans as her whole body goes stiff again.

'It's okay, it's okay.' I pat her on the knee supportively. 'You're doing fine.'

'Aaaaaa*uuh*!'

And then something really amazing happens. As she arches and groans, I grab her other knee for extra support and lean forwards to get a better look at the action down under. Which is when I suddenly realise with a shock that there's movement at the station. Towards me. And if I don't put a halt to these proceedings right *now*, within minutes the miracle of birth is going to be played out virtually in my lap.

'Oh, heavens above!' Stephen grabs hold of my shoulder and leans across my back for a better look. 'It's *just* like that *Alien* movie!'

'Stop pushing!' I shriek at my daughter. 'Stop pushing – *at once!*'

'I. Can't,' grunts Bronte in response.

'You *have* to!' I stare wildly at her while I try to shrug Stephen off me. 'It's coming out! And it's coming out *now!*'

'Nn*noooo!*' But she *does* stop pushing for a minute and instead sits halfway up and glares at me, beads of sweat standing out wetly across her forehead. 'And *stop* telling me what to do! You're *always* telling me what to do! I hate it! JUST STOP IT! AND LET GO OF MY FREAKING KNEES RIGHT BLOODY *NOW!*'

'What?' I stare at her in amazement, momentarily distracted because she has never, *never* spoken to me like that before. Where on earth did it come from? But Bronte doesn't answer; instead, she flops backwards and, with her face going an extremely unbecoming shade of vermilion, starts groaning loudly as she bears down again.

'Aaaah! Aaaaa*uuuhhhh!*'

'Stephen! Get *off* me! And, quick, grab those towels!' I shout with panic. 'Bronte, I said *stop!* Stop pushing!'

But this time there is no response. Abusive or otherwise. In fact, she appears totally oblivious to me. Instead, with her head thrown back and face clenched up in pain, she is making loud guttural grunting noises. I glance across at Stephen for some support but he has reeled back onto his knees and is swaying backwards and forwards, holding one hand to his head and breathing almost as rapidly as Bronte. I reach across and grab his arm but he looks straight past me, takes one more glance at the crowning head and then, turning as white as my dressing-gown, collapses gracefully onto the carpet in a dead faint. Right on top of the pile of towels. I stare at him in disgust but, apart from his chest rising and falling rhythmically, he doesn't move. I'm on my own.

Tucking my hair back behind my ears, I look at Bronte. The exertion she is going through has made the veins in her neck stand out in bold relief, and her fists have begun drumming against the carpet again. Obviously it's pointless appealing to her better nature by begging her to stop pushing, so I let go of her quivering knees and dive back between her legs. And, boy, is there action aplenty happening down there.

Stephen's tumour is *definitely* a baby's head, and a not particularly clean baby's head at that. And it's also just about the whole way out. Having no real idea of what to do now, I flutter my hands about for a few seconds like some dimwit Victorian heroine before deciding the best place for them is in the catcher's position. Sure enough, as soon as I get them cupped, the head slithers all the way out, and twists around slowly like something out of *The Exorcist*. I cradle it in my hands and mutter a series of pleas to anyone who might be up above to help me.

Luckily, heavenly intervention appears unnecessary. With frantic fist-drumming and an undulating bellow that echoes painfully through her body, Bronte bears down one last time and the head is followed (fortunately) by shoulders, arms, a body, and a pair of legs. No penis. In other words, a complete baby girl. In my hands.

I freeze in position. On my knees, between Bronte's knees, with my hands cradled around the marbled-red body of a newborn baby whose umbilical cord still pulsates up into the body of her mother. My daughter.

'Hell,' I breathe as I stare at the baby dumbfounded. 'Flaming hell.'

'Mum? *Mum?*' Bronte struggles to raise herself onto her elbows to see what's going on. 'Is it the baby? Is it all right? Why can't I hear it crying?'

'Crying?' I repeat stupidly, still staring at the tiny newborn who, just at that moment, obligingly stretches out an impossibly small mouth and begins mewling piteously. Two little eyes screw themselves closed as two little fists clench and unclench with each wavering cry.

'Oh, Mum! What is it?' Bronte has raised herself almost all the way to a sitting position and is staring rapturously at her newborn. 'Can I have it? Please?'

'Of course, of course.' With extreme care I pass the tiny, bleating scrap of humanity to her mother. 'Bronte – she's beautiful. A beautiful little girl.'

'Oh, a girl,' breathes Bronte, gazing down at her daughter with instant adoration. 'Oh, I *so* wanted a girl. Hello there, darling.'

With a stupid smile, I wipe my hands on my dressing-gown as I watch the little tableau before me for a few minutes. Bronte continues to mutter welcoming inanities to the baby, who has ceased crying and instead is gazing up at her mother with an intensely interested expression on her scrunched-up little face. Next to them, Stephen is lying on the floor curled up in the foetal position on the towels, snoring quietly.

I can't believe I just delivered a baby. Me! Still grinning, I arrange the umbilical cord a little more neatly across Bronte's belly and suddenly realise my knees are very wet. I get up and my dressing-gown immediately sticks to my legs because it, too, is absolutely soaking. And flecked with stuff that I don't even want to think about. Slowly, I look down at my beautiful carpet and realise that, sure enough, it's in a similar condition to my dressing-gown. Just as I'm flexing my bare toes and listening to the dampish squelch they make, the doorbell rings.

I roll the carpet into the back of my mind, leap nimbly out of the damp patch, and then walk over to the front door with my dressing-gown slapping itself wetly against my shins as I go. Once there, I flick on the outside light, open the door wide and there stand, according to their name-badges, Bill and Sven – the ambulance men. Complete with a large medical satchel and a stretcher on wheels. Better late than never, I suppose.

'Come in,' I say cheerfully as I usher them inside and close the door before the temperature drops too dramatically. 'You're just in time.'

'Excellent!' declares Bill, a short white-haired gentleman who looks like retirement should have been a distant memory. 'I believe you're in labour, madam? Can you tell us how far apart the contractions are?'

'What?'

Sven, a blonde who is about half the age and twice the height of his partner – and a *lot* easier on the eye – puts his hand solicitously under my elbow and attempts to usher me towards the stretcher. Naturally, I resist strenuously.

'It's not me!' I protest as I shake off his hand with some difficulty, smoothing my dressing-gown over my stomach to emphasise my point. 'It's my daughter – *she's* just had a baby!'

'In that case,' says Bill, changing in an instant from considerate and fatherly to dour and disapproving, 'could you please adjust your clothing. Your left breast is exposed.'

I look down and, sure enough, it is. I cover it quickly and

then look up at them with some embarrassment, but Sven grins and gives me a huge wink. After some initial surprise, I return the wink coquettishly. After all, there's nothing like a little innocent flirtation to add a layer of fun to any situation. Bill clears his throat noisily and I glance across at him. The layer of fun immediately evaporates.

'Sorry,' I say quickly.

'Yes,' says Bill sourly, 'and perhaps, madam, you could direct us to your daughter?'

Holding my damp dressing-gown firmly closed, I lead them over to the lounge-room with Bill close behind me and Sven pushing the stretcher alongside. Bronte and baby are still in the same position they were when I left. But then again, I guess it's a tad hard to go for a saunter when you are firmly attached to each other by an umbilical cord. I suppose Bronte *could* drape it over one arm but you'd have to be pretty desperate for a drink, or something, to attempt it. Bill interrupts my musings by pushing past me and squatting down between Bronte and the still prone Stephen.

'What's with this guy?' he asks, inclining his head brusquely towards Sleeping Beauty. 'Is he the father?'

'Highly unlikely,' I reply with a grin. 'No, just a friend. And he fainted – couldn't take it. Men!'

Bill gives me a stern look, takes Stephen's pulse quickly and then, obviously dismissing him, turns to Bronte. And the transformation that comes over his face is nothing short of remarkable. Even though *she* is vastly more exposed than I was, he immediately loses the disapproving look and gives her a huge smile.

'Well! Aren't you the clever one!' Bill gently grasps one of her wrists and starts taking her pulse. 'Well done, young lady! When were you due?'

'Not for about three weeks.' Bronte gazes down at

her daughter beatifically. 'She came early. And isn't she just beautiful!'

'She certainly is.' Bill drops Bronte's wrist and takes a good look at the baby, running his finger quickly over her tiny body. 'A real little beauty – you should be proud of yourself.'

'I helped too,' I add obligingly.

'Really,' says Bill shortly, giving me a disparaging glance before turning back to Bronte. 'Now, Mum, how about we snip off this cord and then we'll be able to wrap up little bub nice and warm.'

'Okay, but I want to donate the cord to the cord bank at the hospital. I've registered and all.'

'And I wish there were more like you,' says Bill approvingly while he takes a pair of curved scissors from Sven, snips the umbilical cord off neatly and pegs it near the baby's belly. 'Now we'll just wrap this little lady up and you'll have her back before you know it.'

Bronte hands the baby over reluctantly and then, as Bill passes her carefully to Sven, suddenly doubles over with pain once more. 'Oh! Oh – not *again*!'

'That'll be the afterbirth,' says Bill as he sets to work. 'Just a couple of pushes and it'll all be over. You can do it, Mum.'

'I'll get the towels!' I yell at no one in particular as I attempt to wrest the pile from underneath Stephen. He immediately wraps his arm around them and mutters crossly. I give up and instead sprint towards the laundry and the linen cupboard. 'Just wait a second!'

I can hear Bronte grunting loudly as I fling the linen cupboard open, grab another armful of towels and head back towards the lounge-room fast, with them pressed against my chest. But, quick as I am, I'm still too late. There, on my red, pink and pale moss-coloured, low-pile carpet sits a placenta in all its glory. And while they might be perfectly functional bits of anatomy, they are not visually appealing at *all*. I pull a disgusted face, drop the towels at my feet and decide that I need a drink desperately.

'Well done!' says Bill encouragingly. 'All finished now. Hey, Sven, do you want to pass that little lady back over to Mum?'

Sven obligingly passes the now snugly wrapped baby to her mother, who stretches out her arms impatiently and immediately begins murmuring sweet nothings into her daughter's ear once more. While she is thus engaged, Sven removes the placenta efficiently and then leans against the stretcher, watching Bill, Bronte and baby bond. I kick the towels over towards the couch and grin wryly at Sven, who grins wryly back. I must say, he is *very* cute. I perch on the arm of the couch, arrange my dressing-gown and cross my legs gracefully. But when I look up to see his reaction, Sven has turned his back to me and is rummaging around in his bag. He grabs a vial of clear liquid and passes it to his partner who, leaning over, wafts it under Stephen's nose. The effect is immediate. Letting go of the towels, Stephen sits straight up and, with his fluorescent beanie askew, stares wide-eyed at the assorted gathering.

'Where *am* I?' he asks melodramatically while he flutters his hands about. 'What's happening?'

'You fainted,' I reply shortly, uncrossing my legs and relaxing. 'Thanks for that.'

'Oh, I *did*? And – Bronte!' Stephen looks around until his gaze settles on the new mother and her offspring on my not-so-clean carpet. He goes pale again.

'Steady on there!' Sven drops to one knee and puts a supporting arm around Stephen. 'Take a few deep breaths and try to relax.'

'Oh, my!' Stephen breathes rapturously, gazing up with

instant adoration at his saviour. 'The name's Stephen. That's spelt with a 'ph', of course, *not* a 'v'. Stephen Rowe.'

'Sven Parkes.'

'Hell,' I mutter, rolling my eyes as I watch Stephen recline in Sven's arms, batting his eyelashes while taking exaggeratedly deep breaths. I wonder if he realises how much he looks like a landed trout.

'Enough.' Bill obviously doesn't think much of Stephen's performance either, judging by the look he sends him. 'C'mon, Sven, give us a hand.'

Sven laughs good-naturedly at his partner before grinning down at Stephen and slowly releasing him. I briefly consider fainting to get some attention but reject the idea because, knowing my luck, Bill would give me mouth-to-mouth. Sven straightens up and, with his partner, pulls the stretcher over next to Bronte. They expertly pull a lever or two and fold it down to floor level.

'Now, young lady, we're going to lift you and bubs up onto this contraption and whisk you off to hospital so you can get the once-over. Okay?'

'And I'll follow in my car,' I say to Bronte as I pass over her tracksuit pants, 'so I'll meet you there.'

'There's no need unless you *have* to,' Bill says, glancing at me again and obviously still not all that pleased with what he sees. 'Your daughter and the bubs will both just be given a check-up and then put straight to bed.'

'Oh. What do you think, Bronte?'

'He's right, Mum,' Bronte says, trying to insert her little finger into her daughter's grasp. 'Like, I'm sure we'll be fine. You should just go back to bed and come in later.'

'*Much* later,' adds Bill, looking at me as if I've been keeping Bronte up needlessly. 'She needs her rest. And, madam?'

'Yes?'

'You are exposing yourself *again*.'

I look down and, sure enough, my left breast has made yet another partial bid for freedom. I readjust my dressing-gown but, because it is so weighted by dampness around the hem, it is difficult to keep it quite as together as usual. Accordingly, I fold my arms across my chest and glare back at Bill.

'Thank you so much for pointing that out,' I say. '*So* helpful.'

'My pleasure,' he replies sanctimoniously as he follows Sven and the stretcher towards the front door. Stephen jumps up quickly and helpfully rushes ahead to open the door. And then, before I can even give Bronte a kiss, they have lifted the stretcher across the threshold and are wheeling it down the garden path. Stephen, who is still propping the door open, suddenly spots his reflection in the hall mirror and gives a shriek.

'Oh, my *lord*!'

'You don't look that bad,' I reply, distracted by the imminent departure of my daughter and her newborn child. 'Just like you've had a bit of an adventure, that's all.'

'My *dear* Teresa . . .' Stephen tucks tufts of dark hair fastidiously under his beanie and then turns this way and that to check the effect. 'I don't want to have *adventures*, schnooks – just adventur*ers*.'

'Really.'

'Yes, just think of me as a reward. Like the spoils of war. And now –' Stephen gives his reflection an approving nod before turning to me with a smug smile '– I'm off to help the guys because I think I'm in with a chance there. Wish me luck!'

'Good luck!' I say agreeably, although I bet it's considered bad etiquette to pick up ambulance guys at the scene. And if it isn't, it should be. Wrapping my damp dressing-gown around me firmly, I hug myself with both arms because it's still pitch dark outside and very, very cold. My toes move past freezing towards that numbness that's the first stage of frostbite. I watch Stephen hurrying up the path to offer his totally unnecessary assistance and wonder if he realises his beanie glows in the dark. What with that, and the fact his black satin pyjamas can hardly be seen, he resembles nothing more than a mobile neon streetlight.

'Bye, Bronte! See you soon!' I call, waving at my daughter as she is lifted into the back of the ambulance. 'I'll be there in a few hours!'

'Bye, Mum.' Bronte finally takes her attention from the baby long enough to give me a little wave. 'Oh! Mum – could you try Nick again for me? But don't tell him!'

'Sure, I'll just breathe heavily.' I start hopping up and down in the foyer to warm myself up because it feels like the dampness around the bottom half of my dressing-gown is starting to ice up. Then, as soon as the rear door of the ambulance is closed securely and Bronte is no longer in sight, I shut my door and lean against it. There's a lump in my throat that was *not* caused by the cold outside. I delivered a baby! *I* delivered a baby! And not just any baby either. I delivered my very own gran . . . grand . . . well, my daughter's baby! I don't think I'm ready for the 'g' word quite yet.

I'm also not ready to go to bed. Adrenalin is coursing through my body and I feel way too hyped up to sleep. In fact, I wish I had someone here I could talk to, to discuss what just happened and to share the miracle with. Apart from Nick, who, given the fact that he was unreachable in a crisis, deserves to wait a little bit for the news. And apart from Bronte's father, who is currently cruising around the Solomon Islands and thus doesn't deserve the news at all. For a brief moment I consider ambushing Stephen before he goes back to bed, but then decide against it. Mainly because I'm fairly sure adrenalin will be coursing through his body too, although for an entirely different reason.

But I can't wait to tell everyone at work about this! And if they don't believe me, well – I've got the proof. In fact, I've got more proof than I really need and would have vastly preferred it on a couple of towels rather than spread across my pale moss-coloured, low-pile carpet right in front of the couch.

## MONDAY

### 0655 hrs

Languidly I reach out, turn off the jets feeding frothy bubbles of foam into the spa bath and lean back, stretching my legs. I take a deep breath of the jasmine-scented air and then smile with sheer pleasure. Because there's plenty to smile about. I've got a lovely home, helpful neighbours, a loving family, a daughter I get along with very well (I'm going to ignore that little outburst earlier, on the grounds she was in extreme pain), great friends, fun boyfriend, reliable job, and now, in addition to all this, I've personally delivered the next generation! I start humming 'She'll be coming round the mountain when she comes', simply because it feels appropriate, and reflect on the fact that, apart from my lounge-room carpet, life is totally under control and I'm coasting along pretty damn well. One hundred percent content – satisfaction guaranteed.

I punch my fist in the air and let out a loud 'yee *hah*!' before taking a deep breath and submerging myself beneath the foamy water while I slowly count how long I can stay under without resurfacing. One, and two, and three, and four . . . I manage to get to sixty-nine, not quite my all-time record, before I've got to emerge and take a big, gulping breath. Then I stretch out again while snowy froth settles cocoon-like around me, and I scoop it up neatly before it can drip off the edge and onto the floor.

After everyone left, I spent quite some time staring at the birthing area and deciding what to do about the stains. Finally, I came to the reluctant conclusion that I'd probably do more harm than good if I attempted to clean it, so I laid some of the unused towels across to soak up the excess moisture and then left it. I'll ring some professional carpet cleaners in a couple of hours and get them over here a.s.a.p.

Then I gave myself a quick wash and shoved my dressing-gown into the bin before, with both breasts on full display, I crawled into bed and tried valiantly to get back to sleep. But it wasn't any good. As I'd suspected, I was much too high to sleep. Instead I just tossed and turned as I replayed the morning's events over and over. I finally gave up the effort just as I came to the conclusion I was a damn hero, despite that sancti- monious pillock of an ambulance man. So, instead of trying to sleep, I made myself a strong cup of hero coffee laced with a liberal amount of hero rum and ran myself a hero bath. And here I am, fully submerged and happily counting life's little blessings.

I sigh contentedly and rearrange myself more comfortably. Like a surfacing submarine, my left breast immediately pops up out of the foam. I give it a disdainful look because this par- ticular breast appears to be misbehaving on a regular basis today. And, if it keeps it up, it'll get the chop – literally. Because, for quite some time now, I've been seriously considering a breast reduction not just for my left breast, but also for the right.

I'm rather well endowed – and that's putting it mildly. And over two decades of being ogled, and whistled at, and having to listen to the same stupid tit-jokes from dorks who think they are thigh-slappingly hysterical (and, to add insult to injury – or vice versa – it's usually *my* thigh they're slapping) is over two decades too long. *Then* there's the problem with buying clothes – as if being nearly six foot tall isn't bad enough! *And* the backache from the uneven weight distribution – I adjust myself in the bath as I think of this and stare down at the offending glands. Then I pick up the soap from the side of the bath and balance it on my recalcitrant left breast – it immediately slithers off and disappears beneath the bubbles with a hollow plop. Yep, totally useless.

I dismiss the irritation of overendowment momentarily as I go back to staring at the ceiling and smiling happily. How can one person have so many blessings? Some people might say I'm tempting fate by counting my blessings, but what's the point of being blessed if you can't feel smug about it? Besides, it's all a matter of control. If you have your life under control, the chances of things going wrong are reduced dramatically.

After I've finished in here I'll have another coffee while I make a few phone calls. First, the library to ask for a few days off – perhaps even the whole week: I deserve it. Second, the carpet cleaners. Third, fourth, fifth and maybe sixth, a few select people to let them know the good news. I flick my foot into the air, sending a cascade of froth floating to the ceiling before submerging myself again to rinse the last of the suds out of my hair. Then I pull the plug, step out and grab one of the enormous white bath sheets to dry myself off vigorously.

These generous towels are capable of wrapping themselves around my body at least twice so, thus clad, I open the door and pad downstairs towards the kitchen to put the kettle on. I left the heat on when I went up to bed earlier, so the unit is toasty warm from head to foot – and so am I. While the kettle is boiling, I run a cloth over the bench-tops and then lean against them, looking out of the kitchen window at the grey dawn and cloudy sky. It looks like another chilly winter day typical of July in Melbourne.

I live in Ferntree Gully, a leafy and charming outer eastern suburb of Melbourne. Ferntree Gully covers a rather large area and ranges from the truly picturesque, brimming with tree ferns, dales and wildlife, to the basically suburban, which is, well, basically suburban. I live in one of the latter areas but an absence of overabundant greenery is more than made up for by the additional absence of trespassing wildlife, such as possums, which would use my roof as a trampoline and relieve themselves in my driveway. I know this for a fact because I grew up in the picturesque, leafy dale part, and not only was I rudely awakened on many occasions by noisy nocturnal wanderings overhead, but it was also my job to clean the possum crap off the car, driveway and porch. No bloody thanks. My mother still lives in the same house, and so do the critters.

So a non-leafy area was a definite priority when I bought my unit (which was actually advertised as a town house but as it's not in town and it's not a house, *I* call it a unit) virtually off the drawing board just over a decade ago when I became single again. It's a two-storey clinker brick dwelling that was terribly luxurious when it was built, and is holding up pretty well – if I say so myself. It has air-conditioning, ducted vacuum and heating, spiral staircase, spa, fireplace, enclosed garden complete with mosaic fountain and cobblestoned barbecue, and every other little mod con you can think of – as well as a few you probably can't. I own it outright and have done so since the moment I moved in. And I'm fully aware that I was very, very fortunate as far as cheated-on wives go. The thing is that *my* ex was a well-established dentist. And he was a well-established dentist so riddled with remorse that at the time he would have done almost anything to alleviate his guilt – anything, that is, except keep his fly zipped during working hours.

The unit is decorated very nicely too. That's the thing about being mortgage-less – you can spend your money on the fun things, like nice furniture and regular re-decorating splurges. My place is currently done in muted pastels throughout. The laundry, kitchen and adjoining family-cum-meals area are a sunny pale lemon, with white cupboards and trim, and the rest of the ground floor, consisting of a lounge-room, powder-room and an enormous entry foyer (lorded over by the spiral staircase), are painted a light dusky-rose colour that contrasts well with my predominantly white furniture and (formerly) pristine, pale moss-coloured carpet. Upstairs is a landing that leads to the three bedrooms – my room (cream), Bronte's old room (sky-blue) and one (sage-green) that I've turned into a book-lined study, complete with a seldom-used computer.

The unit is always immaculate – with everything in its place and a place for everything. Because I'm positively *allergic* to clutter – if my place gets messy or disorganised, it's like my life is messy and disorganised.

I switch off the kettle and pour hot water over the coffee in the plunger. The heady aroma quickly permeates the air and I take a deep breath, hoisting my towel back up and readjusting it as I let my breath out. Then I take a cup back upstairs to my bedroom, where I plump myself on my bed and grin happily at the mirror. It grins happily back.

I lean over to put my coffee down on the bedside chest and promptly lose my towel again. Instead of readjusting it this time, I stand up and frowningly examine myself in the mirror. I turn first one way and then the other. The trouble is that in my daughter I've got a constant reminder of how I used to look twenty years ago – and sometimes I'd prefer to forget.

However, even if I say so myself, I'm not *too* bad for forty-one. Shoulderblade-length blonde hair, largish blue eyes, pale skin, not a bad figure, long legs, nice butt . . . nice butt? It suddenly occurs to me that, even though I'm standing front on, I can see some of my butt. And I'm pretty sure I haven't always been able to do that. I twist around a tad to check my butt is still where it's supposed to be, then bend over and peer between my legs. Sure enough, I can see the bottom end of my bottom end. I straighten up and check out the front view once more before deciding to ignore this visible sign of gravity at work. Perhaps I can get something done about the butt bit when I fix the boob bit. I narrow my eyes threateningly at each appendage before turning away.

Naked, I wander into the walk-in wardrobe and look thoughtfully at the neat row of clothing suspended before me. What I need is appropriate winter wear that reflects the festive nature of this particular day. Eventually I choose a pair of khaki cargo pants, a snug white rollneck jumper, and sneakers. The festive touch is achieved by the addition of a pair of dangly gold earrings. Fully dressed, I walk back over to the mirror and check out the effect. Not bad – casual yet compelling. And, now that it is firmly held in place, I can barely see my rear end at all. I head into the ensuite to brush my teeth, blow-dry my hair and throw on a little foundation.

While I'm in there, I rinse down the remains of this morning's bubbles in the spa bath, fish out the soap and straighten up the shampoos lined along the edge. Then I strip my bed and remake it with clean sheets. This accomplished, I grab the dirty sheets and use them to wipe the coffee ring under my cup before taking them, and my coffee, downstairs, where I deposit the sheets in the washing machine and the coffee in the microwave.

While it's heating up, I grab a pen, write a list of plans for the day and then fasten the completed list on the fridge behind a magnet of a bejewelled Tutankhamen. I stand back to examine it.

## MONDAY

| | | |
|---|---|---|
| *Phone calls* | – | *Library, C/Cleaners, Dennis, Mum, Cam, Diane, Thomas, Uncle Laurie & Auntie June* |
| *Morning* | – | *Shopping: baby present, new d/gown* |
| | – | *Milk, bread, rice, muesli, corn chips, box of chocolates* |
| | – | *Visit Bronte* |
| | – | *Get some videos* |
| *Afternoon* | – | *Drop the chocolates off at Stephen's to say thanks* |
| | – | *Relax/watch videos?* |
| | – | *Do my tax return?* |
| | – | *Start reading <u>Gone with the Wind</u>?* |
| *Evening* | – | *Fergus coming over* |

Looks perfect. I've had *Gone with the Wind* sitting by my bed since Christmas and still haven't got around to reading it. As for the tax return, that's been on top of my 'to do' pile for the past month. So now is my chance for both maybe – and plenty more. Yes, it should be a nice, relaxing day but there's nothing like careful organisation. This is something that I learnt (read: was drummed into me) during the three years I spent in the armed services before marrying Dennis. The six p's: prior preparation prevents piss-poor performance. And if there's one thing we heroes can't tolerate, it's piss-poor performance.

This is going to be just great.

# MONDAY

## 1100 hrs

Flaming hell! Why does nothing ever go the way I bloody well want it to? I slam the gearstick back into third and scream around the corner onto Burwood Highway. Some bloke in a Falcon ute honks at me impatiently but I ignore him because I refuse to indulge in road rage. Normal rage is more than enough for me at the best of times – and today is one of those times. From a great start, my morning thus far has turned out to be a severe trial. The carpet cleaners can't come until tomorrow morning, by which time my carpet should be permanently set in tie-dye pink moss. My ex-husband is on a cruise with one of his string of blonde girlfriends and so can't be contacted. My best friend, Camilla, had already left by the time I got through to her number and then, when I rang my mother, somehow I found myself agreeing to pick her up this morning and take her with me to the hospital to visit. Which means, knowing my mother, that I'll probably end up having her with me for the whole day.

Then, by the time I finished with all these calls and finally rang Diane, not only had she already heard the happy news but she'd passed it on to the rest of the family and was on her way to the hospital as we spoke. Literally – as I rang her on her mobile. Diane is Camilla's eldest sister as well as the mother of Bronte's fiancé, Nicholas, so therefore the new baby is a direct descendant of hers as well as mine. I suppose we're all almost related now. Diane has four boys, of whom Nick is the eldest, and twin baby girls, which probably means she won't be putting her hand up much for babysitting duties. I grimace as this thought hits me because I doubt I'd be much chop at babysitting either, but for very different reasons. Diane is a born mother whereas I . . . well, I'm not.

In fact, I don't even particularly like babies. When other women, and quite a lot of men too, start gurgling over bunny-rug occupants, I just feel a tad bewildered. Sure, they're cute and rather appealing – in a shrink-proof wrapping kind of way – but, let's face it, what can you say about a developmental stage wherein your appearance is actually enhanced by a state of total baldness? And don't even get me started on babies at restaurants, and the way they get all the good parking spots at the shopping centres. Then look at what they do to your figure, your stress levels and your bank balance. No, I don't get it.

In fact, if it weren't for a rather literal misinterpretation of exactly what the rhythm method entailed, Bronte herself wouldn't ever have made her appearance twenty-odd years ago. And it wasn't like I had an awful lot of time to decide whether I wanted kids now, later, or ever, as I'd only been married twelve and a half minutes when she was conceived.

I'm not exaggerating – I went into the reception bathroom to freshen up before the wedding photographs and my new husband, obliging soul that he was, came in to give me a hand – or whatever. So, with the background encouragement of Carole King, one thing led to another, the earth moved and we got into a rhythm that was made all the easier by my hoop-style wedding dress, which flipped up neatly over my head. When, eventually, I readjusted the hoops and went out for photographs, all the while, unbeknownst to me, Dennis's little tadpoles were displaying a total lack of appropriate wedding etiquette and swimming frantically upstream. Nine months later – voila! Baby girl.

Not that I don't love Bronte, I do – very much. But it was never the bells clanging, whistles blowing, life-altering, instantaneous, maternally *magical* experience that I'd read about. Rather, it was a slow process that started with more of a sense of bemusement at her birth, and culminated about four months later when once, during a night-feed, I looked down at her nestled against my breast and suddenly realised oh-my-god, I love her. And that I'd just die if anything happened to her. But that love didn't make me think twice about buying a book which detailed what the rhythm method *really* entailed, and then going on the pill as well just to make doubly sure. And not having any more children certainly didn't count as one of my regrets when the marriage shuddered miserably to a halt about nine years later.

Also, that love has certainly been put to the test this morning. Even apart from the matter of giving birth on my carpet and then telling everybody about it before I could, there was also the fact, as I discovered when I finally managed to get out the door, that Bronte had parked her pink Volkswagen right behind my car when she arrived in the middle of the night. And, as she left with Bill and Sven, of course the pink Volkswagen was still there. I had to execute a seventy-eight point turn and run over my new rosebush in order to extricate my Barina and head off to collect my mother.

I put my blinker on and coast into the left-hand lane in preparation for turning into Forest Road. Several vehicles already *in* the left-hand lane honk furiously so I take one hand off the steering wheel momentarily to send them an appropriate gesture. Then I try to crank the car back into third – but it won't go, so I look down quickly and realise the car is already *in* third. No wonder it was making all those complaining noises coming down the highway. I look back up just in time to brake before colliding with a bus that, very rudely, has pulled out right in front of me, so I honk to let him know his actions haven't gone unnoticed. A couple of teenagers in the rear of the bus copy my earlier gesture but I ignore them blithely and turn up Forest Road towards Ferntree Gully Central.

Then I close my eyes and take a deep breath in an attempt to clear my body of residual stress. When I open them again I'm in Ferntree Gully Central, so I slow down because the little township is a positive mecca for elderly people, and running over a stray one would *really* not help this day pick up. Within a few minutes I'm turning into my mother's street, and then into her driveway.

I park on the terracotta cobblestones and, leaning back to wait for her, feel myself start to relax as I contemplate the weatherboard house before me. I don't think it matters whether you live across the world or across the street, most people experience a sense of coming home, of revisiting roots, whenever they visit the house they grew up in. I know I do – but I also know that, in my case, the days for this are numbered. The rambling white weatherboard I grew up in is far too big for my mother alone, and the block it squats on is far too big not to attract a wealth of developers as soon as the house hits the market. Which means that, sooner or later, in this spot I'll be staring not at a gracious old weatherboard starting to feel her age, but at a row of pea-in-the-pod brick units.

I press down on the horn impatiently and an elderly gentleman who is planting a series of wilting daisies in his lawn next door looks up and frowns at me with annoyance. The front door of my mother's house opens wide and, a few seconds later, my mother herself comes bustling out and down the brick path to where it intersects with the driveway. She is wearing a loud floral pinafore over a purple skivvy, thongs and a huge smile.

'Teresa, darling! How lovely!'

'Sorry I'm late, Mum,' I say as I give her outfit a cursory glance. 'You wouldn't *believe* the day I'm having!'

'Of course I would, honey. You aren't a liar – never have been.'

'Oh. Okay. Hey, you're not wearing *that* are you?'

'What?'

'That –' I gesture at the pinafore ensemble '– to the hospital.'

'But you said eleven o'clock, Teresa!'

'It *is* eleven o'clock. Actually, it's a quarter past.'

'Already?'

'Yes. So could you get changed – quickly?'

'Eleven o'clock!' Mum shakes her head with amazement and wanders back up the path still repeating the time in a disbelieving voice. She slams the door behind her and I roll my eyes and settle down to wait.

When I was a small girl, I firmly believed height had a direct correlation with intelligence. That is, the taller a person was, the smarter they were. And vice versa. I hadn't just plucked this theory out of the ether either, because in my household there was very good reason for believing it. My father was a six-foot-four criminal lawyer who, when he was home, generally wandered around muttering unintelligible sentences and radiating intelligence. Then there was his assorted family, with not one adult non-tertiary educated or under six foot, and all the children rapidly approaching that mark. My older brother and I were in the same mould – both tall, bright and precocious. And then there was our mother.

She is, to be blunt, an idiot. And a tiny idiot, at that. With heels she might break the five-foot barrier, but they'd have to be pretty decent. I don't want to know what it says about my father that he, in his thirties, married a minute eighteen year old with the IQ of a damaged gnat. Obviously, he was one of those men who are fatally attracted to dumb blondes – the dumber the better. And with my mother he hit the jackpot.

Age doesn't appear to have made much difference either; nowadays she's so vague that sometimes even entire conversations seem to pass her by. But, total twit or not, her huge, warm personality more than makes up for her lack in other areas. She is one of the most non-judgemental, kind-hearted, truly generous people I've ever met and, as much as she might frustrate the hell out of me at times, I love her dearly. She did a marvellous job of bringing us up and our snug, loving, *secure* childhood home was due in no small part to her warmth and family devotion. Even today, I know she's always there for me whenever I need her.

And she's also still beautiful. Petite, fine-boned, fluffy and blue-eyed – sort of like a pocket Barbie doll – with her hair now an artfully tinted blonde to hide the encroaching grey. Although, personally, I don't know that I'd bother – if she left it alone then at least she'd have *some* grey matter around her cranial region.

Funnily enough, the predilection for clouding the gene pool must pass through the male gene – because my brother certainly did his utmost to better Dad's choice. Needless to say, I don't get on terribly well with my sister-in-law but I've got to admit their marriage seems blissfully content. Just like that of our parents, who worshipped the ground the other walked on until my father died five years ago. Now Mum just worships the ground that covers him.

I run my fingers through my hair and then glance at my watch, deciding it might be prudent to go inside and hurry her along. The odds are she's forgotten I'm even out here and is having an early lunch or something. Just as I get out of the car, the front door opens again and there's my mother, now dressed in a pair of tailored black pants and a lilac cable-knit jumper, and carrying a brightly wrapped gift.

The gentleman planting daisies pauses as she walks past and doffs his hat politely. If I were on the receiving end of such a gesture I'd stop dead in shock, but she is so used to that sort of reaction she just smiles sweetly back and then walks over towards me. She might be a kangaroo short in the top paddock but, even at the age of sixty-four, men seem to fall all over themselves to protect her. I only wish I had half her good looks and the small bones to go with them. Nobody ever gets an urge to defend you when you're built like one of Wagner's Valkyries. And clothes just don't seem to hang the same either.

'Shall we, honey?'

'Of course.' I get back into the car and start the engine as she settles herself neatly on the passenger side. I reverse deftly and we head off in the direction of the William Angliss Hospital in Upper Ferntree Gully.

'You must've moved pretty quickly,' I say, looking at the gift in her lap. 'I mean, I only rang you a couple of hours ago.'

'Oh, I didn't get it this morning!' says Mum with a laugh. 'I bought this gift *months* ago! It's a baby monitor set but I've already told Bronte so she didn't double up. What did you get her?'

'Um. Well, nothing yet. Because I want to wait and see what she *really* needs.'

'Very sensible.'

'Yes, I thought so.'

'And what chilly weather we're having,' says Mum conversationally as I whip around a string of cars driving very slowly. 'What a lovely surprise.'

'Well, it *is* winter – so it's sort of expected, I suppose.'

'Not the weather.' Mum smiles jovially at me. 'I watched the news last night.'

'The *news* was a surprise?' I ask as I find myself right behind a big black hearse and realise that all the slow cars were actually driving that way for a reason. 'Why? What happened?'

'When?' Mum looks at me with a frown.

'On the news. The surprise.'

'Oh, *I* don't know. I only watch the weather.' Mum opens her window a fraction and the icy wind whistles straight across and zeroes in on my left ear. 'Why? Did something happen?'

'Mum . . .' I take a deep breath and try to focus. 'You just said that it was a lovely surprise. *What* was the lovely surprise?'

'Why, you, honey.'

'*I* was the lovely surprise?'

'Yes, of course – you turning up like that to take me to see the new little baby.'

'But, Mum, we just arranged it this morning!'

'Yes, I know. But the baby was a trifle early, and then – well, so was eleven o'clock. Hadn't you better put your lights on?'

'Why?'

'Well, it's only polite when you're in a funeral procession.'

'But I'm not – all right.' I lean over and flick my lights on. 'So how's Tom? Have you heard from him recently?'

'Yes, I rang this morning to tell him the news. He was thrilled. And they're all fine.' Mum pauses and a slight frown puckers her porcelain brow. 'Although I do worry all the time about that Kleenex Clan and what they might do to him. And to little Bonnie.'

'Mum. Number one – it's the *Klu Klux* Klan. Number two – last time I saw him, Tom was white, Protestant and hetero-sexual. The combination of which renders him fairly safe. Number three – the Klu Klux Klan aren't the be all and end all they once were.' I put my blinker on and try to get out from behind the hearse but the semitrailer on my right refuses to let me in. 'And number four – the only way they'd be a threat to Bonnie would be if they have a branch that's involved in straightening out spoilt brats.'

'Nevertheless, I worry.' Mum folds her arms across her chest and looks at me sagely. 'I've heard things, you know.'

I try not to laugh because I don't want to hurt her feelings. My brother, Thomas, who specialises in corporate law, was sent by his firm over to Atlanta, in the US of A, on a two-year contract ten years ago. The chief reason he is still there is Amy, his southern-born wife whom he met and married during the first year of his contract and who steadfastly refuses to live anywhere else. Bonnie is their *very* spoilt five year old daughter.

'Any plans to visit us in the near future?' I decide to change the subject because this isn't the first conversation we've had regarding the Kleenex Klan and the likelihood of them doing something drastic to Tom or Bonnie. Like forcing them to manufacture illicit, substandard toilet tissue in some sweatshop, I suppose. Amy doesn't really enter the equation – after all, if *she* were nabbed by the Klan, Tom would be free to shift back to Australia with his daughter in tow and visit his mother a trifle more frequently.

'Actually, he thought he might have a meeting over here in a month or so.' My mother turns and looks at me excitedly. 'Wouldn't that be lovely?'

'Yes, it would,' I reply with pleasure, 'but aren't you due over there this Christmas anyway?'

'Am I? Let me see . . .' She frowns with concentration. 'Yes, I *am*! I stayed here last year, so this year it's my turn for America! I'd forgotten – what fun!'

'Yes, what fun,' I reply dryly, wondering how it is possible to forget that, for the past ten years, you have spent one Christmas with your daughter and the following with your son. I make another attempt to get out of the funeral procession but all the cars in the right-hand lane contain extremely selfish drivers and not one will let me in. We lapse into silence but it's not an uncomfortable silence. It never is with my mother because I'll say one thing for her – she's definitely not the type of person who feels they have to fill every conversational gap with inanities. In fact, she's extremely comfortable with long silences and some of my happiest moments with her have been spent without a word being uttered.

I put my blinker on to turn into the road leading to the hospital, and so does the hearse in front of me. Accordingly I resign myself to being lead mourner in the funeral procession all the way through Upper Ferntree Gully, which is indeed what happens. At least it means that, for once, all the other users of the road pay me some respect. And I even have a few elderly gentlemen doff their hats as I drive past. I try to look suitably bereaved but it's difficult with my mother sitting beside me beaming and waving cheerfully at the hat-doffers.

Finally I turn off into the hospital car park and the funeral procession continues on up the hill. Now for the fun part. The William Angliss Hospital is renowned for its lack of parking and is subsequently an extremely rewarding hunting ground for the city's parking inspectors. We drive around and around for half an hour before finding a space which is about four foot shy of being a decent car park. But this is where having a Barina pays off. I let Mum out before manoeuvring the car in with a series of dexterous movements. Then I throw her the keys so she can open the boot and I lock both doors from the inside before clambering over into the back seat, and from there into the boot and out. I dust myself down and lock the hatchback.

'Has Bronte thought of any names?'

'Not that she told me.' I carefully look both ways before ushering Mum over the road and towards the hospital entrance. 'But then, we didn't get much of a chance to chat this morning.'

'Oh, that *is* a shame.' Mum shakes her head ruefully. 'You know, honey, you really should take the time to talk with Bronte more. One of these days you're going to turn around and she'll be all grown-up and gone. And then it'll be too late.'

'Given the fact she spent the morning giving birth on my lounge-room carpet,' I say as I precede Mum through the automatic doors and into the hospital foyer, 'I'd reckon she's pretty grown-up already, wouldn't you?'

'Nothing of the sort,' replies Mum blithely, 'because being grown-up and having babies are not necessarily mutually inclusive, you know.'

I turn and give her an astounded look because, well, sometimes she floors me. Just when I think I've got her pigeonholed, she comes out with something incredibly insightful. We continue in silence to the elevators, where there is a considerable crowd waiting, and I press the 'up' button. Glancing around me, I realise there must be a baby boom at the moment. Everybody seems either to be laden with wrapped gifts and stuffed toys or carrying a blue and/or pink balloon announcing the gender of whatever it is they are going to see.

'Oh!' Mum is staring raptly at the various balloons. 'We should have gotten Bronte a balloon!'

'Not necessary,' I comment, batting one away that was floating dangerously near my face. 'I think she knows what the baby is by now.'

'No, we *have* to! Come on!'

'What, is it some type of rule?' I ask as the metallic elevator doors finally slither open. 'Will we get fined or something?'

'Probably,' says one heavily jowled grandfather type as he passes me laden with both a pink *and* a blue balloon. 'Although odds are the fine'd be cheaper.'

'Don't be such a spoilsport, Bob,' remonstrates his wife. 'If it was up to you, we'd only be giving a card.'

'Damn right,' says Bob grumpily as he enters the elevator, 'and then we could've just posted it.'

'Come on, Teresa.' Mum pulls at my arm as I try to follow Bob into the elevator. 'Let's go and get her a balloon.'

'Mum, she doesn't *need* a balloon!'

'She does so. This isn't something that happens every day, you know.'

'Well, thank god for that,' I say as I wearily watch the elevator doors close with me on the wrong side. 'Otherwise my carpet would be more red than it is green.'

'You didn't tell me you'd changed your carpet!' Mum sets off towards the gift shop at a brisk trot. 'You *never* tell me anything! Although I must say I'm quite pleased. I never did like that other colour. Always reminded me of mildew.'

After an interminable fifteen minutes spent watching Mum minutely examine every single balloon before making her choice (pink with 'It's a girl!' printed cheerfully across it), we head back towards the elevators, where yet another crowd has gathered. Funnily enough, they look exactly the same as the earlier lot. Same gifts, same stuffed toys, same balloons.

This time the elevator arrives fairly quickly and we all crowd in, and then crowd out again at the maternity floor. Everyone else seems to know exactly where they are going. We have to ask at the desk and are directed by a rather harassed nurse to the third room on the left. Accordingly, with Mum's damn balloon floating into my face every few seconds, we wander over to the third room on the left and poke our heads around the door. There are two beds in the room with the one closest to us, by the door, taken up by a bird of a female – tiny, bony and with hair like pale grey-brown feathers. She glances apprehensively at us and then, as she realises we aren't here for her, resumes looking totally miserable once more. I give her a sympathetic smile and turn my attention past the television set suspended from the centre of the ceiling to the bed on the other side of the room. And there's Bronte, dressed in a pair of pink-striped flannelette pyjamas, sitting cross-legged with her long blonde hair loose around her shoulders. She looks clean, and fresh, and radiant. She is also surrounded by presents – and a multitude of pink balloons bearing the words 'It's a girl!'

'Mum! It's about time!'

'I was unavoidably detained –' I glance pointedly at my mother – 'but better late than never. How are you feeling?'

'Fine. And you've brought Gran!'

'Hello, honey.' Mum bustles over, drops her gift on the bed and delivers a firm kiss to Bronte's cheek. 'And congratulations! Where *is* the little darling?'

'Nick's just taken her for a walk. They should be back in a minute or so.' Bronte picks up the gift and rattles it. 'The baby monitor! Thank you *so* much, it's going to come in, like, *really* handy. And just see what everyone else has brought me, Gran! It's fantastic!'

'Oh, show me!' Mum sits down on the edge of the bed and immediately lets go of her balloon, which floats neglectedly up to the ceiling and bobs gently along towards a corner. 'Look, Teresa! The size of these little shoes! Aren't they just precious!'

'Yep, precious,' I comment as I settle myself into an extremely uncomfortable green vinyl armchair. 'Show me more. Please.'

'Well, here's a little twin-set. And just look at this dear mobile! Oh, and what a simply adorable little teddy!'

'Gran, she was being sarcastic,' Bronte says knowledgeably.

'Mum can't stand babies and baby stuff – you should know that by now.'

'It's not that I can't stand them,' I protest defensively, 'it's just that I don't find them as fascinating as everybody else seems to.'

'Oh, Teresa,' sighs my mother pityingly, 'you *are* a duffer.'

'No, she's not.'

This last is said in a deep monotone, just like the donkey Eeyore, out of Winnie-the-Pooh. I turn with astonishment to the little bird in the other bed but, despite having just partici-pated in our conversation, she's staring straight ahead and refusing to make eye contact. I look back at Bronte and raise my eyebrows questioningly.

'Don't worry about her,' explains Bronte in a stage whisper. 'She's a bit, like, *odd*. Just had baby number eight – can you believe it?'

'Eight!' I repeat with horror. '*Eight!*'

'Eight!' says Mum, with a pitying glance at the bed.

'Eight,' sighs Eeyore plaintively, without taking her eyes off the wall.

'Anyway,' I continue after a few minutes, when it becomes obvious that that conversation isn't going anywhere, 'I'd like to know what you were doing at my place this morning, Bronte. I mean, what on *earth* were you thinking of, driving around in bloody labour?'

'Oh, you won't believe it,' says Bronte, slapping her hand to her head. 'How *stupid* was I!'

'I don't know,' I encourage her, 'tell me.'

'Well, I was just off to bed after Nick headed to work at midnight and –'

'I thought Nicholas was at university,' Mum says, confused. 'Nobody ever tells me anything. Did you know your mother changed her carpet, Bronte? *I* didn't.'

'Mum, Nick *is* at university. He's just got a job working a couple of nights at one of those twenty-four hour service stations. And I haven't changed my – oh, never mind. Go on, Bronte.'

'Also, he's put in for some extra shifts because it's semester break, Gran. Anyway, Merrill and her boyfriend were both out, so I was all alone. I was just heading off to bed and I started feeling really queer. Like, *really* queer. And I made myself some herbal tea but it just got worse. There weren't any contractions or anything, I just felt *so* yuck. So I thought I'd come home for the night. And maybe you'd know what was going on.'

'You'd have been better off coming to my place, honey,' Mum whispers to Bronte conspiratorially before grimacing and then rolling her eyes theatrically. 'Your mother wouldn't know the first thing about childbirth. Drugged to the hilt, she was. You could hear her singing from the car park. Rather embarrassing. Your poor grandfather refused to get out of the car.'

'Hello? I'm right here,' I comment.

'The same song, over and over. Something about a mountain, I think it was.'

'But why didn't you ring, Bronte?' I ask reasonably, deciding to ignore my mother's little jaunt down memory lane. 'Then at least I'd have known you were coming.'

'And she's never been able to hold a tune. Never.'

'I didn't want to wake you up.' Bronte looks at me earnestly. 'Like, it *was* the middle of the night, you know.'

'Thoughtful girl,' comments Mum with a nod, forgetting all about my singing abilities whilst she looks at Bronte approvingly.

'But you were going to wake me up when you got there!'

'Oh. Yeah,' says Bronte, frowning. 'You're right. I didn't think of that.'

'Hmm,' adds Mum thoughtfully, with an identical frown. 'Hmm. Yes, I see.'

'Flaming hell.' I look at them both and, not for the first time, marvel at the power of genetics. No wonder they get on so well together.

'Anyway,' continues Bronte, 'on the way, I started having some pains so I pulled over and tried to ring Nick but his mobile was off or something. Then I thought they're probably only those Hexton Bricks ones –'

'Braxton Hicks,' I interrupt.

'Who?' asks Bronte, looking confused.

'Braxton Hicks,' I repeat. 'That's what they're called.'

'Oh, Mum,' says Bronte, rolling her eyes, 'an awful lot has changed since you had me. Like, *everything's* been updated.'

'She's right, honey,' agrees Mum, with a sage nod in Bronte's direction. 'I mean, we didn't have *any* of those when I was having you two. Each generation has it easier.'

'Humph,' says Eeyore glumly.

'Well, as I was saying, I thought they were just those Hexton Bricks things,' continues Bronte, with a challenging glance in my direction, 'but by the time I got home – I mean your place, Mum – I was starting to get really worried. So I let myself in and tried Nick again but still couldn't get through. Then I was going to go up and get you but they started getting *really* bad so I thought I'd sit on the couch and just yell out to you, you know. So I go, like, 'Mum, *Mum!*' And you didn't come but then they were so bad I lay down on the floor. Because I thought it'd make them better, but they just got worse, and then I couldn't get up again. And, like, I didn't think you'd *ever* come.'

'But I did,' I finish smugly, 'and saved the day.'

'Yeah, eventually,' says Bronte with an accusing glance at me, 'but it sure took you ages.'

'Well, *excuse* me for sleeping,' I comment sarcastically.

'Oh, it's not your fault, honey,' chimes in Mum, 'so don't go feeling responsible. All's well that ends well.'

'And wait till you see her!' Bronte's face lights up and she forgets all about my dereliction of duty. 'You just wait! Even you, Mum, you're going to love her!'

Right on cue, a Perspex cradle wedged in a metal trolley is wheeled squeakily through the doorway. It's being pushed by the proud father, looking tall, blonde and masculine as usual. Nick and Bronte make an incredibly well-suited couple in a visual sense, like a romantic version of Viking heroes straight from the folds of Norway – or whatever it is that Norway has.

'Mil, *great* to see you!' says Nick cheerfully, parking the trolley haphazardly by the bed. 'I hear you were something of a lifesaver this morning!'

'You could say so, I suppose,' I say humbly, gratified that at last someone seems to think so. 'But I'm sure Bronte would have managed without me.'

'Nonsense!' Nick bends over to pick up the silent, bunny-rugged occupant of the trolley and pass it carefully over to Bronte's eager arms. 'You were great, admit it.'

'He's right. You were, you know, Mum.' Bronte drops a kiss into the folds of the bunny-rug. 'It might have taken you ages but, like, I don't know what I'd have done without you.'

'Why, thank you, Bronte,' I reply, feeling rather touched. 'I'm just glad I was there.'

'Let me see . . .' Mum edges up the bed closer to Bronte and turns back a corner of the bunny-rug. 'Oh, oh, *oh*! Aren't you simply precious! Hello, you little darling!'

'Do you want to see, Mum?' Bronte tilts the bundle slightly so I can glimpse the baby's face. 'Here you are, sweetie, here's your grandmother.'

'Yech,' I comment shortly as I lean over for a closer look.

'Charming!' says Bronte, pulling the baby back and giving me a hurt look.

'Not the *baby*,' I protest, 'the grandmother bit – I'm not sure I'm ready.'

'Well, you ain't got too much choice,' Nick says with a smile as he sits down on the bed and puts his arm around Bronte. 'So what's it to be? Gran, Nan, Grandma, or do you want to go all modern and stick with Terry?'

'I've no idea.' I roll my eyes and grimace. 'But I think I've got a bit of time to decide, don't you? After all, I can't see her talking for a *few* days at least.'

'Oh, honey! It'll take longer than that!' laughs Mum, shaking her head at my stupidity. 'Babies don't start talking for months and months!'

'Aargh,' groans Eeyore, rolling over and burying herself beneath her blankets.

'And don't forget whose genes she has,' says Nick, ignoring the other bed's occupant as he drops a kiss on his daughter's forehead, 'so you'll have to make up your mind quickly, Mil.'

'Yeah, I'll get onto it tonight.' I ignore the 'Mil' bit, as I've learnt to over the past few months. After they moved in together, Nick decided that calling me Terry was no longer appropriate and rechristened me 'Mil', which stands for mother-in-law – despite the fact they aren't yet married and, indeed, haven't even started to discuss dates. But Nick seems to have a penchant for changing people's names. He calls his twin baby sisters 'Search' and 'Destroy', and has even shortened Bronte's name to 'Bron', which is a nickname I've strenuously discouraged over the years.

'Here you go, Mum.' Bronte leans around Nick and holds the baby out towards me. 'Like, isn't she just gorgeous?'

'Of course your mother will agree,' Mum says, with a challenging frown in my direction. '*Won't* you, honey?'

Ignoring my mother, I tuck my hair behind my ears and lean closer. Just as I'm thankfully noting the fact that the child is considerably cleaner than she was last time I saw her, a really odd thing happens. I'm expecting to feel *something* – because, after all, this infant happens to be a direct descendant of mine – but babies are babies, so I'm only anticipating a mild frisson of pleasure or some such response. Instead, she opens her slate-grey eyes and looks straight into mine – and I fall in love. Instantly, overwhelmingly, and irrevocably.

I close my eyes in shock, but when I open them again it hits me even harder. An all-consuming fierce intensity of emotion that wallops me like a piece of two-by-four to the side of the head. The baby herself seems to be perfectly unaware of the emotional turmoil that's taking place before her, and there are certainly no clues in her appearance as to why I suddenly feel the way I do. She's the shade, and texture, of a boiled beetroot. Relatively lipless, totally hairless and with eyes the same colour as the barrel of a particularly oily SLR semi-automatic after it's been fired several times. Yet here I sit, frozen on the outside and completely melted on the inside – sort of like a Choc Wedge that hasn't been in the freezer very long.

'Want to hold her, Mum?' Bronte seems oblivious to the life-changing event that has just taken place. 'Come on, she won't bite.'

'Humph,' says the mound of blankets on the other bed.

'Oh, okay, Bronte,' I attempt to sound nonchalant, 'if you insist.'

Bronte passes the baby over and I take her gently, nestling her neatly onto my lap. She looks up at me and yawns, her tiny little mouth stretching to the limit with the effort. And, if anything, I fall in even deeper as I hold her. In fact, if you don't count the rather distracted glimpse that I got of her last night (and I'm not), then I've just fallen in love at first sight for the first time in my life. And I don't even *believe* in falling in love at first sight. But she is so incredibly little, so soft, so pliable, so perfect, so absolutely superlatively precious.

'What do you think?' Bronte interrupts my mental inventory of the baby's perfections. 'Isn't she just gorgeous?'

'Do you know . . .' I look up and realise that they are all looking at me expectantly. 'You're right. She's lovely.'

'Oh, I knew it!' Bronte hugs herself with glee. 'I knew you wouldn't be able to resist her! She's just too . . . too *special*, isn't she?'

'She certainly is,' I say slowly, looking back at her tiny face. 'Really special.'

'Damn straight,' agrees Nick with obvious pride.

'So what are you going to call her?' Mum asks Bronte and Nick eagerly while I concentrate on stroking the baby's tiny fingers. 'Have you thought of any names?'

'Yeah, as a matter of fact we have.' Nick grins at Bronte. 'Haven't we, Bron?'

'Yes. We're going to call her —'

'Sherry,' finishes Nick. 'We're going to call her Sherry.'

'But that's *my* name!' Mum looks at them both with amazement. 'What a coincidence!'

'It's no coincidence, Gran,' laughs Bronte. 'We're calling her *after* you, duffer.'

'Oh. Oh, I don't know what to say.' Mum shakes her head and stares at her grand-daughter open-mouthed. 'I'm really touched. I really am.'

'Hello, Sherry.' I put one of my fingers in her tiny palm and she curls an impossibly minuscule set of digits around it. I'm a bit taken aback at their choice of name. What a lovely gesture for my mother. Besides, as if I wasn't already totally infatuated, her parents have sealed the deal by naming her after an alcoholic beverage. It might not be my absolute favourite, but then 'Champagne' doesn't quite make it as a first name.

'I just can't believe it,' Mum mutters, and then gets up off the bed quickly. 'You'll have to excuse me. I'll be back in a minute.'

'I think she's really pleased,' says Nick as he watches my mother clumsily open the bathroom door. 'In fact, I think she's crying.'

'What about you, Mum?' asks Bronte. 'Do you like it?'

'Yes – nice name, nice gesture,' I answer without taking my eyes off Sherry. 'Well done, both of you.'

'Her full name is going to be Sherry Rose Woodmason,' says Bronte. 'The 'Sherry' for *my* Gran, and the 'Rose' for Nick's.'

'Lovely,' I reply supportively. Although, despite the name's obvious liquid attractions, I do have a few reservations about the whole 'Sherry' thing. Because there's a pretty good chance the child will be tall, blonde and blue-eyed like her parents, and there's an equally good chance that she, like her mother and myself, will also be big-breasted. And the thing is that the world is not particularly kind to big-breasted, blue-eyed blondes named Sherry – or, at least, kind in the way I'd prefer.

'Hello? Anyone home?'

'Nick! Bronte! Congratulations!'

'Hand her over! I want to hold my first grandchild!'

I automatically tighten my grip on the baby while I look towards the doorway of the room. David, Diane and their brood are crowding in bearing huge smiles, a variety of gifts, and the obligatory pink balloons. David and his other three sons, Evan, Christopher and Michael, are all built in the exact same mould as Nick. All tall, blonde and Nordic-looking. Diane, on the other hand, looks a lot like my best friend, her sister Camilla. They are both fairly short, around five foot three or so, with light-brown hair, green eyes and a neat figure. They are also both very good value to have around, and have gone a long way towards convincing me that height and IQ don't have to be mutually inclusive.

'Terry! I hear you turned midwife last night.' Diane smiles at me with admiration. 'Rather you than me, I have to say!'

'She'd do anything to be the first to see the baby!' David says with a grin as he shakes his son's hand heartily. 'Congratulations, mate! And now you get to see what life's really all about!'

'Aargh,' says Eeyore from within her blankets.

'Nappies, night-feeds, and never having a top without a stain on the shoulder,' adds Diane, with a curious glance towards the other bed. 'Speaking of which, David, what have you done with *our* two?'

'What?' David looks around distractedly. 'Oh, outside in the hallway. Couldn't get the stroller through the door.'

'So you *left* them there?' queries Diane with a sigh. 'Chris, Michael – can you go and get the twins out of their stroller and bring them in?'

'What kept you?' I ask curiously. 'You said you were on the way when I rang you hours ago.'

'Oh, we stopped to grab some presents for the baby,' says Diane as she unloads the gifts onto Nick's lap. 'And you try taking this lot anywhere near a shopping centre! It's sheer torture.'

The two boys who had left to fetch their sisters come back in with a dark-haired baby girl each. One of the babies has her thumb shoved in her mouth and is leaning against her brother's chest placidly, while the other one is straining to get down and screeching what definitely sound like baby obscenities. The twins, Robin and Regan, were born in February and are, I suppose, about six months old.

My mother chooses this moment to re-emerge, rather

red-eyed, from the bathroom. She shuts the door gently behind her, looks at the now crowded room and smiles happily.

'Did they tell you what they've named the baby?' she asks eagerly. 'Go on, Bronte, tell them!'

'Sherry Rose Woodmason,' announces Nick grandly. 'After Bron's Gran and mine.'

'That's lovely,' says his mother approvingly. 'You *are* a thoughtful boy.'

'So where's the bundle of joy?' asks David. 'Hand her over, Terry, you've had more than enough.'

Although I disagree strenuously, I also realise I've got little chance of hanging on to the object of my desire for now. So I get up reluctantly, and David slides into my seat and takes Sherry. My arms immediately feel weightless and uncomfortably empty. I stroke my finger across her face briefly before retreating to the opposite side of the room, where I lean against the corner cupboard. The Woodmasons all crowd around David and the baby and utter various words of admiration.

Christopher deposits the twin he is carrying on the floor where she immediately flips herself neatly over onto her back. Then, to my admiration, by arching her back and then relaxing it in turn she proceeds to concertina herself along the floor in a slow but steady backward motion. I don't know much about babies but I do believe this is quite an achievement, albeit an odd one, for a baby of her age. I look over at the wonderchild's mother and raise my eyebrows questioningly. Diane just grins and shrugs, then transfers her gaze to her mobile daughter, who has now reached the wall and is changing direction.

Meanwhile, the other twin has also been placed on the floor. However, she is obviously not up to the crawling – or flopping – stage yet. Instead, her brother has just ducked down and thoughtfully laid her out of the way under the bed where she can't be tripped over or trampled on. After gazing at the underside of the bed in opened-mouthed awe for several minutes, the baby slowly rolls to one side, picks up a large bit of fluff, and crams it in her still-open mouth.

'Diane! Don't you watch what your children are eating? Really!'

I turn towards the doorway and there's Diane's mother, making her usual entrance with her husband in tow. Rose Riley is only a shade taller than my own mother and about the same age, although she looks much older. She's also twice as sharp. She keeps her three daughters and each of her nine grandchildren firmly within sight, and does not hesitate to let them know when she disapproves of their actions. Harold, a portly gentleman with tonsured white hair and a permanently worried smile, is her perfect match. He's as round as she is thin and as self-deprecating as she is self-confident. He also happens to be her fourth husband and, as all the others died relatively prematurely, had better enjoy himself while he can.

'Mum! Robin, spit it out.' Diane squats down and inserts a finger expertly into the baby's fluff-filled mouth. 'Here, give it up. *Thank* you.'

'Search and Destroy!' laughs Nick from the bed.

'Hello, everybody,' says Harold, with a general beam all round. 'I hear congratulations are in order. Is that right?'

'It certainly is,' agrees his wife firmly, 'and where is the darling baby?'

I cram myself further into my corner as I watch Rose smoothly take over both the darling baby and the green vinyl armchair. She settles herself in and starts cooing to Sherry, who looks rather bemused.

'Hello there, early bird,' she says to the baby. 'Harold, give them their gift. So, what's her name?'

'It's Sherry Rose Woodmason,' Nick proudly announces again. 'After both her great-grandmothers.'

'Like, we just thought that Sherry Rose sounded a bit better than Rose Sherry,' explains Bronte nervously as she takes a tissue-covered gift from Harold and starts to unwrap it. 'Oh, look, Nick! A sheet-set for the cot! We needed one of these, Mrs Riley, thank you so much.'

'I knew you'd both neglect the practical things.' Rose glances briefly at the ceiling and purses her lips. 'Young people always do.'

'What do you think of the baby's name, Rose?' Mum moves over to stand next to Rose. 'Isn't it a lovely gesture?'

'Why hello, Sherry!' says Rose with obvious pleasure. 'I didn't see you there! You *are* looking well!'

'So are you, honey,' says Mum. 'I like what you've done with your hair.'

We all stare automatically at Rose's hair, which to me looks exactly the same as it always does. Short, wavy and a light Wedgwood-blue colour. Today it matches the twin-set she is wearing with a brown tweed skirt and woollen scarf.

'Yes, I thought I'd try something different. Nice of you to notice.' Rose gives her daughter a fleeting glance. 'Nobody *else* seems to have.'

'So what do you think, Mum?' Diane wisely refrains from commenting on her mother's hair. 'Isn't it nice of Nick to name the baby after both of you?'

'Yes, it is. Thank you.' Rose gives the parental pair on the bed a brief but approving nod. 'Although I can't see that Sherry Rose sounds all that much better than Rose Sherry. But each to their own. After all, who am *I* to comment?'

'You're the matriarch, that's who you are.' Elizabeth, Diane's youngest sister, crowds her way into the room accompanied by her fiancé, Phillip, and yet another pink balloon. 'Isn't that the way it works? When you're a grandmother, you're just a grandmother, but when the next generation starts arriving – well, you get promoted to matriarch and then you can start bossing everyone around.'

'Bit late now,' mutters Diane under her breath to me, 'she's already been doing that for years.'

'Bloody hell,' says David with feeling, and receives a narrow glance from his mother-in-law in response. 'Not you, Mum – I meant Robin. She's crammed a tissue in her mouth. Can you grab her, Di?'

'Sure,' says his wife with annoyance as she bends down to the daughter under the bed. 'I wouldn't want you having to move, after all.'

'Hello, all,' says Phillip, looking exceptionally tall, dark and well groomed, as usual. 'Congratulations, Nick and Bronte.'

'Thanks, mate,' responds Nick, who seems to be in his element. 'Come over and have a better look.'

'Okay.' Phillip grabs Elizabeth by the hand and they move slowly across the crowded room. Elizabeth gives me a smile as she passes and I smile back. She is a taller version of her two older sisters but, apart from that and a tendency to add chestnut highlights to her much longer hair, looks almost identical.

'Is this Bronte Diamond's room?' asks a young female at the door. She has flat black hair, flat black clothing and a large gold hoop through one eyebrow. She is also holding what looks like a badly wrapped pogo stick.

'Merrill!' yell Bronte and Nick in unison from the bed. 'Come in!'

Merrill comes in, and is immediately followed by about four other young females and one extremely reluctant-looking male. They head over to the bed and deliver a series of kisses to Bronte's cheek and a pile of presents to Nick's lap. I'm shoved even further into my corner and the cupboard handle digs painfully into my back. I'd dearly like to call it quits and escape but I don't like my chances of dragging my mother away. She has firmly ensconced herself on the armrest of the green vinyl chair and is deep in discussion with Rose Riley who, obviously taking the matriarch role seriously, is showing no inclination to give up either the baby *or* the only seat. For some reason, which I've never been able to fathom, Rose and my mother get along extremely well and even go on quite a lot of outings together. Perhaps opposites really *do* attract.

One of Diane's boys elbows me in the stomach as he tries to manoeuvre his way past. While I double up in pain, he apologises quickly and then steps over a sister as he continues pushing his way towards his brothers, who are leaning casually against Eeyore's bed-end on the other side of the room. Eeyore herself is still buried.

'Look what I've got!' He brandishes the television remote control at them and they respond with various hoots of encouragement. Within seconds the television is on, the sports channel has been found, and all the males in the room are watching with varying degrees of interest. I glance over to see how Eeyore is taking all this, but she has simply buried herself still deeper and now even her head is covered. Diane follows my gaze and, when she sees the small mound of blankets, takes the remote from one of her sons and turns the volume down as well as shooing them away from the bed-end. But it doesn't make any real difference either to the level of noise in the room or the feeling of claustrophobia.

Meanwhile, the mobile twin has flip-flopped over to me and has her neck bent back at an impossible angle while she looks up at me with interest. After a few moments contemplation, she gives a sudden, sideways jerk and rolls herself onto her stomach. Then she reaches up to hook a finger into the lowest side pocket of my cargo pants and, using this as leverage, slowly but surely pulls herself into a wobbly standing position. Once upright, she looks around for applause.

'Bravo, Regan!' says Regan's mother with enthusiasm as her offspring leans forwards and starts sucking wetly on my knee. 'Did you see that, David?'

'Yes!' responds her husband heartily. 'What a clever girl!'

'Did you know, I only just found out that my daughter has changed her entire carpet?' Mum asks Rose incredulously. 'She never tells me anything!'

'I know the feeling, dear,' says Rose, shaking her head sympathetically as she adjusts the bunny-rug around Sherry and slaps Elizabeth's hand away. 'Always the last to know.'

From my position in the far corner, I can barely see any more of Sherry than her pink bunny-rug. I raise myself on tiptoes and peer over the heads of the various visitors in front of me. This has two immediate benefits. One is that the knee-sucker loses her grip and falls backwards, landing with a solid thump on her behind. And the other is that now I can see the top of Sherry's bald little head.

Diane dives forwards and collects her daughter just as the infant limpet opens her mouth and begins screaming with anger. I don't take much notice because I'm still stretched out and focusing on a glimpse of pink scalp across the room. As my ankles start to send distress signals up towards my thighs, I lower myself down, smiling in amazement as I remember what it was like when I first saw her properly about twenty minutes ago. Who'd have thought that I, of all people, would have such an extreme reaction to a baby? All I want to do now is get rid of these people, sit down with her on my lap, and spend a few hours admiring her in peace.

The child in question, who has been remarkably well behaved so far, now begins to fret and Rose picks her up expertly and pops her up on one shoulder, with her hand behind Sherry's head for support. Then, in answer to yet another query from my mother, Rose turns slightly and suddenly I'm rewarded with a complete facial view of the object of my devotion. For a brief instant it's almost like her eyes lock in with mine and I get a thrill of connection that echoes through my bones and turns my stomach to porridge. I know, on a sensible level, that not only can the baby not see me, but that she's really only interested in where her next feed is coming from. And, in that regard, I'm totally useless. But rationality doesn't matter, and logic doesn't count.

Because I'm in love.

# MONDAY

## 1710 hrs

I flick my right-hand blinker on and slow to a halt while I wait patiently for a learner-driver, and the long line of cars trailing her, to pass by on the opposite side of the road. I congratulate myself on my patience because, really, I haven't had a good day at all.

After finally dragging my mother away from the hospital, I discovered that I'd left my car lights on and the battery was flat. It took three-quarters of an hour for roadside assistance to turn up. Three-quarters of an hour spent leaning against the car in the freezing cold, listening to inane chitchat from the person who was responsible for the lights being on in the first place. At some point I tuned out but apparently during that period, or so she informed me later, I promised I'd take her grocery shopping as soon as we were mobile again. But first, because we hadn't had lunch and she couldn't possibly shop on an empty stomach (apparently this is an economic no-no), we had to visit the pub for a counter lunch. And it *had* to be the pub because after eating she likes to play the pokies for half an hour or so to settle her food down. It certainly didn't work that way for me. After watching various elderly gentlemen push my mother's buttons while I lost twenty bucks in ten minutes flat, my food was anything but settled.

Then, by the time I dropped her off with her twenty-five bags of groceries, it was late afternoon and she insisted on supplying me with coffee and biscuits as a thank-you for running her around all day. So I sat and yawned and ate dutifully while she filled me in on the goings-on of my brother, my uncle, my cousins and each of their families as well as all the gossip from the old neighbourhood. Which, if even half her stories were true, certainly makes my current neighbourhood sound incredibly dull by comparison. Thank god.

The long line of cars continues to crawl by and I idly glance past them and down my street, immediately spotting the rear of Fergus's distinctive yellow panel van parked against the nature strip adjoining my block of units. Hell – I'd forgotten he was coming over this evening! Without really giving it any conscious thought, I flick my blinker off and quickly head back out in the direction that I am pointed. As Fergus usually waits in his car if I'm not home, I very much doubt he saw me in the few minutes I was stationary. Nevertheless, I feel guilty and rude, and downright sneaky. Also a tad confused. Why did I do what I just did? I mean, I *enjoy* Fergus's company – that's why I've been going out with him for almost six months. So why did my stomach just sink at the sight of his car?

All I know for sure is that I'm not changing my mind – my unit is off limits until Fergus gives up and goes home. Which means I've got a few hours to kill because he's a very patient man. I briefly consider going to the supermarket again because, although there's nothing I can think of that I forgot earlier, I'm sure I'd still be able to fill a trolley without much difficulty. It's one of those truisms that grocery conglomerates rely on. But I really don't feel like facing a supermarket twice in one day.

Another option would be a visit to the Tim Neville Arboretum, which is just around the corner, and has some lovely walks that would use up time. If, that is, I felt like taking a lovely walk – which I most certainly don't. Then I suddenly come up with a brainwave. I'll visit Camilla, who lives only about ten minutes past the Arboretum. Apart from the fact that I can regale her with my stint as an obstetrician, I'm absolutely dying to bore someone to death with how damned gorgeous the newest member of my family is. And as the newest member of my family also happens to be the newest member of hers – well, it's perfect.

The only drawback to visiting Cam at this time of day is that at her house it'll be akin to feeding time at the zoo. Except it's like you're *in* the animal enclosure, not just watching. However, my desire to discuss Sherry and avoid Fergus is currently greater than my aversion to children and animals en masse. So I veer into the adjoining lane and take the next corner at a sharp angle that a lesser driver than me would have found positively risky. A few minutes later I'm pulling into Cam's driveway and parking behind her old Holden.

I run my fingers through my hair to comb it smooth before ringing the doorbell and then waiting patiently. But nobody comes to answer it. This is very unusual for Cam's house, so I walk over to the lounge-room window and press my face against the glass to peer in. I can't see anybody watching television but I can hear some music in the background so there's definitely somebody home. Most probably Cam herself, judging by the car in the driveway. I walk back to the door and give the doorbell another try but still no answer. However, my heart is now set on unburdening myself, so I'm not giving up without a fight. I try the door handle and it turns easily so I push the door open and call out softly.

'Hello? Anybody home?' I venture inside and step over a pile of school shoes in the hallway. 'Hello?'

The music is coming from the kitchen area, so I wander up there and check it out. On the radio Roy Orbison is pleading with a pretty woman to look his way, but there's nobody around. Just a large pot of something simmering on the stove and a glass of wine sitting on the bench. I take a look out of the kitchen window into the backyard but it too is deserted. Except for Murphy, their Border collie cross, who is lolling on top of a double-decker hutch containing some rather lethargic-looking rabbits. I pick up the glass of wine and, sure enough, it's still chilled. This is beginning to feel like the mystery of the *Marie Celeste*.

'Hello? Cam? Anybody?' I meander into the lounge-room where, from its glass tank on the sideboard, a blue-tongue lizard flicks a moist dark tongue in and out and watches me suspiciously. As I stand there, trying to ignore the tongue and work out where everybody is, I suddenly realise I can hear some muffled noises coming from the other side of the house. At last. I head back over into the passageway and towards Cam's bedroom where, sure enough, I can hear her murmuring.

'I've been looking everywhere for you!' I exclaim cheerfully as I push the bedroom door open. And immediately freeze in shock – because I *can't* be seeing what I think I'm seeing. I just can't.

There, on my best friend's bed and in full festive regalia, is none other than Santa Claus. And he's not there stuffing stockings either. As I've flung the door open, he has leapt up and, with his bright-red fur-trimmed trousers hanging around his ankles, has executed a perfect tuck and roll and disappeared over the far side of the bed. But before he vanished from sight, I saw enough to be able to vouch personally and definitively for his cheeks being *extremely* flushed and jolly.

Left on her lonesome in the middle of the bed is my best friend, Camilla Riley. She is sitting up with both hands holding a sheet to her neck, and is staring at me with a horrified expression. In fact, she'd look exactly like some Victorian virgin protecting her modesty if it weren't for one little anomaly. Which is the pair of red and green reindeer antlers firmly attached to the top of her head.

'*Terry!*'

'I'm sorry! I'm *so* sorry!' I try to back out but my feet are frozen in position. After all, it's not every day you get to see Father Christmas delivering his presents. Even if it *is* July.

'I didn't hear you come in!' Cam says, appalled, as her antlers wobble with agitation. 'Where did you *come* from?'

'I rang the bell! I called and called!' I say hysterically as I realise with a surge of relief that my feet have started working again. I immediately back straight into the doorframe, bounce off it, and rebound into the hallway.

'Terry! Hang on!' Cam calls and I hear her jump off the bed. Then she appears in the doorway dressed only in a half-buttoned pyjama top and with the antlers still firmly in place. Blushing madly, she looks at me with embarrassment. I look back, with equal embarrassment.

'I'm *so* sorry!'

'Hell's bells! So am I!'

'I thought you'd all be at home! I never thought that you'd . . . that is, it never occurred to me that –'

'No, I *never* usually have the house to myself at this time! I can't believe that the one time I have – my *god*!'

'But I rang the doorbell! Twice!'

'It's not working!'

'Oh, I'm so, so, *so* sorry.'

'Don't be. You weren't to know.' Cam takes a deep breath, glances behind her into the bedroom and then turns back to me with her antlers wobbling. 'Um, do you want a glass of wine or something?'

'God forbid!' I say with feeling because the only thing I want to do is get out of here and rid myself of the visions of Christmas, past, present and future. 'But, Cam – Santa Claus? It's *July*, for heaven's sake!'

'I know. Tacky, isn't it?'

We both look at each other in silence for a moment, and then suddenly burst out laughing. I hold on to the wall as I laugh so hard my side threatens to split.

'I can't *believe* you saw that!' Cam puts her hands over her face. 'God!'

'I wouldn't believe it either,' I say, trying to stop laughing, 'if you didn't *still* have those bloody antlers on your head!'

'What!' Cam puts her hand up and, with a shriek, rips the antlers off and flings them back through the bedroom doorway. Then she looks at me and we both break up again. From the bedroom, a deeper voice joins in the laughter. After a few minutes, I finally get myself more under control and look at Cam with a grin.

'That reminds me. How's Alex? I haven't seen him for *ages*.'

'Fine. I expect he's just fine.' Cam stops laughing and looks at me with narrowed eyes. 'Why do you ask?'

'No reason,' I reply with a smile because I don't have to see Santa's face to know exactly who he is. Alex Brown is Cam's first ex-husband and the father of her two eldest children. He's also a genuinely nice bloke who came back to Australia in February after some years spent overseas, and became Cam's next-door neighbour and a little bit more. That little bit more has now escalated into a full-blown affair with both participants acting like lovesick teenagers with a first crush.

The most entertaining thing about the situation is that both Cam and Alex think they're being totally clandestine. Whenever they're in the company of others they go out of their way to avoid contact but, every so often, they can be seen giving each other long, dark, passionate looks which speak volumes about what they're going to get up to as soon as they have the chance. The whole thing is amusingly ridiculous because, with the exception perhaps of Cam's children, everybody knows exactly what's happening and, furthermore, everybody totally approves. Perhaps they simply like all the secretive extramarital side of things. Maybe it turns them on. Obviously, odd things do.

However, this is the first time anybody has actually caught them in the act, and I don't think Cam will be all that pleased about having their relationship exposed. So, if it makes her happy, I'll just go along with the notion she's having an affair with Father Christmas. Although, personally, I think I'd prefer Alex.

'Humph,' says Cam, who is looking rather embarrassed again.

'Well, tell Alex hi from me next time you see him,' I say as I head for the front door. 'And while you've got Santa in a good mood, could you tell him I'm after new wall-to-wall carpeting for Christmas?'

'What?'

'Never mind. I'll explain later.' I back out the door and wave politely. 'Merry Christmas!'

# MONDAY

## 1735 hrs

It's still too early to go home so I drive aimlessly in the direction of the mountains until I come to the Ferntree Gully National Park lower picnic grounds. I'm not sure if there are any higher picnic grounds – if there are I've never found them. I put my blinker on, turn into the park and coast into a spot opposite the children's playground. Then I unbuckle my seatbelt, wind down the window slightly, stretch out the kinks in my back and prepare to waste time.

About twenty or so people have braved the July cold for some sort of celebration, judging by the balloons and streamers that adorn the rustic wood shelter they're clustered underneath. And if the raucous laughter coming from that direction is any indication, alcohol has been flowing freely for a large part of the afternoon. It'd need to, otherwise the party-goers would be frozen. Apart from that group, the park is only occupied by one hardy family enjoying a midwinter barbecue tea and the playground is crawling with their numerous off-spring. There's just a small amount of light left in the day and the sun has already begun its slow descent, bathing the tree-tops in a soft crimson glow that makes them look almost luminescent.

I watch the sun setting for a few minutes while I run over the scene I just witnessed at Cam's house. And, as soon as I get to the part where I push open the bedroom door, my face goes as red as the sunset. But one thing's for sure, after I've stopped feeling so embarrassed, I'm going to be able to get an awful lot of mileage out of this. Santa Claus indeed! Who on earth deliberately chooses a guy who only comes once a year? I chortle to myself at my wittiness.

But at least Cam has got someone. Not that I don't, but spotting Fergus outside the unit depressed me in some indefinable way. Either that or my *reaction* to spotting Fergus outside the unit has depressed me in some indefinable way. Whichever – I'm still a tad depressed. In some indefinable way.

I frown and then chew my lip thoughtfully while I mull this over for a while. And it hits me. I'll bet my bottom dollar that, subconsciously, I remembered that the carpet was a mess and so was I. After all, I've been running around all day and I didn't get much sleep last night so I'm feeling very tired and not at all up to entertaining. Yes, that's all it was, and nothing more serious. Amazing how the subconscious can work.

I smile happily and resume feeling content once more. What's not to feel content about when you've got a few days off and don't have to get up each morning and work away at your career? Well, if you could call it a career, that is. But I've got no one except myself to blame for the fact I'm destined to remain on the bottom rung of the library ladder.

Unlike my brother, who towed the parental line and became a lawyer like our father, I felt the need to rebel somewhat and joined the services instead. Unfortunately, the irony of my escape from one form of heavy-handed discipline straight to another eluded me at the time. But my three years in the Royal Australian Air Force were some of the most fun-filled of my life. For starters, the ratio of men to women in those days was about one hundred to one and, if I say so myself, I looked *very* good in uniform. I smile with reminiscent pleasure before moving back to the present and sighing.

Because the end result of all this disciplined frivolity is that, while my brother Thomas enjoys high-powered, well-paid employment, I labour in the local library for a rather average wage. And I'm not even a librarian because *that* requires a degree. I'm a Library Officer. A lowly position that's too far away from the glass ceiling even to throw rocks at it with any hope of success. Instead, I'm required by my job description to maintain a helpful demeanour and ensure the requisite smile is plastered on at all times. And, to be frank, my facial muscles are getting very, very tired.

I look at my watch to find that all this deep and meaningful thought has only taken twenty-eight and a half minutes. But the night is rapidly approaching and the picnicking family has begun the long process of packing up and finding children. The father lugs a bag of rubbish over to the bin near my car and glances in at me curiously. I stare straight ahead and avoid eye contact. Then it occurs to me that this probably makes me look even weirder, or perhaps spaced out on drugs, so I whip my head around quickly and grin at him in a reasonably friendly fashion. I immediately realise this was a mistake because he looks back at me askance, shoves his rubbish in the bin and hastily rejoins his wife. They begin a rapid conversation punctuated by several telling looks in my direction. He probably thinks I was trying to pick him up. Huh! He should be so lucky.

And then there's Bronte. Bronte is the most loving, kind, thoughtful daughter anybody could ever want. I can count on one hand the number of problems I've had regarding that girl in the entire time she was growing up. She cleaned her room, studied hard, had nice friends, confided in me – and totally lulled me into a false sense of security. Which was abruptly shattered when she turned twenty, met Nick, fell pregnant and dropped out of university. So now, just like her mother before her, she's a twenty-one year old degree-less parent with a fragile, or at least fledgling, relationship.

But then again, I've got to remind myself that Bronte is not *me*. As Cam has pointed out numerous times, what didn't entirely work for me may well work for Bronte because we are *very* different. In fact, I sometimes think Bronte is like a six-foot, slightly more highly-strung version of my mother. And my mother married young, had children early and lived a very contented life. Still does, actually.

Besides, no matter what does or doesn't happen between Bronte and Nick, they've still managed to create something pretty damn special. It's all rather ironic, really, because when I first heard about the baby's existence, I was devastated – even apart from the realisation I was about to become what is known in certain circles as a *grandmother*. But who'd have guessed that they would produce such a delightful, delectable, utterly *gorgeous* little mound of brand-new humanity? I suppose that's what they mean by silver linings.

I glance back at my watch and note that forty-two minutes have now passed since I parked here. Dusk has given the playground an eerie, deserted look and the only people still remaining are the stalwart party residue, and even they're in the process of gradually packing up. I push my hair behind my ears as I yawn sleepily and then stretch. It occurs to me I've been up for over fourteen hours and it isn't even teatime yet.

A warmly coated elderly couple with a golden retriever walking obediently at their side stroll slowly past, gloved hand in gloved hand, and head towards the thousand steps at the rear of the park. As they pass the playground, the woman turns to her partner, who is wearing a bright-red cloth cap, and says something indistinguishable. Without even looking at her, he raises their joined hands and delivers a kiss to her glove. I smile as I watch them go and then lean back in my seat. Only a little while longer and it should be safe to go home. I put the radio on and Kylie Minogue's voice warbles out so, even though she is a better singer than she is a tennis player, I turn it off again. Instead I decide to close my eyes for a minute, or perhaps a second.

Yep, just a second.

I sit bolt upright in shock as a sharp knock echoes right next to my ear. Then I blink several times and, staring straight ahead, try to place myself. All I know is that it's pitch black and bitterly cold.

'Lady? Hey, lady? Excuse me?'

Still confused, I turn to the source of the gravelly voice and immediately jump as I see a rather distorted face pushed very close to the glass. My adrenalin speeds as my heart threatens to jump out of my mouth and race screaming off into the dark. Then the face backs off a bit and becomes relatively normal. It seems to belong to an elderly gentleman with snow-white hair and a red cloth cap. And I recognise suddenly that it's the same guy who went strolling past with his partner just before I closed my eyes for a second. My heart starts to return to its normal rhythm and I stare at him, still open-mouthed.

'Are you all right?' he asks with concern, his voice muffled by the window-glass.

'Um, yes. Yes, of course.' I wind the window down and slowly realise I must have fallen asleep out here, so I glance quickly at the clock in the dashboard and register that it's past eight o'clock. 'Hell! Look at the time!'

'Exactly,' says the face by the window. 'Bit late for a young lady like you to be out here alone, isn't it?'

'Yes, it is,' I agree. 'I must've fallen asleep.'

'Well, perhaps you'd better head home then.'

'I will. And thanks.'

'No problem.' He straightens up and walks over to join his wife, who is standing on the path holding their dog on a lead. Obviously he'd left them both out of harm's way just in case

I was a raving maniac. I wind my window back up as my heart warms to him and I smile in gratitude. They both smile back and raise a gloved hand each in farewell. Then, hand-in-hand, they stroll down the path to the outer reaches of the park and back towards suburbia. I turn the ignition over and put the heater on full as I rub my hands together and watch the couple go. Every bone in my body aches from cold and stiffness. Forty-one is clearly too old to be able to fall asleep in a car and suffer no ill effects. I might seem like a young lady from that old guy's perspective, but it sure doesn't feel like it from mine. I stretch out painfully and groan.

What on earth am I doing here when I've got a perfectly nice, warm home to go to? I shake my head and sigh. The elderly couple have now reached the highway and are waiting for the lights to change. He lets go of her hand and, instead, puts his arm over her shoulders and pulls her closer. I watch them as I wait for my kinks to warm up and suddenly wonder whether Bronte will still be with Nick at their age – whether she will have someone she's so evidently close to, to wander with hand-in-hand through a tree-lined park in winter.

And I wonder if I will.

# TUESDAY

# TUESDAY

## 0920 hrs

'What did you do, lady, slaughter someone in 'ere?' The carpet cleaner, who could easily be that horrid ambulance man's clone but for his blue bib-and-brace overalls, stares with awe at the big stain in front of my couch. To my untrained eye, it appears to have spread.

'That's right,' I reply jovially. 'That's all that's left of the last guy who couldn't get my carpet clean.'

'Funny,' he says, visibly unamused.

I feel a bit embarrassed now so I speak quickly: 'It's from my daughter. You see, she gave birth there yesterday. On the carpet. So it's a birthmark – get it? A birth*mark*, because she . . . oh, okay.'

I peter out in the face of his stony silence. After I finish rambling, he looks slowly from me to the stain and then back again, obviously having trouble digesting the information. His offsider, a very plump guy who is completely bald and has a gold stud through one side of his enormous hooked nose, comes trundling in dragging some machinery behind him.

'Look 'ere, Matt,' says the first guy, 'some bird 'ad a baby 'ere yesterday.'

'On the carpet?'

'Yep. So they say.'

'On the *carpet?*'

'Yep.'

'Bloody hell.'

'Yep.'

'Haven't they heard of hospitals?'

'Actually,' I chime in, getting pretty irritated, 'we *have* heard of hospitals, thank you. There just wasn't time.'

'Bloody hell.'

'Yep.'

'So, what can you do?' I decide that this could go on and on unless I get them to the point. 'Can you get it out or not?'

'Let's see . . .' Matt props one elbow on the machinery he has dragged in, and contemplates the stain. 'Hmm. Bloody hell.'

'Yep.'

'Perhaps I should just leave you to it?' I suggest with annoyance, 'and you can let me know after you've discussed it.'

'So what're we talking here?' asks Matt, looking at me for the first time.

'What do you mean?'

'Fluids. What're we talking?' Matt points at the stain with his foot. 'I'm guessing bit o' blood, some amniotic fluid – that be about it?'

'Well, we didn't stop for a glass of red wine, if that's what you mean,' I say sarcastically. 'Why, does it matter?'

'Of course!' sniffs Matt. 'And you shouldn't have left it overnight, that's for sure. You'll have set it by now.'

'Yep,' agrees his offsider.

'Well, I *tried* to get an appointment yesterday but I couldn't!'

'Amniotic fluid, mate.' Matt ignores me and turns to his partner. 'Ever had amniotic fluid before?'

'Not personally.'

'Me neither. Bloody hell.'

'Yep.'

'What about coffee or tea?' I ask politely, because sometimes a friendly gesture can have a positive influence on the willingness of people to work miracles.

'Coffee! Tea!' Matt stares at the stain with fresh horror. 'You didn't mention them!'

'Not there! I mean do you *want* a cup of tea!'

'Thank god! Tea's a real bitch,' says Matt with relief.

'So would you like some?' I ask patiently.

'Yeah, great!' says the first guy enthusiastically. 'White and two for me and black with none for Matt.'

'I'm on a diet,' confides Matt morosely. 'Bugger it.'

'Yep, 'is missus won't let 'im 'ave nothing decent.'

'Bloody hell.'

'Yep.'

I leave them leaning on the machinery discussing diets and amniotic fluid, and go to the kitchen to put the kettle on. While it's heating up, I open the window slightly to try to coax some fresh air into the unit. It's pretty cold out there, but it's pretty stale in here. Then I straighten Tutankhamen on the fridge and study today's list to see if I've forgotten anything.

## TUESDAY

Phone calls — Cam, Fergus, Dennis?
Morning — Shopping: baby present, new d/gown
— Get some videos
Afternoon — Visit Stephen & say thanks with chocolates

　　　　　　　　　– *Relax/watch videos*
　　　　　　　　　– *Do my tax return*
*Evening*　　　　– *Visit Bronte*
　　　　　　　　　– *Start reading Gone with the Wind*

It promises to be a much more relaxing day than yesterday so I give the list a nod of satisfaction before reaching out to turn the kettle off. The phone rings just as I'm pouring hot water over the teabags so I tuck one side of my hair behind an ear and answer it.

'Hello?'

'Terry, my love!' Fergus's lilting voice comes through crackly with static from his mobile. 'And what was happening to you last night?'

'Oh, I'm *so* sorry! But, guess what? Bronte had her baby!'

'You're kidding me! A lass or a lad?'

'A lass. They've called her Sherry.'

'Well, isn't that bloody great!' Fergus says cheerfully. 'And they're both after doing fine?'

'Sure.' I think quickly and decide to postpone filling Fergus in on the exact whereabouts of the birth. He'll want to know all the ins and outs, literally, and I just don't have time at the moment. 'And it all went well and she's in the Angliss for a couple of days. I've taken the week off work.'

'Well, I'll have to be getting in there to see her. Perhaps tonight – are you?'

'Um, I don't really know,' I say slowly. 'I haven't decided.'

'Great!' Fergus's voice starts to break up slightly. 'I'll be picking you up then and we'll be going in together.'

'Oh. Okay.'

'It's a date then! I'll be seeing you directly after work.'

'Terrific. See you then.' I hang up the phone and stare for a few moments at the steam wafting up from the two mugs before me. I realise I don't feel terribly enthusiastic about visiting Bronte with Fergus in tow, probably because I wanted Sherry all to myself. I shrug mentally. I can always go in this morning as well – I *am* the mother of the mother, after all.

Matt and his offsider appear in the kitchen doorway and look expectantly at the mugs on the counter, so I fish out the teabags and pass the black tea over to Matt. Then I add sugar and milk to the other and pass that over as well with instructions to please use the coasters on the coffee table. They thank me profusely and wander back into the lounge-room, no doubt to lean on the machinery again. I put some coffee in the plunger, fill it with hot water and let it sit while I call up a mental picture of Sherry's gorgeous face and examine each of her features in turn. The phone rings once more just as I reach her shell-like little ears and I hesitate before answering it, trying to decide whether it's Fergus again or not. Only one way to find out, I suppose.

'Hello?'

'Congratulations, Grandma!' says Cam warmly. 'You didn't tell me about the baby yesterday!'

'Ho, ho, ho,' I reply with relief, 'if it isn't Santa's little helper!'

'Very funny.'

'Besides, it was a bit hard to tell you *anything* yesterday!' I continue cheerfully. 'You were much too busy decking the halls and jingling the bells!'

'Okay, okay. You've had your fun now, so let's drop it.'

'What's the matter? Won't anybody join in your reindeer games?'

'I said drop it!'

'You wish! I'm only getting started!'

'I'll hang up,' threatens Cam. 'I swear to god, I'll hang up if you say one more word about yesterday.'

'There's no satisfying you, is there?' I reply brightly. 'First you have a go at me for not telling you about the baby and now you say you'll hang up if I talk about yesterday at all!'

'You know what I mean,' says Cam darkly. 'Now, tell me about the baby or else.'

'All right,' I laugh in resignation. 'Well, she's very cute.'

'Come on! Even *you* can do better than that!'

'Well, she's small, red, wrinkled and cute. What more do you want?'

'A lot more. But I see I'll have to visit Bronte to find out. Now, I gather you've taken a few days off?'

'I've taken the whole week. I decided I deserve it.'

'Great! Because I'm on semester break, so we'll be able to do some stuff. Starting with lunch today.'

'Okay,' I reply with enthusiasm. 'To celebrate the baby?'

'Yes – that, of course, and also . . . guess who rang me last night?'

'Um, Mrs Claus? And I'm betting she was really peeved, as well.'

'I'll hang up, I will!' says Cam seriously. 'And you can jam your lunch –'

'Now, now!' I say, with mock horror. 'Naughty girls don't get what they want from Santa, you know. No sirree. You'll be stuffing stockings all on your lonesome, and –'

She hangs up.


# TUESDAY

## 1233 hrs

I park my Barina neatly behind Cam's old Holden and stretch happily. I'm really looking forward to this lunch. Apart from the fact that Cam can't hang up on me if we're face-to-face, she's also invited an old friend we haven't seen for over a year. We all used to work together at the Ferntree Gully Library before Cam decided to turn her life upside down, go back to university and start studying again, while Joanne flitted off overseas to some retreat in an effort to find herself and/or inner peace and contentment on some level. It should be very interesting to see if she has succeeded because Joanne has never been known for inner peace and contentment on *any* level. Before she left she was riddled with insecurities, had a temper to match her flaming red hair, and didn't believe in retreating – only attacking.

I open the car door and step out, straight onto the toe of a deserted Rollerblade that flicks up and hits me in the shin with one of its wheels. I curse roundly and kick the Rollerblade over to the garden, where it rebounds off a neglected-looking tree fern and falls onto a shrub. Where, no doubt, it will remain for the rest of its days. I love her dearly, but Cam has three of the messiest children I've ever met in my life – and a messy life to match.

Like me, she is divorced but has two ex-husbands to contend with. The first ex-husband is, of course, Alex, and a really nice guy to have around, whether or not he is masquerading as Santa Claus. But Keith, the second ex-husband, is a real pillock who set a record for obnoxious behaviour during the marriage that he's been at pains to surpass ever since. Unfortunately, he's also the father of Cam's youngest daughter, CJ, whose temperament is showing clear signs of being an inheritance from his side of the family.

I shake myself out of my reverie and rub my shin, which is still smarting. Then I reach back into the car to grab the box containing my contribution to lunch. I slam the car door shut with my butt before crossing the lawn to the porch and knocking loudly on the front door. There's no way I'm *ever* letting myself in again after yesterday. While I'm waiting, I check out my reflection quickly in the lounge-room window. Blonde hair waterfalling down from an oversized bronze clip at the back, black cowl-neck jumper, denim jeans, black ankle boots – not too bad. After a little while the door opens and Cam, dressed in identical jeans but with a cream cardigan, grins up at me.

'You're late.'

'Yes, but I brought cheesecake,' I say as I hand her the brightly coloured cake box. 'It's one of those creamy chocolate ones that makes you put on weight simply by looking at it.'

'Just what I need,' replies Cam with a grimace as she takes the box and shuts the front door behind me, 'but I appreciate the effort you've gone to. Must have taken you hours.'

'That's right. I spent all morning cooking and then packed it in this bakery box so you'd think it was a bought one.'

'Well, it worked. I think it's a bought one.'

'See?' I say as we walk down the passage and towards the kitchen. On the way, I negotiate my way past a single Rollerblade (probably the mate to the one now in the garden) with a purple sock dangling from it, and then step over a Barbie bus loaded with an assortment of well-dressed blonde occupants and a one-armed, naked Ken doll who looks inordinately pleased with himself.

'Sorry about the mess.' Cam kicks the Rollerblade over to one side and then bends down to pick up a lunch-box lid that she balances on top of the cake box.

'What's new?' I comment as we arrive in the kitchen, where various salad vegetables are spread haphazardly across the island bench. 'And, anyway, where's the happy wanderer?'

'She's running late too.' Cam throws the lunch-box lid into the sink, puts the cake box down on the bench and then goes to check the contents of the oven. As soon as she opens it a delicious aroma wafts out.

'That smells good!' I sniff appreciatively and clear some assorted debris from the kitchen table as I settle myself into a chair. 'What's on the menu?'

'Quiche and salad. With fresh-baked bread.'

'Sounds great!' I say with considerable feeling. 'Have you been taking lessons?'

'Of course not! I *can* cook, you know.'

'Hmm,' I reply noncommitally. 'Anyway, I'm starving. Do we *have* to wait for Joanne?'

'Yes. We do,' answers Cam emphatically as she fills the kettle, puts it on the stove and then gestures towards the adjoining room. 'I've even set the table up in the dining-room for the occasion. See?'

I twist around and peer through the doorway at a table beautifully set with a vase of abundant greenery, rattan place-mats, vivid red and green serviettes, and crystal wineglasses. 'Very impressive, and very Christmassy. Is this an ongoing theme?'

'Aargh! I *knew* you wouldn't be able to shut up about that!' Cam turns and tries to look stern, but fails miserably and starts laughing instead. 'God.'

'No, Santa Claus. I distinctly remember.'

'I'm going to kill you.'

'Please!' I put my hands up in mock surrender. 'Don't blame me! You should know by now that you're only meant to sit on his lap!'

'Hey, you're a fine one to talk, anyway!' Cam rallies round for the attack. '*You're* going out with a leprechaun!'

'Ah, yes,' I say sagely, 'but he doesn't dress up as a lep-rechaun. *That's* the rub.'

'Hell's bells.'

'And speaking of rubbing. Tell me, all that fur – didn't you get a rash?'

'Okay – now,' Cam takes a deep breath and massages both temples with the tips of her fingers, 'I think I know the only way I'm going to be able to stop this.'

'By moving on to the Easter Bunny?'

'No,' she smirks at me, 'but do you remember how you told me once that Dennis was much better in the sack than Fergus?'

'Yes! But you promised not to tell – oh, I see. But you know it won't work. Even if you told Fergus, he'd just try harder so I'd still win.'

'It wouldn't be Fergus I'd be telling.'

'Well, then . . .' I trail off slowly.

'That's right,' Cam says smugly. 'I'm sure Dennis would be really chuffed.'

'You wouldn't.'

'Would.'

'Wouldn't.'

'Try me.'

'Wow. Know what you remind me of?' I ask as I smooth the sides of my hair and pretend nonchalance. 'The Grinch, that's who.'

'*Terry!*'

'What?' I ask innocently. 'What did I do now?'

'You know.' She reaches up into a cupboard and pulls out a pair of ceramic mugs. 'Maybe one day I'll be able to laugh about it too – but I doubt it.'

'Okay. Enough's enough,' I nod obligingly. 'But I still think the table looks very . . . um, festive. Perhaps I should have brought champagne?'

'No need because I'm totally organised. There's some in the fridge.' Cam gets out a sugar canister and plonks it down next to the mugs. 'But for now, coffee or tea?'

'Tea, thanks.' I look at her with my head on one side for a few moments. 'Hey! You look different – did you colour your hair or something?'

'Yeah, I got a one-shade lighter put through on Saturday and then a few foils for good measure. I've never tried foils before. Do you like it?' Cam does a slightly off-centre pirouette. 'Well?'

'Hmm.' I look at her critically and then nod. 'Actually, yes, I *do* like it!'

'So do I,' she replies complacently as she continues to arrange tea-making paraphernalia, 'and let me tell you, it's been a *long* time since I've liked anything I've had done to my hair.'

I watch her as she pours hot water over the teabags in the mugs. And she *is* looking good. We may have a lot of similarities in our likes and dislikes but, physically, Cam is almost my exact opposite. As short as I'm tall, she has a neat, rounded figure that is much more in proportion than my rather top-heavy one. Her hair, which is usually a light brown but is now a highlighted dark blonde, is worn very short and never allowed even to creep much past her ears. Apart from that, she has rather average features – but an infectious personality that sort of lights her up.

'Are you staring at me?' Cam looks at me curiously as she puts my mug down in front of me and returns to the kitchen to start assembling salad platters.

'I was just thinking how good you're looking, that's all.' I peer around for a coaster and then give up, instead just wrapping my hands around my mug and blowing at the steam. 'What's your secret?'

'No secret,' she laughs self-consciously, 'just good clean living, that's all.'

'In a pig's ear,' I say shortly. 'So, how's Alex?'

'Alex?' Cam looks at me narrowly. 'Fine, I suppose. Why do you ask?'

'Mummy! C'n I hab something to eat? I'm *starbing* hungry.' CJ, Cam's six year old daughter, wanders into the kitchen with a Barbie in each hand and, ignoring me totally, focuses the full force of her rather imperious gaze on her mother.

'CJ, be polite and say hello to Terry.'

''Lo, Terry.' CJ looks at me briefly and then turns back to her mother. 'Mummy, I'm *really* starbing!'

'Hello to you too, CJ,' I reply politely to her back. 'I thought you'd be at school.'

'School finished last week,' says CJ over her shoulder. 'Mummy? Food?'

'CJ, you'll just have to wait. We're having guests.'

'I'll starb to deaf by then,' replies the plumply rounded juvenile as she stomps over to the kitchen table and slides into a chair opposite me. 'My stomach's eben rumbling, you know.'

I watch CJ with interest as she dumps her Barbies on top of the pile of debris at the end of the table, slides a toy catalogue out and begins to study it intently. CJ is a very attractive little girl with bobbed blonde hair and large blue eyes who is, unfortunately, spoilt rotten by both her mother and her father. We have a rather uneasy relationship, as I'm sure she understands that I see right through her shenanigans. However, we seem to have settled into a tacit understanding of the place each other occupies within Cam's life, and therefore manage to avoid stepping on each other's toes. Too much.

She finds a large blue texta and starts to circle items in the catalogue. Mainly Barbies and related accessories. Perhaps she realises Santa Claus has been around, and is getting ready to place her order. After circling eight or nine items, she pauses and looks up at her mother.

'Mummy, I *need* this Barbie, *and* this one coz she's got lubly brown hair, and this one coz Caitlin's got one. And I *really* need this horse 'n carriage coz it's pink. And my Barbies *really* need this couch thingy and a hairdryer for when I take them in the bath. And I really, *really* need this –'

'Hang on,' her mother interrupts, holding up a hand. 'What have I been telling you about Barbies? They're totally warped! Look at her feet, for a start!'

'What's wrong with them?' asks CJ petulantly, holding up one of her Barbies. 'I think she's got lubly feet.'

'CJ! How can you *say* that!' Cam waves a salad server in the air excitedly. 'They are *permanently* arched! How could she play tennis? Or swim, or even walk normally? I'm telling you, young lady, Barbies symbolise everything that is discriminatory about the way the female body is represented – they extend unrealistic expectations which set cultural goals that are simply unattainable. I mean, look at the size of her boobs, for god's sake!'

'That's not fair! Terry's got eben *bigger* boobies –' CJ points disparagingly at my chest '– and you still like *her*!'

'That's not the same. She's in proportion, for a start.'

'No she's not.' CJ sneers at the region in question and then, folding her arms across her own chest protectively, turns back to her mother. 'What's pro-paw-shon, anyway?'

'Excuse me,' I chime in sweetly, 'could we leave my proportions out of this, please? And what the hell are you taking at uni, Cam? Barbie 101? Let's get back to what we were talking about before.'

'What was that?' asks Cam, thrusting the salad server into a bowl while she frowns at both her daughter and the cultural icon of representational evil she's holding.

'I believe it was Alex. And don't play the little innocent with me. I know –'

'Hey!' Cam interrupts rather rudely. 'You haven't told me about the baby.'

'What baby?' asks CJ, dropping the Barbie back on the pile and bestowing her attention upon me. 'Hab you got a baby now?'

'My daughter had a baby,' I explain to her. 'Yesterday. On my carpet.'

'On your *carpet*!' says Cam, astounded. 'Nobody told me that! What was Bronte doing at your house? Where was Nick? Don't tell me – you *didn't* deliver it, did you?'

'Hang on,' I laugh, 'slow down! Firstly, yes – on my carpet. Secondly, she came around in the middle of the night because she didn't feel well and Nick was at work. And, thirdly, yes I delivered it. And did a pretty good job too, if I say so myself.'

'Wow! How did you know what to do?'

'I didn't. She did most of it and I just went along for the ride. Stephen from next door helped as well. Although he fainted when we got to the main bit. The ambulance guys got there after it was all over. And if you don't believe me, I've got the proof – a bloody great stain right in front of the couch that the carpet cleaners can't get out.'

'Terry, I'm impressed.' Cam is still looking stunned. 'You, of all people!'

'What do you mean, me of all people?' I ask curiously.

'Well, you're not usually the most hands-on type of mother, you know. And you freak if anyone drops a pretzel on your carpet. Let alone a baby.'

'That's not quite fair,' I frown at Cam. 'So I'm a tad neat – so what?'

'A *tad* neat?'

'But, if the baby came out on the carpet,' says CJ slowly, 'then where did it come out *from*?'

'From?' repeats Cam, with a confused look at her daughter. 'What do you mean – from?'

'Well, Auntie Diane had her babies in the hospital so I thought that . . . well . . .' CJ thinks furiously. 'See, if the baby was in Bronte's tummy and it was all ready, and then it came out – well, Terry, you were there, you must hab seen it get out – *where* did it come from?'

'I'm sure your mum will explain the whole process to you later,' I smirk at Cam agreeably. 'I'd tell you myself but I'll be too busy tidying my house.'

'But I want to know *now*. Because there's nowhere big enough for a whole baby to come out from.' CJ pauses for a second, and then continues rather doubtfully: '*Is* there?'

We are saved from answering this age-old query by the sound of a car honking in the driveway. Glancing with relief at each other, we both head towards the front door and, with CJ bouncing beside us and still requesting some answers, go outside to greet Joanne.

The car she is driving is a huge bronze 4WD that makes my little hatchback look like it is in desperate need of steroids. Joanne grins and waves excitedly from up behind the steering wheel before pounding the horn once more for good measure. I flinch and put my hand to my head.

'She's here!' Cam states needlessly as she goes over to greet the new arrival. Even CJ momentarily stops her rather irritating bouncing. I wander over to the garden, pick up the Rollerblade from the top of the shrub and place it carefully on the edge of the porch so that it will be easily found later on. Then I walk over to the 4WD to give Joanne, who has clambered down from the driver's seat, a welcoming smile. But instead my eyes are irresistibly drawn to the apparition that is slowly emerging from the passenger side of the car. Because it looks for all the world like a human praying mantis. Out of the corner of my eye I notice that Cam is now staring transfixed as well and, next to her, Joanne is looking on with a huge grin.

The praying mantis unfolds his various lengthy limbs and gradually turns into a very gangly, very badly dressed adult male of about my age. I focus on his lower half simply because the boniness of his knees demands that I do so. And, even apart from the knees, there should definitely be a law regarding the wearing of shorts by anyone that thin. Especially in winter. They are what my father would have called 'walking shorts', crisply pleated in a pale mustard colour reminiscent of the effluent of breastfed babies. The hideous shorts, and the bony knees below, proceed to advance towards us in an unexpectedly coordinated fashion.

'Richard,' the owner of the knees announces in a deep, melodious voice as he folds Cam's hand within both of his and gives it an enthusiastic shake. 'You're Camilla. Ah, pleased. Very pleased.'

'Likewise,' stutters Cam as she tries to disengage her hand. Joanne beams at them both while CJ scuttles closer to her mother's side and stares up at the apparition with her mouth hanging open. Miracles will never cease – this is the longest I've ever seen her go without contributing to the conversation.

'Mummy, who's *that*?'

'I'd better make introductions.' Joanne is still beaming happily. 'Cam, Terry – this is my friend, Richard. Richard – my old friends, Cam and Terry. And this is Cam's youngest daughter, CJ.'

'Tad less of the old, thanks,' I comment dryly as it's my turn to have my hand enveloped in Richard's and given a vigorous shaking that makes me wish I had worn a more supportive bra. When the shaking eases off, I look up at Richard with the vague intention of muttering something polite and non-committal once I'm able to focus – but instead my world promptly collapses as I fall in love at first sight for the second time in my life.

Everything around me suddenly ceases motion as I literally feel the blood drain away from my face. I can't seem to take my eyes away from the person peering down at me yet, try as I might, I also can't quite register any of his details. Instead, my stomach leaps into my chest cavity where, of course, there's no spare room for it and the subsequent compression causes my breathing to become rather restricted. I gasp for air involuntarily and, as if it was just waiting for some small action from me, the world suddenly comes back into play. I lean against my car in shock.

'Hey, are you all right, Terry?'

With a mammoth effort I pull myself together and close my mouth as I realise Cam is staring at me with concern. So is Joanne, and so is – no, I refuse to go there.

'I'm fine,' I say as I try to get my breathing under control, 'I'm fine.'

'You look *very* pale,' says Cam anxiously. 'Perhaps we'd better go inside – then you can sit down.'

'Help you.'

A large male hand is placed firmly under my elbow and, before I can even draw breath to reject the offer, I'm hoisted upright away from the car. My stomach immediately plops back to the area it's accustomed to hanging around and there's a sudden rush of blood to my cranial region. This makes my head swim – and swim badly at that.

'Are you sure you feel okay?' asks Cam with a frown.

'I'm fine – really,' I reply, trying desperately to get rid of the hand. '*Really!*'

'Well, let's get inside anyway.'

'Yes, let's go!' Joanne says cheerfully. 'Cam, lead the way – I'm starving!'

'Damn! My quiche!' Cam shrieks suddenly as she turns and rushes back inside with CJ running behind, one hand tugging insistently at her mother's cardigan. 'God, god, bloody god!'

Joanne follows them and I'm left with the Good Samaritan, whose hand is *still* positioned under my elbow despite all my efforts to shake it off. To avoid eye contact, I stare at his feet, fully aware I'm acting like a brain-damaged adolescent. He's wearing brown sandals and cream socks with a dinky brown pinstripe running around the tops. I suppose that at least they match each other – and the outfit. Flaming hell.

'Ah, sure I can't help?'

'No, I'm all right,' I insist as firmly as I can under the circumstances. Although just *what* the circumstances are, I'm not quite sure.

'Certain?'

'Positive.' I take a step away from the car and am relieved to find my balance is almost restored. 'Come on, I'll take you inside.'

He follows a step or two behind, no doubt preparing to catch me if and when I collapse in a girlish heap. For the first time ever I feel short and I find that, after a lifetime of wishing fervently to *be* short, it's not a feeling I particularly enjoy. Then again, at the moment the only feeling that I *would* enjoy would be the earth opening up and swallowing me whole. But it doesn't oblige, so we walk slowly inside and make our way past the assorted toys up to the kitchen. Where the quiche smell isn't quite as appealing as it had been and there's now a pall of greyish smoke hovering around the ceiling. Cam is bending over the oven and cursing.

'I can't believe I've done this,' she mutters crossly, 'it's totally ruined. Hell's frigging bells.'

'Mummy said a rude word. Mummy said a rude word,' CJ sings melodiously as she leaves the room and heads down the passage.

I slide into a chair in the corner opposite Joanne and angle it so that I can see the kitchen as well. As soon as I sit down, my rubbery legs send a thank-you message as they collapse with relief. Then I try to take stock of what just happened but I can't. Because it doesn't make any sense.

'Sit down, Richard.' Joanne gestures towards the seat next to her and then, as he settles himself down, gives him a bruising nudge with her elbow and a huge wink. 'So, what d'you think?'

'Ah . . .' Richard flushes and looks at Cam with embarrassment written all over his face.

'Okay, okay! Forget I asked!' Joanne grins at him and then turns to me. 'So, Terry, tell me everything. What's been going on around here?'

'Nothing much,' I mumble as I reflect dourly that Joanne doesn't seem to have changed at all. Still just like a redheaded bull in a china shop.

'Come *on*, something must have happened in the past year!'

'Not really.'

'Absolute rubbish!' Cam says as she turns on the ceiling fan and waves ineffectually at the smoke with a chequered tea-towel. 'Tell her about your new grand-daughter!'

'Bronte had a *baby*?'

'Yes, a little girl. Yesterday.' I sneak a glance at Richard to see if he is paying attention but he is playing absent-mindedly with the corner of CJ's deserted toy catalogue while watching Cam curse in the kitchen. It suddenly occurs to me he must think this is standard behaviour for me. Weak-kneed and feeble-minded.

'Congratulations! So you're a grandmother!' says Joanne excitedly.

'I hate that word,' I reply grumpily as I pull my tea over and then fiddle with the handle of the ceramic mug. The cold tea within has now started to form a film over the top so I pick the mug up and slop the contents sideways to break it. While I'm thus engaged, CJ reappears with an armful of soft toys that she dumps unceremoniously on the floor beside Richard's chair.

'That's *my* Barbies on the table. They hab boobies just like Terry's. And this here –' she holds up a stuffed brown and gold giraffe '– is my giraffe called Lolly and she has a berry long neck.'

'Very nice,' says Richard, who appears to have regained his poise. 'Impressive.'

'And this is my new hippo. I got him from my father. His name is Otto and he has an udder.'

'Ah, your father – or the hippo?'

'The hippo, silly,' says CJ, giggling. 'Men don't hab udders!'

'Something for which I shall be eternally grateful.'

I look at Richard in surprise because that was the longest sentence I've heard him string together so far. In fact, I'm guessing he's not quite as comfortable as he's pretending to be – probably one of those guys who, while not quite antisocial, don't shine in company. So why am I suddenly feeling the way I am? It certainly can't be his dress sense. The hideous shorts are topped with some sort of stretchy cream shirt with two brown buttons directly under the collar, and a loose, dark-brown cardigan. The whole ensemble looks like something the father in *Leave It to Beaver* would have worn – on a bad day.

I examine his face for clues instead. Maybe it's his eyes, because they are very nice eyes at that – deep-set and warm brown surrounded by thick dark lashes the same colour as his ever so slightly receding, ever so slightly greying, shortish hair. And I *love* brown eyes – they always remind me of hot choco-late in front of an open fire, old-fashioned teddy bears, and faithful cocker spaniels.

I tilt my head to the side and chew my lip thoughtfully while I decide that, in fact, Richard looks like an elongated version of Alan Alda with a slightly more prominent nose. I try to pinpoint his best feature – probably those eyes, although he does have rather nicely shaped lips. As if he senses my inspection, he glances across at me and immediately flushes. I turn quickly to stare at Joanne instead.

And her looks seem to have changed as little as her personality. Still the same flaming red hair, numerous freckles and plump body, encased today in a flowing green smock over a long brown skirt. She looks like a bonsai tree that's caught fire. Surely she and Richard can't be an item? They seem totally mismatched. She catches my eye and grins at me.

'So you're a *grandmother*. Unbelievable. How does it feel?'

'Fine.'

'Oh. Well, how's Bronte, anyway?'

'Fine too.' I sneak another glance at Richard but he is staring at Cam again, who is bending over the oven with her denim butt sticking up in the air. Bloody male.

'Look, I'm really sorry everyone, but the quiche is ruined.' Cam straightens up and holds out a blackened pie-dish for our inspection. 'Totally ruined.'

'Now I *will* starb,' comments CJ as she tries to interest Richard in a pair of spotty leopards.

'No matter,' he says helpfully as he pats the leopards. 'I'll fetch something. Ah, in Joanne's car.'

'No, let me see . . .' replies Cam slowly as she opens the fridge door and stares within for inspiration. 'Here we go! I'll slice up this ham and we'll have it with the salad and bread. It's fresh from that deli in Bayswater where they cure all their own. How does that sound?'

'Great,' Richard and Joanne say in unison and then turn to smile at each other.

'Yuk,' replies CJ with considerable feeling.

'Whatever,' I say morosely as I tip my mug over a trifle too far and some of the contents slop out and onto the table. 'Bugger!'

'Are you sure you're okay?' asks Cam as she gives me yet another puzzled frown.

'Yep, sure.' I hoist myself out of my chair and fetch the dishcloth from the sink to clean up the mess. I notice that I've finally got Richard's attention, but I'm guessing it's for all the wrong reasons. I wipe the table, fling the dishcloth back over the bench towards the sink and watch it land with a thud. Then I flop ungracefully back down in my chair.

'Do you want a hand with anything, Cam?' asks Joanne politely.

'No, under control.' Cam stands in the middle of the kitchen and looks around as if she's lost something. 'You lot just sit there and keep out of my way and I'll have it all ready in a jiffy.'

'Ah, Camilla,' Richard says, making an effort to be sociable, 'CJ your only child?'

'No, I've got two others.' Cam bobs down, picks up some metal tongs from the floor and gives them a cursory wipe with the tea-towel. 'But they're a fair bit older – Samantha's nineteen and Benjamin's fifteen.'

'School?'

'Yes. Well, Samantha's finishing this year. She's doing her VCE and wants to join the army next year – apparently.'

'The army!' says Joanne. 'You're kidding!'

'They're not here,' CJ adds helpfully. 'Sam's at Sara's and Ben's at work with Phillip. He's a bet.'

'Good bet or bad bet?' Richard asks CJ with interest.

'A *good* bet of course,' says CJ disparagingly as she starts to collect her toys back up. 'He's going to marry my auntie.'

'Ah – *Ben* is?'

'No, of course not.' CJ now favours him with the look she reserves for complete morons. '*Phillip's* going to marry my auntie. He's the good bet.'

'Well, he's a good bet till he marries her, anyway,' adds Cam with a wry grin.

'Cocky, isn't she?' Joanne says cheerfully to Cam.

'That's one way of putting it,' I mutter under my breath.

'So, Richard . . .' Cam starts carving up the ham and laying the slices out on a large platter. 'What about you? Married? Children?'

'Widowed. One child. A girl.'

'Oh, I *am* sorry to hear that!' says Cam, looking at him sympathetically.

'Don't be, we get along all right.'

'*What?*' Cam pauses in her slicing and stares at him with her mouth open.

'He means his daughter,' I say, rolling my eyes at her.

'Yes.' Richard flashes an appreciative glance in my general direction and then returns his gaze to somewhere around Cam's left shoulder. 'Sorry.'

'His wife's been dead for seven years,' adds Joanne informatively. 'It was a car accident. She was –'

'So Eve's with me now,' Richard interrupts smoothly. 'Seventeen years old. Going on thirty.'

'Oh! My nineteen year old is like that,' says Cam with feeling, obviously pleased to change the subject. 'Can someone take this plate into the dining-room?'

Joanne jumps up and takes the platter from Cam. Which is a lucky break, because I had no intention of moving while the conversation regarding Richard's marital circumstances and residence of offspring was still on.

'So how did you meet Joanne then?' Cam asks with interest

as she opens a bread-maker and the room immediately fills with the heady aroma of freshly baked bread. 'Have you known her long?'

'Funny story, that,' chimes in Joanne, who has just returned from the dining-room. 'I'll tell you when we're all sitting down.'

'Oh. Okay.' Cam looks across at me again and raises her eyebrows expressively. 'Well, then, would someone take this bread in?'

Joanne takes the bread, Cam picks up the salad platter and they move towards the dining-room. I decide I'd better do something apart from sitting here and acting like an idiot so I stand up and make the first excuse I can think of.

'I'm going to the bathroom,' I announce to nobody in particular, and then I make my escape. But when I get there, I just lean against the wall and take several nice, deep breaths. And try to pull myself together.

I can't believe the way I'm acting – usually I'm fairly calm, controlled and comfortable with most situations. And I *am* the sociable type. Maybe I'm having a cerebral haemorrhage or something equally mind-altering. Because I could *not* have just fallen in love like that. This isn't *Sleepless in Seattle* – more like *Flaky in Ferntree Gully*.

Besides, that sort of rubbish simply doesn't happen outside of soppy romance novels, and I'm *already* in love – with Fergus. This guy isn't even my type! The eyes might be nice but I don't *like* dark-haired guys, especially not when the dark hair tops a present-day Ichabod Crane who dresses like the father in a fifties sitcom. And who can barely string three words together! Besides, I'm too young to be interested in widowers.

If I thought I could get away with it, I'd jump into the car and head straight for the safety of home. Or perhaps I could steal the 4WD and go bush. But I've never even watched one episode of *Bush Tucker Man*, so I'd have no idea how to sustain myself once the Fruit Tingles in my pocket ran out. And I also have no idea which direction the bush is from here – or from anywhere, for that matter.

So instead I walk slowly back towards the kitchen and make a resolution to start acting like a normal, relatively mature human being from now on. I can hear the ebb and flow of the conversation from the dining-room as I walk down the passage and realise they must already be helping themselves to lunch. As soon as I enter the kitchen, Cam jumps up from the dining-room table and comes out to join me. I peer around her but can only see Joanne's green back from my vantage point, so Richard must be around the other side of the table.

'What's up?' Cam whispers loudly as she reaches my side. 'You're acting really strangely. Are you okay?'

'Sure I am,' I reply heartily. 'I just had a big day yesterday and it's all catching up with me. I'm fine.'

'You sure?'

'Absolutely. Now let's get back to your guests.'

'Okay – if you're sure.' She looks only half convinced but ready to be persuaded. 'I'll pour you a champagne and that'll perk you up.'

'Sounds great.' We walk out to the dining-room, where Joanne appears to be discussing the value of the Australian dollar at considerably more length than it really deserves. My stomach rumbles and I notice the only empty chair is, naturally, right between CJ and the object of my unexpected attraction. He stands up and pulls the chair out for me to sit down.

'Thanks,' I say politely, and relatively maturely.

'No problem.'

'Mummy, can I hab a glass of that?' asks CJ, pushing her plate away and pointing to the champagne. 'I'm *so* thirsty.'

'No.' Cam leans over and pushes her daughter's plate back in front of her. 'Now, eat up and not another word till you're finished.'

'Not fair,' CJ grumbles as she begins methodically to massacre several lettuce leaves. 'I neber get to drink anything good.'

'You've got juice,' says her mother, 'be happy with that.'

'Bet it's not as nice as that.' CJ nods towards the champagne bottle. 'Not nearly.'

'And you'd be right.' I smile at her as I take a sip of my champagne and decide to drink this glass and settle my nerves before I attack the ham and salad. 'Mmm, *hmm*.'

'Not fair!'

'So, where were we?' Cam ignores her daughter and looks brightly at her guests. 'Joanne – you were going to tell us how you met Richard, weren't you?'

'That's right.' Joanne waves her sandwich in the air enthusiastically. 'Well, there I was, sitting in the departure lounge in Singapore and –'

'Hang on,' interrupts Cam, 'do you mean to say that you've only *just* met?'

'Correct,' says Richard, looking rather amused.

'Oh, I see.' Cam looks at him slightly askance, no doubt calculating the chances of him being an axe murderer. 'Interesting.'

'Well, anyway, I was dog-tired and looking forward to getting some actual sleep. And I was really worried about who I'd be sitting near – you know how you can get stuck next to some really gross people, but for once I got someone decent – Richard! He's a Capricorn, so that explains it. All the way from Singapore to Melbourne and we talked and talked. We must have covered just about everything and anything important that's ever happened to us. I don't think we got a wink of sleep, did we?'

'No,' Richard agrees dryly, taking a sip of champagne.

'We just sat up discussing stuff.' Joanne sends another fleeting glance in Richard's direction. 'And when I found out he was from Tasmania but was going to be stuck in Melbourne for a few days – well, obviously it was the hand of fate. So I insisted I show him around. Isn't that right, Richard?'

'Yep. Right.'

'And it's amazing how quickly you get to know people on trips like that.' Joanne pauses while she finishes off the rest of her sandwich. 'I reckon everybody who plans to get married should go on a long-distance trip together to really work out whether they're compatible. It's the same as knowing someone for about six months in normal time, wouldn't you say, Richard?'

'At least,' agrees Richard as he crumples his serviette on top of his plate and leans back. 'Camilla – delicious. Thank you.'

'My pleasure.'

'For having me too. Thanks.'

'No problem. And it's been lovely meeting you,' Cam replies politely. 'I'm only sorry I burnt lunch and you ended up with this instead.'

'No. Really.'

'But it would have been better with quiche.'

'Don't see how.'

'Well, the bread *was* a bit chewy.'

'Lord, enough already!' Joanne interjects, echoing my thoughts exactly. 'It's nice, you liked it, he's glad to be here – now let's move on!'

'Well, good to see you haven't changed.' Cam glares at Joanne and stands up to start clearing the table.

'Excuse me?' I look up at Cam with my fork still poised over the plate of ham she is about to remove. 'Um, excuse me?'

'Oh, I'm *sorry*, Cam. I didn't mean anything.' Joanne stands as well and picks up the salad platter. 'Sometimes I just say things without thinking.'

'Excuse me?' I say again politely, pointing my fork towards the plates of food in their arms. 'Yoo hoo! Remember me?'

'No, it's okay, Joanne. It's me. I suppose I'm just a bit touchy because I stuffed up the quiche. And the bread *was* chewy.'

'No – my fault totally. Here, let me help you.' Joanne gathers some cutlery with her spare hand. Then they both proceed to remove the lunch remains to the kitchen, where they can be heard continuing to apologise to each other.

'Excuse me?' I say once more, this time to nobody in particular. 'I hate to mention this but *I* haven't had lunch yet.'

'You c'n hab mine.' CJ pushes a plate full of what looks like well-masticated salad in front of me. 'I'll swap for your drink.'

'Hmm. Think I'll pass, thanks.'

'Don't blame you.' Richard slides CJ's plate across and places it on top of his, then unfolds himself from his chair and walks around to collect up the scattering of lettuce from the table near her placemat. He puts these carefully on top of the plates and then takes them out to the kitchen. I'm left with CJ, who is staring at me balefully. I drain my glass and smile at her. After a couple of minutes, Cam comes back into the room with a damp cloth and gives the table a searching glance before turning to me.

'Would you believe they're doing the dishes?' She picks up the empty bottle and looks at me with concern. 'Now, sure you're okay? How's it going?'

'I'm fine,' I reply heartily. 'Who needs food? That champagne worked wonders – got any more?'

'Of course.' Cam drops the cloth on the table. 'In fact, I'll grab it now and you can do the honours.'

I take the cloth, lean forwards and wipe the table down

thoroughly before straightening the placemats. CJ scrambles off her chair and disappears in the direction of her bedroom and, a few minutes later, Cam comes back in loaded with a bottle of champagne and my cheesecake on top of a stack of dessert plates and forks.

'Here's the champers. And could you cut this up too, Terry?' She deposits the lot right in front of me, then plops into a chair and leans forwards conspiringly. 'What do you think – not exactly the chatty type, is he? Can you *believe* they're together?'

'*No!*' I reply, a little more forcefully than I meant to.

'Hey, calm down!'

'Well, how do you know they're together?' I ask in a more normal tone.

'I'm only guessing,' replies Cam, looking at me, puzzled. 'Out in the kitchen she asked me twice what I thought of him. Usually that means they're together.'

'No it doesn't,' I reply shortly.

'Hey, don't take it personally!' Cam looks at me with a frown. 'What *is* it with you today? First you act all weird out in the driveway, then you hardly say a word through lunch –'

'*What* lunch?' I interrupt rudely, hoping to put her off her current train of thought.

'– then you just about bite my head off when all I asked was whether you thought they might be . . . hang on.' She raises her eyebrows as the light begins to dawn. 'I get it! God, Terry!'

'Shut up,' I say through clenched teeth as I pick up the cheesecake knife and hold it in front of me. 'I'm not afraid to use this.'

'I don't believe it!'

'Neither do I.'

'You're jealous!'

'Could you keep your voice down a tad –' I cast a nervous

glance in the direction of the kitchen '– otherwise I'll start singing "Jingle Bells".'

'Really, really jealous!'

'*And* I'll tell everyone about your clever reindeer impersonation. Fooled me.'

'You know, though, what I don't get is that if you're so damn jealous, why don't *you* just do it too?'

'Pardon?'

'Well, why don't you just cut loose and take the plunge? I mean, if you want it so much – do it! Right now!'

'*Right* now?'

'Yes, before you get any older! If Joanne can do it – so can you!'

'So can I?'

'Will you stop repeating the last bit of everything I say?' Cam leans closer, pushes the cheesecake to one side, and grabs my left hand. 'You're just trying to put me off and it's not going to work this time. I mean, if it affects you so much that you're going to start acting all screwy, then you *have* to do something. Otherwise all you'll have are regrets.'

'Are you totally sober?'

'Of *course* I'm totally sober. Well, just about, anyway.'

'So let me get this straight.' I look Cam in the eye. 'You think that the answer is for me to march in there and just *do* it? In your kitchen? With him? Otherwise I'll regret it? Is that what you're saying?'

'*What*? What on earth are you talking about? How can you do it in my kitchen?'

'Well, that's what you said!'

'No, I didn't!'

'Then what *were* you talking about?'

'I'm talking about you going overseas, of course,' says Cam with a frown. 'You've been talking for ages about how miserable you are at the library and how you want a change, or to go overseas, or anything, but you never actually *do* it. And how jealous you were when Joanne up and left, and how peeved you were when we got postcards and – but, if you weren't talking about that, what *were* you talking about?'

'Nothing.'

'Balls,' Cam says rudely. 'Spill it – what were you talking about and what were you going to do in my kitchen?'

'Nothing!'

'Nothing, be damned! Now what was it you thought I was talking about? Let me see . . .'

'Let's not.'

'Hell's bells!' Cam's eyes suddenly grow huge and she flings my hand away. 'You *weren't*! Teresa Diamond! And – with Richard! Haven't you *seen* his knees? Why, you – you . . . and what about Fergus, may I ask?'

I'm saved from answering by Joanne calling out from the kitchen for Cam to come show them where the plates go. She lingers but I studiously avoid her gaze while I grab somebody's half-empty glass of champagne and drain it. My stomach rumbles in protest.

'Don't think I'm letting *this* go!' Cam warns as she gets to her feet. 'I'll be back – never you fear! On my clean lino – well, I never.'

'Perhaps you should,' I mumble to her back as she heads into the kitchen. I open the champagne, fill up my own glass and take a huge gulp. Then I pull the cheesecake back over and carefully cut it into quarters and then into eighths. I examine the sliced cake carefully for the biggest piece and then flip it deftly onto a plate for myself. The first bite tastes like heaven on earth and I groan with pleasure.

'Peckish?' Richard walks back into the dining-room and

looks first at his empty wineglass and then at my largish slice thoughtfully. 'Ah, any spare?'

'Of course,' I mumble around my cheesecake as I feel my face go red with embarrassment.

'Excellent,' he replies as he takes the cheesecake platter and starts to dole slices onto the plates, 'taste good?'

'Yes,' I answer although, in fact, it does not taste quite as good as it had a minute ago. 'Yes, delicious.'

He finishes with the cheesecake and then, taking the champagne bottle from in front of me, fills up the flutes around the table. Cam and Joanne come back in talking animatedly about the idiosyncrasies of out-of-body experiences. Cam sends me a look fraught with meaning that makes me wish I were having an out-of-body experience right now.

'So I swear to you I was floating on the ceiling looking down at my body while it slept. I could see every breath I took,' continues Joanne earnestly as she takes her seat at the table. 'I just stared and stared. It was the weirdest experience I've ever had.'

'But if you actually managed to leave your body, why didn't you do something useful? What was the point of just staring at yourself – I mean, you can do that in the mirror any time,' Cam replies with a certain amount of logic as she too settles down at the table. 'So what's the point?'

'I don't know. I suppose it didn't occur to me.' Joanne pauses to take a mouthful of cake. 'Mmm-*mmm*! This is scrumptious! Did you make it, Cam?'

'No, I believe Terry did, didn't you?'

'Not quite,' I reply shortly as I concentrate on devouring my slice. If I'm going to be thought of as greedy, I might as well make the most of it.

'Mummy! We're habing dessert?' CJ arrives back at the table and looks at our plates accusingly. 'You didn't tell me we're habing dessert!'

'It's not like we never have dessert, CJ.' Cam laughs self-consciously and looks around the table. 'We *do* have dessert, you know. A lot.'

'Here.' Richard pushes a plate across the table to CJ's place as she sits down and looks at him gratefully. 'Enjoy!'

'Thank you!'

I finish off my cheesecake and eye the other three pieces thoughtfully before regretfully deciding that taking another one *would* be thought of as a bit piggy. Then I realise that now I *do* need to go to the bathroom. 'Excuse me.' I stand up and push my chair away. 'Back in a minute.'

After I've used the bathroom, I find some paper and a pen by the hall phone and head down to Cam's bedroom. Then, after chewing on the pen for a few minutes while giving the matter some thought, I write:

> *Rudolph slept here*

I smile at my handiwork and position the paper neatly on her pillow where she will be sure to find it when she goes to bed tonight. Then I sit on the edge of the bed and stare into the standard mirror in the corner. Hell, I feel miserable. I sit like that for a while trying to recover some of my usual bonhomie and general good bloody will towards all. Just as I force my attention away from my reflection and start examining the way Cam's curtain hem has come down and is trailing on the floor, there is a strident knocking at the front door. As I'm the nearest, I drag myself up quickly and go to do the honours.

'Teresa, dear! What a surprise!' Cam's mother stands on the threshold, beaming up at me from her five-foot-nothing height. She is dressed to the nines in a floral frock (people like Cam's mother don't wear dresses – only frocks) and a black, fur-lined coat with a large hat balanced precariously on top of her head. An array of fake multicoloured flowers drips from the hat's brim and obscures her gaze so that she has to peer sideways to see me clearly.

'Why, dear, you're looking a trifle peaky. Is everything all right?'

'Oh, fine thanks, Mrs Riley,' I reply as I groan inwardly. 'It's just a bit hot in here, that's all.'

'Well, you should tell Camilla to turn the heat down then.' She steps into the house, sheds her coat and carefully removes the impressive hat from her head. 'It's positively wasteful, isn't it, Harold?'

'Yes, dear. Is that right?' Harold steps in behind her with an armful of picture frames and awkwardly holds out a hand for me to shake. He is wearing a neat brown suit and his usual anxious expression.

'Have you seen the dear little baby today, Teresa?'

'No. I'm going in tonight.'

'Little darling,' says Cam's mother, obviously referring to the baby, not me. 'Now, is my daughter here? I've been ringing the doorbell for at least ten minutes.'

'It's not working, Mrs Riley,' I state with prior, painfully gained knowledge, 'so she wouldn't have heard it. Come on, they're in the dining-room.'

'Lead the way, dear.'

Obediently I lead the way. At least by being in the front I don't have to watch Mrs Riley ostentatiously avoiding each of the objects strewn across the floor. We walk into the dining-room just in time to hear CJ ask her mother in a very loud voice whether she could have one of the last pieces of cheese-cake before Terry comes back and eats them all.

'Mum!' says Cam with poorly disguised horror as she spots us walking in. 'Mum, you're *here*!'

'Grandma! Grandma!' With considerably more enthusiasm, CJ launches herself out of her chair and races to wrap herself around her grandmother. 'Did you bring me a present?'

'CJ! Don't be rude,' Cam admonishes her daughter half-heartedly as she stares at her mother. 'So, Mum, what brings you over?'

'What? Do I need an official invitation now to visit my daughter?' Cam's mother says in an affronted tone as she bends down to return CJ's hug. 'Is that what things have come to? I've only brought the photos from the wedding I had framed to show you but I can always leave again if you'd rather. I'd hate to put you out, you know.'

'No, I didn't mean that. I just meant – oh, it doesn't matter. Hi, Harold.'

'Hello, Camilla. You're looking well, is that right?'

'Actually, no, Harold. It's *not* right.' Cam's mother straightens up and puts her head on one side to examine her daughter thoughtfully. 'She has obviously coloured her hair and it makes her look – well, cheap.'

'Thanks, Mum. You really know how to build me up, don't you?'

'Well, would you rather I told a barefaced lie? CJ, you're squishing Grandma's middle. Camilla? Is that what you'd prefer?'

'Whatever.' Cam sighs and stands up from the table. 'CJ, leave Grandma alone and finish your cheesecake. Oh, Mum – flowers! Did you bring me flowers? How nice!'

'They are not flowers, Camilla. They are my hat.'

'Oh. Well, anyway, I was just about to make coffee. Would you two like to join us?'

'Only if you can spare the time, Camilla. I wouldn't want to put you out.'

'Too late – I mean,' she adds quickly, 'I mean, it's too late because I was already going to make coffee so an extra two is no big deal. Grab a seat.'

'I think I would prefer to take a seat, Camilla, rather than 'grab' one. I must say your table is looking very . . . festive. Very festive indeed.' Rose sweeps the table with a glance and then sniffs perceptively. 'Did you burn something? You didn't burn *lunch*, did you? And that reminds me, perhaps you could turn the heat down – Teresa is feeling a little flushed.'

'Sure.' Cam turns and gives me an evil look. 'But you'll still be hot, won't you?'

'Do you believe in Santa Claus, CJ?' I ask the child with interest. 'You know, the jolly red guy with the reindeers who shows up around Christmas?'

'Of *course* I do,' answers CJ, looking confused. 'Why?'

'Yes, why?' Cam's mother turns to me curiously. 'Why would you ask something like that? In *July*, of all times?'

'My sentiments exactly,' I reply enthusiastically, 'and I was just saying to Cam before how tacky I thought it was that –'

'Okay, okay!' Cam interrupts rudely. 'If you're staying for coffee, Mum, then I'd better make introductions. Everybody – this is my mother, Rose Riley, and her husband, Harold. And Mum, Harold – do you remember Joanne? I think you met her at a barbecue I had last year. We used to work together at the library.'

'Pleased to meet you, dear.' Harold smiles pleasantly at Joanne. 'Don't quite remember, but never mind. Is that right?'

'*I* remember.' Cam's mother fixes Joanne with her gimlet gaze. 'You're the young lady who dresses in different colours to suit your mood. Do you still do that?'

'Actually, yes, I still do, Mrs Riley,' answers Joanne with some trepidation. 'And how are you?'

'Fine. So you're wearing green today – what does that mean?'

'Um, well – it's to signify trees . . . life,' stammers Joanne. 'You know, um, renewal. Yes, renewal – friendships, that's it.'

'Hmm. Interesting. And who is your friend here?'

'Oh, Mum, sorry, this is Richard.' Cam waves airily in Richard's general direction. 'Richard – meet my mother, Rose Riley, and her husband, Harold.'

Harold immediately walks around the table with his hand outstretched and Richard begins his unfolding trick until he stands at his full, rather impressive height in front of him. They shake hands and smile politely at each other. Then Richard turns to Cam's mother and, with his hand still out, smiles at her. But she doesn't shake hands. And she doesn't smile back. In fact, I suddenly notice, her face has turned a peculiar shade of mottled greenish-white and she has grasped the back of a spare chair for support. She also appears to be at a loss for words and it is probably this, more than her pallor, which causes everybody's attention to focus on her with varying degrees of bafflement.

'Mum, are you okay?'

'Mrs Riley – would you like my seat?'

'Rose, Rose –' Harold goes pale himself as he studies his wife. 'Rose, are you not feeling well? Is that right?'

All through this medley of solicitous concern, the subject has not batted an eyelid or moved a muscle. Rose Riley is still standing rigidly behind the chair she has grasped, her knuckles showing white through the skin with the force of her grip. But they look positively rosy compared with her face, the colour of which makes her eyes look sunken and staring. Actually, staring they most certainly are. They have not wavered in their intense focus across the room, so I follow their gaze and suddenly I, too, am staring – at Richard.

I look back at Rose to make sure that it *is* Richard she's staring at, and then I look back at Richard to see how he's taking all this. And I get another little shock when I register that, out of all of us, he seems the least surprised by what is going on. In fact, he is staring straight back at Cam's mother and the only difference between the two of them is that Richard is actually smiling.

# TUESDAY

## 1730 hrs

I open the door for Fergus and, for the first time in our relationship, immediately notice how much shorter he is than me. Until now, I've never really thought of Fergus as short: his larger-than-life personality seemed to fill the room regardless of his lack of actual inches. If there was anything about Fergus that bugged me, it's probably the fact that he's also cuter than me. A *lot* cuter. Because Fergus has one of the most elfin-looking faces I've ever seen on a man. He also has shaggy blonde-streaked hair, a gold earring in his left ear, and wacky taste in clothes. Today he has on his lemon overalls with an emerald-green t-shirt underneath. Green is Fergus's favourite colour – he claims it reminds him of the hills of Ireland, even though I suspect he has never physically been there. Apparently, it's all in the genes.

'I'm having to take a raincheck –' Fergus shuts the door behind him and rubs his hands together to warm them '– and be off over to Maggie Brown's instead.'

'How come?' I ask curiously. Maggie is a friend, Alex's sister, and Cam's former sister-in-law. 'What's she done now?'

'Well, hasn't one of her best clients gone and pulled off the doorhandle a half-hour ago? The flaming great eejit.'

'That doesn't sound like much of an emergency,' I say doubtfully.

''Tis when he and the lass are stuck on the other side,' replies Fergus pragmatically.

'Really?' I can't help grinning at the thought. 'But then hadn't you better get straight over there?'

'No. Didn't Maggie tell me to take my time? It's all profit, she says. So I've time for a drink, my love.'

'Great.' I lead the way through the lounge-room with my still-stained carpet, and into the kitchen. Fergus sits at the table, runs his hand wearily through his already dishevelled mop and yawns. He looks really tired. I get the bottle of scotch down from where it lives on top of a cupboard and pour a generous splash into two glass tumblers. Then I top Fergus's up with ice, and mine with Diet Coke *and* ice. Lastly I grab a bag of corn chips from another cupboard, fill a glass bowl with them and get two coasters out of a drawer.

With all these preparations done, I look across at Fergus and realise with amazement that he's fallen asleep at the table with his head on one arm. I try to decide whether to leave him be or to wake him up for the drink and, while I'm thinking, an unbidden image suddenly flits into my mind of an impossibly tall, ridiculously thin and badly dressed man with the most gorgeous eyes I've ever seen. I flush with a mixture of guilt and annoyance and, to compensate, dash over to the table and give Fergus a hearty kiss on the mouth. He immediately puts a hand at the nape of my neck and kisses me back, which goes to show he wasn't all *that* deeply asleep. He tastes of peppermint and cigarettes.

'Why thank *you*, lovely lady,' he says as he releases me, 'and isn't that more like old times!'

'What do you mean, "old times"?' I reply tersely. 'These *are* old times!'

'Whatever you say, to be sure. And what would you be saying to skipping the drink and –' Fergus pauses, wiggles his eyebrows about and gives me what he obviously sees as a seductive look '– taking this little discussion upstairs?'

'Don't be ridiculous.'

Fergus doesn't reply, just looks at me expressionlessly for a moment before getting up and transferring the drinks from the counter to the table. I stand there awkwardly, holding the coasters and wishing I'd phrased that rejection a trifle more subtly, but am momentarily unable to think of a damn thing to make it better.

'All righty then. Shall we be drinking to the little lass?'

'Certainly,' I say heartily as I raise my glass. 'To Sherry!'

'To Sherry,' repeats Fergus. 'May she live long and prosper!'

We both take a drink and I pass him his coaster before he puts his glass down. Then I fetch the corn chips and settle myself in the chair opposite him. We sit in silence for a few moments while I run my finger around the rim of my tumbler and try to think of something to say. Has it been this hard for a while and I just haven't noticed?

In the first few months of our relationship it seemed we couldn't find time for all the things we *wanted* to say. And the laughter! Fergus has the most amazingly wacky sense of humour. He was just such good company. We'd have afternoon sessions on the weekend where we just lay around in bed for hours, talking and laughing at everything in between bouts of really fun sex. Yet here we sit, in total silence. How did this happen? How can we get it back on track?

I take out my hairclip and run my fingers through my hair haphazardly then, pulling it together roughly, reclip it at the back. The results are probably less than attractive, but it bought me time to think of something scintillating to say. 'Um, so how's work going? Apart from Maggie's handle dilemma, that is.'

'Flat out. It's a holiday I'll be needing soon.'

'Sounds like it.' I take a sip and then play with my glass again. 'So, what about today then? What did you do today?'

'You're not really wanting to know all this.'

'Yes I am. What did you do today?'

'Terry –'

'No you didn't. I'm sure I'd have remembered.'

'All right then, if you're insisting.' Fergus throws his hands up in mock surrender. 'What did I do today? Well, wasn't I stuck for the entire day in a house up at Tecoma replacing floorboards? Terrible termite damage.'

'Interesting.'

'Not very,' Fergus laughs. 'But what about you? And how are you after spending your time off?'

'Well, let me see. Today I had lunch at Cam Riley's place.'

'Camilla!' Fergus slaps himself on the forehead. 'Wasn't I supposed to fix her doorbell last week!'

'Ah! So I can hold *you* responsible for . . .' I trail off as Fergus looks at me curiously. 'Never mind.'

'For what?' he asks, his eyes bright. 'Come on, you can be telling me.'

'No, sorry.' I grin at him, amused as always by his love of gossip. 'But actually something curious *did* happen today that you might be interested in. See, we were having lunch with this old library friend when the strangest thing happened.'

'Strange, how?' Fergus asks, right on cue.

'Well, Joanne – that's the old library friend – brought this guy with her. Apparently she'd only just met him on the plane back from overseas. He was about six and a half foot tall and as skinny as a beanpole. And he was wearing these ghastly shorts, one of those stretchy shirt things and sandals with socks. But he had quite a nice face, hair was a sort of dark brown, with a tad of grey over the ears, and a bit receding. Largish nose – but nice. *Really* thick eyelashes, and his eyes were –'

'Terry, my love?'

'Hmm?'

'It's getting the picture I am. Because haven't you spent ten minutes describing the man and none telling me what your Joanne is looking like – and isn't *she* the one who's after being your friend?'

'I'm just getting to that! She's shortish, plumpish and has red hair and freckles. Okay? Happy now?'

'Ecstatically so. Haven't I a weakness for redheads?'

'Whatever. Anyway, so there we were having lunch when there's a knock on the door and it's Cam's mother.'

'Oh, sweet Jesus.'

'Exactly. So she comes in and starts off in her usual manner, but then when Cam introduces her to Richard she suddenly shuts up. In fact, not only does she shut up, but she goes really pale and looks like she's going to faint.' I pause for effect, and to take another sip of scotch.

'I'm guessing Richard is being the tall, skinny guy with the big nose?' Fergus is finally looking interested. 'And were you finding out why?'

'Well, not really. Everyone bustled around her and got her to sit down and have a drink of water. And his nose wasn't that big. But I thought poor old Harold was going to have a heart attack. And the weird thing was that she just kept staring at Richard and he just kept staring back, and sort of smiling at her. Like he knew *why* she was acting strangely but he wasn't going to say anything unless she did first.'

'So, did she?'

'No. And when she'd sort of gotten over her turn, everyone was asking what had happened but all she said was that it was a combination of the heat in there and Camilla's coffee.'

'Hmm, and isn't that possible? I've *tasted* her coffee.'

'But that's the thing, Fergus.' I lean forwards to give my words added emphasis: 'She hadn't *had* any yet.'

'Well, isn't that strange,' says Fergus thoughtfully as he takes a handful of corn chips. 'Very odd indeed.'

'Yes. And then about five minutes later she made up some excuse about a meeting somewhere and they left.'

'So were you lot asking this fellow Richard whether he knew what was going on?'

'Of course. Cam just about gave him the third degree. But he said he had no idea – just that he has that effect on women sometimes.'

'And does he?'

'Yes – no, I mean, of course not. He was only joking. And that's about all he'd say on the matter. So we had coffee and Joanne talked about Tibet, and meditation, and how she's discovered that she was several of Henry the Eighth's wives in previous incarnations.'

'Why is everybody always being from someone famous?'

'Exactly. But Richard hardly said anything. And that was that.'

'So you'll never be knowing then?'

'Maybe not,' I reply slowly, 'unless Cam can get it out of her mother. She was going to ring her later.'

'Well, hey.' Fergus leans forwards, his eyes alight with curiosity. 'And why don't you ring Cam now and be finding out?'

'Can't – it's Tuesday night.'

'Ah, to be sure.' Fergus leans back again and grins. 'And isn't that their night for neighbourhood watch?'

'That's one way of putting it.'

'Well, let me see. Hmm, why would a woman be paling at the sight of a fellow?' Fergus pauses to consider the various possibilities. 'To be sure it doesn't happen to me all that often.

Hey, didn't they maybe have a passionate but doomed affair in the past?'

'That's ridiculous,' I reply shortly as my stomach does its happy wanderer act again. 'There's too much of an age gap.'

'Really?' Fergus raises his eyebrows and then finishes off his scotch.

'No, I mean a real lot,' I add quickly as I remember that there is a fair age gap between the two of us as well. 'Like about twenty-odd years. *That* sort of age gap. Besides, he doesn't look the part.'

'Hmm,' Fergus says sagely as he glances at his watch. 'You'll have to be finding out for both of us and letting me know. And now I'll be heading off.'

'To rescue Maggie's client.' I stand up and collect the glasses. 'Well, they should be heartily sick of each other by now.'

'Not necessarily,' says Fergus with a leer as he levers himself out of his chair.

We walk over to the front door in silence and I open it for him. He leans up and kisses me on the cheek before giving my arm a clumsy, and rather uncomfortable, squeeze.

'I'll be ringing you, okay?'

'So you're not coming back over here tonight?' I ask awkwardly, not sure what I really want the answer to be.

'And isn't that a tempting thought?' says Fergus with a grin. 'But, no, don't I have to be up at the crack of dawn – so it's to me own little bed, I think.'

'No problem.' I wave at him as he walks over towards his van and smile cheerfully when he waves back. Then I shut the door and lean against it, taking a deep breath. A couple of months ago it would have made absolutely no difference to Fergus that he had to get up at the crack of dawn, he would have stayed regardless. And, a couple of months ago,

I would probably have put up a stronger fight to talk him into it.

# TUESDAY

## 1930 hrs

'So, after her feed, she slept straight through until seven thirty this morning. Like, I couldn't believe it! Mum, she's an angel.'

'She sure is,' I agree as I look down at the little angel nestled in my arms. Sherry is fast asleep, sparse lashes fanned out across the tops of her cheeks and her chest rising and falling ever so slightly as she breathes. I can see tiny veins threading just under the surface of her eyelids, and every so often she smiles tremulously, as if having a particularly good dream. Bronte has dressed her in one of the new jumpsuits she received yesterday; it's a lemony yellow and covered with vivid red cherries. She looks beautiful.

'I mean, there's all the other babies carrying on and everything. And, like, I was talking to that weird woman from the other bed.' Bronte gestures towards the empty bed by the door. 'It's okay – she's gone for a walk. But anyway, she had her baby on Sunday and she said she is *so* tired she can barely think straight! They're *all* so jealous of me because Sherry is just so good!'

'She sure is.' I put my hand lightly on Sherry's chest and watch as it rises up and down. Then I rock her gently backwards and forwards. At first, without opening her eyes, her little hands splay outwards but then she gets into the rhythm and relaxes once more.

'So we had a lesson on giving the babies a bath. And, Mum, I was, like, *so* nervous that I'd – oh, I don't know, drown her or something. And some of the other babies screamed so much you couldn't even concentrate. But Sherry – she loved it! She was terrific!'

'She sure is.' I stop rocking the baby and she immediately flutters her eyelids open and stares at me for a second before tiredness forces them back down. She yawns hugely and then sighs as she settles into sleep again.

'And then the lady from the cord bank came up and, like, *personally* thanked me for donating the umbilical cord. She said she wished there were more socially aware mothers like me around. Because apparently the donation rate is, like, *really* low and half the cords are just thrown away because people can't be bothered.' Bronte pauses to take a breath and looks down at me looking down at Sherry. 'Mum, you really *do* love her, don't you?'

'I sure do,' I reply as I force myself to stop staring at the baby and look at Bronte. 'Why, did you think that I didn't?'

'Well, no. Not *really*. But I know what you think about babies so I was a bit worried, you know.' Bronte looks down at Sherry and smiles. 'But you can't help but love her, can you?'

'No, you certainly can't,' I grin at Bronte reassuringly. 'And, believe me, I wouldn't be sitting here with her on my lap for so long if I wasn't totally smitten. So when do you get to take her home?'

'Actually, they said I could've got out tomorrow but I was, like, no way! So it's Thursday morning.'

'Thursday morning,' I repeat with astonishment. 'That *is* quick!'

'Well, it's not like I had a caesar or anything.'

'True,' I say as I look back down at the baby. 'And has Nick got everything ready for you at home?'

'Well . . .'

'What?' I ask suspiciously, because I *know* my daughter. 'What is it?'

'Well . . .' Bronte hesitates and starts playing with one of her bracelets. 'We were going to speak to you about that.'

'About what?'

'About going home.'

'Yes?' I'm no longer looking at the baby at all as Bronte has got my complete attention. 'Yes? What *about* going home?'

'So you've told her?' Nick comes bouncing in through the door and throws himself onto the bed next to Bronte. 'Excellent! Then it's all sorted.'

'What's all sorted?' I ask, with some foreboding.

'I *haven't* asked her yet,' says Bronte crossly, 'I was just leading up to it.'

'Knowing you, it'll take till Thursday to get around to it,' comments Nick cheerfully, 'so let's get it over and done with. Mil, because it's semester break, I've got all these extra shifts at the garage for the next two weeks. Mostly nights. And, to be perfectly frank, we need the money. So, we were thinking that perhaps it'd be better all round if Bron and the baby go back to your place for a week or so. For support, you know. What do you reckon?'

'My place,' I repeat dumbly.

'Yeah, your place. I mean, she's already got her own room there and you've got the week off. And you've got great heating and, besides, it'll be really excellent for her to have you around for the first little bit. Well – top idea, huh?'

'Hang on a minute.' I try to stem the flow of words, or at least slow them down so I've got a chance to think. 'I thought you had your unit all set up for the baby?'

'We *do*, Mum,' says Bronte, 'but with Nick working most nights, well, I just won't feel right. I mean, I hate it anyway but with the baby – oh, it'd be awful.'

'And Merrill's thesis is due in a month so she's working at home – flat out.'

'I see,' I say slowly.

'And I *would* really love to have you around for the first week or so, Mum.'

'I see,' I say, even more slowly.

'So? What do you reckon?' asks Nick impatiently. 'Top idea, yeah?'

'Well . . .' I look across at Bronte's face – and smile. 'Yes, it's a top idea. You're more than welcome. You *and* Sherry.'

'Fantastic!' Bronte beams at me with relief. 'I didn't know what you'd say – what with a baby, and nappies and night-feeds, and all that. But don't worry, I won't be asking you to do too much! Like, you're a legend, Mum! Thanks so much!'

'No problem. Hey, hang on.' I look across at Nick as something occurs to me. 'What about you? Are you staying over as well?'

'No, that's fine,' he laughs. 'So you can take that look off your face! I'll stay in the unit and come over whenever I've got a day off. I'll probably pick up Bron and we'll go out. Give you a break.'

'Okay,' I smile at him. 'Not that I would've minded, of course!'

'Sure,' he says with a grin.

'Mum, can you look after Sherry for a tick?' Bronte clambers down off the bed. 'I need to talk to Nick.'

'No problem.' I start rocking the baby again as they leave the room and shut the door behind them. I can hear them talking furiously just outside in the corridor but it doesn't make much sense so I concentrate on Sherry instead. She's probably more interesting anyway. Although I hadn't quite planned on spending as much time with her as it looks like I'm going to. I might be in love with the child, but I'm not stupid. I *know* how much work a new baby demands in the first week or so. I remember.

I look up as the door is pushed open again but it's only the room's other occupant returning from her walk. She pokes her feathery head through, peers around and then sidles in and looks at me questioningly.

'Nurse been here?' she asks me in her flat, Eeyore voice.

'Ah, no,' I reply, slightly confused by her behaviour. 'Did you want her?'

Instead of answering, she turns and pulls the door open a fraction again. Then she peers outside and, obviously not liking what she sees, suddenly jumps back and flattens herself against the wall. Almost immediately the door is pushed fully open and obscures her as a plump nurse, pushing a fully loaded Perspex baby trolley, bustles through and stares around the room with a frown.

'Have you seen Mrs Cobb?'

'Mrs Cobb?' I repeat stupidly, trying to work out what the hell is going on.

'Tsk. Never mind.' The nurse sighs with annoyance and then, after having another good look around, backs out of the room pulling the trolley along with her. The door swings shut again as she leaves and Eeyore, or Mrs Cobb as I now suspect she's called, is revealed once more. She hops up and down for a few seconds, counting under her breath, and then heads for the door herself.

'Going for a walk,' she mumbles to nobody in particular before slithering out through the door. I'm beginning to think the woman has severe psychiatric problems. Whatever, she's left the door ajar and I can now hear every word from the corridor.

'I said *no* – we'll ask her tomorrow!'

'But it'll be fine, Bron – she won't mind.'

'I tell you – not yet!'

'But don't you reckon she'll want as much notice as possible?'

'Like, no *way*.'

123

'Hey, guys?' I call out to Bronte and Nick. 'You do realise I can hear every word you're saying, don't you?'

'Oh, can you?' Bronte pokes her head around the door-frame and looks at me sheepishly. 'How much did you hear?'

'Enough that you might as well ask me whatever it is now, and get it over and done with.'

'I *told* you so.' Nick comes in pulling Bronte along by the hand. 'Come on, Bron.'

'Anyway, I thought you *had* just asked me,' I say as I look at them both with my guard well and truly up. 'Wasn't that what went on before?'

'No, this is something else,' says Bronte as she leans against the bed.

'Yeah, another favour.' Nick puts his arm around her and looks at me. 'But just a little one.'

'No it's not.' Bronte looks at him with irritation. 'We might as well be honest – it's, like, a really *big* favour.'

'I can't see it,' Nick says, shaking his head. 'What's so big about it?'

'That's because you won't be doing any of the work,' says Bronte. 'I *know* you.'

'Still don't reckon it's that big.'

'Well, it is.'

'Not.'

'Is.'

'Hey!' I look at them both with amazement. 'Will you two grow up! And why don't you let *me* decide if it's big or not. So what the hell *is* it?'

'*Shh*, Mum,' whispers Bronte as she leans over to check on Sherry. 'You'll wake the baby!'

'*I'll* tell you.' Nick plumps up a pillow and makes himself comfortable on the bed. 'It's like this. Bron and I decided ages ago we didn't want the baby christened, like in a religious ceremony or whatever. But we wanted *something* instead. Then a friend of ours had a naming day for their kid and it was exactly what we were after. Something to celebrate the arrival with family and friends and all, but with no religion involved.'

'I know all this,' I say impatiently, 'Bronte told me.'

'Did she also tell you we wanted the same celebrant?' asks Nick. 'Because she was *really* fantastic.'

'Yes, she did,' I reply, rocking Sherry gently. 'And I thought you'd already booked the woman, so what's the problem?'

'Well, we *had* booked her.' Bronte starts playing with her bracelets again. 'But we booked her for about six weeks from now because, like, Nick had this stupid theory that the baby would be late, because he was.'

'Well, I *was*,' says Nick defensively.

'Yeah, but *she* wasn't.' Bronte gives him a disparaging look. 'Anyway, we really wanted to have the naming thing for when she was about a week or two because it's all about being, like, a welcome thing, and if you wait till they're months old, then what's the point?'

'Okay, I think I see what you're getting at,' I say as I put one hand up to my temple and massage it lightly. 'But I still don't see the problem. Why don't you just rebook her for a couple of weeks time?'

'Because we can't!' wails Bronte. 'She's going away next Monday to Europe for five weeks!'

'And we don't want to wait five weeks,' adds Nick, 'because it's supposed to be a welcome thing so if she's that old, well . . .'

'Then what's the point?' I finish for him. 'Yes, I get it. What I *don't* get is where I come in. What's the favour?'

'Well, I rang her today, and she goes, "You've really only got this Sunday". But that'd be it – until she gets back, that is.'

'I see,' I say slowly, because I think I *do* see. 'And you want to have it this Sunday. And you want to have it at my place because you'll be there then.'

'And because it's so much nicer!' says Bronte eagerly.

'And warmer!' adds Nick.

'Hmm.' I look down at the sleeping baby and sigh. 'How many people?'

'Oh, only family,' says Nick dismissively, 'so not that many.'

'And it'd be only a little afternoon tea.' Bronte is finally looking at me. 'I'd help you, of course.'

'Of course!' adds Nick. 'And so will I!'

'I can't believe I'm doing this,' I say, shaking my head, 'but – all right. You can use my place.'

'Oh, *thanks*, Mum!' Bronte leans forwards and kisses me on the cheek. 'You're the best! Thanks so much!'

'Yeah – thanks, Mil!' Nick grins at me and then turns to Bronte. 'See? I told you she wouldn't think it's a problem!'

'And I promise you won't have anything to worry about, Mum. Like, I know how you are about your place, and we'll take really good care of it.'

'We sure will.'

'*And* we'll clean it after,' adds Bronte earnestly, 'every inch.'

'Every inch!' repeats Nick.

'Oh, and your carpet!' says Bronte, 'I *know* how you are about your carpet. Well, you won't have a *thing* to worry about!'

'Not a thing!'

'Not a mark!'

'Not a spot!'

'Like, it'll look exactly the same as it does right now!'

'Absolutely perfect!'

# TUESDAY

## 2305 hrs

I'm just drifting happily off to sleep when my father comes wandering over from the edge of my consciousness and looms large behind my closed eyelids. I smile at him and he smiles affectionately back before sitting his tall, angular body down and looking thoughtfully at me, his chin resting on one bony hand.

He looks much the same as he did in life. Hasn't lost any more hair, hasn't got any more wrinkles, hasn't even put on any weight – which he could probably do with. In fact, he's looking remarkably good. His darkish hair is only just tinged with grey and is only slightly receding. His nose is a tad larger than I remember but his eyes are still that deep-brown colour that I've always wished I'd inherited. And it's pretty obvious he hasn't been receiving any fashion tips up beyond the pearly gates either. He's dressed in a beige pullover and a pair of over-sized brown corduroy pants, which I bet are fastened around his thin waist with his favourite black belt.

'Hello there,' he says with a smile.

'Hi,' I whisper softly, willing him to stay for a while and chat. 'How's it going?'

'Fine, fine.' He shivers as he rubs his hands together. 'Bit chilly here, isn't it?'

'I've turned the heat off,' I reply, 'but I suppose you're not used to the cold anymore, are you?'

'Don't know about that.' He frowns slightly. 'Gets pretty chilly where I'm from.'

'*Does* it?' I ask, puzzled. 'I thought it'd be sort of even all the time there.'

'Not at all.' He raises his eyebrows questioningly. 'Why would you think that?'

'Well, that's what it says in all the books.'

'Not the ones *I've* read,' he replies. 'In fact, sometimes it gets so damn frigid that you'd sell your soul for some heat.'

'Oh no!' I exclaim with horror as something suddenly occurs to me. 'You're not in heaven at all, are you? You're in *hell*!'

'We prefer to call it Tasmania, thanks,' he says evenly. 'We find it attracts more tourists that way.'

'Tasmania?' I reply, confused. 'What on earth are you doing in Tasmania?'

'I *live* there.' He looks at me as if I've mislaid a few marbles. 'I thought I told you that this afternoon?'

'This afternoon?' I repeat dumbly. '*When* this afternoon?'

'When I met you,' he explains patiently, 'at your friend's place. Camilla. I was with Joanne and we all had lunch. Remember?'

'What!' I lean forwards and examine his face. 'It's *you*!'

'Of course it is. Who did you think it was?'

'My father! I thought you were my father!'

'Well, that's odd,' says Richard, frowning at me as he stands up. 'That's very odd indeed. Do I *look* like your father?'

'Yes! Yes, you *do*!' I shriek and, in doing so, wake myself up totally. I sit bolt upright and stare wide-eyed around the room as I convince myself there is nobody else here with me. Not my father, and certainly not Richard. What was *that* all about? I lie back down and will my heartbeat to return to normal. Then I go back through the dream slowly and call up an image of both my father and Richard. I stand them next to each other and examine them carefully.

And it's true. Richard *is* my father! Well, not *exactly* my father, which would be impossible as the man was buried five years ago. But he looks *very* much like my father – the same tall, thin build, the same expressive eyes, the same air of intelligence, the same dated sense of dress. Then *that's* why I turned into an adolescent! It wasn't anything to do with something ridiculous like falling in love at first sight! It was just a simple reaction to a man who has the same body type and overall look my father possessed.

I take a deep breath and let it out with a whoosh of relief. I feel better already. I no longer have to do any sentimental soul-searching or mope around carrying an unrequited love like a millstone around my neck. My father! No wonder I felt so disorientated and weak-kneed. Who wouldn't when their sub-conscious recognises and reacts to a likeness the conscious doesn't pick up on?

I grin at the two images superimposed on my mind's eye and then make them turn and shake hands politely with each other. After which my father gives me a wave and fades away, leaving Richard, in all his praying-mantis glory. His image hovers for a few seconds and then turns to give me a truly heartbreaking smile before walking slowly back into the recesses of my mind. Where I'll swiftly shove him into an unused cupboard and lock the door tightly. And then all I've got to do is wait it out until the man returns to Tasmania and all will be well.

I bury my head in the pillow and then roll over, clutching the doona up around me. My father! It occurs to me that Sigmund Freud would probably say all of this means that I'm lusting after my own father. Because I *did* have a rather physical reaction to Richard this afternoon, not just emotional. And that's pretty twisted. I frown to myself, and then my brow clears as I recollect a certain image of Santa Claus and his loyal reindeer. Lusting after a guy who looks like one's father is positively healthy compared with that little number.

# WEDNESDAY

*Handy Household Hint No IX:*

*Always walk a mile in someone else's shoes before you judge them. That way, apart from gaining valuable insights, you'll be a mile away when you judge them and you'll have new shoes.*

# WEDNESDAY

## 0845 hrs

I'm lying in bed enjoying the decadence of sloth and tossing up whether to invite Scarlett O'Hara to join me when the phone rings. I reach out languidly and pluck the receiver off the reproduction antique phone by my bed.

'Hello?'

'Terry!' Pat, one of my Saturday tennis partners, shrieks happily in my ear, 'I hear congratulations are in order, *Grandma!*'

'How did you know?' I ask curiously, sitting up in bed and pulling my doona to my chin. 'I haven't even told any of you lot yet!'

'Oh, news travels fast,' continues Pat in her slightly-too-loud voice. 'Debbie saw your daughter's name on the hospital admissions list, and she told Mary, and she told Joyce, and then Joyce was playing tennis on Monday night with Marg and Jan, so she told them, and then I go for walks with Denise, and she lives next door to Val, whose cousin is married to Jan's son. So there you are.'

'I see,' I answer rather untruthfully as I hold the receiver a little way off from my ear. 'Nothing's a secret for long, is it?'

'Not a chance,' agrees Pat cheerfully. 'And there's another reason I'm ringing. I hear you've got the week off.'

'How did you – never mind.'

'Anyway, I know you don't play midweek tennis because you work but, seeing as you've got today off, how would you like to join us? We're having a round robin and then our annual general meeting. Which you don't have to stay for, of course, but the tennis is fun and then we have a cup of tea and everyone brings a plate. You'll enjoy yourself. Want to come?'

'Um. What time?'

'Starts at nine thirty. But you don't have to be there right on the dot. And don't bother bringing anything yourself, you're a guest. C'mon, what do you say?'

'Well, I *would* like to stretch my legs,' I reply, mulling it over.

'Okay! You're on. I might be a tad late but I'll see you down at the club. Sure you don't want me to bring anything?'

'No, just you and your racquet. See you there.'

I lean over to hang up the phone and then, yawning, stretch myself out across the bed and pull the doona snugly around me. After my rather disturbing dream last night, I couldn't get back to sleep for quite some time. Which was odd because, once I had discovered the root of my reaction to Richard yesterday, I fully expected I would immediately fall into the deep, blissful slumber of the truly deserving. But it wasn't to be. Instead I lay awake till the early hours before drifting into a restless sleep that's left me full of kinks this morning. Hence my agreement to join in the round robin at the tennis club. Because normally I steer well clear of the midweek lady brigade, as they're a rather odd bunch. And that's putting it mildly.

I stretch out once more before hefting myself up and, shivering in the brisk morning chill, make my bed quickly and neatly before having my shower. Ten minutes later I'm clad in a towel and selecting a tracksuit, skirt and top from my wardrobe. After careful deliberation, I choose a navy-blue and white Sfida ensemble that matches my runners perfectly. I examine my fully dressed self in the mirror and wonder why Richard didn't even give me a second glance. Because although quite a lot of men find my height a bit of a turn-off, my measurements alone usually warrant a raised eyebrow or two. But with Richard – nothing. He obviously likes his women smaller, judging by the extra attention he paid Cam throughout the afternoon. I wonder if I can get a height reduction while I'm getting my butt reduction and breast reduction. And, if I'm getting four things reduced, perhaps I'd qualify for a bulk discount.

I shrug philosophically and walk back into the ensuite to blow-dry and then brush my hair back into a ponytail. Next it's just a splash of deodorant, a touch of moisturiser, a dash of foundation and I'm all ready for some physical exertion. Although, given the fact it's the midweek ladies I'll be joining, I doubt I'll get too much of a workout.

I tidy my ensuite briskly before leaping down the stairs two at a time and heading towards the kitchen to put the kettle on. On the way, I turn the heat on full and stop in front of the couch to stare at the dull pink stain on my carpet. Slowly, I look from the stain to the lounge-room walls and back again, and realise they actually match. Interesting – but still unacceptable.

In the kitchen I light the gas under the kettle and, while it's busily heating itself up, I pour a generous serve of muesli into a bowl and add some skinny milk. Then I make my coffee, grab a coaster, a pad of paper and a pen, and take all the assorted items over to the table, where I settle myself down. It's time to write today's list while I have my breakfast.

## WEDNESDAY

| | | |
|---|---|---|
| *Phone calls* | — | *Fergus, Bronte, Cam, another carpet-cleaning mob* |
| *Morning* | — | *Round robin with the midweek ladies!* |
| | — | *Shopping: baby present, new d/gown* |
| | — | *Get some videos* |
| *Afternoon* | — | *Visit Stephen & say thanks with chocolates* |
| | — | *Relax/watch videos?* |
| | — | *Do my tax return* |
| *Evening* | — | *Visit Bronte* |
| | — | *Start reading <u>Gone with the Wind</u>?* |

It occurs to me that today's list is very similar to yesterday's list, which was very similar to Monday's list. So I make a mental vow that I *will* get all these things done today. It would be simply too ridiculous if I ended up going back to work next week with my tax return still not completed. And it's equally stupid that the only person who hasn't supplied Bronte with a gift is her own mother. *And* an afternoon spent with my feet up watching videos is just what the doctor ordered. *And* I don't want to spend another evening minus a dressing-gown. *And* everybody keeps telling me what a fantastic book *Gone with the Wind* is, so it's about time I found out for myself.

So these are my aims for today and if anything else comes up, it will just have to wait. Because frankly, my dear, I don't give a damn.

# WEDNESDAY

## 1215 hrs

'But then we'll have to buy all new plates. And is that *really* economically responsible? I don't think so.'

'Perhaps *not*, Val,' replies a hatchet-faced female sarcastically, 'but I for one have had enough of trying to squeeze a slice of quiche and some salad onto those bread-and-butter plates we're using at the moment. It's a ludicrous situation.'

'Well, they're fine if you just have rolls for lunch.'

'But who on earth wants rolls for lunch *every* single Wednesday?'

There are nods and murmurs of agreement all around the tables as everybody starts to discuss what they would like for lunch on Wednesdays if they had their choice and/or larger plates. While the discussion takes place, the secretary, a pleasant-looking woman of about my own age, frantically writes something down in the large ledger before her. Val sighs deeply and looks sulkily at her cup of tea, muttering under her breath.

'All right then,' says the secretary looking up at the assorted ladies, who immediately fall quiet. 'Have we a general consensus that new, larger plates are required?'

Everybody, except Val, nods in agreement. The secretary scribbles again for a few minutes while a middle-aged woman wearing a hot-pink tracksuit and bright-red lipstick wanders around the table offering a plate of lamingtons. When she reaches me, I take one and put it on my plate with the other assorted goodies I've been collecting. The meeting might be excruciatingly boring but the food is scrumptious. The women are all sitting around three or four octagonal tables, which have been lined up in a row and covered with food. Sponge cakes, meringues, sausage rolls, tiny quiches, scones, rumballs, pikelets – everything homemade and everything delicious.

And even if it wasn't for the food, I don't think I'd be capable of moving anywhere for a while as I'm totally and absolutely knackered. What I expected to be a mild workout turned into a test of endurance that I failed miserably. In fact, when they were asking for volunteers for the last group of sets, I hid in the bathroom. Because these midweek ladies could run rings around the Saturday mob I usually play with – they are fitter, more consistent, and a great deal more feisty. They also have a collective killer instinct that would make Lleyton Hewitt's knees tremble.

'All righty then,' says the secretary, 'any other general business?'

'Yes.' A tiny female with Asian features puts her hand up. 'Has anybody else noticed the smell in the big urn? Well, I did *and* I investigated. Apparently, it was utilised by the Monday night men's team as a vehicle for boiling frankfurts.'

'*What!*'

'You're kidding!'

'That's Siewyee,' Pat, who is sitting on my right, whispers to me. 'She's the club champion. Killer forehand.'

'Dis*gus*ting!' The hatchet-faced woman who had put Val in her place earlier shakes her head in disbelief. 'Something *has* to be done!'

'Quite right. I'll bring it up at the club annual general meeting next week,' says the secretary, writing furiously. 'Now – anything else?'

'Yes, I've got something!' calls the lamington lady in the hot-pink tracksuit from the far end of the table. 'Could you please ask the section one girls to stop allowing their toddlers to play musical instruments while competition is in play?'

'Hear, hear!'

'Yes, *please*!'

'And, while we're on the subject, could you ask Caron from section one to keep her twins out of the clubhouse at *all* times. They went through my handbag last time and posted my car keys down the ball-chute!'

This time the agreement around the table is particularly vociferous, with several of the ladies embarking on lurid tales of exactly what Caron's twins had got up to during the season. The secretary writes furiously on her paper before picking up her spoon and hitting it on the side of a cup in a request for silence.

'Okay, anything else?'

'Well, I'd like to bring a motion for new tables,' pipes up Val, with a sidelong smirk at the hatchet-faced woman. 'After all, if we're to have these new large plates, then the current tables are going to be awfully crowded.'

Once again, there are murmurs of agreement around the table and several women nod sagely as they break into discussion. The hatchet-faced woman narrows her eyes at Val while she tries to think of something appropriately cutting. I reach across for the teapot and top up my cup before taking a deep sip. Doesn't taste of frankfurts at all.

'You know she's right, Jan,' says Pat to the secretary, 'these octagonal tables only just hold eight of the bread-and-butter plates each, so with normal dinner plates they're going to be all hanging over the edge. And you couldn't possibly have any guests, there wouldn't be the room.'

'But we can't afford new tables,' replies Jan, looking increasingly stressed as she checks her books. 'They'd be terribly expensive.'

'Quite so,' agrees the hatchet-faced woman sternly.

'Well, then —' Val isn't giving up so easily '— perhaps we ought to save up for the tables *before* we buy the plates. Makes much more sense.'

139

'I'll put it to the vote,' says Jan, and she hits the cup with her spoon once more. 'All those in favour of saving up for the tables and *then* buying the plates, please raise your hand.'

The majority of the women raise their hands, so, because I don't want to be left out, I put up mine too. Val beams proudly and the hatchet-faced woman sends her a truly malevolent look before leaning back and staring thin-lipped at the ceiling, her arms folded across her chest. I do hope they don't play against each other in the near future. I wouldn't bet much on Val's chances of surviving the encounter intact.

'Moving on,' says Jan, performing her cup trick again, 'we've arranged for Deb to take flowers up to Lorraine, who's in hospital for a breast reduction tomorrow – oh, *stuff* it!' Jan claps her hand to her mouth and, with a horrified expression, looks up and around the gathering. 'I wasn't supposed to say *what* she was having done. Could everyone please pretend they didn't hear that?'

'Oh, sure!'

'No problem.'

'Didn't hear a thing.'

'Great.' Jan doesn't look all that convinced but continues regardless: 'Then I think that's about it. Oh, except that Genny has asked whether some others, apart from just her, could take the tea-towels home to be washed occasionally.'

'Hear, hear,' says Genny with feeling.

'And we'll need a volunteer to price some bigger tables so we know exactly how much money we don't have. Anybody got some free time?'

'I'm sure Val would be happy to oblige,' says the hatchet-faced woman quickly, 'wouldn't you, dear?'

Val opens her mouth and then closes it again, no doubt deciding that a partial victory is better than nothing. I take advantage of the lull in conversation to select a piece of decadent-looking cream-cake with pineapple icing and a couple of tiny meringues. If this is standard fare for midweek ladies, I think I'm going to sign up. Perhaps I could even get to meet Lorraine and ask her if it was worth it.

'Thanks, Val – much appreciated. And that finishes it then.' Jan closes her ledger and lays her pen across the top with a sigh of relief. 'That is, unless anybody has anything else to add? No? Excellent. I declare this meeting closed.'

There is a smattering of applause around the table and then the level of conversation immediately increases as small groups of women begin discussing various topics, the standout favourites being Lorraine's impending breast reduction and Caron's terrible twins. As I don't know either of these ladies or their appendages, I eat my cream-cake in silence, looking out at the row of en tout cas courts shimmering in the low winter sun. I wonder if Richard plays tennis? And, whether or not he plays tennis, I wonder if he has left for Tasmania yet? I finish off my cream-cake and Pat offers me a platter of sausage rolls. I take two, one for now and one for my plate.

'Too small, aren't they?' the hatchet-faced woman asks me politely.

'Actually, I thought they were perfect,' I reply, eyeing the sausage roll I'm about to devour. 'Exactly a mouthful and no more.'

'I meant the plates.'

'Oh, hmm,' I answer diplomatically as I catch Val's eye on me from across the table. 'Not sure about that.'

'So, enjoying yourself yet?' asks Pat with a grin. 'Not quite what you're used to, hey?'

'Not at all,' I agree truthfully, 'but it's surprisingly entertaining.'

'Yeah, they're a good bunch.'

'And the tennis was *really* great.'

'You sound stunned,' interjects a youngish female who

looks just like one of CJ's Barbies, complete with meticulous make-up and an elaborate blonde hairdo. 'What did you expect?'

'Well, I . . . um . . .' I look around and realise that there is considerable interest in my answer. 'Actually, I don't know *what* I expected.'

'Fair enough,' says the blonde, laughing as she looks away.

'Can't stand her,' Pat whispers loudly to me. 'Look at her *hair* – it's got that much hairspray on it, it doesn't move at all. One of these days I'm going to hit a ball right into it, and I bet it'll get stuck.'

'I can't believe Lorraine is getting a breast reduction,' exclaims a redhead whose own combination of bra-lessness and buxom figure I'd personally found very off-putting when I played tennis against her earlier. 'Why would *anybody* want to have a breast reduction?'

'My husband'd kill me if I had one of them,' interjects Blondie. 'Really *kill* me.'

'Maybe she's doing it for herself,' says Pat, 'and not her husband?'

'Hmm.' Blondie seems intrigued by this novel concept for a second before shaking her head in dismissal. 'Nah.'

'So who won the round robin?' asks a white-haired, bushy-browed woman from across the table. 'Does anyone know?'

'I think it was Siewyee,' replies Pat.

'Siewyee *again*!' says the woman, bringing her abundant brows together so that they look like an oddly positioned mohawk. 'Then who came runner-up?'

'Heather came runner-up,' calls Jan from the end of the table. 'Cathy came in third and Sue was fourth.'

'What about fifth?'

'Helen.'

'Sixth?'

'Glenys.'

'Mandy, you *must* give me the recipe for these scones!' the slim brunette on my left leans across in front of me and yells up to the other end of the table. 'They're delicious!'

'No way, Sharyn,' replies Mandy emphatically, 'it's a family secret. Sorry.'

'Bitch,' mutters Sharyn under her breath as she takes another mouthful of scone. 'They're not *that* bloody good.'

'Did I come seventh then?' asks the bushy-browed woman of nobody in particular. 'Or eighth?'

'So, are you ever going to join us?' Pat asks me. 'Lots of these women work full-time, they just have Wednesdays off, that's all.'

'Do you know, I wouldn't mind,' I reply, surprising myself by actually meaning it. 'There certainly seems to be a lot more going on than with Saturday tennis.'

'There sure is!' laughs Pat.

'Ninth?'

'Can I have your attention, please!' Jan, the secretary, is standing up and holding out an ice-cream container. 'It's time to draw the raffle. And the winner will get this, um, lovely plant that Joyce so kindly donated. So, first of all, a round of applause for Joyce's generosity.'

Everybody claps agreeably while Joyce blushes and looks suitably humble. I stare transfixed at the 'lovely plant', which appears to be some kind of cactus that has been inbred to the point of deformity. Standing about three feet tall, it's covered with incredibly large, fleshy protuberances that are each topped with a red, bulbous, carnivorous-looking flower. If the ladies were to place this particular plant in the vicinity of Caron's twins, I don't think they'd have to worry about them being around for too long.

'And I thought we'd ask Terry, as our guest here today, to

143

draw out the winning ticket.' Jan comes over to me and holds out the ice-cream container. 'Terry, would you like to do the honours?'

'Sure.' I reach up and pull out a ticket, which I then pass over to Jan. 'There you go.'

'And the winner is . . .' Jan makes a great show of unfolding the ticket while everybody holds their breath. '*Terry!* The winner is Terry!'

'*Me?*' I splutter around a mouthful of lamington. 'Are you *sure?*'

'Absolutely!' Jan shows me the raffle ticket with my name written in large letters. 'See? So Terry wins the cactus!'

'Rigged!' calls out Blondie loudly.

The room breaks into fractured applause, punctuated by laughter, and Jan lugs over the dreadful cactus and deposits it onto the table in front of me. I eye the plant doubtfully, and move my plate of food out of its reach.

'Look, that's really rotten,' I say with feeling. 'You know, pulling my own name out and all. Let's redraw it.'

'No way,' replies Jan emphatically, with a sidelong glance at the cactus. 'You won it fair and square.'

'Yes, it's *all* yours,' adds Blondie. 'You can think of us when you water it.'

'Christ,' mutters Pat to me, 'that girl's a total flake.'

'Damn,' I mumble, chewing my lip while I look at the cactus warily.

'Here, put it on one of these so it doesn't leak,' says the hatchet-faced woman, passing me over a plate. 'They're just the right size. For a plant, that is.'

'Tenth?' asks the bushy-browed woman. 'Did I maybe come tenth?'

'So what exactly do they take off?' inquires Sharyn, holding the neck of her top out so that she can get a good view of her almost flat frontage. 'I mean, how do they get to the . . . flesh? I don't get it.'

'Has anybody seen my car keys?' calls Val. 'I left them over here near Joyce's plant. Has anyone picked them up?'

'Eleventh? Or what about twelfth?'

'So I'll let you know when we have our next round robin,' says Pat, 'and see if you can get the day off.'

'And you never know your luck,' adds Jan, with a grin at my plant, 'because Joyce donates a cactus each time. So, if you're *really* lucky, you could win another one.'

Double damn.


# WEDNESDAY

## 1433 hrs

Looking at myself in the changing-room mirror, I frown and strip off yet another dressing-gown. It joins the growing pile in the corner. Why is it that all the dressing-gowns I like are too short? Why is it that all the dressing-gowns I *don't* like are too short? I tug on the last one, a leopard-print number that makes me look as if I should be out stalking zebras on the African plains. And it's too short as well.

I smooth my hair down, drape all the dressing-gowns willy-nilly on their hangers and stomp out of the changing-room in disgust. Then I dispose of them en masse at the first available rack and stand there, wondering what to do next. Because I've now exhausted every shop in the centre that stocks dressing-gowns and haven't had any luck at all.

While I'm thinking, I notice a stand overflowing with thick flannelette pyjamas and decide that a pair of those will have to do. After all, in about a decade or two I'll probably

145

start to shrink and then I can come back and buy myself a lovely dressing-gown that will flow on the ground around me. Until then, it'll be pyjamas all the way. I select a particularly fetching pair decorated with a multitude of hands. Interesting concept.

I take my selection up to the registers and join a queue that stretches mid-store. In front of me is a young woman with so many preschool-aged children that it defies belief. She definitely needs my flannelette pyjamas more than I do, *and* a chastity belt to go with them. There's one child sitting at the front of the trolley, three sitting inside the trolley, two holding on to the trolley, and one unwrapping chocolate bars at a display next to the trolley. She also doesn't seem to have any actual purchases as the only things in her trolley *are* her children, so I'm not sure what she's doing in the queue. Maybe she's after a refund. Good luck.

'*Terry!*'

'Diane! What are you doing here?' I grin down at Cam's sister, who has joined the queue behind me with a super-wide trolley that holds her twins and an assortment of purchases. The twins are dressed identically in lavender woolly jumpsuits and matching padded jackets. They are both sleeping peacefully.

'I had to grab a couple of work-shirts for David and a pair of footy boots for Michael. And then, of course, I found some clothes for the girls that I couldn't resist. Here, look!' Diane holds up a small bright-red tracksuit with diagonal green stripes and a matching beanie. 'What do you think?'

'Very nice,' I reply, shading my eyes, 'and you won't lose them in that either.'

'Oh, do you think it's too bright?' Diane eyes the tracksuit doubtfully.

'No, it's fine,' I lie encouragingly. 'Hey, have you seen Bronte today?'

146

'Yes, I popped in this morning.' Diane puts the tracksuit back in the trolley. 'And you've saved me a phone call now.'

'I have?'

'Yes, because Bronte tells me she's staying with you for a week or so. Which, incidentally, I think is an excellent idea and it makes me feel a great deal better about the whole thing. But anyway, she also says you're hosting their naming day for the baby. And good on you – that's *very* generous.'

'I thought so.'

'Well, of course I don't want you left with everything so I offered to do the ringing around. Because obviously it's too late for proper invitations. So Bronte and I put our heads together and came up with a tentative list for the party. I've left it at home but I really want you to cast your eye over it and see if there's anybody we've missed.'

'*Excuse* me?'

Diane and I both turn to look at the speaker, an elderly lady behind us in the queue who is leaning on a metallic walking frame. She frowns at us and points, with a shaky finger, towards the registers. When we turn to see what she's on about, we notice that a big gap has formed in the line between us and the fertile female with the trolley full of children. But while we're registering this, a young bearded man comes strolling along and, humming pleasantly, deposits himself neatly in the gap.

'Hey!' I exclaim with justifiable annoyance.

'Yes?' he replies politely, turning to look at me. 'What can I do for you?'

'You've jumped the queue!'

'I think you're mistaken,' he says, smiling at me. 'There *was* no queue.'

'There certainly was!' interjects Diane, leaning across. 'And it was here!'

'No, sorry.' The young man turns his back on us and resumes humming.

'I'll deal with this.' The elderly woman from behind hobbles slowly around us and then, by tilting her walking frame, manages to jab the young bearded guy deftly in the ankle with one of the legs. When he gasps with pain and turns to see what's going on, she gestures wildly to the back of the queue.

'Get in line – *now*!'

The young guy glares at his assailant for a second or two while he patently decides whether to stand his ground. Then, obviously coming to the conclusion he's outmatched, he hops over to the adjoining queue and stands at the end with a face like thunder. Diane and I watch the elderly lady with stunned admiration as she hobbles slowly back into place. Looking up, she sees us watching and gestures impatiently towards the registers. Hurriedly we move forwards.

'That's what I want to be like when I'm old,' I say with awe. 'A force to be reckoned with.'

'Hmm,' says Diane. 'She reminds me too much of my mother.'

'True.'

'Anyway, your computer's online, isn't it?'

'Yes,' I say doubtfully, 'why?'

'Well, I'll send you the list by email. Hey, quick, move forwards, Terry.'

'You can try,' I reply, shuffling forwards obediently, 'but I'm not very good at that sort of stuff.'

'But you work in a library!'

'And?' I question, keeping an eye on the slow-moving queue. 'Your point is?'

'I see.' Diane raises her eyebrows at me. 'Well, I'm sure you'll manage. I'll get your email address off Cam and send it over to you tonight. Then, if you think of any more names, you can just let me know.'

'Okay, but I'm sure Bronte's covered our family so it should be fine.'

'What about Dennis?' Diane looks around me at the registers. 'Terry – you're up!'

Sure enough, the female in front has moved away with all of her numerous offspring still in tow and it's finally my turn. I shoot the elderly woman behind a quick glance of apology for not being quicker off the mark and move forwards, putting my singular purchase on the counter. After I've paid and collected my bagged pyjamas, I move over to one side and wait for Diane to get through her transaction. A few minutes later she joins me and we pick up the conversation where we left off.

'According to his receptionist, Dennis is off cruising at the moment.'

'Cruising?' Diane looks at me, confused.

'Cruising as in *on* a cruise,' I reply. 'Not as in trying to pick someone up. Although . . .'

'Yes,' says Diane sympathetically, 'hmm.'

'Anyway, he's supposed to be back by the weekend so she's going to pass on the message about Bronte. And then, when he rings, I'll let him know about Sunday.'

'Good,' says Diane, tucking her purse securely into her handbag. 'And I'll handle all the rest. Just let me know what you want me to bring.'

'Hey, Diane?' I ask as something occurs to me. 'Did Cam tell you about your mother yesterday? At lunch?'

'Yes!' Diane hangs her bag on her shoulder and looks at me, nodding. 'She did! That is *so* weird. I can't wait to find out what it's all about.'

'Then you don't know?' I ask, disappointed. 'No ideas?'

'Not a one,' she replies. 'I mean, it sounds like she knows him – otherwise why have a reaction like that? But as far as

I'm aware, she's never even *been* to Tasmania so I've got no idea. But I'm going to find out.'

'When you do, can you tell me? I'm just curious.'

'No problem.' Diane looks at her watch as one of her twins starts to yawn, stretching herself out and bopping her sister neatly on the side of the head. 'Hey, Regan! That's not very nice, sweetheart!'

The bopped twin immediately starts to scream blue murder while Sweetheart looks on imperturbably. Diane hurriedly unclips the restraint and picks up her injured offspring, nursing her against one shoulder and murmuring appeasements. As the baby's sobs turn to hiccups and she starts to calm down, I watch Regan with considerable interest. She is now paying absolutely no attention to her sister and has instead started to examine her fingernails carefully. Then, as if she senses me looking at her, she turns, cocks her head on one side, and stares evenly back. And it suddenly hits me that this must have been exactly what Cam's daughter CJ was like six years ago. Oh, the power of genetics!

Poor Diane.

# WEDNESDAY

## 1600 hrs

With some difficulty, I fill out all the blanks through to the end of Section Three of Part B, and then follow the instructions directing me to Section Four of Part D. However, when I read through the first two paragraphs of this section, I discover they seem to be in direct contradiction to the circumstances outlined in Section Two of Part A. Accordingly, I flick back to Section Two of Part A, and examine the tiny print at the bottom of the page, which now tells me to go straight to Question Six of Section One of Part E. And I'm quite sure it didn't say that before.

But my particular tax return form doesn't seem to *have* a Question Six of Section One of Part E. In fact, try as I might, I can't even find Part E. I flick the pages backwards and forwards, naively assuming that Part E would be sandwiched between Parts D and F. But it's not. So I flick back to Section Two of Part A and re-read the tiny print. And now it says to skip Questions One to Eleven of Parts C, D and E and instead read Question Twelve of Part F to see if it applies. I briefly consider attempting to flick forwards to Part F, and decide instead to flick the lot. So I do. Right over to the other side of the room. Then I flick the pen for good measure.

Pushing my ponytail over my shoulder, I stare balefully at the bundle of papers now scattered over the floor by the television set and decide that perhaps investing in a tax agent mightn't be a bad idea. Instead of wasting my time on such stressful matters, I'll start reading *Gone with the Wind*. I'm pretty sure Scarlett never had to bother her head with Parts A to F of annual tax returns. Fiddle dee dee to that.

So I stretch out on the couch and open the book to immerse myself in the days of buggies and courtship and whalebone corsets. But it's a tad difficult because I can see the scattered papers out of the corner of my left eye and their haphazardness offends my sense of order. I re-read the first paragraph three times and then give up. Hauling myself off the couch, I head towards the offensive paperwork just as the doorbell rings, so I change direction to answer it.

'Teresa!' Stephen bounces through the door dressed in jeans and what looks like a velvet smoking jacket with padded shoulders and enormous braided pockets. 'Or should I say *Grandma*?'

'No,' I reply emphatically as I close the door behind him. 'You shouldn't.'

'Got time for a coffee?'

'Sure.' I lead the way through the lounge-room towards the kitchen. 'And I've been meaning to drop in and say thanks, so you've saved me the trip.'

'Thanks?' asks Stephen, following in my wake. 'Thanks for what?'

'For Monday morning, of course. Helping out with Bronte.'

'Oh, pffft.' Stephen waves his hand airily. 'Lord – what are all these?'

'My bloody tax return.' I stop at the entrance to the kitchen and watch Stephen bend down and retrieve the crumpled papers from the floor. 'I *hate* it.'

'Odd filing system you have, schnooks,' he replies as he joins me with the tax return paraphernalia in one hand. 'What happens when the whole floor's covered?'

'Hardy ha ha.' I put the kettle on and spoon some coffee into the plunger while Stephen sits at the table and tucks my group certificate and other loose pages in the tax return booklet. 'I swear those things are designed by the same people who invented the Rubik's cube.'

'Oh, I *love* the Rubik's cube!' says Stephen. 'What fun!'

'Yeah.' I roll my eyes at him as I get out a couple of coasters and pop them on the table. 'A real barrel of laughs.'

'Do you want me to do it for you?' Stephen opens up the booklet, has a look at what I've written and starts to laugh.

'What's so funny?' I ask, rather offended.

'Here, this.' Stephen starts to chortle again. 'What you've written for Question Two of Section Three of Part B. Ha ha ha!'

'I'm going to ignore you.' I add some milk to the two cups

and carry them over to the table with a plate of chocolate-chip cookies. 'Because anybody who finds tax returns amusing has to be sick.'

'Don't sneer at people just because they're different,' replies Stephen evenly, still reading the tax return. 'Now, do you want me to do it or not? I'm pretty cheap.'

'Do you actually *do* tax returns?' I sit down in the chair opposite and wrap my hands around my hot mug. 'I thought you were an actor.'

'Haven't you *seen* my acting?' says Stephen, looking at me with amusement. 'Do you *seriously* think I'd make a living from that?'

'Um, well . . .' I reply carefully, because I *have* seen his acting and I *have* always wondered how he managed to put food on the table.

'Quite right. No, acting's just a hobby – sometimes it pays, sometimes it don't.' Stephen takes a sip of coffee. 'But my paying job is accountancy.'

'You're an accountant?' I ask in disbelief. 'An *accountant*?'

'Actually, it's a great lurk,' says Stephen, a trifle defensively. 'I just do the books for a few small businesses and then, at this time of the year, make a bit on the side with tax returns. So, yes or no? I'll do yours at a cut rate because of the entertainment value.'

'Yes, yes, *yes*!' I say, nodding eagerly. 'And thank you! Just give me the bill when you're done.'

'No problem.' Stephen folds the papers in half and puts them in one of his ample pockets. 'And don't forget to give me your receipts before I go.'

'Receipts? What receipts?'

'Ah, I see.'

'Good, then we'll change the subject – did you get lucky Monday morning or not?'

'No, not *then* exactly. But –' Stephen looks across at me with a self-satisfied smirk '– I hope to on Saturday night.'

'Don't tell me you got a date with him?' I ask as I take a bite of biscuit.

'I most certainly did, and isn't he *just* the cutest thing you've ever seen with a stretcher? Almost as cute as that little Irishman of yours, hey?'

'Almost,' I mumble around my biscuit, 'but, yes, he *was* cute. Not my type – but well done, anyway.'

'Well, I should *think* he's not your type!' Stephen laughs. 'Otherwise, lordy, have I got my wires crossed!'

'Oh, no problem there,' I reply, with a knowledgable nod. '*That* was pretty obvious. And I hope it all works out well for you.'

'Schnooks, so do I. So do I.'

'And really – thanks for Monday morning.'

'Oh no.' Stephen puts his hand to his heart and looks at me earnestly. 'It's me that has to thank *you*!'

'What on earth for?'

'Well, I've always wondered what it would be like –' Stephen reaches over and grabs a biscuit, which he waves at me to emphasise his words '– you know, with a *woman*. Just out of curiosity, you see, because *so* many people seem to think it's the dog's dinner! But after I saw what I saw on Monday morning, oh my *lord*! I will *never* wonder again!'

'But, Stephen, she was giving *birth*!'

'No matter – it was scary.' Stephen shudders. '*Really* scary.'

'Oh, come on!'

'Yes, scary!' He shakes his head and points the biscuit at me. '*Yech!* I don't know *how* you people cope! Then again, I suppose you don't spend a lot of time down there – so I should say, I don't know how your *men* cope! Oh! And let me tell you about the nightmare it gave me that night!

Absolutely terrifying! There I was, just bouncing on a trampoline and –'

'Bouncing on a *trampoline*?'

'Yep. And I was having a perfectly lovely time, looking at
the blue, blue sky and getting higher and higher. Up and
down, up and down. Then, when I was at the highest point I
possibly could be, I looked down and you'll never guess! It
wasn't a trampoline anymore!' Stephen pauses for effect and
looks at me, shaking his head. 'No, it was this absolutely *huge*,
monstrous –'

'I don't want to know!'

'Exactly! And while I was realising this, it was like slow
motion and I was poised up in the air. But I knew that any
minute the spell would break and I was going to have to go
down and, when I did, I was going to plunge right into the
middle of it!'

'I'm not listening!' I cup my hands over my ears to stress my
point. 'And I *don't* want to know!'

'Okay, okay.' Stephen leans over the table and removes one
of my hands. 'I won't tell you the rest.'

'Thank god, otherwise *I'll* be getting nightmares!'

'You sure would! But –' he shudders theatrically and then
wags the biscuit at me again '– I tell you, schnooks, I had *such*
a job climbing out! And I've *certainly* been reassured that I'm
on the right path.'

'Glad to be of service.'

Stephen takes a sip of coffee and pops his biscuit in his
mouth, lost in thought. And if he is thinking what I *think* he's
thinking, I hope that he doesn't decide to share that with me
either. However, all this talk about whatever it was we were
talking about has reminded me I'm overdue for my two-yearly
pap smear. I make a mental note to arrange an appointment
while I've got the week off.

'*Teresa!*'

'What!' I exclaim, startled. 'What is it?'

'That *plant.*' Stephen is staring at the kitchen counter where the cactus squats in all its glory, bulbous flowers at the ready. 'It's gorgeous! Where *did* you get it?'

'Why, Stephen,' I exclaim, struck with brilliance, 'it's for you! A present to say thanks for your help.'

'Oh my lord!' He gets up and walks slowly over to the counter. 'For *me*? You *shouldn't* have!'

'Of course I should,' I reply, smiling graciously, 'even if you did faint at the end. I don't know what I would have done without you.'

'I'm speechless!' Stephen reaches out and, completely without fear, strokes one of the fleshy-looking stems. 'Absolutely speechless!'

'No,' I say teasingly, 'never!'

Instead of answering, Stephen picks up the plant and carries it over to the table, where he deposits it gently next to his coffee. Then he comes around the table and, before I can even respond, envelops me in a huge hug and delivers a kiss to my cheek.

'Thanks, schnooks,' he says, visibly touched. 'I'll treasure it.'

'No problem,' I reply, feeling a little guilty now. 'My pleasure.'

'But where *did* you get it?' Stephen turns the pot around to examine the cactus from each of its ugly angles. 'It's *absolutely* spectacular!'

'Oh, it was the last one left and they're not getting any more,' I say airily, in case he wants to rush out and buy the lot. 'Hey, another cup of coffee?'

'No thanks – but I *will* have the last one of these biscuits, if you don't mind?'

'Help yourself.'

'Ta.' Stephen drains his coffee and pulls the biscuit plate towards himself. 'By the way, I dropped in to see Bronte yesterday. She *is* looking well. Considering.'

'Yes, she is. And that reminds me – are you doing anything on Sunday?'

'All depends on the success of Saturday night,' Stephen replies with a leer. 'Why do you ask?'

'Bronte's having a naming day for the baby here in the afternoon. Just family and close friends. Can you make it?'

'Indubitably.' Stephen nods as he gazes at his plant with adoration. 'Wouldn't miss it for the world.'

'Great. I'll let you know a definite time when they tell me.'

'Excellent. Hey –' Stephen looks at the empty biscuit plate and then up at me. 'I thought you said the last one was for me, Miss Piggy?'

'*I* didn't eat it!'

'Well, I certainly didn't.' Stephen lifts up the plate and looks underneath it. 'And it was here a minute ago. C'mon, fess up.'

'I swear I didn't eat it!' I raise both hands and shake my head. 'Really!'

'Then who did, hmm?'

I shrug at Stephen and get up to fetch the biscuit barrel from the kitchen cupboard. I fill a fresh plate with chocolate-chip cookies and carry it across to the table, where I place it in front of Stephen, who immediately helps himself to one and begins eating. I *know* I didn't eat the other biscuit. I flick my ponytail back, look at Stephen, and then slowly move my gaze to the cactus. I watch it distrustfully – but it doesn't bat a blossom. Instead, with its fleshy protuberances bulging grotesquely, it just sits there – obviously biding its time.

# WEDNESDAY

## 1900 hrs

'So Mrs Woodmason is going to do all the ringing around *and* she's going to help on the day. You know, with the setting up and all.'

'That's great, Bronte,' I reply as I lean over and look down into the Perspex capsule again. 'But when is *she* going to wake up?'

'I don't know, Mum, but hopefully not for a while.'

'Why?' I glance at her curiously. 'Has she been playing up?'

'Like, not exactly.' Bronte leans back on her pillow, looking tired. 'She just seems to have been awake an awful lot today, that's all.'

I look down at Sherry again and tuck her little blanket in securely around her. As the only visitor, I'm sitting in the green armchair and have pulled the baby trolley over next to me, just waiting for Sherry to show a sign of wakefulness. Any sign will do. But she's fast asleep with her eyelashes fanned out along the top of her flushed cheeks and her rosebud lips ever so slightly open. One tiny hand, which has escaped from her cocoon-like wrappings, is clutched around a corner of her blanket and there is a droplet of milk from an earlier feed poised in a fold at the corner of her mouth. Whenever she breathes out, it quivers.

On the other side of the room, the only evidence of Mrs Cobb is a scrawny-looking lump in the centre of the bed that hasn't moved since I've been here. And I'm beginning to think she doesn't have a baby at all – certainly I haven't seen one and I've been here a few times now. I turn my attention back to Sherry and stroke her fingers gently.

'You wouldn't be wearing your mother out now, would

you?' I say in a singsong voice. 'No, you wouldn't do that. Not you.'

'Surely that's not our *Teresa* talking like that?'

I look up at the doorway in surprise and Rose Riley smiles at me playfully. And, as if that wasn't scary enough, my own mother pops out from behind her like she is auditioning for a scene from *The Sound of Music*, and gives me a huge smile. Rose is dressed in her usual skirt and twin-set, shades of lavender today, and my mother is wearing a petal-pink track-suit, matching headband and runners.

'Teresa, honey! Fancy seeing you here!'

'Ditto,' I reply, getting up from the armchair before I'm asked to. 'And, Mum, why do you look like the front cover of an aerobics tape for senior citizens?'

'Because Rose and Harold kindly picked me up from the gym. I was doing my Pilates.'

'Yes, we thought we would bring your mother over to visit the baby,' adds Rose Riley, settling herself down in the chair. 'Somebody has to.'

'I brought her on Monday!' I reply, stung. 'I spent the whole day with her, too!'

'And it was lovely of you, honey.' Mum bends over the crib and coos to the baby. 'Oh, you're asleep, you little precious.'

'Like, don't wake her, Gran!' says Bronte, looking worriedly towards the baby. 'She *really* needs some sleep.'

'And you look like you could use some too, dear,' Rose says, examining Bronte keenly. 'You look tired. Where's that grandson of mine?'

'Nick's at work, Mrs Riley.'

'I think it's about time we dropped the 'Mrs Riley', don't you?'

'Oh!' Bronte looks horrified. 'But then what do I call you?'

'Well, perhaps you can just call me what Nick and the

others call me – Grandma.' Rose turns to my mother and looks at her questioningly. 'That is, if you don't have any objection, Sherry.'

'Certainly not, Rose.' Mum beams briefly at them both. 'I think it's a lovely idea.'

Bronte nods, looking at me rather miserably. I give her a huge grin and a wink.

'And we heard about your little ceremony on Sunday, Bronte –' Rose purses her lips slightly before continuing '– although I must say that, in my day, we simply had a proper christening and were done with it.'

'Times change, Rose,' says my mother.

'And who am I to say anything?' Rose throws her hands up and shrugs. 'But, nevertheless, I'm quite happy to offer my assistance. Just tell me what it is you would like me to bring and I'll be sure to bring it.'

'Why, thanks Mrs Ri– I mean, Grandma,' stutters Bronte.

'So?' inquires Rose, with her head on one side.

'So what?' asks Bronte, confused.

'So – what would you like me to bring,' says Rose slowly, enunciating each word clearly, 'to the ceremony?'

'Um – I'm not sure . . .'

'That's lovely of you to offer,' I interject, looking at Bronte's reddened face, 'and I believe Diane's helping to organise the food and everything while Bronte's in here. So perhaps it'd be best if you speak to her so that there's no doubling up?'

'Excellent idea. I'll phone her tonight.'

'Thanks, Mrs – um,' says Bronte.

Harold chooses this moment to come wandering through the door, looking, as usual, rather anxious. He walks over to his wife and positions himself behind her chair before nodding politely at everybody.

'Hello, Teresa. Good evening, Bronte. I finally found a car

park, dear,' he says, looking at his wife, 'but it's miles away. Is that right?'

'Good,' replies Rose approvingly. 'But you'll have to fetch the car to the entrance for us when we leave then.'

'Is this baby ever going to wake up, honey?' Mum asks Bronte. 'Because I didn't get a chance to hold her on Monday, you know.'

'Here, have my chair, Sherry, and I'll pass her to you.' Rose gets up and straightens her skirt fastidiously. 'If that's all right with Bronte, that is. Yes?'

'Well, um. I suppose so – like, yeah sure.'

'You realise that you are going to have to be a bit more defi-nite with your answers, dear,' says Rose, frowning at Bronte, 'if you're going to raise a child. They pounce on *any* indecision and before you know it – *they* are the boss and not you. And, let me tell you, that spells disaster.'

'Um, yeah. Okay.'

Rose shakes her head almost imperceptibly and turns to raise her eyebrows at my mother, who beams back happily from where she has secured herself in the chair. While Rose is thus occupied, I grab the opportunity to get a brief hold of Sherry and dart forwards to pick the baby up gently from her crib. As I lift her, she stiffens momentarily before relaxing and settling back into her sleep. I rock her slowly, drinking in her adorability and feeding off it like some sort of parasite while, once again, she melts me. After a few moments, when my mother's outstretched arms start to shake, I realise my time is up. So I reluctantly pass the baby down to her great-grandmother. Leaning back in the armchair, Mum smiles beatifically at us all before tucking Sherry's blanket around and then cradling her against her chest, her attention now focused totally on her charge.

'Excellent.' Rose steps back and takes me firmly by the elbow. 'Because I wanted to talk to you, Teresa.'

'To *me*?'

'Yes, to you. About yesterday.' Rose ushers me over to the other side of the room as she talks. This seems a particularly pointless exercise as the room isn't exactly huge and whispering has never been one of her strong suits. Accordingly, we are still well within earshot of everyone else and they immediately all stop whatever it was they were doing to listen in.

'Yesterday? Oh, great!' I gently shake my arm loose and look down at Cam's mother with considerable interest. 'Actually, I'm so glad you've brought that up because I *really* wanted to ask you. What *happened*?'

'What do you mean?' Rose looks at me with slightly narrowed eyes.

'Well, yesterday . . .' I hesitate, unsure how to continue. 'When you went all – well, strange.'

'*Strange*?'

'It was the coffee,' interjects Harold, from across the room. 'Is that right?'

'Yes,' says Rose emphatically, 'it was.'

'But –' I look at her in confusion '– I thought that's what you wanted to talk about.'

'No,' says Rose.

'Oh, okay. Then what *was* it you wanted?'

'All *I* want to ask,' Rose continues, straightening herself in a futile attempt to measure up to my height, 'is whether you know that girl Joanne very well.'

'Joanne? Well, I suppose so.'

'Well enough to have her phone number?'

'Of course,' I reply, frowning. 'Why?'

'No reason. Could I have it, please?'

'Sure.' I shrug again. 'But I don't have it on me. Anyway, Mrs Riley, Cam'd have it as well, you know.'

'No, I've already asked Camilla and she only has her old one. Apparently, she was overseas for a while and isn't in the same lodgings now.'

'Of course!' I try to look apologetic, instead of incredibly curious. 'And that means *I'll* only have her old one as well. I never thought to ask her where she was living now.'

'Oh.' Rose looks at me expressionlessly. 'No matter.'

'But I can get it from her on Friday, if you like. One of the girls from the library is moving to America so we're having a goodbye party. And I believe Joanne's coming. So's Cam.'

'Excellent!' Rose brightens up noticeably. 'That's excellent.'

'But can't you tell me why?'

'No.'

'Oh, Rose, why don't you just tell her?' my mother pipes up from the armchair. 'It's nothing to be ashamed of, after all. You did *nothing* wrong.'

'No.' Rose shakes her head emphatically. 'Definitely not.'

'Oh, Rose,' sighs my mother, looking at her sadly.

'Sherry, be quiet,' snaps Rose. 'I'll tell if *I'm* ready and not before. And it certainly won't be until I tell my own daughters, thank you very much.'

I follow this exchange while being eaten alive by curiosity. After Rose finishes talking, she glares at my mother while Harold quickly crosses the room and puts his arm around her. I watch amazed as she leans against him and he holds her tight. I've never *ever* seen this woman show any sign of weakness, or of needing support – until now. I catch Bronte's eye and she looks at me with her mouth open, obviously just as stunned as me. Then I look across at my mother, who is still sitting in the chair with Sherry fast asleep in her lap. But she's just looking sadly at Rose.

'I *am* sorry,' Mum says apologetically. 'I didn't think. I'm such a fool, of *course* you'll want to tell the girls first. Of course.'

'No, *I'm* sorry, Sherry.' Rose straightens up, but with Harold's arm still securely around her. 'You meant well and there was no need for me to snap like that. Inexcusable.'

'Well, you are under a lot of strain, honey.'

'Still inexcusable.'

'Why don't I get us some tea from the canteen?' Harold looks at his wife with concern. 'And I'll get another chair for you, dear. Is that right?'

'That would be lovely, Harold.' Rose smiles at him and his face immediately brightens. 'In fact, I'll come with you.'

'Excellent!' Harold beams.

'And would anybody else like some tea?' Rose asks politely, her moment of weakness obviously behind her, at least temporarily.

'No thanks,' Bronte and I reply in unison.

'Yes please,' says my mother, with a smile at her friend.

Harold removes his arm from around his wife and, instead, grasps her hand and folds it within both of his. Then, somewhat awkwardly, they leave the room and Rose's heels can be heard tapping down the corridor in the direction of the elevators. Once I'm quite sure they're not coming back, I walk over to the bed and sit down next to Bronte. Then I flick my hair back, prop my elbow on a pillow, and fasten my mother with an evil eye.

'Okay. Spill the beans – what's going on?'

'Sorry, honey.' Mum tucks the blanket around the baby fastidiously to avoid looking at me. 'I've promised.'

'Can you just give me a hint?'

'No.'

'Does it involve Richard?'

'How did *you* know?' Mum looks at me with astonishment as Sherry starts to stir.

'I know more than you think,' I reply sagely, hoping to trick her into a disclosure. 'So if *you* tell me what *you* know, then *I'll* tell you how *I* know what *I* know.'

'Um . . .' Mum jiggles the baby. 'You've lost me.'

'Me too,' says Bronte, looking from me to her grandmother and then back again. 'I have *no* idea what's going on at all! Who's Richard?'

Instead of answering, my mother puts her finger and thumb together and runs them across her lips as if she is closing a zipper. Then she holds the pinched digits out in front and, after making sure that we are both watching, flicks her hand to indicate the throwing away of a key. I shake my head and sigh.

'Hell, Mum. How old are you?'

'Old enough to keep a secret,' replies Mum, obviously forgetting her lips are supposed to be zipped, 'and I *won't* tell you, honey, so please don't even try. Because it's not my secret to tell.'

I watch her narrowly as she transfers her attention back to the baby and starts singing a soft, low lullaby that I remember dimly from my own childhood. Sherry looks at her great-grandmother with a daft expression on her face and a thin trickle of milk threads its way from her open mouth and down her chin. Actually, the daft look makes them look a lot like each other, except that the baby's eyes are beginning to cross ever so slightly.

Bronte nudges me and, when I look at her, nods towards my mother before shrugging and raising her eyebrows at me questioningly. But I've got nothing to tell her because I don't know that much more than she does. However, if there's one thing I'm determined on, it's that I'm going to find out. Even if what it takes is getting my mother alone in a dark room with a swift application of some truth serum, perhaps a bottle of Bailey's Irish Cream, or even an electrified cattle prod. One way or the other, I'm going to find out what the hell is going on. And soon.

# WEDNESDAY

## 2050 hrs

Username? <u>Diamond</u>
Password? <u>              </u>

The message flashes at me impatiently while I rack my brains attempting to recall what on earth I *did* use as a password. I take a sip of my hot chocolate and stare at the computer, willing it to tell me – but it remains stubbornly mute. Just flash, flash, flashing. So I chew my lip and tap my fingers on the desk in irritation as I try to remember. Unfortunately, it was quite some time ago and there have been a lot of passwords under the bridge since then. In fact, it often feels like everything I do requires either a password or a PIN number – or both.

I distinctly remember the technician leaning over the desk after setting up the internet for me, and directing me to enter a username and password. I distinctly remember him mainly because he had an extremely well-rounded butt. I type the word 'butt' in the password box and hit enter, and then wait with my fingers crossed.

The password you have entered is INCORRECT
Please enter your correct password <u>           </u>

Bugger, bum, bitch. I take a deep breath, lean back in the study chair and play with my ponytail while I try to empty my mind. The theory being that if the brain is a blank, then the password will just light up centre-stage and obligingly blink on and off until it can be memorised. But the only thing blinking on and off is me. So, while I take another sip of hot chocolate, I go through the laborious process of refilling my mind. Then I type in the word 'Teresa', and hit enter.

The password you have entered is INCORRECT
Please enter your correct password _____

I enter 'Terry' and 'Bronte' and 'Sherry' and variations of my address. Then I try the name of a pet dog I had as a child, the name of the base I was stationed at during my RAAF years, the name of my first boyfriend and, for good measure, the name of the guy I lost my virginity with. I even, in sheer desperation, try the name 'Dennis'. After each attempt I hit the enter key and hold my breath as I watch the screen.

The password you have entered is INCORRECT
Please enter your correct password _____

My brains now thoroughly racked, I get up and walk around the study, straightening a few books and idly running my finger over the shelves to check for dust. Then I readjust the curtain folds and align Bronte's framed VCE certificate. I end up in front of the filing cabinet and, hit with sudden inspiration, pull the drawer open and remove the file marked 'computer'. I flick quickly through the contents in search of a password, any password – but all that's there are bills, receipts and an old school project of Bronte's called 'The Perfect Computer Design'. It seems Bronte's perfect computer was coloured three shades of pink, with enormous speakers and a mouse shaped like a high-heeled shoe. Or, at least, that's what it looks like.

I *could* ring Bronte at the hospital and ask her what the pass-word is but, judging by the way she looked earlier, I wouldn't be all that surprised if she was already asleep. And she's going to need every bit of rest she can get. So I sit back down and, with my chin resting in my hands, send various ESP messages through the flashing screen and straight to the hard drive. Some of the messages are polite, and some not so polite. However, after a few minutes concentration, I'm rewarded by an image that flashes onto the blank slate of my mind so, after I examine the vision from all angles, I lean forwards and type the word 'Richard' on the keyboard.

The password you have entered is INCORRECT
Please enter your correct password _____

Well, so much for ESP. I try kicking the side of the com-puter in frustration but, even with the threat of further torture to all its bits and bytes, it still doesn't buckle under pressure. Instead the phone rings so, with a baleful glance at the com-puter, I flick my ponytail back and answer it instead.

'Hello?'

'Hello yourself!' Cam sounds particularly upbeat and jovial. 'I've been trying to ring you all day, where've you been?'

'Well, let me see –' I reach out, turn the computer screen off, and settle in for a chat '– I played tennis this morning, then I went shopping. Actually, I ran into your sister as well.'

'*Which* sister?'

'Diane. She was out with the twins. Anyway, then I was here the rest of the afternoon so you couldn't have tried too hard.'

'No, I went over to visit your daughter this afternoon. That's why I was ringing, I thought we could have gone together.'

'So what did you think of the baby?'

'Cute, *very* cute,' Cam sounds enthusiastic, 'and she looks like you and Bronte, too. Made me feel all clucky.'

'Why, because she looked like me?'

'No, in *spite* of the fact she looked like you,' Cam laughs. 'But I thought Bronte seemed a bit tired.'

'Yes, I did too,' I agree readily. 'Reality must be starting to hit. Did you hear she's bringing the baby here for a week?'

'Yes!' Cam laughs again. 'But I don't see why. Doesn't she know what you're like with babies?'

'Hey!' I exclaim, stung. 'I'm perfectly fine! Besides, I don't have to *do* anything; she's just coming home for the company. You know, some support.'

'Hmm, interesting concept. Oh, and thanks for the note!'

'What note?' I ask, puzzled.

'The one you left on my pillow that CJ found,' replies Cam evenly. 'The one that she thinks is proof I have a boyfriend named Rudolph who sleeps over. And the one she showed her father to *prove* that I have a boyfriend named Rudolph who sleeps over.'

'Oh, that note!' I say merrily. 'No problem.'

'Hmm. Anyway, what're you doing tomorrow?'

'Let me see. I've got some carpet cleaners coming in the morning, then I've got a doctor's appointment, and Bronte's coming home at some stage but I'm not sure of the time yet. Oh, and then I might pop in and see my mother because I need to ask her something.' I narrow my eyes as I briefly envisage the coming interrogation. 'Which reminds me, Cam, when you've finished telling me why you want to know what I'm doing, just say the word 'Rose' so that I remember to tell you the *very* interesting thing that happened at the hospital.'

'It sounds like it involves my mother,' says Cam suspiciously. 'Does it?'

'Sure does. Now, what's up tomorrow?'

'Well, I've had this free gym membership for months now, and I haven't activated it because I haven't had time, but I thought I might go tomorrow. That is, if you want to come along?'

'You mean because you know I used to belong to a gym, I can show you the ropes and you won't look such a dingbat?'

'Exactly!'

'Okay.' I smile to myself. 'How about I pick you up around two?'

'Sounds good. But . . . um, I'll drive. And now – Rose!'

'Well! There I was, visiting Bronte, when who should arrive but your mother and mine. Oh, and Harold. Anyway, after the usual stuff about the baby and all, your mother pulled me aside and asked me for Joanne's phone number.'

'Is that it?' asks Cam, sounding disappointed. 'She asked me for that the other day as well.'

'Yes, so she said. But she got terribly excited when she thought I had it, and then when I remembered that all I had was the old one – I swear she nearly fainted!'

'Fainted?' Cam sounds disbelieving. 'My *mother*?'

'Yes! Harold had to prop her up. And my mum turns around and says, "Rose, just tell her" – meaning me – "what's going on because it's *nothing to be ashamed of* and you've done *nothing* wrong." There! What do you think *that* means?'

'I don't know,' replies Cam slowly, 'but something really strange is going on.'

'Yes. And I'm going to find out.'

'How?'

'Well, *my* mother obviously knows so I'm going around there tomorrow to torture her. I'll let you know the end result at the gym.'

'Excellent. Because it's got me stumped. I was talking about it with Diane and Mum hasn't ever *been* to Tasmania. So how on earth would she know him?'

'I don't know. But she does.'

'Yes, she sure does. And, speaking of him, what was the deal with *you* the other day?'

'What do you mean?' I ask defensively.

'You know! That was some extreme reaction!'

'It was your coffee, that's all.'

'Will everybody *stop* blaming my coffee!'

'Okay then,' I laugh agreeably. 'And, yes, I did have a rather odd reaction. But I worked it all out later. Do you remember my father?'

'Your father?' repeats Cam with confusion. 'Well, yes – vaguely. But I only ever met him once or twice.'

'See, my father was very similar in looks to Richard,' I explain earnestly. 'Same body type, same eyes, same sort of aura. Do you know what I mean?'

'No, but continue.'

'You do so. Anyway, I suppose I miss my father. That is, I *know* I miss my father, and I think when I saw Richard I just reacted to the resemblance, that's all.'

'Well, that makes sense,' says Cam sarcastically, 'and it explains perfectly why you wanted to jump him on my kitchen floor.'

'I did not!'

'You did so!'

'Did *not!*'

'Did –' Cam stops, and starts laughing instead.

'It's not funny,' I say sulkily.

'No, it's not,' she agrees with a smirk in her voice. 'It's actually a sign you need therapy. And soon. I can recommend a good one, if you like.'

'Yes, I saw how together *you* are the other day!' I say nastily. 'Together with *Santa*, that is.'

'Terry –'

'Didn't the antlers get in the way when you –'

'Two o'clock,' she interrupts shortly, and hangs up.

I put the receiver back into its cradle and resume staring at the computer while I play with my ponytail. How dare she mock my theory? It's a perfectly good theory and I'm sticking with it. I lean forwards and switch the screen back on. Then, simply because it feels appropriate, I type in a four-letter word beginning with 'F' and hit enter.

The password you have entered is INCORRECT
Please enter your correct password _____

If only it were that easy. If only *life* were that easy – if life itself had a password, and all you had to do was type it in your own personal console and everything would be revealed. In easily understandable language that you could then take and apply wherever necessary. So that nothing was awkward, nothing difficult and nothing incomprehensible. You'd just coast along, changing programs at will.

And each key on the keyboard would have an appropriate purpose – like 'delete' for those people who are particularly annoying, 'alt' for when you want to live outside the square, 'shift' and your new house is all set up, and 'backspace' to erase that really stupid thing you just said. Escape, control, home, insert – they would all have a specific use much more in keeping with actual life. And all you would need is your password.

But then again, what would be the use? I'd probably forget it, anyway.

# THURSDAY

*Handy Household Hint No 111:*

*Never forget that the sooner you fall behind, the more time you'll have to catch up.*

# THURSDAY

## 0715 hrs

'I didn't wake you up, did I? Because I'm just so *bored*, Mum! Like, I've been up for hours because I'm *so* excited about getting out and I've already packed everything and Nick's not going to be here to pick me up till about four! Oh, and Mum, he'll be grabbing my V-dub from the front of your joint sometime today. But you should *see* all the balloons and crap I've got here! You know, where are we going to *put* them all? And, Mum, Sherry played up so bad last night that I almost tore my hair out. She just wouldn't settle, didn't matter what I did – fed her, sponged her, changed her, I even gave her a massage at two thirty! Like, I'm *so* looking forward to getting home, giving you this baby and having a sleep! Mum, I *can't* thank you enough!'

# THURSDAY

## 0825 hrs

### THURSDAY

| | | |
|---|---|---|
| Phone calls | – | Fergus!!!! Diane (re email) |
| Morning | – | Carpet cleaners @ 9.00am |
| | – | Shopping: baby present |
| | – | Pap smear appointment @ 10.20 |
| Afternoon | – | Visit Mum and don't leave without some information!!! |
| | – | Cam's @ 2.00pm for the gym |
| | – | Tidy Bronte's room |
| | – | Bronte and Sherry after 4.00pm |
| Evening | – | Relax/watch videos or attack <u>Gone with the Wind</u>? |

# THURSDAY

## 0842 hrs

'No way known, I'd only be robbing you, lady. Because, I'm tellin' you, that there stain's set in bloody concrete. Although, hmm – I shouldn't be telling you this coz my boss'll kill me if he hears I've been giving work to the opposition, like. But the only guy I know who might have a chance with this 'ere is my cousin. He's bloody amazing with stains. I've seen carpets I wouldn't have given a chance in hell of comin' clean, then in walks Matt, and afore you can scratch yourself – bloody beautiful. I'll give you his number. Great bloke, bald as an egg, bit plump, always on a bloody diet . . . if he can't get it out, no one can.

# THURSDAY

## 0925 hrs

'So we're grandparents! Unbelievable! I only wish I'd been there – you always get *all* the good stuff, Terry love. But hey! Don't feel bad about it, I'm sure I'll get to see a lot of the little tacker, too. Now, we'll – I mean, *I'll* be back in town tomorrow morning. Just need to pop into the office for a bit then I'll come straight over to your place to see Bronte. Hey, I know! Let's have lunch together. What's on the menu? How about some of those chicken vol-au-vent things you used to do? Maybe with some risotto, and some scalloped potatoes? I tell you, I'd *love* something simple after all the stuff I've been eating for the past week! Unbelievable!'

# THURSDAY

## 0943 hrs

'Hi there, Terry my love. I was thinking that I might be getting a call from you last night? Ah well, never mind. Now, I just thought I'd better be letting you know that I'm up at Daylesford for a couple a days to help a mate out with some work. So you can think of me as I'm tasting the spas and dabbling me toes in the magic water! I would've been asking you up here with me but . . . um, of course! You've got the lass and the baby to be looking after, to be sure! And I know all about the partying to be taking place on Sunday – so I'll be there with bells on. And you'll be after me bringing you some of this here fountain of youth, so I'll fetch as many bottles as you'll be needing, and a couple more! Never you mind about that!'

177

# THURSDAY

## 1105 hrs

'Well, that's it! All done, Mrs Diamond, and sorry we're running a bit late today. But I told you it wasn't so bad, didn't I? You only made it worse by being silly and clenching yourself up like that. Now, up you pop, get yourself dressed and I'll send this off to the lab. You'll be getting the results pretty soon and next time you come in for this, just remember to relax, all right? These procedures don't *need* to hurt at all. Okay, now – *hey*! Watch your foot there! You're going to knock the slide off the – *damnation*! Look what you've done! See? Now we're going to have to do the whole thing again. Come on, come on, I can't do it with you standing way over there, pop back up on the bed and remember – just relax.'

# THURSDAY

## 1155 hrs

The same old guy is out in his front garden next door, watering his now-planted daisies, as I walk up the path to my mother's front door. Despite his best efforts, a gusty wind keeps redirecting his water spray so that the only things around that remain dry *are* the daisies. He pauses in his endeavours to give me the once-over and then turns away, obviously recognising me as a non-criminal type who intends no harm to his neighbour. If only he knew.

I open the security door and use the lion's-head knocker on the front door. While I'm waiting, I pull my coat around myself tightly and hop up and down to keep warm. A few seconds later the door opens wide and my mother, dressed in a long-sleeved midnight-blue caftan, beams up at me.

'Teresa, honey! How lovely!'

'Hi, Mum. Just thought I'd drop in to say hello.'

'You look like you've been out running,' my mother says, looking at my outfit, which even I've got to admit is rather weird. I've got my black calf-length coat over a big red track-suit jacket over a snug black tank-top and three-quarter length lycro hipsters. Odd combination – but I'm planning on going straight to Cam's house after I finish with my mother. With or without Mum's body in the boot.

'Not yet,' I reply, peeling off my coat. 'First I'll have a coffee with you, okay?'

'Of course! What a treat!' She stands back and, after I manoeuvre myself around her, shuts the door behind me. I hang my coat and my shoulder bag on one of the brass hooks by the door before following my mother into the kitchen. She heads straight for the kettle while I sit down at the rectangular formica table that has been here since I was a baby.

The kitchen is of a country design. Square and huge, with benches and cupboards all around the perimeter and the table and chairs in the centre. There is a large, old-fashioned window covered by white net curtains, which match the tablecloth hanging almost to the floor over the table. Framed photographs and children's drawings cover every available bit of wall space, behind which can be seen wallpaper of an orange and brown, pots-and-kettles design. You can't *buy* wallpaper like that anymore – with good reason. Every counter in the kitchen is cluttered with plants, canisters and assorted bowls of fruit. And the whole feel is homely and comfortable – an excellent place to unwind and tell secrets. I rub my hands together in anticipation.

'Cold, honey?' asks Mum as she pours hot water into a coffee mug and looks up questioningly. 'Sugar?'

'Warming up now, thanks. And just one sugar, Mum,' I reply, reflecting on the fact that I've *always* had one sugar. It'd be nice to come around here just once and not have to explain how I have my coffee.

'Milk?'

'Just a tad.' And I've always had just a tad of milk. Never mind, there are more important things than a retentive memory. I decide to make some polite conversation to lull her into a false sense of security before I move in for the kill.

'So, what have you been up to?'

'Oh, this and that.' Mum moves over to the table and puts my coffee in front of me with a plate of fat, heart-shaped biscuits. 'Bit of gardening, bit of bingo, bit of yoga. Have a biscuit.'

'Yoga? Really?' I say, slightly taken aback because I've never heard her mention yoga before. 'What's it like? Tell me more.'

Mum sits down opposite me with her own coffee. 'Well, it's down at the scout hall. Go on, have a biscuit, honey.'

I wait for a minute or two but she's obviously not going to add anything, so I take a biscuit and, while I eat it, gaze around the kitchen for inspiration. Almost immediately I notice a new set of drawings from my five year old niece tacked to the wall by the stove. The subject seems to be something resembling a pink and grey horse – but with several more appendages than one might expect, that may or may not be legs.

'I see that Amy is still doling out her daughter's pictures to unsuspecting relatives. When did you get those?'

'Oh, only last week,' replies Mum, following my gaze and focusing on the set of drawings. 'Aren't they just wonderful? I think Bonnie's going to be quite the little artist one day.'

'Really?' I ask doubtfully, putting my head on one side and looking back at the pictures to see if I missed something. Some portent of greatness, perhaps. Nope, just a six-legged male pink-grey horse thing with large teeth. I take a sip of coffee and then try another of the homemade biscuits. 'Yum! These are really delicious, Mum!'

'Aren't they? Mr Hood next door bakes every Wednesday and brings me over a container full of the most wonderful things. You should have come over last week: I had éclairs and profiteroles.'

'Wow!' I make a mental note to drop in more often on a Thursday. Why can't I have neighbours like this? All I get is a guy who has my taste in men and who faints at the sight of birthing babies.

'Have some more, honey.' My mother pushes the plate over towards me. 'I always get too much for just me.'

'Thanks, I will.' I help myself to another couple of biscuits and decide that, as soon as I finish stuffing myself, I'll launch the attack. In the meantime, I let my glance wander over the walnut-framed photographs hanging by the door and home in on the one of my father. Grimly staring slightly off to the side and with one hand resting majestically on his lap, he is in full court dress complete with wig. And, yes, the resemblance is quite striking. I spare a condescending thought for Tuesday's me, imagining that she was falling in love with a man she'd only just met and then behaving like a complete pillock. Well, next time something like that happens, I'll simply take advice from my subconscious — it's obviously more in control than the rest of me. I finally finish my biscuits and, brushing my fingers off, regretfully decide to leave the others on the plate. It's time to crumble my mother's pitiful defences instead.

'Mum, about yesterday —'

'*Teresa!*'

'What?' I reply, startled. 'What is it?'

'Look at the time!' Mum points to the wall-clock. 'I'm

terribly sorry but you'll have to go, honey. Because I promised Mrs Carstairs from two houses over I'd go for a walk with her. Poor thing, she needs the exercise. She's got a wall eye.'

'You need *exercise* for a wall eye?' I ask, astounded, 'Why?'

'Why what?'

'Why do you need exercise for a wall eye?'

'Is this a joke?' asks Mum, looking at me quizzically. 'If so, I don't think it's in particularly good taste, honey.'

'No, it's not a joke,' I say, exasperated. '*You* said that Mrs Whatever needed exercise because she had a wall eye.'

'No, I did not,' replies Mum emphatically.

'Yes you – oh, doesn't matter.' I take another sip of coffee and reflect that should my mother ever get dementia, it'll probably be quite a while before anyone notices the difference.

'Well, it was lovely to see you.' Mum stands and starts to clear the biscuit plate and coffee cups away. 'Always a pleasure.'

'Hey! I hadn't finished that!'

'Oh, honey, it's cold. It'll give you indigestion.'

'Cold coffee gives you indigestion?'

'Yes, of course it does.' Mum tips the remaining biscuits off the plate and into a canister. 'Everybody knows that.'

'Well, what about iced coffee then?' I ask smartly. '*That's* cold.'

'Oh, iced coffee's different, of course.' She lifts out a step-stool from next to the fridge and, after unfolding it, clambers up to put the canister away into a top cupboard.

'Different how?'

'Because it's never *been* hot. It's only coffee that's *been* hot and then gets cold that gives you indigestion.' She clambers down off the step-stool and folds it back next to the fridge. 'So there you go.'

'There I go?'

'Yes, because now I have to leave for my walk.'

'You're kidding. Right now?'

'Yes, I just *told* you – Mrs Carstairs is expecting me and I still have to get changed. Do you know, sometimes I think you don't take in a word I say. See, we go up the trail out the back to the national park and then walk to the water tower and down again. It takes about an hour but it's very refreshing, especially in this brisk weather. You should try it sometime.'

'But, Mum, I wanted to talk to you!'

'Oh, I *am* sorry,' says Mum apologetically as she walks towards the door. 'I tell you what! Why don't you join us?'

'I can't. I'm going to the gym for some exercise.'

'Ah! The great indoors versus the great outdoors. Well, there's no competition, is there?'

'No,' I mutter crossly. There goes my interrogation. Straight up the trail to the water tower and down again. I push my chair back roughly, get up and follow my mother, who is already at the front door holding out my coat and bag. After I take them from her brusquely, she opens the door wide and stands there beaming at me.

'Always a pleasure, honey,' she says as I shrug on my coat. 'Such a shame you can't join us.'

'Perhaps you'll be home later?'

'Of course I will!' Mum nods agreeably. 'But don't you have Bronte and the baby coming home this afternoon?'

'Bugger!'

'Anyway, I'm sure we'll get a chance to talk on Sunday at the party. I'm planning on sitting in that lovely little courtyard of yours all afternoon with Rose. And you're welcome to join us. We can talk about whatever you want then. Okay?'

Somehow I've ended up on the front porch in the gusty wind and, as I open my mouth to respond, my mother smiles, waves and shuts the door gently but firmly. So there I stand – cold, open-mouthed, and none the wiser. But at least I'm not hungry.

# THURSDAY

## 1435 hrs

'Hell's bells! What on earth *is* that?' Cam points at a shiny metallic contraption that sprouts from one wall of the gym. It has several padded parts, several handles, and several pedals. There is also a suspicious number of scuff marks on the wall behind it, almost as if past patrons have struggled frantically to free themselves at some point.

'No idea. But we'll give it a miss, I think.'

'Thank god.'

'Maybe we'll start with an exercise bike,' I suggest, looking at the row of vacant bikes. 'How does that sound?'

'Manageable.'

We wander over to the bikes and I show Cam how to adjust her seat downwards to suit her height. Then, reaching over, I press her control pad to set up a slow and relatively easy climb for ten minutes. I watch her settle into a rhythm while I pull my hair out of its ponytail and redo it roughly into a spiky-looking bun. As long as it stays away from my face, I don't care. This accomplished, I set up my own controls and soon we are cycling away in unison. I glance over at Cam and chuckle to myself because exercise gear doesn't do a thing for her. At least, the exercise gear she is *wearing* doesn't do a thing for her. An oversized green t-shirt and baggy orange tracksuit pants that make her look very much like a well-rounded carrot. I, on the other hand, have shed my coat and jacket and am looking fairly dangerous, if I say so myself. That's one thing about my figure – it may not look all that great in street clothes, but it's just *made* for the gym.

I've never been to this particular place before but I'm quite impressed. It seems to have all the necessary equipment, and a little bit more. Rows of exercise bikes, treadmills and stair-climbers fill two rooms, while in another an incredible range of weird and wonderful apparatus allows for straining abs, curling biceps and flexing thighs. Large, almost impossibly luscious plants adorn every little nook and cranny, and the latest hits blare out from hidden speakers at a decibel level just loud enough to ensure privacy in conversation without having to shout. We've obviously come at a good time too, because the place is nearly empty.

'Okay, now tell me again how you didn't get *anything* out of your mother?' Cam looks at me disparagingly as she cycles. 'I mean, Terry! *Your* mother?'

'I don't know. I was just winding up for the attack, and then somehow I was outside staring at the door.'

'Well done,' Cam comments sarcastically.

'Hey! I don't see you finding anything out!'

'You want *me* to speak to your mother?'

'No, I want you to speak to *your* mother!'

'Well, it looks like I won't have any choice,' Cam says grimly, 'because that's exactly what's going to happen.'

'Really?' I look at her in disbelief. 'You're actually going to tackle your mother about Richard?'

'I think it's more that she's going to tackle me.'

'What do you mean?'

'Exactly what I said.'

'Okay, enough with the woman of mystery stuff,' I say in exasperation. 'God! It must be hereditary!'

'Don't scare me!' Cam grimaces. 'But all right, I'll tell you *my* news.'

'Shoot.'

'Well, I'm not *sure* it's got anything to do with Richard, but I'm just putting two and two together – although I *might* be wrong.'

'Shoot,' I repeat impatiently, 'or I will!'

'Okay, okay,' she laughs. 'See, Mum rang just after lunch trying to arrange some sort of meeting. That is, she started off trying to arrange a morning tea tomorrow with me and Diane, saying it's ages since she spent any time with her daughters and –'

'What about Elizabeth?' I ask curiously, as Cam has a habit of forgetting her younger sister or, when she does remember her, referring to her as 'Bloody Elizabeth' in a manner that speaks volumes about their relationship.

'Her too. Anyway, she says how it's been ages since just the four of us spent any time together. Without husbands or fiancés or whatever. But when I told her I was busy, because I'm taking CJ to the zoo with her friend Caitlin and her mother, she suggested lunch instead. Like, I'm going to get all around the zoo and back by lunchtime? So then she got really snappy and said she'd ring back.'

'And did she?' I ask while Cam takes a breath.

'Yes, about five minutes later.'

'Sounds like someone wants a little more than a get-together, doesn't it?'

'My thoughts exactly.' Cam slows her cycling pace down so much that I can see the little red light blinking on her console warning her she's way under what she should be doing. 'Anyway, it turns out her options were pretty limited because Bloody Elizabeth is busy Friday evening and Diane's busy at your place on Saturday afternoon.'

'She *is*?'

'Yep, something to do with Bronte's thing on Sunday. Anyway, we ended up with ten o'clock Saturday morning – at my place.'

'You'll have to ring me immediately afterwards. Promise?'

'Promise.'

'Or I could ring and you could leave your phone off the hook,' I suggest, only half joking, 'then I could listen in.'

'She'd have me flogged,' Cam replies shortly.

'Maybe that's it!'

'What, me being flogged?'

'No, maybe he was her hit-man back when she headed the Mafia!'

'Well, I have to say,' Cam puffs, finally getting up to pace and banishing the little blinking light, 'that's the most logical explanation we've come up with so far.'

'Fergus thought he might have been a previous lover,' I comment, checking out my pulse rate on the console. 'You know, like a toy boy.'

'Fergus is a twit.'

'Well, it *is* possible.'

'Nah. I'm sticking with the hit-man,' Cam pants. 'It's more feasible.'

'He didn't *look* like a hit-man,' I say slowly as I try to picture his face again.

'He sure sounded like one! *And* he won't meet your eyes!'

'So?' I speed up again to get back into rhythm. 'He's just a tad shy.'

We continue cycling for a while in silence, both lost in thought. An elderly guy gets on the bike next to me and, after setting up his program, starts to cycle at a rate sure to guarantee a coronary within minutes. Then the bell pings on Cam's bike and, as the pedals slow down, she collapses against the handlebars. A few seconds later, my bike follows suit so I leap off and glance towards the exercise room.

'Come on!' I wave my hand at Cam impatiently. 'Quick, it's all empty. We'll have it to ourselves.'

'And that's good, why?' Cam follows me, breathing heavily.

I head straight over to the LAT pulldown and adjust the

kneepads for a shorter person. Then I pull down the metal bar and gesture to Cam to sit down.

'Here,' I say, passing her the bar. 'Put one hand at either end like that and just pull it slowly towards your chest and back up again. Two lots of about fifteen should do it. Have a break between the sets. When you've finished that, have a go on the biceps curl over there, it's pretty self-explanatory.'

'It'll need to be.'

I grin at her woebegone expression, and then grab a gym ball from the rack overhead. I put myself through a series of squats and stretches before heading over to the leg press and attacking that with gusto. I'm really glad Cam suggested this workout now because the more energy I expend, the better I feel. Besides, it seems that my curiosity about Rose and Richard will be satiated within a few days. And satiation always puts me in a good mood. I finish with the leg press and position myself at the bench press to lift some weights. A few minutes later, I sit up and wipe my face with a corner of my tank top. Then I look around to see what Cam is up to. But she's still sitting at the LAT pulldown, and seems to be in exactly the same position as she was when I left her fifteen minutes ago.

'What *are* you doing?' I ask in amazement. 'Haven't you even started yet?'

'Of course I have!' she snaps back. 'I'm just resting.'

'How long have you been just resting?'

'Not long!' Cam gets up with a groan, letting go of the metal handle too quickly so that it snaps back against the wall with a loud, echoing thud. I look at the wall with interest but it still seems intact, merely slightly dinted.

'Are you all right there, love?' A six and a half foot Adonis materialises next to Cam and looks at her helpfully. 'Need any assistance?'

Cam stares at him open-mouthed, her gaze travelling slowly from his chiselled facial features down past his black singlet and bulging muscles to his loose, *very* high-cut black shorts – before shooting back to his face again. She blushes.

'Need any assistance?' he repeats slowly, obviously having decided she's not the full quid. 'You're a new member, are you?'

'Yes, yes I am.' Cam puts out her hand and, after looking at it with some surprise, Adonis laughs and shakes it agreeably.

'In that case may I suggest you sign up for an assessment?' he says, reclaiming his hand with some difficulty. 'It's free of charge and that way you'll be given a personalised routine to follow and get shown all the ropes at the same time.'

'Sounds like a great idea.' I sidle up to the pair of them and, with my hand resting on the metal LAT handle, lean against the wall nonchalantly.

'*Hello* there,' says Adonis, looking impressed. 'Are *you* interested as well?'

'Very interested.'

'And have *you* ever been assessed?'

'Not lately.'

'Ex-cellen*te*!'

'What do we have to do?' Cam interrupts rudely. 'You know, for the assessment.'

'Assessment?' Adonis looks back at her in confusion. 'Oh, assessment! Yes, I'll just need to slot you in. I'll go grab my book.'

Cam and I watch Adonis walk out of the exercise room towards the front desk, and then turn and grin at each other.

'Wow!'

'Ex-cellen*te*!'

'You're *such* a flirt, Terry,' Cam says, shaking her head. 'Just can't help yourself, can you?'

'Well, I needed a bit of an ego boost,' I reply with feeling, 'especially after the week I've had.'

'Huh! I'm going to the front desk to book myself in for one of those assessments. And don't bother coming along because you're not even a member here. Forgot to mention that, didn't you?'

I watch her stalk out of the room and, chuckling to myself, sit down at the LAT pulldown and, after adjusting it, perform two sets of lifts. When I've finished, I fetch my water bottle from a shelf nearby and take a huge drink.

'Good idea.' Cam grabs her bottle and follows suit.

'How are you feeling?' I ask solicitously. 'Getting sore yet?'

'A bit,' Cam replies, putting her bottle back. 'Actually, a lot.'

'How about we spend twenty minutes on the treadmill and then call it quits?'

'Sounds ex-cellen*te*.'

We choose two treadmills side by side and a judicious distance from the speakers, which are currently blaring out a medley of rap music. At least I *think* it's rap music. I set up Cam's control pad, show her where to stand and demonstrate how to work the different settings for speed, time and climb rate. Then I press start – and she immediately shoots backwards, straight off the end of the treadmill and into a heap on the floor.

'Hey!' I press pause and turn to look down at her. 'You're supposed to walk *with* it! Did you think it was going to do all the work?'

'Of course not!' Cam replies with annoyance as she picks herself up. 'I just wasn't ready!'

'Ready now?' I inquire sweetly.

'And look!' She points to the instructions on the console. 'It says stop if you feel faint or short of breath. I'm feeling both, so it's obviously unsafe for me to use it. Medically speaking.'

'Get on.'

'If I die, I'm going to come back and haunt you. I'll sit on your bed and stare at you wistfully every night.'

'It'll be just like being married again.' I wait while Cam steps gingerly back onto the treadmill and then, staring straight ahead, grasps the front handles so tightly that her knuckles go white. She nods so I press start again and this time, when the machine starts rolling slowly, she walks stiffly with it. I watch her for a few minutes until she starts to relax, even removing one hand and waving it at me confidently.

'Hey, look – one handed! This isn't so bad!'

'It's not supposed to be,' I reply with a laugh as I set up my own control pad and get my machine going. I walk my way through the slow start and settle into a brisk walk of about six and a half kilometres an hour, before turning to check on Cam. She seems to have grasped the workings of the machine and is now not only walking swiftly, but has also released the handles entirely.

'How's it going?'

'No problem,' she replies, grinning at me. 'In fact, I really like this!'

'Good.'

'Hey, are you going to Barbara's farewell tomorrow afternoon?'

'Yes, what about you? Do you want me to pick you up?'

'No! Um, I mean no thanks – because I'm not sure I can make it. Uni stuff. But I *am* going to try.' Cam starts experimenting with the different settings on her control pad. 'I'd really like to say goodbye to her before she goes.'

'Fancy moving overseas to live with a guy you met over the internet.'

'I know. I hope it works out for her.'

'Hmm.' I rotate my shoulders as I walk, loosening them up. 'I've got *no* chance of an internet romance – I can't even remember my password!'

'Twit.'

'No, I'm serious.' I spot Adonis leaning casually in the door-way, watching me walk. I flash him one of my super-wattage grins but he just gives me a wry half-smile and turns away.

'What did you tell that guy?' I ask Cam distrustfully.

'Ha! Just that you were entering a monastery next week!'

'Dork! Only *guys* join monasteries!'

'Exactly,' she smirks at me. 'He was shattered.'

'You realise I'll have my revenge, don't you?'

'I was doing you a favour. You've got too much on your plate already.'

'Hmm,' I reply thoughtfully. 'About Barbara's thing, do you think Joanne'll be there?'

'I'd be surprised if she isn't.'

'Your mum wanted you to get her phone number.'

'Okay – remind me.'

'Do you think she'll bring him?'

'Nah,' says Cam, without having to ask who I mean. 'He'd be gone by now.'

'*What!*' I turn to face Cam in disbelief, and come danger-ously close to shooting off the end of my own treadmill. 'What do you mean – gone?'

Cam looks at me curiously. 'Joanne *did* say he was only here for a few days. And that was on Tuesday, so I'm guessing he'd be gone by now. Certainly by tomorrow, anyway.'

'Bugger.' I concentrate on getting back in rhythm as my stomach does its free-fall act again. 'I'd forgotten about that.'

'And why, may I ask, has it upset you so?' Cam inquires pleasantly, her eyebrows raised. 'After all, he only *looks* like your father, remember?'

'Of course I remember!' I snap back. 'It's only the whole mystery thing with your mother. I'm curious about it, that's all!'

'Sure you are,' says Cam smugly as she plays around with her control pad again. 'Hey, this thing's really cool!'

I ignore her while I adjust my own controls, turning up the walk pace until I'm forced to start jogging to keep up, my feet pounding the conveyer belt underneath with a loud thump, thump, thump. For some reason I had forgotten about Richard only being here for a few days. Of course I knew he lived in Tasmania and would be going back eventually; I just thought that it wouldn't be for a while. Not until after we'd had a few meetings at least, got to know each other a tad, perhaps even had a conversation or two where I *didn't* act like a complete pillock.

I decide that the best course of action at the moment is to stay on my treadmill, running until I'm totally exhausted and incapable of thought. Then Cam can carry me home and pour me a glass of something mind-numbing. I lean forwards, increase my time setting and keep on jogging while I concentrate on blocking all external stimuli. Which is why I don't actually register Cam's increasingly panicked shouts for a good few minutes. As soon as I do, I turn to see what's up – and almost flip myself over my handlebars in surprise.

Somehow, Cam has managed to set her machine onto such a steep incline that it is pointed roughly towards the ceiling, yet still running at a very fast pace. Which she's having considerable trouble keeping up with but can't escape from, because her shoelace has caught in the front edge of the conveyer belt. So there she is, yelling at me while staggering frantically uphill with one hand flailing helplessly towards the emergency stop bar on the console.

I turn my machine off and coast to a stop. Then I lean against the console and watch her curiously. Her hand keeps hitting at the front of the stop bar but, because of the severe angle, doesn't quite reach it.

'Having fun?'

'No! No! Turn it *off*!'

'What was that?' I inquire solicitously. 'Did you say turn it up?'

'No!' She tries to rip her shoelace loose and ends up hopping at a run. 'I'm going to kill you!'

'We can't have that!' I say, throwing my hands up in mock horror. 'Don't forget I'm taking my vows next week.'

'Turn the damn thing off! *Please!*'

'Ah, the magic word.' I reach across, turn the machine off and it slows to a halt as it lowers itself back to the ground and levels out. As it is coasting down, Cam flops down on the belt and, still panting heavily, tries to get her shoelace loose. But it's stuck tight. She leans back and puts her hand to her chest as she tries to get her breathing under control.

'I'm going. To kill. You.'

'I could always turn this thing on again, you know,' I comment as my hand hovers over the console pad. 'So be nice, you hear?'

Cam makes a grunting sound that is halfway between a laugh and a pant.

'Okay.' I bend down and take hold of her shoelace. 'Let's have a look.'

But despite my best efforts, and then our joint best efforts, we can't get the shoelace out. It's stuck tight. So Cam removes her shoe and leaves it sitting on the treadmill as she backs away and sits on the floor, still recovering from her ordeal. I look around curiously to see if there were any witnesses to this little debacle but even Adonis isn't in sight.

'I'll go and get someone to help in a minute,' I say to Cam as I sit on the floor next to her and start to laugh. 'Your face! I wish I had a camera!'

'Bitch,' says Cam as she begins laughing too.

The elderly guy from the exercise bikes comes into the room, wiping his face on a towel, and stops short when he sees us sitting on the floor laughing. He looks from Cam to me to the shoe in the middle of the treadmill. Then, obviously changing his mind, he leaves again.

'When I get this shoe loose,' says Cam, holding her side and groaning, 'I'm going to beat you to death with it.'

'Should I start running now?' I ask with interest. 'Or would a slow walk suffice?'


# THURSDAY

## 1736 hrs

'I thought you said you were getting picked up at four,' I say petulantly as Bronte answers her mobile phone. 'It's nearly six!'

'I know, sorry, Mum.' Bronte's voice cuts in and out of a fair amount of static. 'Nick was running late and they couldn't find my paperwork, then Sherry was an absolute pain. Like, it's just been one of those days.'

'So where are you now?'

'Um —' she hesitates for a minute '— in your driveway.'

'*What?*' I run over to the lounge-room bay window, pull back the curtain and peer out the side into the driveway. Sure enough, there they are, standing next to Bronte's pink Volkswagen in the near dark, unloading mountains of gear onto a now flattened flowerbed.

Bronte looks up, the mobile against her ear, and waves enthusiastically. 'Hi, Mum!' she says into the phone.

'How long have you been there?'

'Oh, about five minutes.'

'Then why on *earth* are you talking to me on the mobile?'

'Because you rang, of course!'

'Bronte. Hang up.' I take a deep breath and put the phone back in its cradle before I head for the driveway. The cold hits me as soon as I leave the house and I breathe puffs of vapour out into the evening dusk. Bronte, still with the mobile at her ear, glances up at me, frowns at her phone and disconnects. Then she pops it into the side pocket of her jeans, which are altogether too loose for someone who's just given birth. Ah, the rejuvenation of youth!

'Hey, Mil!' Nick pokes his head up from the boot and grins at me. 'Like your outfit!'

'Thanks,' I reply, pulling my jacket together.

'Yeah, but your hair looks really weird,' adds Bronte, giving my spiky bun a disparaging glance as she tugs a bright-blue crate out of the car boot.

'So, you got room for all this?' asks Nick.

'Actually – I'm not sure.' I cast a dubious glance over the mound of baby-related paraphernalia, through which a desperate rhododendron is gasping for air. 'Is it all really necessary?'

'Oh, *yes*, Mum!' Bronte stops what she is doing and turns to me with an earnest expression. 'I asked Nick to pack everything, just in case.'

'Great,' I reply dryly as I walk around the growing pile and open the back door of the car. And there she is – the light of my life – sleeping peacefully in her brand-new capsule. I push the flotilla of pink balloons to one side so I can get a better look. Bronte has fastened a ridiculous hair-band around her bald little head and dressed her in a frilled and laced concoction that would look more appropriate on a fairy floss stick. Apart from that, though, she is all pink, soft, rounded flesh – simply irresistible. She gurgles and spits in her sleep. I gurgle back but hold the spit. Then, with the formalities out of the way, I unhook the capsule and lift it out carefully.

'Hello there, Sherry Rose. Are you going to spend some time at my house?' Even as I speak, I know I sound just like one of those dingbats who turn into saccharine as soon as they see anybody under the age of one.

'Hey, Mil, tear yourself away for a second. Where do you want all this stuff?'

'We'll start taking it inside,' Bronte answers for me as she begins the second stage of the removal process. 'Quick, it's freezing out here.'

'Put it all in the lounge, thanks.' I follow her with the capsule in my arms and go back into the house where I deposit Sherry gently on the floor by the couch.

'We'll have to work out how to use some of this stuff,' says Bronte as she dumps a colourful rocker/walker thing next to me. 'Like, it's pretty tricky.'

'You sit down, Bron,' says Nick solicitously as he comes in with his arms full of bags and boxes and dumps it all right on top of my new rug in front of the couch. 'You shouldn't be doing this.'

'No, you shouldn't!' I agree, suddenly remembering her condition. Although, as she is standing right next to the evidence, I don't know how I could forget.

'Whatever,' says Bronte, flopping back on the couch and tucking her legs under herself. 'I'm stuffed!'

'Do you two want something to eat?'

'No thanks, Mum. Not hungry.' Bronte leans back and sighs. 'But it's good to be home.'

'That's the last of it!' Nick appears in the doorway with a couple of bags and a bunch of balloons, which he immediately releases so that they float up to the ceiling. 'And I'd better get going.'

'How?' I ask curiously. 'Are you taking Bronte's car?'

'Nah, one of my brothers is picking me up,' Nick replies as, right on cue, a honk sounds from the driveway.

'See you.' Bronte leans forwards and Nick kisses her cheek perfunctorily. 'Are you coming around tomorrow?'

'Sure am.' Nick grabs her hand and squeezes it. 'I'll give you a ring, okay?'

'Okay.'

'Bye, Scotch – be good for Mummy and Granny.' Nick leans over the capsule and kisses the top of his daughter's bald head. 'See you, Mil – and thanks for this.'

'No problem,' I reply to his retreating rear before I turn back to Bronte. 'Scotch? What's that in aid of?'

'Oh, he's decided he prefers Scotch to Sherry.'

'Hmm, I see.' I nod thoughtfully because I sympathise with his preference. 'But what's the rush? Doesn't he want to spend some time with you and the baby?'

'He starts work in half an hour,' says Bronte, yawning over the sound of a car reversing noisily out of the driveway. I walk to the front door, which Nick has considerately left wide open, and watch as a blue ute screeches around so that it's parallel to the kerb before it takes off up the darkened street, leaving skid marks behind as a farewell.

'Which brother was that?' I ask as I close the front door securely and walk back into the lounge-room, turning up the heat as I pass the thermostat.

'Dunno,' replies Bronte, getting up off the couch and manoeuvring her way through the pile of paraphernalia. 'Look, Mum, would you mind if I just had a little nap? Sherry'll be fine where she is, she's not due for a feed for a couple of hours and, like, I'm so tired I can't think straight. Do you mind?'

'No, that's fine,' I reply agreeably and, before I can even blink, Bronte is off and up the stairs towards her old bedroom.

I'm left with a capsule full of newborn baby, a ceiling spread with balloons, and a mound of baby goods that stretches all the way from the couch to the doorway.

There's a porta-cot, porta-highchair, porta-playpen and even, unbelievably, a porta-potty. There's a largish suitcase, a smallish suitcase, a pile of bunny-rugs, a jam-packed nappy bag and three plastic bags full of soft toys. Each of the plastic bags has 'DO NOT GIVE BAG TO BABY' written on it in shaky black texta. Just in case I was tempted, I suppose. There's the rather weird-looking red, blue and yellow contraption that Bronte brought in, which resembles a baby-walker without wheels but with more bells, whistles and knobs on it than I've ever seen gathered together in one place. Then there are three colourful plastic crates – the red one holding cloth nappies, the blue one full of disposable nappies, and the yellow one housing a sterilising unit, assorted bottles and a tin of formula. And last, but not least, are the parts of a pram. Or, at least, I *think* it's a pram; it could just as easily be some type of automated lunar exploration vehicle.

I grimace unhappily because this is *exactly* the sort of clutter I hate most – in fact, it almost makes me feel physically ill. Accordingly, I pour myself a glass of scotch and then get stuck into the mess.

I start by moving the pram pieces into the foyer, and the sterilising unit, formula, bottles and accessories into the kitchen. Then I read the instructions and make up the unit before submerging a few bottles and dummies in case they are needed. Next the suitcase, bunny-rugs and smaller bag of clothing are lugged upstairs, and put just outside Bronte's room.

While I'm up there, I strip off my gym clothing and jump into the shower for a brief wash before drying myself and pulling on my new pyjamas and a pair of fluffy red socks. I run a brush through my hair quickly before collecting the dirty clothing and padding downstairs to the laundry. On the way I pick up a lone white sports sock from the lounge-room floor and take it with me. Here five minutes and she's already marking her territory. And that's the thing about sharing – it immediately opens the door to odd socks. I *never* have odd socks when I'm here by myself, just matched pairs that enter the washing cycle together and exit as neatly folded little bundles with a smile at one end.

I walk back into the lounge-room, tiptoe over to the capsule and check on Sherry before deciding what to do next. Perhaps another drink. This accomplished to my satisfaction, I remove the porta-highchair and the porta-potty into the broom cupboard because they are totally useless for a four day old infant. Then I fix up a corner of the lounge-room as a play area with the porta-playpen, weird-looking rocker/walker thing, and crates of assorted nappies. I use the box that was holding the sterilising unit as a repository for the toys and rattles. Finally, I dispose of the empty plastic bags to minimise any chance of me being tempted to GIVE BAG TO BABY.

Now the only things left are the porta-cot, and there's no point putting that up till it's in Bronte's room – and all the balloons. I duck energetically around the lounge-room, climbing on furniture and bopping balloons until I've got them all herded into a corner. Then it's just a matter of tying the strings together and dragging the whole lot into the powder room to abandon them.

I take a gulp of scotch and lean back against the wall, surveying my work. Not bad at all. I put my glass down on the coffee table and then straighten up my new rug, which I bought after we'd finished at the gym this afternoon. It's a semicircular high-pile with a rose and white swirled pattern that actually blends in quite well with its surroundings. I stand back to admire it and nod with pleasure. Admittedly, I'd prefer the unblemished carpet, but beggars can't be choosers. Or so they say.

I tiptoe back over to the capsule and peer down at Sherry, who is showing signs of restlessness. I quickly slip her hair-band off, tucking it away under her mattress as she stretches one arm out of her wadding and flexes her impossibly small fingers. I tuck my hair back and reach down, putting my own finger within her palm and then watching with delight as she folds her hand around it, grasping tightly.

And then, when she has me well and truly lulled, she opens her little mouth and lets out the most piercing shriek possible. This initial cry is followed by a series of loud mewling noises as she scrunches up her face and shudders her body through each cry. I take back my finger and run over to the stairs.

'Bronte!' I look back at the capsule and wonder how so much noise could possibly come from such a small container. '*Bronte!* Bronte!'

Giving up on the chances of her responding in the near future, I take the stairs two at a time and then run over to Bronte's room, flinging the door open. But she's not there. That is, the bed shows mute evidence of having been lain in recently, but Bronte is not in sight. I knock on her ensuite door and, when there is no answer, open it and peer inside. No Bronte.

I walk back onto the landing and stand there, wondering where on earth she could be. Sherry's cries echo up the stair-well and hinder my thinking processes dramatically. Before I run back downstairs, I throw open the study door without expecting any success. And there she is – at the computer, playing arcade games.

'Bronte! What *are* you doing?'

'Hi, Mum,' she replies without turning around. 'I woke up

before and thought I'd have a go at this. *Damn!* He got me again.'

'Bronte! Can't you hear the baby?'

'Baby?' Bronte swivels the mouse around and taps her fingers rapidly across the keyboard. 'Ha! Got you!'

'Yes – *your* baby!' I exclaim, getting thoroughly irritated. 'You know, the one you left downstairs who's now screaming her lungs out.'

'Sherry? Screaming?' Bronte jumps up and looks at me accusingly. 'Why didn't you say so!'

'What?' I ask, dumbfounded by the unfairness of that last remark. But Bronte doesn't answer; instead, she just pushes past and runs down the stairs towards the lounge-room. I follow at a distance, cheering myself with the thought that now she too has a daughter and therefore, sooner or later, she'll pay.

By the time I arrive, Bronte has ensconced herself on the couch with her windcheater up and Sherry at her breast. The sight of this stops me dead in my tracks. Because there sits *my* daughter, with her own daughter feeding at her breast. What an unbelievably touching, nostalgic moment. The sort of moment one files away and then retrieves in one's dotage. A lump forms in my throat.

'Can you turn the TV on, Mum? Like, this is dead boring.'

Luckily, I filed the moment away before she opened her mouth. I walk over to the television set and turn it on, then pass Bronte the remote control so that I won't be called upon to change channels for her. The screen comes to life and fills with a weatherman who is waving a stick excitedly at a map of Australia.

'Hang on, Bronte.' I put my hand in front of the remote control she has aimed at the set. 'I want to see the weather for tomorrow.'

'Okay.' She puts her hand down and glances across at me. 'Hey – cool PJs, Mum. What's with the hands?'

'They just mean I'm touched,' I reply, '*totally* touched.'

We watch as the weatherman recites the boating conditions for the next day. Personally I believe that anybody lucky enough to own a boat should source his or her own weather forecast, and not take up so much of ours. I pick up my glass from the coffee table and have a sip of scotch while I wait. Finally he gets to the actual weather: 'There will be showers in Sydney, rain in Adelaide, drizzle in Perth, some precipitation in Alice Springs, several downpours in Brisbane, squally in Hobart, and some psychotic activity up in Darwin –'

'Did he say '*psychotic* activity' in Darwin?' I ask Bronte, baffled.

'Yeah, so?' she replies, moving Sherry over to her other breast. 'And shh! I thought you wanted to watch this?'

'I do!' I retort, annoyed. Psychotic activity. I've never actually been to Darwin, but surely they're not so bad up there it requires a warning as part of the weather report? Perhaps he meant 'cyclonic' activity.

'. . . and as for Melbourne, expect a cloudy day with occasional squally showers, some drizzle and several downpours. And that's it from me; now it's over to Mike with a fascinating story about the mating ritual of pandas.'

Unfortunately, Bronte works the remote control before I can observe the fascinating story about the mating ritual of pandas. Instead, a cartoon featuring a one-eyed female spaceship pilot comes on and she settles in to watch it. I grimace at the thought of rain tomorrow because I had planned on doing a little gardening. But, I suppose, at least we don't live in Darwin.

'How about I take the porta-cot upstairs and set it up?' I ask Bronte. 'And then you can put the baby straight to bed when she's done.'

'Cool.' Bronte glances at me for a second before returning her attention to the television. 'Thanks, Mum.'

I pick up the porta-cot by a handle embedded in the side and lug it up the stairs awkwardly. When I get to Bronte's room, I put it down by the side of the bed and then fetch in the bags and bunny-rugs that I'd placed outside earlier. Next I open the bag containing the porta-cot and examine the rectangular padded interior for clues on how to assemble it. There are none. After about ten minutes, I find some Velcro underneath the padding and, when I pull it apart, the entire contraption unfolds and *voila*! I've got a porta-cot and a mattress lying in front of me. I smile, flushed with success.

Unfortunately, however, it appears my flushing was a little premature. Try as I might, I can't get the four sides of the porta-cot to stand upright simultaneously. Finally, I decide to get a little more forceful and show the damn device just who's boss. Shortly afterwards there is a loud snapping noise and the entire rear end of the porta-cot collapses in a heap. A broken heap.

'Where did you get all that baby stuff?' I ask Bronte when I arrive back in the lounge-room. 'Who gave it to you?'

'Oh, Nick's mum gave me some stuff the twins didn't need anymore and Dad gave us most of the rest,' replies Bronte, without looking up from the television. She has Sherry up on her shoulder and is patting her back rhythmically but the child is totally out for the count. Her mouth is slightly open with her tongue protruding wetly and a thin dribble of milk is running all the way down Bronte's windcheater.

'What about the porta-cot?'

'That's one of the things Dad bought.' Bronte finally looks at me. 'Cool, isn't it? Why do you ask?'

'Well, I was just wondering if you still had the receipt. Because it's broken.'

'Broken!' Bronte stares at me, aghast. '*How*?'

'Obviously faulty,' I reply with righteous indignation. 'Bloody rubbish. So, have you got the receipt or not?'

'Well, yes, I can get the receipt,' Bronte says as she gently lowers Sherry and then nestles the baby into her arms. 'But, like, where's she going to sleep tonight?'

'I'll think of something,' I say confidently as I finish off my scotch and then take the glass out to the kitchen sink. While I'm rinsing it, I suddenly remember neither of us has had tea yet. As soon as this realisation hits, my stomach rumbles and I feel weak from hunger.

'Do you want anything to eat?' I put my head around the corner and look at Bronte. 'A sandwich or something?'

'No thanks!' she whispers loudly. 'Nick and I grabbed some Maccas on the way from the hospital.'

No wonder they were so late! I check out what's available in the fridge and then fix myself two ham and salad sandwiches, which I carry upstairs on a plate, thinking furiously all the way. When I get to Bronte's bedroom, I repack the porta-cot haphazardly and then shovel it into the plastic bag before storing it by her wardrobe. Then, while I eat my sandwiches, I look around for inspiration – and find it among her bookshelves.

First I remove Bronte's seldom-used encyclopedia set from its shelf and stack the volumes on the floor. Next I cover the books, in sets of five, with bunny-rugs, and use the sets as impromptu bricks to build a rectangular enclosure on the floor. Finally I fold up an adult-sized blanket, put it in the enclosure as a mattress and pop in an old stuffed giraffe of Bronte's as the pièce de résistance. Am I good, or what?

I bounce down the stairs and into the lounge-room, where I find Bronte still watching television with the baby asleep on her lap.

'All done,' I say with pride, 'and I think you'll be impressed!'

'What did you use?'

'You'll see!' I grab a couple of extra bunny-rugs from the capsule and head back upstairs to put them in the middle of my invention as coverings. But the first thing I see when I get to the bedroom is that one side of the enclosure has caved in. Bugger. I look at it thoughtfully and decide that if the encyclopedias can't stay in place *without* a live baby in the middle, then it's probably not worth the risk of trying it out with her there. She'll be smothered by knowledge.

Accordingly, I dismantle my encyclopedia barricade and return everything to its rightful place. So now I've wasted another half-hour and still haven't accomplished a thing bedwise. I run my fingers through my hair in consternation.

'I thought you had something set up?' Bronte materialises in the doorway with the baby in her arms. 'I've changed her and she's all ready for bed.'

'It didn't work,' I reply with a sigh.

'Why don't we just use the porta-playpen?' asks Bronte. 'Here, you take Sherry and I'll go get it.'

I'm left there holding the baby and cursing myself for a total dork. Why didn't I think of the playpen – or even the pram, for that matter? Maybe because I'm always looking for complicated solutions when the simple ones suffice just as well. And usually better.

Bronte comes back in bearing the porta-playpen bag and dumps it on the floor. Within seconds, she has it out of its bag and completely set up by her bed. Then she grabs the pile of bunny-rugs and throws them inside the playpen before reaching out her arms for her daughter.

'Now say goodnight to – what *do* you want to be called, Mum?'

'No idea,' I reply as I kiss the top of Sherry's head. 'Goodnight, precious.'

'And I'm turning in myself, Mum,' says Bronte, lowering her daughter gently into her makeshift bed. 'So goodnight, see you in the morning.'

'Goodnight, Bronte. Sweet dreams.'

Shutting the bedroom door, I leave them alone and walk back down the stairs slowly, carrying my empty sandwich plate. After I rinse it off and put it in the drying rack, I lean against the counter and look out at the darkened night sky. The window has clear droplets scattered across it, evidence of an evening drizzle that now seems to have ceased.

I yawn tiredly, automatically glance at the clock on the microwave and get a real shock when I register that it's past eleven. I can't believe the entire evening has whizzed by and I haven't even had a chance to relax. I've been running up and down the stairs, putting away baby paraphernalia, setting up baby barricades and tending to baby needs. I suppose that at least it's kept my mind busily away from mystery men, and mystery meetings, and mystery mental meanderings. But still, how do parents cope with this stuff, day after day after day? How did *I* do it? I feel so exhausted that even my bones ache.

Boy, am I going to sleep like the dead tonight.

# FRIDAY

*Handy Household Hint No XIV:*

*For a severe headache: take a large coconut and split it open.*
*Discard contents and fill with 1 cup Bailey's Irish Cream*
*and 1 tablespoon low-fat milk.*
*Use concoction to wash down two painkillers.*

# FRIDAY

## 0053 hrs

I'm sitting on an old wooden swing in the corner park, being pushed by my father and screaming with delight. Up and down, higher and higher – my blonde plaits streaming forwards as I descend and then trailing behind like the tails of a kite as I shoot towards the cloudless blue sky. I'm going *so* high that I think there's a chance, a *very* good chance, I'll be able to duplicate the incredible feat performed by Sebastiana Poxleitner of Grade 3B, and go all the way over.

I pump my legs furiously, tucking them underneath as I approach the ground and flinging them out at the apex of the lift. I shriek at my father to push harder, faster, higher – and suddenly someone else starts shrieking with me. I look around in confusion and immediately lose my momentum, my speed rapidly decreasing until any hopes of equalling Sebastiana Poxleitner of Grade 3B remain exactly what they've always been – a dream.

But even as I stop screaming, the other person continues. Over and over – shrill, penetrating infantile bleats that echo around the park and send the birds flocking up into the sky. As the cries continue, a misty fog drifts in and slowly encroaches on the park, the swing, and my father. I watch wide-eyed as its hazy tendrils reach me and then find myself having to fight through the murkiness in order to surface. When I finally do, I open my eyes and stare groggily around my bedroom.

Same room, same bed, same shadowy grey outlines of furniture. But different noises. I reach out, flick on my bedside lamp and sit up, rubbing the remains of the mist from my eyes. Of course – it's the baby screaming, but why hasn't Bronte answered her yet? I glance across at the time and grimace before burrowing back down under the doona, waiting for Bronte to do something.

Unfortunately, this takes several minutes and by the time I hear Bronte murmuring to the baby, I'm wide awake. But at least the screaming has stopped. I fling back the doona and, grateful that I decided to leave the pyjamas on for sleeping, pad softly downstairs to get a drink of water. When I get back, I pay the ensuite a brief visit and then crawl thankfully into the warmth of my bed. All is quiet next door so I turn off my light and curl up, trying to will myself back to the swing in the park with my father.

But it's long gone.

## FRIDAY

### 0213 hrs

This time I recognise the screams the instant they infiltrate my consciousness. Mainly because it took me quite some time to get back to sleep and I don't think I had even got close to that soul-deep level where you wake feeling all groggy and confused. Instead I reach out, flick on the light and check the time. Bugger.

Fortunately, Bronte appears to respond a little quicker on this occasion and the screams subsist within minutes. And I don't even hear any murmuring happening so I'm guessing the baby has gone straight back to sleep.

It's all right for some.

# FRIDAY

## 0338 hrs

She is crying once more. Physically, mentally and emotionally, I drag myself into a sitting position and glare at the wall separating Bronte's room from mine. I don't bother turning on the light but, unfortunately, I can still make out the time which just depresses me even further. I groan and then flop back down and stare at the darkened ceiling, waiting for the crying to stop. And it's a long wait.

# FRIDAY

## 0542 hrs

I think *I'm* going to cry. And then that would make two of us. I lie in bed listening to Sherry's wailing and find myself temporarily unable to summon the motivation even to curse. Each cry stretches forever and then, as it fades, becomes a shuddering reverberation that sends shock waves through the marrow of my bones. My head is thumping and my eyes feel like somebody has lifted each eyelid and poured in a teaspoon of sand.

Instead of crying, I pull the doona over my head and push my face into the pillow. But it doesn't matter what I do, I can still hear the shrill, mewling wails coming from what was, just yesterday, the love of my life. At the moment she is simply the bane of my existence.

# FRIDAY

## 0932 hrs

I'm hit by the deathly quiet of the house the instant I open my eyes. An unnatural, eerie stillness that is strangely at odds with the daylight filtering through the curtains. Instead of indulging in my customary spread-eagled stretch, I fling the doona back and, pulling my fluffy socks on, pad next door to Bronte's room. The door is open and there is nobody inside.

I hurry downstairs and, by the time I reach the foyer, can hear a muffled but relatively calm voice coming from the kitchen area. I slow down with relief although I'm not quite sure what I was worried about – perhaps that Bronte had posted her perpetually wailing daughter down the laundry chute in the early hours of the morning? As I cross the lounge-room, I note that the curtains have all been drawn back and the heat switched on. Then I turn the corner towards the kitchen and the first thing I see is the capsule, balanced on the island bench.

'So today we'll practise how to be a good girl for Mummy, all right?' Bronte, dressed in yesterday's jeans and windcheater, has her back to me and is washing dishes in the sink. 'And then tonight, if you sleep *all* night, I'll let you watch MTV in the morning.'

'If she sleeps all night, I'll let her do anything she likes,'

214

I comment dryly as I peer inside the capsule. Sherry, dressed in a pink and lime-green striped romper set with a matching hair-band, blinks up at me and blows a rather impressive saliva bubble.

'Mum! Good morning!' says Bronte brightly, wiping her hands on a tea-towel. 'Would you like a cup of coffee?'

'Love one,' I reply, yawning.

'Oh, Mum, did we keep you up last night?'

'Well –' I run my finger over Sherry's little hand. 'No, no – I'm fine.'

'Good. Because Sherry did play up a bit and I was, like, really worried she'd wake you up.' Bronte puts the kettle on and gets my coffee plunger ready. 'But obviously she didn't, so that's cool.'

'Yeah, cool,' I reply as I stroke the baby's head gently. 'Bronte, what on *earth* is up with all these hair-bands?'

'Aren't they great?' says Bronte happily. 'Like, *so* cute.'

I refrain from answering while I tickle Sherry on the stomach. She immediately scrunches up her face and goes an unbecoming shade of red.

'Look, Bronte!' I point at the baby's face. 'Take the bloody thing off! She's embarrassed!'

'No she's not.' Bronte glances at her daughter and sighs. 'She's filling her nappy again. And I've only *just* changed her!'

'Ah,' I say wisely, as the accuracy of Bronte's guess is evidenced by the infiltration of a certain aroma. 'Yech!'

'I'll take her out in the lounge and change her.' Bronte hefts the capsule off the bench. 'You'll have to finish making your coffee. I'll have one too.'

I watch her leave the room and absentmindedly wonder whether Sherry's contribution will be the same colour as the shorts Richard was wearing on Tuesday. Then, with a jolt, I register what I'm wondering about and shake my head in disgust. Sick, sick, sick. I rechannel my thought processes towards coffee and concentrate on the kettle instead. And while I'm waiting for the water to boil, I put myself through a few stretches to loosen up my muscles. Because I'm *definitely* feeling the effects of yesterday's gym routine. I spare a thought for Cam who, I'm willing to bet, woke up this morning barely able to move. The thought turns into a chuckle when I remember her face as she floundered around on the end of the treadmill.

'What's so funny?' calls Bronte from the lounge-room.

'Nothing.' I pour boiling water into the plunger and assemble a couple of mugs. 'Hey, how many sugars do you have?'

'Two!'

'Milk?'

'Just a tad!'

I make the coffees and take them over to the table with a couple of coasters. Then I settle myself down contentedly, ignoring the complaints coming from my thighs. Through the French doors and beyond the enclosed courtyard, I can see that the sky is heavy with low-hanging grey clouds that promise heavy rain in the not-too-distant future. It's the sort of day that you should spend curled up on the couch in front of an open fire with a good book in one hand, a block of chocolate in the other and a blanket across your lap. Maybe today's the day to accompany Rhett and Scarlett through the pages of *Gone with the Wind*.

I lace my fingers around my mug and yawn. That last solid four-hour sleep has done wonders, and I feel twice the person I did just before six this morning. But I'm also pretty amazed that I slept in for so long – I *never* sleep in!

'Toast?' asks Bronte, putting the capsule down by the table and going back into the kitchen.

'Mmm, yes please.'

'Hey, Mum, what's with the stain in front of the couch?' Bronte glances at me as she pops some bread into the toaster. 'Did you spill something?'

'Did *I* spill something?' I ask, astounded.

'Yeah, I looked under that new rug.' Bronte gets the butter out of the fridge. 'Because I don't like it. Big pinkish stain, right in front of the couch.'

'Yes, I *know* where it is.'

'So, what did you do?'

'I didn't *do* anything! It was . . .' I peter out, looking at her face, and then go on slowly: '. . . me. Yes. Red wine, you know.'

'Mum! You should know better!'

'Yeah, I suppose I should.' I take a sip of coffee and watch Bronte deftly catch the toast as it shoots enthusiastically out of the slots in the toaster. Then she proceeds to spread each slice liberally with butter and, putting mine on a plate, brings it over to me.

'Here you go!'

'Thanks,' I take a big bite and then dab up the hot melted butter as it dribbles down my chin. 'Delicious!'

Bronte puts her own plate next to her coffee and sits down. 'Do you know, Mum, I'd forgotten what weird slept-in hair you have in the morning.'

'Thanks,' I say sarcastically, running my fingers through my hair in an attempt to straighten it. 'And I'd forgotten how great you are for my self-confidence, too.'

'And now you've got butter in it,' says Bronte, watching with interest. 'You look like that Mary chick in *There's Something About Mary.*'

'Haven't seen it,' I comment while I attempt to clean *and* straighten my hair. 'Did she have butter in her hair too?'

'Yeah, Mum. That's right – butter.'

'But why?'

'*I* don't know. A fetish, I suppose.'

We lapse into silence as we devour our toast. I'm beginning to think I'm really going to enjoy this week. I'll buy earplugs today, which should take care of the nights, and then all I've got to look forward to is coffee and breakfast each morning, and the sight of Sherry whenever I wish. I push my plate away and pick up the mug.

'Just tell me if we get in your way,' says Bronte, obviously thinking along similar lines. 'Like, I don't want to be a nuisance.'

'Far from it!' I look her in the eye to emphasise my point. 'It'll be a pleasant change for a while. And, in fact, I've decided to take next week off work while you're here as well. I'm going to ring the library later – perhaps it'll qualify as carer's leave or something.'

'Great,' says Bronte, without quite the level of enthusiasm I was expecting.

'Hey, whatever happened to that weird woman who was in the bed next to you?' I ask curiously. 'You know, the one who talks like Eeyore from Winnie-the-Pooh.'

'Oh, you mean Mrs Cobb.' Bronte rolls her eyes and leans closer. 'You wouldn't *believe* it, Mum. She left the day before me and her husband came in to pick her up and, like, he was even worse than her! So, there they are, getting all her stuff together and not saying anything and that baby is just, like, crying nonstop. He did that, you know – *all* the time. Anyway, so I'm reading a magazine and I think that baby's been crying forever! So I look across, and you wouldn't believe it!'

'Try me,' I say encouragingly.

'Well, they'd left!'

'And . . . ?' I ask, a trifle confused because that doesn't seem all that unbelievable.

'*And* they'd left the baby there!' Bronte grins at me. 'I'm serious. They'd taken her bags and just walked out. So there

I am with two babies! So I press the nurse's buzzer and, when she comes in, I go, like, "Hey, they've left without the baby", and she goes, like, "No*ooo*", and I go, "Yes, they have", and she goes –'

'Come on, Bronte,' I interrupt impatiently, 'cut to the bloody chase!'

'Okay, well she goes – the nurse, that is – she grabs the capsule and goes running after them and I can hear her going: "Mrs Cobb! Mrs Cobb!" all the way down the corridor. And I asked her later if she found them and she, like, goes, "Yeah – in the car park". Can you *believe* that? All the way to the car park!'

'Hell,' I say, with a sneaking sympathy for Mrs Cobb.

'Yeah.' Bronte nods and then takes a sip of her coffee and stares down at her own capsule, lost in thought.

'Hey, Bronte.' I follow her gaze, peering into the capsule where Sherry has drifted off to sleep. 'I didn't think you were supposed to use those things for non-car use. I thought they were bad for their backs or something.'

'Really?' Bronte looks at me with astonishment. 'I didn't know that!'

'Well, I'm not sure, I –'

'See? Like, that's *exactly* the reason I wanted to stay here for a bit.' Bronte jumps up and heads over to the foyer, where she starts putting the pram together. I finish off my coffee and get up to carry it, and my plate, to the kitchen sink. I rinse out the mug and the plunger then sit them on the bench ready for my second cup.

'Another coffee, Bronte?'

'No, haven't finished this one yet.' Bronte comes back in, pushing a navy-blue pram with a sparkling silver framework and enormous wheels. She parks it next to the capsule and, bending down, lifts Sherry up gently and deposits her within. Then she covers the baby warmly and rocks the pram until she settles again. While she is occupied, I turn the kettle back on and then sit at the table with my pad and pen.

'There we go.' Bronte leaves the pram and joins me. She grins. 'Still making your lists?'

'Of course.' I pick up the pen and start writing. 'Your father's coming for lunch today, did you know?'

'Yeah, he rang yesterday. He said you were, like, cooking something special?'

'Fat chance.' I glance at the microwave clock. 'Actually, you could give him a ring and tell him to bring lunch with him. For all of us.'

'Cool.' Bronte drains her mug. 'I'll get him to bring pizza. So did you want me to do anything else this morning, Mum?'

'No, all taken care of.'

'Great. Then I'm off to play on the computer.' Bronte pushes her chair back and heads upstairs, leaving the pram parked beside the table. I look at it with interest. Does that mean I'm in charge? Well, there's not a peep coming from that direction so I turn to my list and start to put it together.

## FRIDAY

| Phone calls | — | Cam re lift to library function, library re next week off, Fergus |
| Groceries | — | Milk, bread, something for tea, fruit, earplugs |
| Morning | — | Clean house |
| Lunch | — | Dennis to supply |
| Afternoon | — | Library function |
| | — | Richard? |
| | — | Back in Tasmania? |

Richard & Joanne?
Richard & Terry!

I come out of my fuguelike trance and stare down at what I've written with open-mouthed amazement. Where did all *that* come from? The last thing I remember was writing about the library function and then tapping my pen on the table as I idly wondered who would be there. Next thing I know, I've zoned into an artistic fifth dimension where the pen moves of its own free will! Maybe this is what Joanne was referring to when she was carrying on about leaving her body. I look again at what I've written and grimace.

'Mum! The kettle's boiling!' Bronte ducks into the kitchen, turns the kettle off and looks at me accusingly. 'And, like, it's boiled totally dry!'

'Hell.' I rip my piece of paper off the pad and screw it up. 'I didn't notice.'

'No kidding.' Bronte gingerly lifts the kettle off the stove and puts it on the sink. 'I think you'll have to let it cool down for a while.'

I wait at the table while she fills a glass with water and then, with a wry grin at me and a cursory glance at her daughter, takes it back upstairs with her. After she leaves, I get up and cross over to the sink with my scrunched-up piece of paper still in my hand. I smooth it out, re-read it, and then use the gaslighter from the stove to set it alight. I watch the edges burst into flame and then curl in on themselves as they blacken and crumble. The glow creeps towards the centre and I drop the burning paper into the sink just before it is totally engulfed. It sizzles when it hits and then the blackened ashes break apart and scatter themselves across the damp metallic surface.

Flaming hell.

# FRIDAY

## 1242 hrs

'Hey, listen to this, Dennis.' I start reading from the gilt-edged menu before me: 'A pastille of salmon pate peeks coquettishly between a fan of sensitively cooked slivers of lobster and fibres of crystallised seaweed.'

'Sounds delicious,' replies Dennis as he tucks the bunny-rug a little closer around Sherry and readjusts her on his lap.

'I bet the lobster didn't think it was all that sensitive.'

'Still sounds delicious.'

'Have you always been such a pretentious prat?'

'Yep – you just never noticed,' replies Dennis equably as he tops up each of our glasses with white wine. He is dressed in his usual conservative fashion: a light-grey suit with a deep-blue shirt and matching tie. It's a style that flatters his large frame and almost conceals the few extra kilos that he's carrying nowadays. But, all things considered, he's ageing quite gracefully. A few years older than me, he isn't particularly jowly or wrinkly and still has a full head of sandy hair that's showing no intention of receding in the near future.

'Why'd we have to come here, anyway?' Bronte looks around the restaurant disparagingly. 'Like, I left a message for you to bring pizza and some wine over to our place.'

'But when I heard your mother didn't want to cook, I thought I'd take you out for a treat. And this is a great place!'

'You didn't *take* us out,' Bronte mutters, playing with a corner of the discarded menu. 'I had to drive here myself!'

'Well, *I* could have driven,' I comment righteously. 'I did offer.'

'Yeah, right.' Bronte rolls her eyes.

Dennis winks at Bronte, probably in an attempt to cheer her up, but it has little effect. 'Besides – pizza and wine! You must get that from your mother's side. Tell me, love, exactly what wine would you choose to go with pizza?'

'When you haven't been able to drink for nine months,' replies Bronte smartly, 'any wine'll do.'

'Definitely from your side,' Dennis says to me as he lifts his glass and holds it up to the light before taking a sip. 'Mmm, delicious.'

'And no more for me, Dad, because I'm breastfeeding.'

'Fine, love.' Dennis grins at Bronte before tickling Sherry under the folds of her chin. 'And I'll just have to take it upon myself to train you to appreciate the finer things in life, won't I, precious?'

Precious doesn't answer, choosing instead to yawn wetly and then squint her slate-coloured eyes at her grandfather. Her head flops to one side as if she can't quite believe what she's seeing. I don't much blame her.

'Dad,' says Bronte, reaching over to straighten her daughter out, 'watch her head, she needs support.'

'Sorry, love.'

A ridiculously cheerful young waitress bounces over to our table to deliver the meals. She gets the order right first time and departs with a smile that shows more teeth than seems humanly possible. But the food smells delicious. Angel-hair pasta draped with a chicken sauce for me, chicken schnitzel for Bronte, and medallions of something brown and glutinous with a pasta salad for him. No sensitive lobster or coquettish pate to be seen.

'Great teeth,' comments Dennis, watching the waitress leave. 'Not bad at all.'

'Are we still talking about the teeth?' I ask sweetly.

'Of course. And how about some of my pasta, you adorable little thing, you?' Dennis tucks Sherry in a little more securely so that he can eat around her. 'Do you like pasta?'

'Dennis, don't feed her pasta.'

'What about peas then, my little sweet-pea? Do you like peas?'

'Dennis, don't feed her peas.'

'How about Grandma's pasta then – angel-hair pasta for an angel-haired girl.'

'Dennis, don't feed her angel-hair pasta, don't call me Grandma, and look, she doesn't *have* any hair.'

'Okay, what *can* I feed her then?'

'Nothing! She's a baby, you dork!'

'Now that's what I call a bummer,' Dennis coos down into Sherry's face, and she responds by blowing several saliva bubbles in his general direction. In deference to the occasion, Bronte has changed her into an orange and white polka-dotted pair of cotton rompers and a matching skivvy. Unfortunately, Bronte did not extend the same courtesy to herself and is still clad in the jeans and windcheater she had on earlier. I, on the other hand, have dressed to kill, with my waterfall hairstyle set off by gold-hoop earrings, a low-cut peasant blouse and snug black jeans. I've even disguised the smell of Dencorub with a liberal amount of perfume. Because, although the last thing I want is a rekindling of intimate relations between us, that certainly doesn't mean I don't want *him* to want a rekindling of intimate relations between us. I think that's a rule of thumb when any female is meeting with an ex. Especially when the ex in question spent the latter half of the relationship propositioning anything wearing a skirt. Or not.

Like most females, Sherry has quickly fallen for Dennis's rather superficial charms. He's got a way about him that makes whoever he's with at the time feel very, very special and, if there's one thing women of all ages love, it's being made to feel very, very special.

'So, Bronte –' Dennis turns to his daughter '– how's it feel being a mother?'

'Cool, actually.' Bronte brightens for the first time since we got here.

'No regrets?'

'None at all,' says Bronte emphatically, no doubt remembering the grilling she went through when we found out about the pregnancy. 'Like, no – none at all.'

'Well, that's good anyway.' Dennis looks at his daughter impassively for a minute or two before turning to me. 'And how are things these days for you, Terry? You're looking well, I must say.'

'Why, thank you.' I pause as I swallow my pasta and replenish my fork. 'How kind of you to notice.'

'It's hard not to,' replies Dennis as he leers at my peasant-shirted cleavage. 'You have obvious assets.'

'Gross, Dad!' says Bronte, putting her cutlery down in disgust.

'Don't be a pig, Dennis.' I unload the fork into my mouth and savour the taste of the creamy pasta sauce. 'It's terribly old-fashioned.'

'Okay,' he laughs good-naturedly as he tickles Sherry again. 'So, still got that Fergus hanging around?'

'Of course I have,' I reply defensively. 'Why wouldn't I?'

'Let's see – holidays are over and he's back in school?'

'It's holidays now, you pillock.' I note with disappointment that I've almost finished the entire contents of my plate. And I'm still *very* hungry.

'Oh! So he *is* on school holidays then?'

'That's not what I meant and you know it.'

'Well, kick up your heels – enjoy. You go, girl.'

'Fergus is okay,' says Bronte with a frown at her father. 'Better than some.'

Dennis laughs and I glare at him across the table but he busies himself with trying to keep Sherry still while he butters a roll one-handed. I take a sip of wine and wish, not for the first time, that I'd never introduced Fergus to Dennis. Ever since, I've had to put up with smart cracks about his age, his height, his accent, and especially his taste in clothes. I wonder what Dennis would have to say if I turned up with someone like Richard on my arm? Anyway, it's just so damn hypocritical.

'You've got such double standards, Dennis. You spend most of your waking hours drooling over blondes half your age and making a total idiot of yourself – but when *I* do it, well, that's totally different, isn't it?'

'Actually, yes, it is.' Dennis looks at Bronte quickly before smiling at me like the cat that's got the proverbial cream. 'It's a man's world, my love. And a successful older guy with a good-looking young woman on his arm isn't going to raise eyebrows like a good-looking older woman with a pink-clad little handyman just out of grade school. It might be double standards but it's also life – face it.'

'Oh, shut *up*, Dennis.'

We sit there in non-companionable silence while Bronte picks at her food, Dennis finishes off his roll and I occupy myself by imagining how he would cope if someone did a Lorena Bobbit on him. It doesn't help that I know Dennis has a point. I mop up the remainder of my pasta sauce with half a bread roll and then glance over at Dennis's pasta salad and indistinguishable lumps of meat. I wonder if he is going to eat it before it goes cold.

'I wonder if you're going to eat that before it goes cold?'

'Well, I would if I could manage. As you're finished, why don't you take bubs here and I'll have something to eat.' So saying, he gently hoists Sherry up and passes her around the table to me. 'Ah, that's better. I suppose she's too little for a highchair but why didn't you bring the pram? We could have propped her in there while we ate.'

'I didn't think of it,' replies Bronte as she pushes the vast majority of her vegetables off to the side. 'Because, like, I didn't realise we were going out till the last minute, you know.'

'Well then, what about the capsule? You must have it in the car.'

'Of course I do. But it's bad for her back.' Bronte turns away from her father to look at me. 'Do you want me to take her, Mum?'

'No, wait till you've finished eating.' I readjust Sherry and tuck her into the crook of one arm. Then I concentrate on mopping up the remains of my chicken sauce with the remains of my bread roll. I've got to say, for a place specialising in pasta dishes, they're a tad skimpy with the actual pasta. Instead it looks like they have spent this month's food budget on dental work for the waitresses – every single one of them is walking around beaming as if she has had surgical implants. Perhaps Dennis was here.

Sherry distracts me by becoming restless so I pick up the menu and wave it gently in front of her face. Then, after she relaxes, I rest the menu on top of her bunny-rug so that I can help myself to another bread roll. Dennis also reaches for one at the same time and grins at me when our hands touch. I snatch my hand away as if it's been burnt and, reaching across, he drops his bread roll on my plate before grabbing another one and returning to his meal. I stroke Sherry's head absent-mindedly, sending her ESP messages regarding chauvinist pigs and double standards.

'Tell you what, after we get through Bronte's naming day, let's double date.' I give Dennis an evil look as I break my roll awkwardly.

'Are you *kidding*?' Dennis puts his fork down and stares at me.

'No, I'm not. It'll be fun,' I smile reassuringly. Because it *will* be fun – and it'll show up the obvious differences between *my* ditsy blonde and *his* ditsy blonde – and *my* ditsy blonde is witty and very entertaining. And he certainly won't need help reading the menu.

'Well, don't include me,' says Bronte, looking horrified. 'We're busy that night.'

'Okay, if you want.' Dennis grins at me and shrugs philosophically. 'Weird, but what the hell.'

'Excellent! Ring me in a week or so and we'll set it up.'

'Sometimes you flabbergast me, love,' Dennis comments as he takes a mouthful of the gelatinous brown lumps on his plate. 'Mmm! These are damn delicious!'

'Well, they certainly don't look it.'

'Hey, guess who I saw last week?' Dennis glances up from his plate at me.

'Do I have to – or could you just tell me?'

'Maggie Brown! I haven't seen her in years. Do you know her? She's your friend Camilla's ex-husband's sister.'

'I know who Maggie Brown is,' I say impatiently, 'so what's the problem? Can't get it for free anymore? Did you get a discount?'

'What are you talking about, woman?' Dennis looks at me in total confusion as Bronte puts her hand over her mouth and splutters helplessly.

'It's a joke, Dennis. You know, about Maggie and what she does for a living.'

'What does she do for a living then?' Dennis takes another mouthful of medallion and proceeds to talk around the food. 'I thought she was a schoolteacher or something.'

'Dad, you *must* know.' Bronte wipes her mouth with her serviette. '*Everybody* does!'

'Obviously everybody except me.'

'You're kidding?' I look at Dennis in some surprise, as usually he knows more intimate secrets about people than they do about themselves. It must be the gas he uses in the surgery.

'Look, all I know is that she was in yesterday for an extraction. Impacted molar. Nasty little bugger, too.' Dennis puts down his cutlery and starts picking at the remainder of his salad with his fingers. 'But the woman's made of stone. No injections and didn't even flinch when I ripped it out.'

'Too much information.'

'So, tell me what you're both on about then.'

'Okay. Well, she *used* to be a high school teacher, but she had one of those midlife career changes years ago and went into business with a friend of hers. They own a brothel in Ferntree Gully.'

'*Maggie* owns a brothel?' Dennis's mouth has dropped open in disbelief. Luckily for us he has no food in it.

'Yep.'

'You mean, she . . . that is, *she* –'

'No, if you mean is she one of the workers, then no. She's the owner.' I laugh at the expression on his face but I can understand his reaction because it's very similar to mine when I first discovered what Maggie did for a living. She's one of the nicest, most loyal friends a person could possibly ask for – but she isn't exactly the sort you could imagine decked out in high heels and suspenders, or whatever it is that ladies of the night normally wear. In fact, she most closely resembles a beach ball with arms and legs.

'I was going to say . . . But, bloody hell! Unbelievable.'

'Yep.'

'It sure takes all kinds.' Dennis shakes his head slowly. 'But, no, I took cash for the molar extraction yesterday.'

'Pity. Missed a good opportunity there. And that's not like you.'

'The day I have to pay for it is the day I give it up.'

'Yadda, yadda, yadda,' I say rudely. 'You'll never give it up.'

'*Gross*, Mum!'

Dennis pushes his half-empty plate away and has a sip of his wine. 'Terry, do you want to pass that baby back over again?'

'I'll take her, Dad.' Bronte puts down her cutlery and reaches out her arms. 'Here, Mum, pass her over.'

'Oh, love, could I take her for a bit?' asks Dennis. 'After all, I've got some catching up to do.'

'Okay,' replies Bronte grudgingly as I stand up and carefully deliver the now dozing baby into Dennis's lap. 'But, like, watch her head.'

'Fine.'

'And, Dad, that porta-cot you bought me was faulty. Do you still have the receipt?'

'Somewhere, I'll search for it tonight.' Dennis looks annoyed. 'God, they make some serious crap nowadays. Sorry, love.'

'Well, it's not your fault if it was broken,' I comment generously as I pick at the remains of his salad. 'And it was nice of you to buy it for her.'

'Yeah, I'm a nice guy. Spread it around.'

'I think you already have.'

'I do my best.' Dennis leans back with Sherry in his arms and smiles at us both. 'Now, what do you two say to some pavlova?'

'Yum,' exclaims Bronte enthusiastically, pushing her plate away.

'Do you mean sensitively whipped egg whites?' I ask in a husky voice. 'Topped with a coquettish pastille of fresh cream beaten so severely that it begged for mercy?'

'That's the one,' says Dennis, laughing.

'I say bring it on.' I take a sip of wine and then make some space in front of me for pavlova. An even more cheerful-looking waitress quickly materialises next to Dennis, methodically takes our order and then clears the table.

In an impressively short time Bronte and I are each tucking into an enormous slice of pavlova dripping with whipped cream, strawberries and kiwifruit. The slice in front of Dennis remains untouched as he waits for one of us to finish and take the baby, who is becoming restless again. I smile at him and roll my eyes to indicate the dessert's delectability.

'I must say, it's good to see a woman with a healthy appetite.'

'Yep,' I reply around a mouthful of pavlova, 'that's one thing I've never had a problem with. Unlike your appetites.'

'Do you know, Terry, you really should put the past behind you.'

'Easy for you to say.'

'I wish you two would stop it,' says Bronte crossly. 'Like, just for once.'

I continue eating my pavlova in silence while Dennis plays with Sherry's fingers and then tries my trick of waving the menu gently across her face. Every time we meet I swear to myself that, this time, I won't bring up the past. And every time I end up doing it just the same. Which is odd because I'm really *not* bitter nowadays and, what's more, I can't imagine anything worse than still being married to the man. In fact, we seem to have reached a stage in our lives where all the animosity that tinged the last two years of our marriage, and at least the first five years of our separation, has evolved into a healthy acceptance of each other as friends. Friends with a lot of baggage, but friends nevertheless.

'If you've quite finished devouring that pav,' Dennis says, looking at me with exaggerated patience, 'could you take our mutual grandchild so that I can eat mine?'

'Sure,' I answer obligingly around my last mouthful. I push

my plate away and stand up to fetch Sherry, who should be starting to feel like an unwanted postal parcel by now. As I lift her up, the menu gets stuck within the folds of her bunny-rug and is dragged across the table, creating a creamy trench through Dennis's plate of pavlova. Bronte gasps and Dennis smiles at me ruefully.

'Lord, I'd forgotten all this.'

'Me too.' I lift Sherry a tad higher, away from Dennis's dessert, and then carefully lower myself into my chair. Unfortunately the menu comes too, leaving a trail of cream down my low-cut peasant blouse and across the lap of my jeans. Holding Sherry securely in my lap, I pluck a strawberry off my right breast and pop it into my mouth.

'Be still my heart!' Dennis gives an exaggerated groan and then looks around for a waitress.

'Oh, Mum!' Bronte pushes away her dessert plate. 'Here, I'll take Sherry.'

I lean back so that Bronte can get both arms underneath the baby, who she then lifts up and takes with her back to her seat. One of the cheerful waitresses appears with a damp cloth in her hand. She begins to mop me up.

'Hey, thanks – but I'll do that.' I snatch the cloth from her.

Meanwhile, Sherry has progressed from being merely restless to downright agitated. While her mother tries in vain to pacify her, she begins a low undulating wail that causes every head in the restaurant to swivel in our direction. I take a gulp of wine and stand to finish my clean-up, brushing off the flakes of meringue shell and mopping up the cream. I now look like I'm auditioning for a wet t-shirt competition but at least it means that half the heads turned in our direction are no longer staring balefully at the baby.

Bronte removes Sherry from her bunny-rug and lifts her up, placing her against a shoulder. Then, supporting her head and back with one hand, she uses the other to pat the baby's padded bottom. At the very first pat, an extremely offensive smell issues forth and, when I turn automatically to look at its source, I notice that Sherry's nappy hasn't been entirely successful in retaining its contents.

'Oh, dis*gust*ing!' Dennis grimaces and waves one hand in front of his nose.

'No,' wails Bronte plaintively, 'not again!'

'Give her to your father,' I suggest, sitting down and passing the sticky cloth to the hovering waitress. 'He's just been saying that he has to make up for lost time.'

'Good idea,' agrees Bronte readily, 'here you go, Dad.'

'Sorry.' Dennis glances at his watch and stands up. 'Love to help out but I have to be back at the surgery by two thirty. I've got a root canal.'

'That'd be right,' says Bronte darkly as she stands up with Sherry still on her shoulder. 'Here, Mum, like, can you take her while I get the nappy bag from the car?'

'Okay,' I reply, less than enthusiastically, as the wailing baby is lowered back onto my lap. I grab the bunny-rug and try to arrange it around Sherry's lower half while Bronte fishes her car keys out of her pocket and leaves the restaurant at a trot. After watching her exit, I pop the semi-wrapped Sherry up onto my shoulder and immediately the combined odour of strawberries, cream and a shitty nappy nearly knocks me out.

'Dennis – give us a hand,' I say threateningly, 'or I'll give *you* a root canal.'

'Promises, promises. And I would if I could, but –' he shakes his head ruefully as he pulls his wallet out from his back pocket '– I'm afraid duty calls.'

'Dennis, don't you *dare* leave,' I grind out through clenched teeth.

'Do you know, that's *really* bad for your bite. Which reminds me, you're late for your check-up. Give me a ring and I'll slot you in. Here –' he fishes a few notes out of his wallet and passes them over to the waitress '– this should cover the bill. Keep the change.'

'Dennis!'

'No – I insist on paying, it's the least I can do. And I tell you what, Terry –'

'*Dennis!*'

'Just because I like to cater to *your* appetites –'

'DENNIS!'

'You can finish off my pavlova.'

# FRIDAY

## 1742 hrs

'. . . and so we'd all like to farewell Barbara as she moves on to bigger and better things in the States. We wish her all the best with her new husband and fully expect to hear soon that the American library system has been completely overhauled by our indefatigable colleague here! So, here's to Barbara! Good luck and best wishes!'

Alan, the big boss, beams as loud applause echoes through-out the library. One of the teenage shelvers pushes a madly blushing Barbara forwards and Alan leans over to shake her hand. Then he turns behind him and picks up a small but brightly wrapped gift, which he passes over to Barbara with a flourish.

'Just a token of our gratitude,' he says, looking straight over Barbara's head towards the crowd of library employees, 'to take along as you enter this new, and no doubt challenging, phase of your life. And seriously, folks, I for one would like to tell Barbara how much I've enjoyed working with her all these years, and that I'll miss her friendly face every morning . . .'

I quickly slip around the corner of the new releases display, and walk over to the row of fiction books behind a planter at the far end of the library. Then I choose one at random, and settle myself on a seat beside a large overhanging palm where I can't be seen. Because, as much as I like Barbara, I can't *stand* Alan and his interminable speeches. Any chance that man gets he will drone on and on, delighting in the sound of his own voice. Missing Barbara in the mornings, hell! He probably didn't even know who she was until she put in her resignation. What a hypocrite.

I push myself back into the chair and smooth down my jeans. My *clean* jeans, as I took the time to get changed before I came over to the library to farewell Barbara. Besides them, I'm now wearing my black boots and a red angora square-cut jumper, without a bit of pavlova to be seen. Just as I make myself comfortable, there is a loud tapping on the glass to my right so I look over towards the rain-splashed window. To my astonishment, I see a dripping wet, middle-aged, rather rotund female dressed in a see-through rain poncho standing outside the library. With the rain running in rivulets off her hair and down her face, she's drumming her fingers on the glass, waving a hardback at me, and mouthing what look like obscenities. Using hand gestures, I indicate that the library is closed and for her to return the book via the after-hours chute. She immediately uses a few hand gestures back and continues mouthing what I now realise definitely *are* obscenities. And impressively inventive ones at that.

Rather than engage in an exchange of X-rated lip-reading, I decide to ignore this shining example of what I've got to deal with day after day in my chosen career. Instead I turn my back and reflect on the chosen career itself. The choosing of which is made even more stupid by the fact that I don't particularly like dealing either with the public or with the books. I don't mind *reading* them, if I get the time, but I find the haphazard piles and untidy shelves of the library more than a little frustrating. *I* like my books all in a line, categorised by size, not author, and with their spines about six centimetres from the edge of the shelves. Give or take a millimetre.

I idly flick the pages of the book in my lap, wondering why Cam hasn't shown up. Or Joanne. Or – I sigh deeply and lean back in the chair, my hairclip immediately digging itself into the back of my scalp. I straighten up and mutter a few choice obscenities of my own.

'Want to be alone?'

I glance up and my mouth falls open. For, peering down at me from his rather impressive height, is none other than Richard. And he looks exactly as I remembered, apart from a slightly more coordinated outfit of bone corduroy pants and a burgundy cable-knit v-neck. One look and I immediately realise that after three days of thinking about him, analysing my reactions, dissecting my responses and justifying my emotions – nothing has changed. He still makes me feel like a gawky teenager with a first crush. Without taking my eyes off him, I close both my mouth and the book in my lap.

'No, I mean, yes. No, I mean –' I pause, take a deep breath and pull myself together. 'I mean, please join me if you'd like. And how are you? I thought you'd have left for Tasmania by now.'

'Ah, would have.' Richard folds his thin frame into the chair next to me and starts examining his fingernails. 'But something came up. Leaving Sunday now.'

'Oh.' I pat my hair surreptitiously as I rack my brain for something intelligent to say. Just as I open my mouth to emit

236

what would no doubt have been words of wisdom, there is another series of sharp raps on the window to my right. I look up automatically and, as soon as she sees she has my attention, the middle-aged, plump female proffers me a rather damp finger.

'Friend?' asks Richard curiously, looking over as well.

'Not quite.' I watch the woman stomp off towards her car through the rain, which is now positively pelting down. 'But we take our overdues seriously here.'

'Ah.'

'Just look at the rain out there.' I turn again to Richard, and fall back on the age-old conversation filler: 'Horrid weather, isn't it?'

'Ghastly,' he agrees with a grimace. 'We got soaked.'

'We? I see – Joanne. How is she?'

'Fine, fine. Nice girl.'

'Yes, she certainly is.' I look at him curiously because he didn't sound much like a man in love, or in lust, or whatever. 'So she was okay with you staying on longer?'

'Joanne?' Richard glances at me with his eyebrows raised. 'Why not?'

'I don't know.' I play with the book nervously and, after a few seconds of silence, Richard reaches across and plucks it out of my lap, holding it up and looking at the cover.

'*Lust in the Desert,*' he reads before looking at me with interest. 'Fascinating.'

'No, no.' I snatch the book back and fling it over onto the returns trolley. 'I'm not *reading* it, I just picked it up because I was bored.'

'Wouldn't work, anyway.'

'What?'

'Lust in the desert. All that sand.'

'Yes! And the dust-storms – yech!'

'Communal tents.'

'No showers!'

'Curious camels?'

We look at each other, burst out laughing – and I'm hooked. One hundred percent, totally, absolutely hooked. The only thing missing as far as I know has been that all-important sense of humour, and it seems not only has he got one, but it's also on the same wavelength as mine. Albeit slightly more monosyllabic. Now visibly relaxed, Richard leans back in his chair and stretches while I tuck my legs underneath me and make myself comfortable. A few moments of fairly companionable silence go by, and then I decide to throw caution to the wind. After all, I'll probably never see him again.

'Just out of curiosity, do you remember Camilla, the woman we had lunch with on Tuesday? Remember how her mother turned up? Well, we were wondering – did you by any chance already know her from somewhere?'

'Who, Camilla?'

'No, her mother.'

'Already *know* her?'

'Yes.'

'Ah, no . . . not *really*.'

'Oh, I see,' I reply, although I don't actually see at all. The mystery is no clearer and now I also have to wonder why he put emphasis on the word 'really'. I puzzle over how to frame my next question without it appearing that I'm sticking my nose into what is none of my business, while still doing exactly that.

'Nice city, Melbourne,' says Richard, obviously trying to change the subject. 'Enjoyed myself.'

'Haven't you ever been here before?'

'Never.' Richard smiles at me without quite meeting my eye. 'Ah, might visit more now.'

'And why would you do that?' I query quickly in my best Sherlock Holmes manner. 'Have you met someone you might want to catch up with again?'

'Pardon?'

'Have you met . . .' I peter out as I realise that what I've just said could be construed several ways, when really I was just referring to Rose Riley. I chew my lip thoughtfully.

'Met someone?' Richard turns towards me but still doesn't quite look me in the eye. 'Ah, maybe.'

'I see,' I reply slowly, with a heavy feeling that the conversation might just have taken a sharp turn in a direction I was not quite ready for.

'Yes.'

'Well then,' I say brightly, deciding that another change of subject is called for, 'where has Joanne taken you?'

'Ah!' Richard groans, leaning back again. 'Everywhere!'

'Sounds like you've been busy.'

'Understatement.'

'And has she introduced you to everyone here?' I wave my arm to indicate the library, not all of Melbourne.

'Tried to.' Richard crosses one corduroyed leg and I notice that he is wearing red socks. 'But, ah, the speeches . . .'

I laugh and roll my eyes expressively. 'No wonder you found cover! That Alan is a pompous dork.'

'A dork?' Richard turns to me and finally meets my eye as a smile lights up his face. 'You know what a dork is? Really?'

'Sure! An idiot, or a twit, or . . .' I trail off when I see the amusement crinkling around his eyes. 'Why – what is it?'

'Whale's penis.'

'*What*?'

'Whale's penis,' he repeats. 'You know, a –'

'I know all about whales' penises!' I exclaim, at which he raises his eyebrows. 'What I mean is, I don't actually know *all* about them, like I don't know what one really looks like . . . I mean – hell! I can imagine.'

'Really?'

'Sort of,' I say with embarrassment, trying to work out how on earth I've ended up sounding like I spend my spare time conjuring up images of whales' penises.

'Ah, interesting,' he smiles in my general direction.

'Not really.' I grin back as I shove the embarrassment away. 'In fact, I'd prefer lust in the desert any time.'

'Quite right!'

'Even with the sand –'

'And the dust-storms –'

'And the curious camels!'

Looking at each other with pleasure, we laugh again and I notice that his warm brown eyes actually develop a distinct twinkle when he is amused. He certainly seems to be more relaxed now than the last time I saw him, if the number of words he is stringing together is any indication. If I can keep this conversation going for another twenty minutes or so, it may well get to the stage that I've got to interrupt him to get a word in edgeways.

I smile with contentment and look down at his loose corduroy pants. He *definitely* looks a lot better with his knees covered – less like he should be standing on one leg in shallow water searching for fish. My gaze travels slowly up to the burgundy v-neck, which has seen better days. Although, by the looks of it, not for quite some time. I get a sudden urge to lean across, rip it off him, throw it to the floor – and then drag him off shopping for some decent clothes. Taking a deep breath and looking away before I do something stupid, I glance through the palm towards the throng of people over on the other side of the library. There appears to be a tad more action happening there and I note that the chatter has started to build up: a sure sign the speeches are over and the fun has begun.

'Do you miss your wife?' I blurt, and then blush fiercely when I realise what I've said. 'Sorry! None of my business!'

'That's okay.' Richard looks down at his fingernails again. 'Yes – I do. But we were separated before. She died. For five years or so. Still miss her. So does Eve.'

'Oh,' I say, when it becomes obvious he isn't going to add anything further. 'I see.'

'Ah, Terry –' Richard abandons his fingernails and stares at my right ear instead.

'Yes?'

'How long are these things? Usually?'

'Oh, a couple of hours, that's all.'

'You doing anything? Afterwards?'

'Afterwards?' I repeat idiotically as my heart slips a cog and then tries to compensate by increasing its pump-rate dramatically. 'You mean, after this?'

'Richard!' Joanne shrieks excitedly as she pops her head around the potted palm. 'I was *wondering* where you'd got to! And, look! Here's Terry! Oooh, what are *you* two up to?'

'Nothing,' I mumble as I feel my face go red. 'Nothing at all.'

'Hey, Barbara, I found her!' Joanne yells over her shoulder. 'She was hiding out with that guy I was telling you about.'

'Terry!' Barbara's round, plump face joins Joanne's. 'Well, well, well. What *are* you doing tucked away behind here? And what would Fergus say?'

'Nothing,' I repeat with irritation as I untuck my legs and sit up straight, 'because there's nothing *to* say!'

'Who's Fergus?' Joanne looks from Barbara to me curiously.

'Nobody!'

'Well then, we might just have to tell him and find out,'

laughs Barbara, obviously under the mistaken impression she is being amusing.

'Fine!' I snap, now thoroughly annoyed. 'You *do* that!'

'Hang on! I was only teasing, you know.' Barbara does a double-take and then looks at me apologetically. 'Hey, I'll grab you some wine to make up. Don't move!'

'And I'll grab a couple for us, Richard,' says Joanne, 'then I'll join the two of you. Terry can tell me all about this mysterious Fergus of hers. It's got to be better than making small talk with Alan and Co!'

To avoid looking at Richard, I twist my head around and watch the two of them walk away. They make an odd pair – red-headed Joanne in a flowing red outfit that's not quite the same red as her hair, and Barbara with her generous frame clothed in her usual black. They head towards a large trestle table that has been set up near the autobiographies and loaded with several opened packets of chips, a couple of wine casks and a stack of plastic tumblers. This library is one class establishment, that's for sure. My neck starts to ache so I sit back and massage it lightly.

'Good while it lasted,' Richard says wryly.

'The peace, you mean?'

'What else?' He looks at my right ear with his head tilted to one side. 'Who's Fergus?'

'Fergus?' I give up on my neck and start massaging my fore-head instead. 'Fergus who?'

'Fergus your boyfriend, of course,' says Barbara helpfully as she passes me my tumbler of wine and pulls over a seat. 'The cute blonde with the Irish accent.'

'Ah,' comments Richard expressionlessly.

'And I don't believe we've been introduced. I'm Barbara.' Smiling, she leans forwards to shake Richard's hand. 'You must be Richard. Joanne's told me all about you.'

'Ah, hmm . . .' Richard half rises out of his seat to shake her hand and then sits back, staring at the large-print books in the distance.

'And congrats to you, Terry!' Barbara turns to me and raises her tumbler. 'Here's to the grandma!'

'Thanks,' I say as I put my wine down and start rotating my thumbs in little circular motions around my temples. 'Thanks a heap.'

'Have you got a headache?' Barbara asks with concern.

'I have now.'

'Hey, Barbara, have you told Richard how you met Chuck?' Joanne chimes in as she settles herself on Richard's armrest. 'Go on, tell him.'

'How did you know?'

'Cam wrote and told me. Anyway, Terry, where *is* Cam?'

'I don't think she was able to make it. Busy with uni, you know.'

'Bummer.' Joanne looks at Richard and raises her eyebrows. 'Bummer.'

'It's not all that unusual nowadays, you know,' Barbara says defensively as she turns to Richard. 'Not uni – I mean me and Chuck. See, we met over the internet. Ages ago.'

'Ah.'

'We clicked. And it's just like a normal friendship, you know, when you get to know each other slowly and then realise there's something more. We've exchanged photos and everything, and we talk almost every night. I bet we know more about each other than most other couples ever do!'

'Ah.'

'And that's it.'

'Ah.'

'Well, *I* think it's really romantic,' declares Joanne, nodding emphatically, 'and what's more, last night I read Barbara's tea-leaves and they spelt out success in all her spheres whilst the waning moon is in Uranus.'

'Ouch,' says Richard, taking a sip of his wine.

'Pardon?' asks Joanne, frowning at him. 'Don't you like the wine? I'm afraid it's only cask but then the library's so mean, we're used to it. Would you rather a coffee?'

'No, no. Wine's fine.'

I stop massaging my temples for a minute to glance across at him and he sends a fleeting grin towards the vicinity of my eyebrows. My insides warm and I grin back with pleasure. Bugger, bugger, bugger.

'Hey, you lot!' Margo, the tiny dark-haired liaison librarian, leans around the corner and looks at us all accusingly. 'You're hogging Barb from her own party! Come on, up you get and mingle!'

With remarkable strength, she levers Joanne off her perch on Richard's armrest and then grabs Barbara's elbow, hoisting her considerable bulk upright. Finally she turns to me and I narrow my eyes threateningly.

'I can get up myself, thanks.'

'Interesting,' says Richard mildly.

'Then do so immediately, Terry!' Margo grabs Barbara's hand so she can't escape. 'And over you come, Barb. You can tell the mob from the mobile library how you met Chuck.'

'Come on, Richard.' Joanne takes his wine to encourage him out of the chair. 'She's right, we should be mingling a bit. I'll introduce you around.'

'Sure.' Richard unfolds himself upright and then turns back to me. 'Nice to meet you. Again. Thanks for the company.'

'My pleasure,' I reply politely as I also stand up and realise once more just how short he makes me feel. 'Any time.'

'Ah.' Richard looks down at me impassively.

Then Joanne tugs impatiently on his arm and he turns away to be led over to the nearest huddle of librarians, who appear to be having a very loud and enthusiastic conversation about the suspected marital indiscretions of the Adult Literacy Coordinator.

I lean lazily against the nearest bookshelf and just observe the crowded room for a few minutes. Most of the people here are good friends of mine and usually I'd be in the thick of it – socialising, gossiping and helpfully pointing out the numerous failings of the executives. But this evening I'm simply not in the mood.

Margo has dragged Barbara over to the audiovisual display where Alan is holding court and explaining to a very bored-looking group the positive ramifications of a reorganisation of the Dewey decimal classification system. Over by the trestle table, the elderly audiovisual aide from our Boronia branch is trying to pour wine into her plastic cup and, judging by the difficulty she is having, has already had more than her limit. Waiting their turn behind her are the Head of Acquisitions and Cataloguing, and the Organisational Development Executive Office Manager, who are both silently passing the time by staring balefully in Alan's direction. Obviously they're not in favour of a reorganisation of the Dewey decimal classification system. Beside them is a more cheerful group who have begun a party game that appears to involve balancing plastic tumblers in a pyramid and then throwing potato chips at them. Looks like fun.

I take a sip of my wine and continue gazing around the room. Now and then somebody catches my eye and either waves or grins. I'm not altogether surprised Cam doesn't appear to have made it to the function because, with her increased involvement at university, she has begun a gradual move away from the library that probably isn't even conscious.

Eventually I work my gaze around to the group that Joanne and Richard have joined. And as I look over in that direction, I can't help but focus on Richard, because he's so tall. And then I can't help but notice he's looking straight back at me. My heart hiccups as, for once, our eyes lock and for a few long seconds we simply stare at each other. And then I do the stupidest thing I've done so far this week – and that's saying something. Without even thinking about it, I wink.

Richard looks back at me with amazement and I return the favour. In fact, it's difficult to know who is the *more* amazed, the winker or the winkee. I'm not normally known for spontaneity and, if this is an example of what it leads to, I don't want to be known for it. I feel my face go a beetroot colour, which is sure to clash with my jumper, so I blink several times and then realise doing *that* probably makes it appear as if I'm still trying to wink, just more spasmodically. So I widen my eyes and forbid them to close at all for the near future. Richard tilts his head slightly to one side and continues to look at me curiously. So I do what I should have done five minutes ago.

I leave.

## FRIDAY

### 2046 hrs

'So you like him – what's the big deal?'

'What do you mean – what's the big deal?' I turn and look at Cam indignantly. 'Of *course* it's a big deal!'

'I didn't see you getting this hot under the collar when you met Fergus, that's all.'

'Well, that was different.' I lean forwards, pick up my champagne and take a sip.

'Different how?' Cam tucks her legs underneath her and regards me curiously.

I reach out to put my glass down on the coffee table and

then lean back on the couch, ignoring the hairclip that imbeds itself in the back of my head while I think it over. The thing is I'm not quite sure how it's different – I just know that it is. But I don't seem to be convincing Cam of this. I filled her in on our conversation at the library and tried to be descriptive, but the actual *connection* I felt, and that I *think* he felt, didn't translate well at all. So I decided not to share the wink with her – that didn't even seem sane when I did it. In fact, every time I cast my mind back to the bloody wink, I get this unpleasant porridgey feeling and I need to have a drink.

Accordingly I have another sip of champagne and then, instead of answering Cam's astute question (which I've now actually forgotten), I let my gaze wander over her lounge-room. Which is in its usual state of disarray. An empty biscuit packet is balanced on top of some discarded clothing by the coffee table, with a sprinkling of hundreds and thousands around it. Cushions are piled with a blanket next to the television, as if one of the kids had nested there earlier in the day, and a wobbly looking stack of books by the armchair indicates somebody's attempt to study at one point. But the positively worst thing in the lounge-room would have to be Cam's bottle-green velour beanbag with the mustard pinstripes. It looks a lot like one of those huge lumps of molten seaweed you often find washed up on the beach. And immediately take a wide detour around.

I avert my gaze from the beanbag and instead lock eyes with the blue-tongue lizard on the sideboard. He flicks his tongue out suggestively and then tilts his head to regard me quizzically, as if he's also waiting for my answer to whatever the question was.

'Well?' Cam smiles at me pleasantly. 'I can wait all evening, you know. I have children; therefore, I have patience.'

'What was the question?'

'As if you don't know. I *asked* you why this guy is different from Fergus.'

'I don't know,' I mumble, reaching forwards and picking up a water cracker from the platter Cam has placed on the coffee table. 'So let's change the subject, shall we?'

'Fine.' Cam shrugs philosophically. 'You brought it up.'

'I know.' I finish off the cracker and brush the crumbs from my chest. 'Never mind. And anyway, what happened to *you* this evening? You know, your no-show at Barbara's function?'

'God! I was so stuffed after the zoo that I wasn't going *anywhere!*' Cam looks at me and grimaces. 'That place is enormous! And they had to see every single animal, bird and damn insect. Then, you wouldn't believe it, just as we finish – we realise that one of the kids is missing.'

'CJ?' I ask hopefully.

'No, her friend's little sister. Anyway, we retrace our steps and yell and yell and yell. By this time Caron, the mother, is almost in tears, so we find the office and get them to call out over the loudspeaker. You'll never guess where she was?'

'Where?' I ask, because obviously it's expected of me.

'There's a cave in one of those underground tunnels near the wombats – she'd crawled in there and gone to sleep. Unbelievable. The only good thing that came out of it was CJ ended up so exhausted, we didn't have one argument all afternoon and she went out like a light after tea.'

'Well, at least that's something!'

'Yeah – but it was a high price to pay.' Cam takes a deep sip of her champagne. 'So tell me, how was the internet sex kitten?'

'Yech.' I make a face as an image of Barbara, dressed in pink fluff and reclining on a couch with a come-hither smile, flashes across my cerebral screen. 'And double yech.'

'Hmm,' Cam grimaces, obviously struck by a similar image. 'But I'll have to ring her tomorrow to wish her luck.'

'After your meeting with your mother, of course.'

'Of course.' Cam looks at me strangely. 'I can see that all roads are going to lead back to Richard tonight, aren't they?'

'Bugger!' I sigh and then shrug philosophically. 'It's just that I don't understand it. I *never* have this sort of reaction to guys. Never!'

'True,' Cam says thoughtfully, 'and I must admit I don't quite understand it myself. It's not like you at all.'

'No, it's not.'

'I mean, it's not like he's Prince Charming, is it? Can't string two words together, can't look you in the eye, and that body! He'd make a model look plump. And he's not exactly what you'd call good-looking either.'

'Hang on!' I look at her huffily. 'That's not quite true.'

'Yes it is,' she continues. 'Although maybe he wouldn't be too bad with a makeover. Something that would drag him into the twenty-first century.'

'Do you know –' I can feel myself getting defensive on Richard's behalf '– I never realised you were so superficial. Sure, he's got a problem with his fashion sense, but once you take the time to get to know him, he's *very* pleasant to talk to – a really nice guy. So maybe he's a tad shy, but since when has that been a crime? And he's *not* that bad looking either. I mean, just his eyes for a start – they're really . . . really –'

'Really?' Cam grins and raises her eyebrows. 'You *are* quite hooked, aren't you?'

'Yes!' I wail, flinging myself back against the couch. 'So what do I *do* about it?'

'Nothing.'

'*Nothing?*'

'That's right – nothing.' Cam takes a sip of her champagne. 'Because you never do.'

'What do you mean by that?' I ask her with amazement.

'Well – look, you're not going to get all offended, are you?'

'No, why would I?'

'Because usually when I bring this sort of stuff up you either change the subject or get all huffy. And I don't want to ruin the evening, but if you're going to go on and on about Richard, and ask my advice, then I'm just going to tell you, that's all. So – promise you won't get offended and I'll say my piece and get it over with.'

'Well . . .' I chew my lip thoughtfully, torn between a desire to hear what she has to say and a sneaky suspicion I already *know* what she has to say – and that I don't want to hear it. 'What the hell? Go on. I'll stop you if I start getting offended.'

'Okay. Well, it's like this – you've been coming over here now for months every Friday night and going on about how you feel and –' Cam holds out her hand as I open my mouth. 'Don't get me wrong – I *love* our Friday therapy sessions and wouldn't change them for the world. All I mean is that I've been listening to you saying the same stuff week after week.

'And now, with this thing about Richard, I can't see it'll be any different. Because the bottom line is that you will never – *never* – risk changing your life. Not even to have that boob job you keep carrying on about. That's why you always talk about going overseas, but never do it. And why you go on about wanting more education but never do it. And also why you carry on about how miserable you are at the library, but you'll never quit. And that's probably also why you pick the sort of guys you pick. Like Fergus. I mean, I love Fergus – he's fun, and charming, and great company. But he's not your type and anybody with two eyes in their head can see that. You're like odd socks together. But I bet that's why you picked him, subconsciously, and that's why you picked that last guy of yours, and the one before that as well. None of them are your type and so none of them are a threat and so none of them are ever going to mean that you have to commit or change anything in your life.'

'Hell,' I say softly, staring at her stupefied.

'And you want to know why you only choose options that are safe?' Cam continues without waiting for an answer, obviously warming to her theme. 'You only choose options that are safe because you were hurt once – and badly – and you'll never risk that again. See, commitment equals hurt. So if you don't change anything in your life, and you only pick guys who aren't going to touch you on a deeper emotional level, then you'll never run the risk of repeating that hurt and the whole emotional, physical, psychological upheaval that it caused.'

'*Flaming* hell.'

'And that's it.' Cam looks at me questioningly. 'So are you still talking to me?'

'Well, well, well . . .' I take a deep gulp of my champagne and lean back. 'So that's where taking psychology at university gets you?'

'It's true. In fact –' Cam pauses and looks over at the pile of discarded clothing next to her '– do you know what you remind me of?'

'No idea,' I reply shortly. 'Enlighten me.'

'You're like a t-shirt that's got marks all over it and, instead of soaking it in something, you just keep throwing it in the wash. But of course the stains don't come out and, in fact, the more times it's washed, the harder it will be to get them out when you finally do the right thing. Which is to stop just repeating the surface cleaning and give it a right proper soaking. It's risky because it might get discoloured but it's also the only thing that'll get rid of them.'

'You're bonkers.' I look at her incredulously. 'So I'm either an odd sock or a dirty t-shirt. Thanks very much.'

'Only figuratively speaking,' Cam mutters defensively.

'I know,' I exclaim sarcastically, 'why don't you write a list of everything that's wrong with me? Hey?'

'*No!*' Cam shouts before continuing in a more moderate tone of voice. 'You and your lists! That's half the problem! You write lists for everything – why don't you just do something *without* a list for once? Be spontaneous!'

'I need a drink.' I get up, take my champagne flute and stalk out to the kitchen where I refill my glass from the bottle in the fridge. Then I walk over to the kitchen window and push the net curtains aside to stare out into the dark, damp backyard. I can see the shadowy outline of a few trees that frame the fence dividing Cam's house from Alex's. Sipping my champagne slowly, I put one finger up to trace the rain as it spatters across the pane.

'I'm sorry.' Cam comes out into the kitchen and puts her empty glass on the table. 'I didn't mean to go that far. And I *knew* you'd get offended.'

'Don't worry,' I answer without turning, 'I'm not offended.'

'Yes you are.'

'No I'm not.'

'Well, you should be.' Cam slides into one of the kitchen chairs and props her chin in her hands. 'After all, who am I to give advice?'

'I don't know.' I turn to face her. 'You seem to have your life pretty well on track, don't you?'

'Yeah, I suppose so. But it's a bit unconventional, isn't it?'

'Who cares? As long as it works for you.'

'I suppose.'

'I *know*.' I fetch the champagne bottle from the fridge and take it, and my glass, over to the table. 'And you were right, as well.'

'I was?' Cam looks at me with disbelief. 'Are you *sure*?'

'Yes, I'm sure.' I fill Cam's glass almost to the brim, then put the bottle on the table and sit down opposite her. 'But the funny thing is that I used to be a real risk-taker. I mean, that whole Air Force thing was a rebellious gamble against Dad, and even marrying Dennis after only having known him a few months was a huge risk. *That* was spontaneous.'

'So what changed? Or was I right about that too?'

'I think you might have been,' I reply slowly as I unclip my hair and shake it out. 'But there's not much I can do about it now.'

'I was right!' Cam shakes her head in wonder. 'I was right!'

'Don't let it go to your head,' I suggest, running my fingers through my hair to comb it, 'unless you can suggest a remedy.'

'Of course I can!' Cam says eagerly. 'Do something outrageously adventurous! Quit your job, or at least take extended leave, and go overseas – live a little!'

'But that doesn't help me with the whole Richard thing.'

'Tasmania is sort of overseas, isn't it?'

'Sort of.' I grin at her. 'But it's not a terribly adventurous type of overseas, is it?'

'Now, *that* depends on whether you take the risk with Richard, doesn't it?'

Rather than answer, I fiddle with the stem of my champagne flute and stare out into the dark, damp night. Cam's outside light only illuminates a small slice of her backyard and the falling rain slithers silverly through the patch of light. Her dog, a Border collie cross, is sitting in the middle of the glow, like an actor centre-stage within a personal spotlight. Dripping wet, he is staring mournfully up at the window.

'Look at your poor dog!' I exclaim. 'Don't you have a kennel?'

'Yes, a perfectly good one,' replies Cam, following my gaze to the dog, 'but that animal is an idiot.'

'I'm surprised that Ben hasn't dragged him in here.'

'He probably would have if he was here.' Cam looks away from the dog and back towards me. 'But he's over at Jeff's for the night and he's going to St John's with them in the morning. And Sam's at a friend's as well so it's just me and CJ. Want another drink?'

'I'll have one more and then I'd better switch to coffee.'

'Why don't you stay the night?'

'Pardon?'

'I'm serious.' Cam pauses, with the champagne bottle poised over my glass. 'Look at the weather! It's revolting. Besides, you can have a few more drinks then. And you can sleep in Sam's room; she won't mind.'

I watch her continue to pour the drinks as I reflect on this unexpected offer. I've been coming over to Cam's every Friday night for an awfully long time and have never stayed the night before. But, then again, I've also never had a week where I've fallen in love twice – and where one of the objects of my attraction is at home, ready, waiting and primed to keep me awake for most of the night. And it's the wrong one.

'Go on,' urges Cam, putting the bottle back down on the table. 'But make up your mind quickly so you can ring Bronte before it's too late to let her know.'

'Okay!' I grin at her. 'Why not?'

'Why not indeed? You know where the phone is.' Cam gets up and grabs the bottle. 'I'll put this in the fridge and then go make sure Sam's room is relatively neat while you're ringing.'

I walk my chair backwards until I reach the island bench and then stretch up and unhook the wall-phone. I dial my number and listen to the phone ringing at the other end. When a sleepy Bronte answers, I explain the situation and promise I'll be back home mid-morning. As I hang up, I reflect

254

on the fact she definitely became a lot more lively when she realised I wasn't coming home.

'Everything all right?' Cam walks back in carrying the platter from the lounge-room and puts it down on the table as she sits. Then she takes a long sip of wine as she watches me curiously.

'Just a minute.' I lean backwards, unhook the phone again and redial my number which, just as I suspected, is engaged. I laugh as I hang up.

'What's so funny?'

'I wondered why she got all chirpy when I said I was staying here.' I pick up my chair, move it back over to the table and sit down. 'I bet she's ringing Nick and inviting him over.'

'You don't mind, do you?'

'No, and it'll give him a chance to see what night-feeds and bad-tempered babies are all about.'

'The baby wasn't that bad last night, was she?' asks Cam curiously, helping herself to a cracker piled with dip.

'She was *worse*,' I say with feeling as I remember trying to burrow my way into my mattress. 'She woke up every hour or so and screamed the whole damn house down.'

'Ah, so *that's* why you agreed to stay here so quickly.'

'Exactly.'

'She is pretty cute, though.'

'Actually, she's not just cute – she's gorgeous!' I smile at the thought of Sherry's physical perfection. 'And apart from last night, she's *perfectly* behaved as well. And she's really placid, and alert, and bright-eyed – really inquisitive, and –'

'Well, well, well,' Cam interrupts rudely, 'who would have thought that you, of all people, would be carrying on like this about a baby? Wonders will never cease.'

'Well, she is,' I mutter crossly.

'I'm not saying she's *not*,' continues Cam with a grin, 'I've just never seen your eyes light up quite like that before. Hang on! Yes, I have!'

'When?' I ask curiously.

'About twenty minutes ago – when you were talking about Richard!'

'Ha, ha.' I raise my eyebrows derisively. 'You're just hysterical.'

'No, actually I'm serious.'

'Oh,' I say with some bafflement, because I really *did* think she was trying to be funny. I cast my mind about for an appropriate change of subject. 'Did I tell you we had lunch with Dennis today?'

'Really?' She curls her lip scornfully. 'And how *is* the oral playboy?'

'Cam, you dag,' I chortle with amusement. 'What the hell's an *oral* playboy?'

'I meant because he's a dentist,' says Cam, as she too starts to grin. '*Not* what you're thinking!'

I'm incapable of answering because I'm laughing too hard. After a few seconds, Cam starts to laugh as well and the moment rapidly turns into one of those occasions where you feed off each other's laughter, and every time you start to wind down, you catch sight of the other's face and break up once more. Even though what actually *started* you laughing wasn't really all that funny to begin with. Accordingly we roll around in our seats, gasping for breath in between near hysterical shudders of hilarity. Finally, I clutch my stomach and bend over as tears run down my cheeks.

'No more,' splutters Cam. 'Don't look at me!'

'You dag!'

'That's twice you've called me that!' Cam wipes tears from her eyes and groans.

'It's my new word.' I start laughing again, this time because

I remember my old word and am hit by the image of a whale's penis.

'Mummy?'

Our laughter abruptly ceases as we both look towards the kitchen doorway, where a pyjama-clad CJ is staring at us uncertainly. She rubs her eyes hard, yawns and then wanders over to crawl into her mother's lap.

'CJ!' Cam wraps her arms around her daughter. 'What're you doing up?'

'You woke me,' mumbles CJ, 'with all your screaming. I thought you were here with that Rudolph.'

'I keep telling you that there *is* no Rudolph!' says Cam, sending me an accusing glance. 'It was just a joke!'

'It's not a bery funny joke.'

'Quite right. And now it's back to bed you go.' Cam tries to lever herself out of the chair with CJ wrapped around her like a limpet. 'Terry and I'll be going to bed ourselves in a minute.'

'Whoa!' I hold up a hand. 'I'm not bedding *anyone*, and especially not you! What's the matter, Santa gone off the boil?'

'Shut *up*, Terry!'

'*Who's* boiling Santa?' CJ, now rather wide awake, looks at her mother, horrified. 'And what'll happen to Christmas if Santa's all boiled?'

'Nobody's boiling Santa.' Cam manages to get herself upright. 'It's just an adult expression. Christmas is definitely still on, and now – you're off to bed. Thanks, Terry.'

'No problem.' I watch them go and then finish off my champagne as I stare out of the window at the dog, who is still sitting in the spotlight and looking miserable. I wonder if I *should* do something spontaneous? Something adventurous? Unfortunately, an overseas trip now is out of the question – babies of Sherry's age change too much, too quickly. And I don't want to miss any of it. But I *could* look around for another job, I suppose. Something more challenging, more interesting, more intellectually fulfilling. But then again, it's not like I *hate* my job – and how stupid would it be to give up a reasonably paid job that is not only tolerable, but also nice and close to where I live?

Perhaps I could move. *That* would be something adventurous, and then I could change jobs because the nice and close bit would no longer be applicable. But I like my house, despite the carpet. It makes me feel secure, and permanent. Maybe I could keep the house, and the job, and instead just do a course to inject something challenging into my life. I've always wanted to learn lead-lighting, or pottery, or even self-defence.

'Well, she's settled,' says Cam, coming back into the room and flopping down onto her chair. 'But we'd better keep it down for a while.'

'What do you think of karate?'

'In what context?'

'For me.' I slide my empty glass over towards her as a hint. 'To add a bit of challenge to my life.'

'*That's* your answer?' Cam looks at me quizzically as she goes over to the fridge. 'Taking up martial arts?'

'Well, it'd be something different,' I say defensively, 'and probably pretty useful too.'

'Yeah, you could kick my butt next time I psychoanalyse you.'

'Yet another plus,' I say brightly. 'So when are we going to the gym again, anyway?'

'Never,' says Cam shortly, putting the bottle on the table and sitting down.

'Next Tuesday's good for me.'

'I'm still in agony from yesterday! God, you should have seen me this morning!'

'Exactly why you need to persevere,' I say unsympatheti-
cally, because I'm not going to admit that every muscle in my
body is still complaining as well.

'Okay then,' she sighs, and looks at me threateningly. 'But
I'm not going near that damn treadmill again. You can forget
about *that*!'

'Excellen*te*!'

'Humph. Hell's bells, look at that damn dog,' groans Cam,
doing exactly that. 'I give up.'

She gets up again and goes over to the laundry, where I can
hear her opening the back door and whistling. The dog pricks
up his ears and looks around for a few moments before registering that hearth and home are calling. He leaps up and goes
racing across the backyard and in through the door. Cam backs
out of the laundry and closes the door quickly. She comes over
to the table and looks at me ruefully as we listen to the unmis-
takable sounds of a medium-sized dog giving himself an
almighty shake to rid himself of accumulated water, mud and
general sludge.

'Great.' She flops down and grabs the champagne bottle. 'I
only cleaned that room last week.'

'I don't even know why you got that dog.'

'Oh, Ben's had his heart set on a puppy for years.' Cam fills
up our glasses and passes mine over. 'I don't think I've ever
seen him as happy as when he got Murphy.'

'Exactly how many pets has he got now?'

'Not that many,' says Cam defensively. 'Murphy; the rabbits,
of course; Sonic the blue-tongue; his fish; his hermit crabs –
and whatever's out in the shed.'

'Is that all?' I ask sarcastically.

'Oh, and that.' Cam gestures towards a rectangular
polystyrene box on the floor by the island bench. 'But it's only
temporary.'

'What is it?'

'A guinea pig he's looking after for Phillip for some reason.' Cam gets up and, bending over, picks up the box gingerly. 'Here, have a look. He's quite cute.'

'Okay, if I must,' I say unenthusiastically, moving my champagne glass quickly as Cam slides the box onto the table in front of me. On one side of it is a large colourful sticker bearing the name of Phillip's veterinary practice and a picture of a cat and a dog, who look a little too friendly for my liking. Phillip is engaged to Cam's sister, Elizabeth. He is very tall and rather good-looking, in a clipped Errol Flynn type of way that I must admit doesn't do an awful lot for me. But Cam's son, Ben, who wants to be a vet, has adopted Phillip as a mentor of sorts and spends a lot of his spare time helping out at the Boronia practice.

'You must.' She levers the lid off the box with a hollow scraping sound and then stands back. 'See? He's one of those cute ones with chunks of fur sticking out everywhere.'

I look down into the box before me. Sure enough, nestled in a mound of yellow straw is a medium-sized, multicoloured guinea pig who is obviously having a bad-hair life. Tufts of dark-brown fur stick out at right angles to tufts of black fur, with tufts of white, chestnut and mustard-coloured fur in between. This rodent has serious coiffure problems. I suspect that it also has serious health problems, judging by the lethargic way it is lying flat on its back with its head lolling to one side.

'Cam?' I give the guinea pig a gentle prod, to no avail. 'I think it's sick.'

'What?' she shrieks, shoving me back as she leans over to take a look. 'God! I didn't *do* anything!'

'No one said you did.'

'You're my witness! I never even *touched* him, did I?'

'Not that I saw. Perhaps it's hungry?'

'Ben fed him before he left,' Cam says distractedly, running her fingers through her short hair, 'and he's got water and all. What's wrong with the damn thing?'

'I don't know.' I reach in and place one finger gently on the pig's chest. 'It's breathing quite rapidly.'

'At least he's breathing. Do you think I should ring Phillip?'

'It's pretty late,' I reply, glancing at the clock, 'but it *is* his guinea pig, I suppose.'

We both lapse into silence as we stare into the box at the supine rodent. Its eyes are closed and I can see its chest rising and falling at a rate that surely can't be good for a long-term prognosis. And then I see something else as well.

'Cam?'

'What?'

'Are you sure this thing's a boy?'

'No, why?' Cam looks at me. 'What difference does it make?'

'Quite a bit, I think.' I gesture towards the rodent's nether regions. 'See?'

Cam follows my gaze and her mouth falls open. Because between the tufts of multicoloured fur, a small pink thing can be seen emerging. I can't believe that, twice in one week, I'm about to witness the miracle of birth. At least this time I don't have to take an active part.

'Hell's bells,' breathes Cam as she watches fascinated. 'She's having babies!'

'She sure is.'

'Ben's going to be thrilled. Oh!' Cam turns to me questioningly. 'Do you think I should wake CJ up?'

'No!' I reply quickly. 'Only because it might take ages, you know.'

'I suppose,' Cam says reluctantly, 'but she'd love this.'

We watch as the rodent continues to pant shallowly, and the small, pink, hairless thing continues to emerge. I think it might be one of the baby's legs. However, after some minutes I note that the birthing process doesn't seem to be making much progress. In fact, just as it looks like the leg is about to be followed by something more substantial, it appears to get stuck and almost disappears only to begin its slow re-emerging all over again.

'Cam?'

'I know,' she says worriedly, 'something's wrong, isn't it?'

'Looks that way.'

'God, I think the baby's stuck.'

'Looks that way.'

'Well, what can we do?' Cam glances at me with concern. 'Because if I stuff *this* up, I'll never hear the end of it.'

I transfer my gaze back to the guinea pig. 'I think you might have to give it a hand.'

'Why me?' Cam squeaks. '*You're* the one who's got experience!'

'Exactly why it's your turn,' I reply firmly. 'Go on, just help – I don't know, *guide* it.'

'All right,' says Cam grimly as she rolls up her sleeves. 'Here goes.'

She reaches one hand into the polystyrene box and starts by gently patting the guinea pig's exposed belly. Then, after a few moments, she takes a deep breath and moves her hand down to the little pink leg, which is emerging once more. Gingerly she takes hold of the leg and tries to guide it out but, just when it seems she's going to be successful, it slips out of her fingers and disappears once more.

'Bugger!'

'Try again,' I say supportively. 'You nearly had it then.'

So she tries again, and again, and again. For about fifteen

minutes or so. But each time she has the little pink leg in a firm grasp and it looks like the rest of the baby is about to follow, it seems to hit an obstacle and slips straight from her fingers and back into the body of its mother. I sip my champagne and watch with concern. Because, although I don't know much about the reproductive habits of rodents, I'm guessing prolonged labour doesn't bode well for the survival chances of the infants. And I can tell by the increased desperation of Cam's attempts to assist the birth that she's thinking much the same thing.

'You'll have to ring Phillip.'

'I know,' she sighs heavily as the leg slips out of her grip one more time. 'This is going on too long.'

'Yep.'

Cam rubs the guinea pig's belly gently. 'Hang in there, girl, help's on the way.'

'Here, have a drink first.' I pass Cam her champagne and she takes a gulp before putting it down and heading over to the phone. While she dials, I look back into the box and watch the poor little rodent as she pants with her legs splayed and her head sagging to one side. I feel a rush of camaraderie for what the valiant little creature is going through. All right, *I* might have had considerable help of the narcotic variety, but I did still go through a birth myself. It creates a bond. Maybe I should sing to her?

'Hello?' says Cam into the receiver. 'Phillip? Oh, I *am* sorry to be ringing you so late but it's that guinea pig you left with Ben. It's in trouble. It's giving birth and it seems that one of the babies is, well, stuck and it can't – what? What? *What?*'

I look up in consternation as Cam shrieks into the phone and then lapses into silence, nodding every so often as she listens to what Phillip has to say. Her eyes open wide and then narrow.

'I see. Yes, I understand and I think it's damn disgusting. No, of course not. Okay, I'll remember. Sorry to disturb you so late. Thanks, Phillip – bye.'

Cam hangs up the phone slowly and walks over to the sink where she washes her hands thoroughly for a good few minutes. Only then does she turn towards me and, with her mouth set into a thin, hard line, walks determinedly across to the foam box on the table and peers balefully within.

'I hate you,' she says with considerable venom to the prone guinea pig. 'I *really* hate you.'

'*What?*' I put my hand protectively over the box's opening. 'What's *she* done? What on earth did Phillip say?'

'She isn't a damn she, that's what he said,' spits Cam, still staring at the guinea pig malevolently. '*She's* a he.'

'Is not,' I reply with exasperation. 'How can she be giving birth if she's a he?'

'Exactly.'

'What do you mean?'

'Because she's *not* giving birth, that's why! She's just . . . just . . .'

'For god's sake – just *what*?'

'Just *masturbating*, that's what!'

'*What?*'

'Precisely what I said.' Cam smiles grimly. 'Apparently those disgusting pig males just lie on their backs and, well, masturbate!'

'But then what was the pink –' I hesitate as the ugly truth hits me between the eyes – metaphorically speaking.

'Exactly.'

'And when you were –'

'Exactly.'

'Flaming hell.'

Cam doesn't bother answering this time. Instead she casts one more venomous look into the box before picking up the lid and forcefully ramming it back onto the polystyrene container. Then, with considerably less care than she had shown earlier, she picks up the box and deposits it back onto the floor by the island bench. I can feel the laughter starting to bubble up within me and I'm not game to meet her eyes.

'Don't you dare.' Cam slides into her seat and polishes off her champagne with one gulp. 'Don't you bloody dare.'

'Damn, I wish you *had* got CJ up now. I would have loved to hear you explain this little number!'

'Shut up.'

'No wonder he was panting!'

'Shut up.'

'He must have thought all his Christmases had come at once!'

'What did I tell you about mentioning Christmas?' asks Cam grimly.

'Hmm. You realise you've gone from satisfying Santa to gratifying guinea pigs within the space of four days? That's not what I'd call an upward trend.'

'God, I *hate* that furry rat.'

'Well, I think he likes you – I could tell.' The laughter that has been bubbling away within me for the last few minutes finally spills over and, putting my arms on the table, I lower my face into them and let it out. My shoulders heave as the laughter wracks me, and tears drip onto the tabletop. After a few minutes, as my head starts to thump and my cheeks start to ache, I realise I can hear an echo. I roll my head to one side and see that Cam has folded up with laughter as well.

'A *leg*!' she splutters helplessly. 'We thought it was a leg!'

'Well, Ben can never say that you won't do anything for his animals!'

'Mummy?' asks CJ sleepily from the doorway.

'Damn.' Cam stands up and, wiping her face, gives me an apologetic look. 'Back in a minute.'

'No problem.' I watch Cam drape an arm around her daughter's shoulders and guide her out of the room and back towards her bed.

I groan and pat my cheeks to cool them down. Then I run my fingers through my hair and try to tuck it neatly behind my ears to return some semblance of normality. I decide that what I need is some champagne but, when I grab the bottle to refill my glass, I discover it's empty. An examination of Cam's fridge is rewarded by another bottle of champagne so I open it and fill both our glasses before putting it down on the table within easy reach.

Just as I'm sitting back down, I hear some thumping coming from the polystyrene box by the island bench. I move my chair a tad closer and, leaning down, lever the lid off and peer inside at the recipient of our earlier good graces. Well, he is certainly no longer looking at all unwell. In fact, he is scurrying around his container very happily, his multicoloured tufts positively bristling with vitality and his beady little eyes twinkling. Yes, he looks extremely pleased with life in general. As well he might. Suddenly he registers that he is being watched and freezes, mid-scurry, for a few seconds before darting over to the corner and under a pile of straw. Then he pushes his head back out and, with his whiskers twitching, looks up towards me.

And winks.

# SATURDAY

*Handy Household Hint No VIII:*

*If you've made your bed, for goodness sake don't lie in it — it will only mess it up.*

# SATURDAY

## 0839 hrs

Somebody is watching me. I knew the instant I woke by a certain prickling sensation between my shoulder blades. I slowly un-embed my face from the pillow, turn sideways and open my eyes. And am rewarded by a squinty view of a roomful of furniture and fittings I do not recognise. A white dressing-table covered with odds and ends of make-up. A matching tallboy. A corner desk with stacks of books and a daily planner poster above it. A wall-shelf holding a neat row of smiling porcelain dolls. A floor covered with clothing remnants and several odd socks.

It only takes me a few seconds to tune into reality and remember I stayed at Cam's place last night. And that I slept in Samantha's room. Then it automatically follows that I *am* probably being watched. And I even know by whom.

'Good morning, CJ.' I flop over in the bed so I can face her. 'And how are you this fine morning?'

'Okay,' answers CJ, who, dressed in denim overalls and a pink skivvy, is leaning in the doorway eating an apple.

'Is your mother up?'

'Yep.'

'Is she in the kitchen?'

'Yep.'

'Is she making coffee?'

'Dunno.'

'I see.' I sit up in the bed, yawn, and then stretch vigorously.

'Did you sleep ober last night?'

'Yep.'

'In Sam's room?'

'Yep.'

'Why d'ya do that?'

'Dunno.'

CJ rewards my chattiness with a narrow look before stalking away. I smile at her retreating back and then, after one more stretch, heave myself out of Sam's bed. I'm dressed in a spare pair of Cam's pyjamas that leave very little to the imagination on top, and about six inches of naked ankle flesh at the bottom.

I find my socks from last night and pull them onto my feet to stop them freezing. Because it's very cold in here this morning. I'd forgotten Cam doesn't have central heating. And it's also still pouring. Even though the curtains are closed, I can hear the rain drumming on the roof and splattering across the windows.

Once my socks are in place, I remake Samantha's bed quickly, making sure that it now features hospital corners, before running a comb through my hair and securing it into a tight, albeit messy, bun. Then I pad out of the bedroom and up the passage to the kitchen. From which a most heavenly aroma is issuing forth.

'Ah, coffee!'

'*There* you are.' Cam, fully dressed in jeans and a burnt-orange windcheater, hands me a steaming mug and waves me over to the table in the meals area. 'I sent CJ to tell you that coffee was on ages ago.'

'Really,' I reply dryly as I settle myself down and blow at the steam coming off my mug. 'It must have slipped her mind.'

'Well, while I was waiting for you, Bronte rang to say someone called Pat from tennis phoned to say today's been declared a wash-out already. So no tennis, and you've got a free day.'

'Great! I *really* wasn't looking forward to standing around and mopping courts between showers. It's the worst bit about tennis.'

'Good for you. So, anyway, how did you sleep?'

'Excellent.' I put my mug down and grin at her happily. 'And did I need it! I went out like a light and didn't wake once – I feel *great*.'

'Well, you know what my mother always says.' Cam turns to me and adopts her mother's slightly acidic tone: 'One hour of solid sleep is worth two hours broken – and don't you forget it.'

'No wonder I feel great!' I wrap my hands around my mug. 'Seeing as we went to bed around one-ish, then that's about seven and a half hours solid, which equates to fifteen hours of broken sleep. I'm a regular Rip Van Winkle.'

'I don't think it works that way.' Cam smiles as she pops some bread into the toaster. 'Toast?'

'Yes, please – I'm starving!' I pat my stomach to emphasise my words. 'And then I'll have a shower and get out of your hair before your mother's mystery meeting.'

'No rush.' Cam glances at the microwave clock. 'We've got an hour.'

While she busies herself making toast, I sip my coffee and watch the rain pelting down in the backyard. The dog is back outside, and back in the middle of the yard, watching me mournfully. As I turn away to avoid feeling guilty, CJ comes wandering into the kitchen and helps herself to the toast her mother has just finished buttering.

'Hey,' Cam protests, 'those were for Terry!'

'Sorry,' says CJ around a mouthful of my toast. 'Can I hab some too, then?'

'You might as well have those now,' replies her mother, putting some more bread into the toaster. 'But sit down at the table with them.'

CJ slides into a chair opposite me, and proceeds to nibble the edges of her toast wordlessly while she watches the dog watch her. Suddenly the front door is flung open and a few seconds later Benjamin, dressed relatively neatly in his St John's uniform, arrives in the kitchen out of breath. He looks around wildly.

'Hello, Ben!' says CJ brightly.

'Ben!' says his mother, holding my toast out on a plate. 'What're you doing here?'

'Where's my guinea pig?'

'What?' asks Cam, going red. 'Why?'

'Because I'm taking it to St John's, that's why.' Ben looks at his mother suspiciously. 'I left it near the front door – c'mon, they're waiting for me out there, what've you done with it?'

'*Nothing!*' exclaims Cam, as she avoids looking at me. 'I just moved it in here yesterday so it'd stay warm, that's all. It's next to the island bench.'

'Oh!' says CJ, putting her remaining slice of toast down. 'Can I see it?'

'Excellent!' Ben dives around the island bench and picks up the polystyrene box carefully. Then he places it on top of the island bench, takes the plate his mother is holding and puts it on top of the box. He grins at her.

'Haven't had any breakfast. S'okay, isn't it?'

'Yeah, sure.' Cam gives him a rather resigned smile and turns away to put another two slices of bread in the toaster. 'It was Terry's, that's all.'

'Cool.' Ben sends an apologetic grin in my direction and starts shovelling toast into his mouth.

'Hadn't you better hurry, Ben?' asks his mother as she looks back at the clock. 'Especially if they're waiting for you?'

'I can't go out there with this toast, can I?' says Ben reasonably. 'It'd be rude.'

'Ben, can I see your guinea pig?' asks CJ pleadingly. 'Please?'

'Ben doesn't have time,' replies his mother, 'now eat, CJ!'

'Okay.' Ben suddenly dives across to the table and, lifting up his astonished sister's arm, proceeds to suck on it noisily.

'Yaaah!' screams CJ, trying to fight her way loose. '*Mummy!*'

'Ben!' Cam stares at him, astounded. 'What on *earth* are you doing?'

'Just doing what I'm told,' replies Ben equably, letting go of his sister's arm. 'You said "eat CJ", so I was.'

'Yuck, yuck, *yuck*!' CJ wipes angrily at the soggy spot on her skivvy. 'I hab got bits of toast all ober me now! I *hate* you, Ben! You're rebolting!'

'Yes, you *are* rebolting,' says Cam, scowling at her son as she takes his now empty plate off the box and drops it in the sink with a clatter. 'Grab your box and go to St John's before I beat you up.'

'Okay, okay!' Ben laughs cheerfully as he leaves his sister and picks up the box carefully. 'But, CJ, be warned – I'll be back for lunch!'

'*Mummy!*'

Ben grins at her and then exits the kitchen. Shortly afterwards, the front door slams. I take a sip of my coffee and stretch as I watch CJ unhook her overalls clumsily and pull her skivvy over her head. Her mother ducks next door into the laundry and comes back out holding a lemon windcheater that has a lost-looking Paddington Bear on the front.

'Here, CJ.' Cam drops the windcheater on the table in front of her daughter before returning to the kitchen to wait for the toast to pop. 'You can put this on.'

'I *hate* Ben. And I wanted to hold the guinea pig,' grumbles CJ, dropping the skivvy on the floor. 'Guinea pigs *like* me.'

'They like your Mum too,' I observe mildly.

Cam sends me a grim look as she holds the butter knife up threateningly. 'That'll be quite enough from you, Terry.'

'I haven't even started.'

'That's what I'm worried about.'

At this point the front door can be heard opening once more, albeit not as loudly. A few seconds later, Samantha, dressed in a slinky black number and with a pair of black high-heeled shoes dangling from one hand, arrives in the kitchen. Her face still exhibits streaks of smudged make-up and her eyes look like those of a racoon after a wild night out. She smiles generally at us all and grabs a piece of buttered toast off the plate her mother is holding.

'Hi all! Just have to get dressed for work – see you in a tick.'

'Here, Terry – grab this toast before someone else does and I'll put some more on.' Cam dumps the plate containing the remaining slice of buttered toast in front of me and reloads the toaster as Samantha leaves the kitchen in the direction of her bedroom.

'Thanks.' I take a quick bite of my toast before it can be filched.

'I wanted some more too, Mummy,' complains CJ as she redoes her overall straps. 'I hab only got one bit left and I'm starbing.'

'Sure, CJ, just wait a sec,' Cam fills the kettle and puts it on the stove. 'More coffee, Terry?'

'Most definitely.' I drain my coffee and take the empty mug over to Cam before returning to polish off my toast. 'Oh, I love being waited on!'

'Enjoy it while it lasts.'

'Okay.'

'Yum! More toast!' Sam helps herself to one of the just popped slices and proceeds to butter it. She has performed miracles in minutes, with the black outfit now replaced by a burgundy uniform with the words HOT 'N HEAVENLY emblazoned across the front in gold lettering. Her face has been scrubbed free of make-up and her long dark hair has been pulled back into a smooth bun that is encased within a black hairnet.

'Do you need a lift to work?' asks Cam as she inserts more bread into the toaster and then butters the remaining slice of toast.

'I can take you,' I offer politely. 'I'll be leaving soon anyway.'

'No!' Cam says rather loudly, before continuing in a more normal tone. 'I mean, no thanks because –'

'Dad's taking me.' Sam takes her plate over to the table, where she sits down next to her sister. 'But thanks anyway.'

'D'you know Terry stayed in your room last night?' CJ puts her two cents into the conversation. 'In your bed?'

'I guessed by her clothes in there.' Sam grins at me. 'Hope you found it comfy. And, by the way, love your jammies. Totally sick.'

'Just what I've always wanted – sick nightwear,' I comment, 'although personally I'd prefer them a tad longer, and wider, and less revealing.'

'Can't say as I agree there.' Alex comes wandering into the kitchen and, after raising his eyebrows at me suggestively, sends such a warm smile in Cam's direction I turn green with envy.

'Hi!' she beams back, and her whole face lights up. 'I didn't even hear you come in!'

'That's because I am as sure-footed as a panther, and as stealthy as a tiger.' Alex proceeds to demonstrate by creeping across to CJ with his arms outstretched for capture. 'All the better to get *you*!'

'Yaa*ah*!' shrieks CJ with delight as he grabs her and, lifting her out of her chair, flips her neatly over his shoulder. Bits of toast fly everywhere but Cam doesn't say a word. She just stands in the kitchen, wiping her hands on a tea-towel and watching the proceedings with a beatific smile on her face.

'And now, come on, Sam,' says Alex, depositing CJ back onto her chair with half a piece of toast mashed against the front of her overalls, 'otherwise you'll be late.'

'Okay.' Sam dumps her plate on the island bench, grabs another piece of toast and kisses her mother quickly on the cheek. 'See you later, Mommie Dearest.'

'Likewise.' Alex grabs the remaining two slices, which Cam has just buttered, and grins at us all. 'Good to see you, Terry – *especially* like that.'

'Thanks.'

He turns to give Cam a meaningful look. 'I'll see *you* a little later. By the way, your answering machine is having a blinking attack down there. I bet you've forgotten to check it for days. Again.'

With one last grin all round, the sure-footed panther/tiger leaves with his stealthy offspring. The door closes behind them and Cam puts another two slices of bread in the toaster. The kitchen smells warm and friendly and delicious. I yawn and reflect that, although it might smell pretty good, life certainly runs at a more frenetic pace in this house. I don't think I could stand it.

'How many have you got coming tomorrow?' asks Cam as

she passes me over the hot buttered toast. 'Do you want me to bring anything?'

'Mummy!' says CJ, staring at my plate crossly. 'What about me?'

'Of course you're coming. Why wouldn't you be?'

'Coming where?'

'To the party.' Cam frowns at her daughter as she loads the toaster once more. 'Tomorrow. At Terry's.'

'*You're* habing a party?' CJ looks at me with disbelief. 'With *people*?'

'No, CJ. With animals,' I reply sarcastically, 'and your mum's bringing the guinea pig.'

'Can't *I* bring the guinea pig, Mum? Please?'

'No, CJ, you can't.' Cam looks at me narrowly. 'I suppose you think you're funny?'

'Yep,' I reply, taking a mouthful of toast. 'Yep, actually I do.'

'But I'll look after it! I will!'

'Enough!' Cam waves the butter knife in the air. 'CJ, *nobody* is bringing animals tomorrow. It's a party for *people* – to cele-brate Bronte's baby.'

'Then how come *you* get to bring the guinea pig?' asks CJ sulkily.

'*Aaaah!*' responds her mother, looking briefly towards the heavens for guidance. 'Terry was only joking! Here's your toast.' Cam slides another two slices of toast onto CJ's plate. 'And that's enough for now, so eat up.'

'Good!' CJ picks up a slice and waves it at her mother. 'Coz I asked for these *before* Terry got hers!'

'Don't be rude.'

'About tomorrow,' I say, 'don't bother bringing anything. There's only family coming.'

'Really? The way Diane was talking, I thought it was going to be biggish!'

'I think she might be exaggerating just a tad.' I take a bite of my toast and continue talking around it. 'Bronte promised me there'd only be a few.'

'Okay.' Cam looks at me doubtfully and then shrugs. 'Whatever.'

'A few what?' CJ asks her mother distrustfully.

'A few *people*, CJ.'

'But I suppose I'd better talk to her about it at some stage today.' I chew my toast thoughtfully. 'I mean, I don't even know what time the shindig is on!'

'Three o'clock,' replies Cam promptly, 'it says so on the invitation.'

'Invitation? *What* invitation?'

'Just an email one. I think Di sent them.'

'Really?' I'm still looking at her in surprise. 'Wow, she *is* organised.'

'She sure is.' Cam puts a fresh cup of coffee in front of me. 'Now, you'll have to excuse me for a second: I'm going to go and check those damn messages.'

I concentrate on devouring the remainder of my toast and then get up to deposit my empty plate in the sink. CJ, who has only taken one bite out of the middle of each slice of her toast, abandons her plate on the table and wanders off in the direction of the lounge-room. Shortly afterwards I can hear the manic sounds of a cartoon on the television. I can also hear a medley of voices issuing forth from the answering machine by the front door and it certainly appears Alex was right: there *were* an awful lot of messages there. I've just sat back down at the table and picked up my fresh cup of coffee when Cam comes back into the kitchen and looks at me with a frown.

'It just occurred to me that maybe we're on the wrong track about the meeting being about Mum and Richard.'

'Why?' I ask, looking at her with interest. 'What's happened now?'

'Well, there were two messages on my answering machine from her telling me not to forget about Saturday morning and to keep lunchtime free as well, one message from Diane telling me that Mum's rung her three times to remind her and what's the go about lunch, one message from Bloody Elizabeth asking me if I know what it's all about, and even a message from Harold telling me to be especially nice to my mother because she's a bit fragile at the moment.' Cam grabs her coffee and slides into the seat opposite me. 'So, what if she's sick or something? What if *that's* what it's all about?'

'What would her being sick have to do with Richard?'

'Nothing, you twit!' Cam looks at me with exasperation. 'That's what I'm saying! Get your mind away from that damn Richard for a minute or two, will you?'

'Hey, no need to get snappy!'

'Sorry.' Cam holds up a hand in apology. 'I'm sorry. It's just that I've got myself a bit worried now. I mean, what if she's sick? What if she's *really* sick?'

'I don't know,' I say slowly, thinking through this theory. 'I can't imagine your mother sick, can you?'

'No, but that doesn't mean she can't be. And I suppose she *is* getting on now, after all.'

We lapse into an uncomfortable silence while we drink our coffees. I can't really think of what to say because, now that I mull it over, there's a very good chance Cam may be right. Certainly an elderly mother calling an urgent meeting with her three children, minus their significant others, does not bode terribly well. Especially when the said elderly mother's husband makes a point of ringing to say his wife is 'a bit fragile' at the moment. Bugger.

'When did all those messages get left?'

'Must have been yesterday while I was at the zoo. Because, despite what Alex says, I *do* check my messages most days,' Cam says defensively, 'it's just I hardly ever use the hall phone, and that's where the answering machine is.'

'So, move it,' I reply pragmatically, knowing full well she'll never get round to it. 'Anyway, it doesn't matter now. And don't tie yourself up in knots about it, you'll soon find out what's going on.' I glance over at the clock on the microwave. 'Look! It's twenty to ten now!'

'Hell's bells!' Cam bounds out of her seat, gathers up the dirty plates and cups, and dumps them in the kitchen sink. Then she starts filling the sink while wiping down the benches haphazardly.

'Do you want a hand?' I get up and put my own half-empty cup in the sink. 'Or do you want me just to get out from under your feet?'

'Do you mind?' She turns to face me, looking apologetic. 'Go have a shower and I'll make a fresh batch of coffee.'

'No, don't bother.' I pick up some bits of toast off the floor and put them in a pile on the bench. 'I'll just have that shower and get dressed. Then I'll be out of here.'

'Coward,' says Cam with a half-smile.

'Guilty as charged.'

## SATURDAY

### 0957 hrs

Cam's shower is one of those old-fashioned ones that hang over the bath – but what it loses in terms of actual space, it makes up for with the size of the showerhead itself. Obviously invented back when saving water seemed as ridiculous as recycling rubbish, it gushes forth a heavy spray that encircles my body as *well* as all of its more extreme appendages. The water is hot, soothing and positively orgasmic. I sigh and tip my head, wiping my hair back with one hand. I could stay here forever.

But that's not a viable option. So, after a thorough wash, I reluctantly turn the shower off and step out of the bath, grabbing the small thin towel hanging on the rail. Now that the drumming of the shower has ceased, I realise I can hear voices outside the bathroom. And not just the voices of Cam and CJ, either. Which means that, unfortunately, the other participants in the mystery meeting have begun to arrive.

Well, there's no point hurrying if they are already here, so I start to dry myself off slowly with the mini towel and decide that some of my large, luxurious bath sheets would make an excellent Christmas present for Cam this year. I must remember to tell Santa next time I see him.

I dress myself in yesterday's jeans and red angora jumper before finding a blow-dryer in the depths of a cupboard and drying off my hair. While I'm doing this, I look around and reflect that perhaps a new bathroom would be a better option for Santa. This one is disgusting. The walls are covered with dark brown-flecked mosaic tiles that clash dreadfully with the chestnut vanity and pastel-pink bath. The only decent things are the imitation slate floor-tiles, which Cam had laid earlier in the year.

I finish with my hair and then continue my search, this time for moisturiser and a bit of foundation. I want to make myself look half decent as I've decided to visit my mother on the way home. Because if she sees that I'm concerned about Cam's mother perhaps being seriously ill, then surely she will feel compelled either to fill me in or tell me what the meeting's *really* about to ease my troubled mind. It's a win-win manoeuvre.

Eventually I find some rather sticky-looking bottles at the back of the cupboard with a yellowing neck brace, a stack of assorted shampoo samples and a singular cardboard-stiff grey sock. I locate what I need among the bottles and apply them to my face in the correct order. Finally, a brief examination in the mirror reminds me what I already know – it's all psychological.

I clean up the bathroom by mopping up water with the towel before wrapping it with my discarded pyjamas and opening the bathroom door. The first thing I see is CJ, who is leaning against the passage wall and staring at me steadily.

'You're not allowed down there.' She inclines her head towards the kitchen. 'Not anymore. No one is.'

'Why not?'

'Dunno. Just not.'

I don't bother continuing the conversation. Instead I walk down the passage towards the kitchen and turn the corner with a smile ready. Which is more than I can say for the four women sitting around the table in the meals area. Facing me, in the seat I occupied earlier, is Cam, who is busily pouring tea from a porcelain teapot and passing the cups around. In the short time I was in the bathroom, she has transformed the table into something out of *Home Beautiful*. Draped with an ecru lace tablecloth, it bears matching linen napkins, a crystal platter of shortbread biscuits, and an enormous vase of what look like fern fronds. Obviously she decided that the royal treatment was in order. In the chair next to her and half hidden by the greenery is Diane, who is playing with a napkin ring and looking like she would rather be anywhere else. Opposite her and with her back towards the kitchen is the youngest sister, Elizabeth, and next to her is Rose Riley her-self. Everybody either looks up or turns around and stares at me in surprise as I enter.

'Terry!' Cam pauses with the teapot poised over a rapidly filling cup.

'Cam!' I reply brightly.

'Camilla!' says her mother. 'Look at what you're doing, for goodness' sake!'

'Damn!' Cam straightens the teapot and puts it down on the table before mopping up the spillage with some of the napkins. 'Sorry.'

'Hello, everybody.' I smile at them all. 'I'll just dump these in the washing machine and then I'll be off.'

'Terry stayed here last night,' adds Cam, by way of an explanation. 'In Sam's room.'

'Hi, Terry,' says Diane, peering around the fern fronds as she fastidiously transfers the tea-soaked napkins onto a spare saucer and pushes it over to a corner of the table. 'I'm coming over to your place this afternoon, did Bronte tell you?'

'And you're not going to offer her a cup of tea?' queries Rose of her middle daughter, with her eyebrows raised. 'That's not very polite, darling.'

'It's all right, Mrs Riley,' I say quickly, 'I've already had coffee.'

'Nonsense.'

'Would you like a cup of tea?' asks Cam politely. 'Here, have my seat – I'll get one from the lounge-room.'

'Sit,' says Rose Riley with what she obviously thinks is a welcoming smile, 'and tell us all about that adorable great-grand-daughter of mine.'

'Um, okay.' I offload my armful of dirty washing onto the machine in the laundry and then return to the table to do as I'm told, casting Cam an apologetic grimace as I take her seat. 'Let me see . . . Um . . .'

'Now you're beginning to sound like Bronte.' Rose frowns at me. 'I don't understand why you youngsters hum and hah instead of speaking clearly and concisely.'

'Perhaps it's your imposing presence, Mum.' Diane sends me a sympathetic smile. 'You scare them into silence.'

'Absolute rubbish.'

'She's got a point, Mum,' adds Elizabeth, who I can't see at all behind the copious greenery. 'You probably don't realise it.'

'Hurrumph.' With that Rose dismisses this theory abruptly and, leaning over, assumes control of the teapot. 'Take that full cup away, Camilla, and fetch Terry a clean one, will you.'

'Fine.' Cam, who has just come back from the dining-room carrying a chair, deposits it next to the table and gingerly takes the brimming cup over to the sink. She empties it out, rinses it off, and brings it back over.

'I *did* say a clean one,' sniffs her mother, taking the cup and examining it closely. 'But never mind, this one will have to do.'

'Fine,' repeats Cam, sitting down at the end of the table on the chair she has just brought in. 'And I see you're doing the honours?'

'Well, I'm less likely to spill it,' replies her mother as she pours me a cup and passes it over. 'Now, is that everybody?'

Her daughters each nod while I add some milk and a spoonful of sugar to my cup. I feel rather awkward sitting here with them, almost like I've pushed my way into a secret society. Much as I want to know what's going on, I don't really want to be here. I decide to drink quickly and make my escape.

'Well, here we all are.' Rose looks around at Elizabeth, then Cam, then me, and frowns at the fern fronds obscuring her view of her eldest daughter. 'For goodness' sake, Camilla! Will you please move that ridiculous vase? I can't see Diane at all!'

'That's okay,' says Diane, 'I don't mind.'

'Well, I do! Camilla?'

'Yes, Mum. Just a minute, Mum.' Camilla reaches across and, with Diane's help, pushes the vase over to the end of the table under the window. 'Is that better?'

'Much, thank you,' nods Rose approvingly, 'and now I suppose I'd better get started and tell you all why I've asked you here today.'

'No!' I splutter, holding out my hand to stop her. 'Wait till I go, Mrs Riley!'

'Nonsense.'

'But I shouldn't be here!'

'What difference does it make, dear?' She looks at me quizzically. 'After all, I'm sure Camilla would be on the phone to fill you in as soon as I leave. You might as well hear it from the horse's mouth, so to speak.'

'I'm sure she wouldn't.'

'Of course I wouldn't!'

'Nonsense. Besides, the sooner you know, the sooner you will stop harassing your poor mother.'

I try to look taken aback at this scurrilous accusation, but am actually at a bit of a loss as to how to counter it, given that I *had* been planning to head straight to my mother's house after I left here. Well, that's certainly off the agenda now.

'So, that's settled.' Rose takes a sip of tea and then fiddles with the cup handle, not looking at any of us. 'Now, this isn't easy . . .' she sighs and then, obviously making an effort, straightens up in her chair. 'But it has to be done, so here it is. Girls, I've got something very difficult to say.'

'Is it Peter Piper picked a pickled pepper?' asks CJ brightly, sticking her head around the kitchen door, 'coz we learned that at school. Do you want me to say it again?'

'No!' yells her mother, 'I thought I told you you were to stay away till I told you?'

'How come *she's* here then?' CJ points at me, and then puts her hands on her hips. 'That's not fair!'

'Christine Jain!' Rose turns around slowly in her chair and fastens her grand-daughter with a glittering eye, 'you will go down to your bedroom and you will play there until you are called. Sometimes adults need to talk about things that are just for adults and this is one of those times. Is – that – understood?'

'But –'

'And I'll give you two dollars,' adds Diane.

'Cool beans,' CJ nods agreement to this arrangement and then disappears down the passage. As soon as her footsteps have receded, Rose turns back around and faces us once more.

'All right then. As I was saying before I was interrupted, this is not an easy thing at all to tell you girls. And it's something I probably should have told you quite some time ago.'

'You're dying!' blurts Cam, visibly distressed.

'You are?' Diane looks at her mother in shock. 'My god! Mum – *no!*'

'You can't be!' Elizabeth shakes her head, then closes her eyes and puts her hands up to cover her ears. 'No! No! *No!* I'm not listening to this!'

'STOP!' Rose stands up and waves her arms like Moses parting the Red Sea, 'I AM NOT DYING!'

'What?'

'Really?'

'You are all ridiculous!' says Rose crossly, frowning at each of her daughters in turn. 'Elizabeth, uncover your ears. Camilla, what on earth possessed you to say that I was dying?'

'So you're not?' Cam looks at her mother wide-eyed.

'Of course not! I only just got married!'

'You idiot!' says Diane to Cam angrily, 'you scared the life out of me there!'

'Then you're sick?' asks Cam, ignoring her sister.

'No! I'm as healthy as a horse and I plan to stay that way for quite some time.' Rose, still looking very annoyed, reaches across and physically removes her youngest daughter's hands from over her ears. 'Elizabeth! I am NOT dying!'

'Oh! Thank *god*!' Elizabeth opens her eyes and sags with relief. 'But then why'd Cam say you were?'

'Because she's a fool.'

'Well, pardon me for being concerned,' Cam says sarcastically, folding her arms across her chest and glaring at her mother. 'I'll just sit here and shut up, shall I?'

'Perhaps that's best,' says Rose, nodding, 'and I shall tell you why I asked to see you all before anybody else comes up with any wild theories.'

'Excellent,' Diane says.

'Good,' Elizabeth says.

'Um,' I say, unwilling to add too much to the family dynamics.

Everybody sits in silence while we wait for Rose to continue. But now the moment has actually arrived, she seems reluctant to proceed. Instead she sighs and then stares either at the fern fronds or the view out of the window, it's difficult to know which. The rest of us take advantage of her distraction to share a variety of facial contortions, such as grimaces and raised eyebrows. After a few moments of this, Rose turns back towards us and picks up her cup of tea to have a sip. I notice, with a jolt, that her hands are trembling slightly.

'Mum?' asks Diane gently, 'are you all right?'

'Yes, of course.' Rose takes a deep breath in and then lets it out in a rush. 'All right. Firstly, I'd just like you all to remember that we are talking about very different times here. In my day, things were done differently, *women* were treated differently. And we didn't have quite the same choices you girls have now. Not that I'm using that as an excuse, I'm just saying that's how things were. Well, anyway – you know I have, of course, been married before.'

'Naturally,' answers Diane, on behalf of her sisters, 'because of our father, for starters.'

'I meant *before* your father. My two earlier marriages. What I want to talk to you about now is my second marriage. And don't forget that although I was a widow, I was still only a girl. Twenty-one when I met him and we married within the year. He wasn't much older than me and everything was quite . . . quite lovely . . .' Rose pauses and a tiny smile flickers across her face and then vanishes as she continues. 'We were together for three years before he was sent to Korea. The war was on, you see, but the stupid thing was that it was almost over when he went. He got there in April, was killed in June and it was all over by July.'

'Oh, Mum.' Diane reaches across and puts her hand on her mother's as Rose lapses into silence. 'How terrible for you.'

'Wasn't his name Dick?' Cam frowns, obviously trying to remember details.

'Certainly not. It was Jim – Jim Berry. And it's a long time ago now.' Rose moves her hand away from Diane's and straightens her back. 'In fact, I wouldn't even be telling you all this if it weren't for something that happened this week. But I'll get to that in a minute. So, there I was, in our flat in the city with a telegram telling me I'd just been widowed again.'

'Oh, Mum.'

'Yes.' Rose pauses and looks up at her three daughters. 'On the very same day that I found out I was pregnant.'

'What!'

'Pregnant!'

'Exactly,' says Rose grimly. 'I don't mind telling you that I didn't know what to do. I had no money. The family business had just gone under and my parents were doing it tough with two daughters still at home to feed. They were sympathetic but they made it quite clear I was on my own.'

'Mum, that's awful!'

'What'd you do?'

'I wrote to Jim's parents. They lived in Tasmania, in a little country town called Strahan. I told them about my situation and they took me in. They owned a small dairy down there and Jim's two brothers were still at home, but they made room for me and made me welcome. I worked in the dairy doing the books to help pay my way but they never forced me to – it was my choice. They were really good people. And on the first of January, on New Year's Day, the baby was born.'

'I don't believe this.' Cam looks at Diane for back-up. 'Do *you* believe this?'

'So what was it?' Diane is totally focused on her mother. 'A boy or a girl?'

'A little boy. Lovely little thing – as bright as a button. Looked just like his dad. And the parents were as pleased as punch when I named him after Jimmy. They made it clear I was welcome to stay for as long as I liked, forever if I wanted. But, girls, oh – I *hated* it there. They were hoping I would marry one of the other boys because they saw that as the perfect solution. But I didn't – at all. You see, they were all lovely people but they were *different* from the people I had always known. More staid, more settled. I was still only in my mid-twenties and I felt, well, *stifled* by the country.' Rose shakes her head and grimaces at the memory. 'Funny when you think that I ended up on a farm with your father anyway.'

'But you were older then,' says Diane supportively.

'Not much older,' continues her mother with a shake of her head, 'but I wasn't to know that at the time. All I knew was that if I stayed there I would . . . die. So I left. I came back to

Melbourne, moved into a flat with another girl and even got my old job back. As a machinist.'

'But who looked after the baby while you were at work?' asks Elizabeth with a puzzled frown. 'And what happened to him? Where is he?'

'You left him there,' Cam says slowly, looking at her mother. 'You left him in Strahan.'

'Yes, I did.'

'Mum!' exclaims Diane, aghast. 'You *didn't*!'

'I did. They knew I was unhappy so they offered to look after him while I got myself settled back here. You see, it was only supposed to be temporary – or maybe they realised how hard I would find it to get into a position where I *could* take him. I don't know. Anyway, *I* thought I could do it. But I couldn't. Don't forget these were the days before child-care, and crèches, and government assistance. Oh, I missed him *so* much . . .' Rose pauses again and gazes for a moment at the far wall between Cam and Diane. Then she gives herself a little shake and continues: 'And I put some money aside but it was never enough. So they wrote and told me how he was going, and what he was doing. And I even went back once, but that was worse . . .'

'Why?' asks Elizabeth, leaning forwards as her mother trails off.

Rose takes a sip of tea and then puts her cup down, fastidiously straightening it in the saucer. 'It was his first birthday and I remember he was already walking. Into everything, he was. And he was so at home there. He was even calling Jim's mother "Mummy" – he didn't know me at all.'

'Oh, Mum,' says Diane, horrified, 'how awful!'

'Yes it was,' continues Rose matter-of-factly. 'It *was* awful. So I never went back again. And, after a while, the letters petered out. My fault as well as theirs. I suppose they thought the longer I wasn't in touch, the more chance they had of keeping him. As for me, there is no excuse. I was young, and selfish, and stupid. And I decided that if I couldn't have him, it was easier not knowing him. Eventually I met your father and married him. He was a good man, and I have no doubt he would have taken the boy in. But *I* decided that it was too late, and he was better off staying where he was. So I never even told your father.'

'This is unbelievable,' Elizabeth says, shaking her head. 'We have a *brother*?'

'How old would he be now?' asks Diane pragmatically. 'And has he ever got in contact with you? Have you ever met him?'

'And where does he live?' Elizabeth looks at her mother curiously. 'Does he know about us?'

'One thing at a time.' Rose holds up her hand. 'Let me finish. When I married your father and decided against telling him, I also decided against telling Jim's parents. Right or wrong, I made a clean break. That doesn't mean I never thought about the boy, or wondered what he was doing. But, no, I never contacted them again. As for your questions, well – he is forty-six now, he still lives in Tasmania, he knows about you three and, yes, I've met him.'

'When?'

'What does he look like?'

'*I* know,' says Cam slowly, glancing at me. 'And you know too, don't you?'

'Yes, I think I do,' I reply, looking at Rose as everything continues to tumble into place. 'It's Richard, isn't it?'

'Yes – it's Richard.' She smiles thinly at both of us. 'Richard James Berry, named after his father. Except that everyone called his father Jimmy.'

'*Oh!* That's the Richard from your lunch, isn't it?' Diane says excitedly as she turns to Cam. 'The one that you said made Mum go all odd.'

'How come everybody knows who he is except me?' wails Elizabeth.

'So I had lunch with him yesterday,' Rose continues, looking relieved the worst is over, 'and he seems perfectly pleasant. In fact, I do believe they did a *very* good job. He's polite, charming, very well brought up. Ask me what he does for a living. Go on – ask me.'

'What does he do for a living?' asks Elizabeth obediently, before suddenly screwing up her face. 'Eech! He doesn't still do . . . milk, does he?'

'No.' Rose dismisses the milk industry with a wave of her hand. 'Of course not.'

'Then what?' I finally find my voice because I really want to know, and I wouldn't have cared if it *was* milk. I quite like milk myself.

'He is a doctor,' announces Rose, sitting up straighter as she beams at us and waits for the applause. 'A doctor of philosophy, that is. A university lecturer.'

'Christ,' mutters Cam, 'his lectures must go for hours. The man can't string three words together.'

'But when did *you* speak to him? How come you've met him?' Elizabeth stares at Cam. 'And why wasn't *I* invited?'

'Pfft,' replies Cam shortly.

'Are we going to see him?' asks Diane.

'Yes, you are,' answers her mother. 'For lunch – today.'

'Lunch!' says Diane.

'Today!' says Cam.

'Wow,' says Elizabeth, 'a *brother*!'

'But how did he know Joanne?' I ask Rose, thinking ahead. 'I mean, they told us they met at some airport lounge. Surely that's a bit, well, coincidental, isn't it?'

'Who's Joanne?' asks Elizabeth with a frown. 'Do I know her? And why does everyone know everything except me?'

'I have to admit,' replies Rose thoughtfully, looking at me, 'that's the strange part.'

'I'll say,' grumbles Elizabeth crossly.

'That?' says Cam, looking at her mother with disbelief, '*that's* the strange part? You hit us with the news we have a brother we've never met, that you had a baby forty-six years ago who you haven't seen since – and yet the bit about the airport, *that's* the strange part?'

'There's absolutely no need to get snippy,' Cam's mother looks at her disapprovingly. 'I'm only trying to be honest, that's all.'

'About time,' mutters Cam.

'Don't mumble, Camilla. If you have something to say, just say it.' Rose stares challengingly at her daughter for a few moments and then, when no response is forthcoming, turns away and continues: '*As* I was saying, it was a rather odd thing. It's true that they met at an airport lounge. In Singapore, I believe. He was on his way back from London and had a four-hour stopover and it seems Joanne heard his Australian accent and introduced herself. Apparently, she had been at some type of retreat where they weren't allowed to speak and so she was making up for lost time. Funny, she's never very chatty when I see her. Never mind. Well, by the time the plane was ready she had been telling him all about her life to date and had happened to mention you, Camilla – something about working with you at the library. Anyway, he recognised the name so he swapped his business class seat for the seat next to her. She was in economy.'

'Oh,' comments Elizabeth, '*that* was silly.'

'Yes, well, on the way to Melbourne he asked her about us and then explained why.' Rose takes another sip of tea and pulls a face at its coolness before pushing her cup away. 'So she came up with the idea of him staying a few days and meeting us all. Although I believe he was not going to tell us who he was. But I recognised him . . . he looks just like his father, you see.'

'God!' says Diane. 'That must have been a shock, Mum!'

'Yes,' replies Rose slowly, 'it was.'

'You mean his *father* looked like that?' says Cam incredulously. 'Tall and beanpoley?'

'Yes,' replies Rose, 'he certainly did.'

'And you *fell* for him?'

'But hang on – why didn't he want us to know?' Elizabeth finds her voice again. 'I mean, what's wrong with us?'

'And how did he recognise Cam's name?' Diane looks at her mother with a frown. 'How did he know who *she* was?'

'Good question!' Cam looks towards their mother for illumination.

'Well, that's easy. Apparently his daughter – he has a teenage daughter named Eve – was interested in family history a few years ago so he helped her look it all up and make a genealogy chart. So he was well aware of who we all were and even where we all were.'

'But he wasn't ever going to look us *up*?'

'I believe not.' Rose looks at her spot on the wall again. 'You see, he feels he had a good childhood – a *great* one, he said – and didn't really feel the need to, well, complicate his life. He said there were no *gaps* that he felt needed filling. And that probably would have been the way it stayed if he hadn't run into Joanne. He said she piqued his interest and suddenly he got curious.'

'So is he upset that we know now?'

'I don't think so. He didn't say anything like that and he was surprisingly honest about how he felt.' Rose smiles with obvious pride. 'A very *together* young man. Lovely manners too. And I do believe he's looking forward to this lunch with the three of you.'

'But I'd still like to know how come almost everybody has met him except me,' complains Elizabeth, taking a shortbread biscuit and waving it at Cam. 'That means you all get a head start with him.'

'I think I'm in shock.' Diane starts collecting the teacups together and stacking them at the end of the table. 'I don't know what to say.'

'C'n I come in now?' CJ's blonde head pokes around the corner of the kitchen doorway. 'Are you all finished with talking?'

I don't know about the rest of them, but I certainly am. In fact, I've been incapable of speech for quite some time now. Because there are too many ramifications here for me to get my head around, and the atmosphere in Cam's meals area at the moment is not conducive to anything resembling clear thinking. Rose looks like a balloon that has been suddenly deflated, all pinched and drained and sapped of strength. Nevertheless, while not exactly defensive, she is obviously still on her guard and unwilling to relinquish control of the situation. Diane, on the other hand, has given up on the conversation entirely, electing instead to collect the crockery and wash it. Elizabeth is sulkily shredding fern fronds and Cam is just looking bitter.

While CJ, taking the lack of response as an affirmative, runs across to the table and clambers up onto her grandmother's lap, I begin to plan my escape. I don't want to be here anymore. In fact, I seem to remember that I didn't want to be here in the beginning. I run my fingers through my hair, flop it back and tuck it behind my ears. So Richard is Rose Riley's son. So Richard is my best friend's brother. So Richard is forty-six years old. So Richard is meeting them all for lunch today.

And so Richard and Joanne probably aren't an item.

# SATURDAY

## 1213 hrs

I let myself into my house slowly, expecting to hear either the television at full volume, the stereo blaring, or the baby exercising her lungs. Instead there's just the sort of eerie silence I was quite fond of until my daughter and her offspring moved in two days ago. As I shut the door behind me, I allow myself a small frisson of hope that said daughter and offspring might not be currently in residence. I love them both fiercely, but at the moment I'd love some peace and quiet even more. I put my keys down on the foyer table, wander into the lounge-room and immediately rethink the fierce love bit as, my eyes widening, I survey the damage.

And damage there is aplenty. In fact, if this were a gung-ho crime show, I would be able to say the lounge-room betrays definite evidence of a struggle. A struggle between chaos and order, that is – with chaos the obvious victor. All the couch cushions have been piled in a heap in front of the television set with my new rug draped over the lot of them. The coffee table is heaped with empty pizza boxes, dirty glasses and scrunched-up chip packets, there is a bunny-rug spread across the carpet in the corner with enough toys and rattles to stock a small toy-shop, and an open Billabong backpack on the armchair dangles entrails of jumpers and jeans over the armrest and onto the floor. There is even a lone toothbrush sitting on top of the stereo. And there's a god-awful stain on the carpet.

I take all of this in slowly as I gaze from one side of the room to the other in amazement. Then I wander, slightly stunned, into the kitchen area. And immediately realise this is obviously where the largest battle was fought – and chaos, once again, reigned supreme. The sink is full and what couldn't fit in there has been piled haphazardly onto the bench-tops. There's a plastic bag holding what I suspect might be a dirty nappy sitting on top of the island bench, along with an opened box of cereal, an opened tub of fried rice, an opened jar of Vegemite and a singular sock. An assortment of discarded baby clothing is scattered across the floor by the table, while on the table itself are several neatly lined-up empty Coke bottles and one half-full baby bottle – almost as if someone was planning an impromptu game of skittles. There's also a note.

> *Hi, Mil! Bronte had a really bad night with the baby so I've taken her out to cheer her up. Don't worry about the mess – she'll clean it up as soon as we get back.*
>
> *Cheers, Nick*

I put the kettle on automatically, and then decide I don't want a hot drink after all. I had enough coffee and tea at Cam's place to last me for quite some time. As soon as I think of Cam's place, by automatic association my mind works its way across to the scene with her mother – so I shut it down. I'm not ready to go there.

What I *really* feel like is a drink but it's a tad early for that, so I turn my back on the kitchen and walk carefully through the lounge-room with my eyes closed, only opening them when I feel the bottom step of the spiral staircase with my left foot. I go upstairs expecting a similar chaos vs order sort of thing to be happening up here – but it's surprisingly neat. Bronte's bed is even made and the only thing remotely resembling a mess is the stack of CD computer games that have been left next to the computer in the study. I put these away before sitting down at the computer and staring at the screen.

For now at least, I'll pile the state of my lounge-room and kitchen with the other things I don't want to think about just yet. Instead I'll concentrate on extricating the email Diane sent a few days ago so I've got an idea of the number of guests tomorrow. Then I'll do a shopping list and work out what I need in terms of fodder. And, of course, it's vitally important that whatever I get takes only a few minutes to prepare – but looks like it's taken hours.

I lean forwards, pick up a stray computer game disc that has slid half under the monitor, and place it neatly on the side of the desk. Then I pause, staring at the disc as it suddenly hits me that Bronte has been playing games on this computer quite happily ever since she arrived home. Ergo she *must* know the password.

I dial her mobile phone number on the study phone and listen to it ring.

'Hello! Hello!'

'Bronte, it's Mum.'

'Hey, Mum! Like, where are you?'

'At home.'

'Oh, um . . .' Bronte puts her hand over the phone and whispers quite audibly to someone else: 'She's home! Shit – I *told* you we should have cleaned up first!'

'Bronte?'

'Mum, hang on, will you?' Bronte forgets to put her hand over the phone again so I hear Nick quite clearly as he advises her to pretend the signal's breaking up. They proceed to have a heated, and perfectly distinct, discussion concerning the advisability of this slight fabrication.

'*Bronte!*'

'I'm here! And look, sorry about the mess – we'll clean it up as soon as we get home, I promise. It's just that Sherry was so dreadful last night that Nick said we needed a break – so we're at the Healesville Sanctuary! Like, it's *so* cool – I haven't been here for years!'

'Great,' I reply, 'glad you're enjoying yourselves.'

'Oh, we *are*!'

'Well, we'll talk when you get home, okay? What I really want is the password for the computer – do you know it?'

'Of course!'

'Well?'

'It's "Diamond" – you know, like our surname.'

'I *know* our surname, Bronte,' I snap irritably, 'but that's the *username*, not the password.'

'No, no – it's the password as well! Truly! Hey, you're break-ing up, Mum! Lots of static – zzzz, zzzz. Can't hear you – ring you later. Bye!'

I hang up the phone and go back to staring at the com-puter. Surely it couldn't be? With not much to lose either way, I switch the computer on and wait till the screen flashes its mocking little message at me:

Username?  Diamond_____

Password?  _____

Leaning forwards, I type in the word 'Diamond' and wait pessimistically for the reject message. But it doesn't come. Instead, the screen flashes a rainbow of colours, plays some corny music, and then covers itself with an array of neat, square icons. I'm in! Feeling a bit like a successful computer hacker, I click on the inbox icon and scroll through the unread emails, watching their little envelope icons flip open – all thirty-three of them, one after another – plink, plink, plink.

There are chatty emails from my brother, Thomas; infantile emails from my niece, Bonnie; chain-mail emails from friends who obviously dislike me; semi-pornographic emails from friends who obviously do; joke emails passed on from acquaintances; and annoying spam from people I don't even know. I scroll down through the electronic debris until I find the email sent from Diane the day before yesterday. The subject line reads: 'Proposed guest list for Sunday shindig.' I double-click to open it and then read:

---

Hi Terry,
Have attached a word.doc with the proposed guest list for Nick & Bronte's naming thing on Sunday. I am going to start emailing invitations and/or ringing around tomorrow so pls get back to me <u>quickly</u> with any changes or additions. If I don't hear from you I shall assume that everything is fine – although we did end up with a few more than I expected. So let me know quickly.
Thanks, Diane

---

I tap my fingers absentmindedly on the mouse while I look at this email. What does she mean about 'a few more than expected'? Family is family – and it hasn't grown overnight, for god's sake. Except, of course, for Richard. But I'm not going there.

With more than a sliver of apprehension, I double-click on the attachment and wait till the Word document flashes up on the screen. But it's blank. Well, *that* certainly suits me – no guests at all. Perfect.

Unfortunately, it's also unlikely. So I tap my fingers on the mouse again for a few minutes while I try to work out what's happened to the list. Then, on a hunch, I close down the attachment, the email, and the inbox before opening Microsoft Word and voila! There's a document titled 'Guest List'. I don't know how it got here, and I don't much care. I decided long ago that the workings of computers will always be beyond me. I double-click on the document and, a few seconds later, my screen fills with the guest list for the Sunday shindig. And I let my breath out with a whoosh of relief after I quickly count the names and only get to twenty-six. Well, that's not too bad – I *expected* almost that many. So I read through the list a bit more slowly and suddenly realise there are some key players missing – like my mother, Cam, two of Nick's brothers, and . . . me.

I cup my hand over the mouse and scroll down, hoping to see at least *my* name creep onto the screen. But it doesn't. Instead, another ten names adhere themselves to the bottom of the list and show no signs of moving. So I continue scrolling. And scrolling. While name after name after name makes the quantum leap from obscurity to invitee. And my mouth goes through the gamut of slightly ajar, to falling fully open, to unattractively agape.

But still the list shows no sign of ending so, with a sinking feeling, I glance towards the little dubrick at the side of the screen that indicates how far down a document you are. And my sinking feeling gets the bends when I realise it's only sitting at about the two-third mark.

There must be over one hundred names here. Over one hundred people crammed into my unit. My pristine, beautiful unit. With people jam-packed in my kitchen, people cheek to jowl in my lounge-room, people squished in my courtyard, people popping out of the windows. Because there simply isn't the room for that number of people here. Well, at least I no longer care whether my name is there or not. In fact, I rather hope it isn't.

# SATURDAY

There is a loud knocking on the door just as I finish vacuuming the carpet in the lounge-room. Then again, because I *had* been vacuuming the carpet in the lounge-room, there's probably been a loud knocking for quite some time. I place my new rug carefully over the offending stain once more and then jog over to the front door to fling it open. Diane, holding what appears to be the leaning tower of Tupperware, beams up at me.

'I come bearing gifts!' she declares merrily.

'You'd need to,' I reply, less than merrily, 'with the number of people you've organised to come here tomorrow.'

'What do you mean?'

'Just what I said.' I wave her through the doorway and take the top three levels of the tower before it topples. 'I mean, Diane, how on earth am I going to fit all those people in here?'

'But why didn't you email me back if you weren't happy?'

'Because I couldn't, that's why,' I reply shortly, shutting the door behind her.

'And besides, who on that list could I *not* invite?' Diane follows me into the kitchen. 'They're mostly family, after all.'

'That's a bloody big family you've got.'

'Not really.' Diane puts her load down on the table and frowns at me. 'No bigger than most, anyway.'

'Well, my question still remains – where am I going to put them all?'

'Terry . . .' Diane pauses as she looks at me thoughtfully. 'How many were on the list you read?'

'You ought to know.'

'Tell me anyway.'

'Well, I gave up at around the one hundred mark, put it that way.'

'One hundred!' Diane falls backwards onto a chair and looks at me aghast. 'One *hundred*! Did you say one hundred?'

'At least.'

'Oh my lord!'

'Hang on.' I sit down opposite her. 'Why're you so surprised? *You* sent the list!'

'No, no, *no*. I sent a list of exactly forty-three that Bronte and I worked out in the hospital. I mean, I was a bit stunned we got to forty-three but there wasn't really anyone we *couldn't* invite. So I sent it off to you and told Bronte the other day to go over it and add anyone she thought of later on . . .' Diane trails off as we both stare at each other and are simultaneously enlightened.

'Bronte!'

'How *could* she!'

'I'm going to kill her.'

'See, I told her I'd invite the ones we had agreed on and it was up to her to follow up on any you or she added,' Diane continues, 'so she's obviously just used the Word document I sent. And followed up. Oh, my lord! One hundred people!'

'I have a feeling that whatever those Tupperware containers are holding isn't going to be enough.'

'I have a feeling you're right.'

We sit there in silence, both staring at the Tupperware tower as if waiting for it to re-enact the miracle of the loaves and fishes. I desperately want to ask her how their lunch went today, but I also desperately don't want to go there. With over one hundred people turning up on my doorstep tomorrow, I've got more than enough on my plate. Thinking of plates reminds me of the problem of feeding all these guests. And feeding all these guests reminds me of eating, which reminds me of lunch on Tuesday. Which reminds me of Richard. I sigh, chew my lip thoughtfully and decide to go there anyway.

'How was your lunch?'

'Lunch?' Diane is still looking at her Tupperware with a frown. 'Oh, lunch! Of course! Well, it was interesting, to say the least.'

'In what way?' I ask, trying to sound nonchalant.

'Well, my mother for starters. It was really sort of *sad* watching her watching him. She was all proud and beaming, but she's really done nothing to be proud of, has she?'

'I don't know,' I reply slowly. 'Perhaps seeing he has turned out so well helps her feel vindicated. Like she made the right decision after all.'

'Oh.' Diane looks at me with a frown. 'I hadn't thought of it that way.'

'But did you *like* him?'

'Yes, actually I did.' Diane sounds taken aback. 'I really did. But he's shy, isn't he? And thin, *really* thin.'

'A bit,' I say stiffly. 'And what about everyone else? Did they like him?'

'They certainly seemed to. I know David did, and so did Michael – the other boys were all out. But you know David – he'll get anyone to relax.'

'What about Cam?'

'I *think* she liked him too, but she was a bit quiet about it all so it was hard to tell. And I haven't had a chance to talk to her since, what with all this –' Diane waves towards the Tupperware '– but I don't think we'll be seeing him again anyway, so it probably doesn't matter.'

'Why not?' I squeak, my heart skipping a beat.

'Well, because it wasn't mentioned. In fact, it was like he was avoiding it.' Diane frowns at me. 'Hey, are you all right?'

'Oh yes.' I try to sound airy. 'Just a tad worried about tomorrow, that's all.'

'Don't blame you.' She looks back at her Tupperware and sighs. 'Over one hundred people. Wow.'

'Yes. Wow.'

We sit in silence once more while I decide how to broach the Richard subject again. There's probably not all that much else I'll discover about the lunch, but I just like hearing his name. I'm still working out a good approach when I register the fumbling sounds of a key in the front door. Diane and I look at each other with narrowed eyes and speak in unison.

'Bronte!'

'Someone say my name?' Bronte bounces into the kitchen and smiles at us happily. 'And, Mum, I see you've cleaned up – thanks so much. You didn't have to, you know.'

'Bronte?' Diane looks at her future daughter-in-law with carefully controlled annoyance. 'Exactly how *many* names did you add to my list?'

'Oh . . .' Bronte's smile dies a quick death and she chews her lip nervously. 'The list.'

'That was my fault, Mum.' Nick comes in with the baby capsule dangling from one hand. 'Bronte was starting to get worried about the number of people so I went, "What the hell, you only have a baby once, don't you?"'

'That's not strictly true, Nick,' I comment pedantically. 'Look at your mother.'

'Like, no *way*!' says Bronte with feeling. 'One's enough.'

'Anyway, you *know* what I mean.' Nick grins at me disarmingly. 'So, what's the problem? It's only a few extra. You guys don't mind, do you?'

'Don't mind?' I manage to squeak. 'Don't *mind*?'

'What Terry's trying to say,' chimes in Diane, in a considerably softer tone than she used with my daughter, 'is that perhaps one hundred-odd people might be a bit of a squeeze here.'

'*Very* odd people,' I mutter crossly, 'judging by some of the names.'

'Are numbers all you're worried about?' Nick laughs cheerfully. 'Because if *that's* the problem, don't stress. Most of our friends'll be hanging around outside, anyway.'

'And what are you going to feed all these people?' continues his mother. 'Because one hundred people eat an awful lot of food, you know.'

'Again – no problemo.' Nick passes the capsule to a rather silent Bronte and wags his finger at us. 'Stay right there! Wait till you see what we've bought!'

We watch him exit the room and then hear the front door being opened again. Bronte puts the capsule down carefully beside my chair and I'm rewarded by a glimpse of Sherry, sleeping like the angel she is. Diane leans over and musters a smile as she looks at the baby too.

'Sorry, Mum,' mutters Bronte, looking at me. 'The truth is that, like, we just got a bit carried away.'

'I noticed.'

'But Nick's right – wait till you see what we've bought!'

'Okay.' I bend over the capsule and touch the top of Sherry's little bald head. I can see the fontanelle beating rhythmically against the top of her scalp. How vulnerable. How precious.

'Here we go!' Nick bounds back into the room carrying three bags of groceries, which he dumps on the ground next to Bronte. They both squat and start to pull out the contents.

'Look!' Bronte waves a double packet of potato chips in the air. 'See?'

'And crackers!' Nick flourishes a packet of them at us and

then dives into the bag for some more. 'And party pies! And pizza!'

'Oh my god,' says his mother, leaning over and pulling the third bag open. '*One* packet of pretzels! *One* packet of Cheezels! *Chewing gum!* I don't believe this!'

'Told you so.' Nick gives us a smug, even supercilious look. 'Nothing to worry about! It's *all* taken care of.'

## SATURDAY

### 1635 hrs

'Hey, Mum, it's me! No, Terry. Yes. Look, you know your big white china set – the one with all the place settings and the matching teapots and serving plates and all? Could you please get it down and Nick'll be there later to pick it up. And also your embroidered white tablecloths. And some of those big crystal vases. We need to borrow them for tomorrow. What *else* could you bring? Well, let me see – how about some of those homemade sausage rolls you make, and a platter of those chilli mini-shashliks, and what about some of those little potato pancakes? Are you writing all this down?'

## SATURDAY

### 1648 hrs

'Hi, this is your loving wife. Well, I *will* be – if you do the following things for me. First I want you to get those white chairs from the shed. You know, the ones we bought for Evan's eighteenth. Yes, all of them. And the two white folding tables. And the super-big Esky. I want you to load them all in the car and bring them over here. No! Don't bring the girls! Get Chris or Evan to look after them. Now, on the way I want you to stop at that big grog shop on Maroondah Highway. Yes, I thought you'd know the one. And I want you to hire two boxes of multi-purpose glasses. Then I want you to stop at the shops and get me some balloons, and streamers, and serviettes. *I* don't care if you can't fit it all in! Do two trips, for goodness' sake!'

## SATURDAY

### 1659 hrs

'Hello, Dennis. Sorry, was I interrupting something? Oh, it sounded like it. Anyway, I'll only keep you a minute. I just had this awful feeling I forgot to tell you that you were providing the drinks for this do of Bronte's tomorrow. I *did* forget? Bugger – so sorry. Well, some beer should do it – make sure you get light *and* regular, and we'll need some champagne, and perhaps a few bottles of chardonnay, or riesling. Oh, and don't forget the soft drink! At least five dozen. Yes, I know it's a tad late in the day but you could have offered anyway, you know. And then I would have remembered to tell you. How many people? Oh, just a little over a hundred . . .'

## SATURDAY

### 1711 hrs

'Hi, Mum – it's Diane. No, stop! *That's* not why I'm ringing. Listen, you know those little vol-au-vent things you make? Do you think you could possibly whip some up for Nick's thing tomorrow? Yes, I know I didn't ring you back when you offered to bring something. Yes, I know that was dreadfully rude. Yes, I know. But could you still do some of them for us? And maybe some of those open sandwiches you do so well, and some of those puff pastry mustardy-cheese things, and you know that celery dip that Harold does? Perhaps some of that too. How many? Well, say one hundred of each – that should be enough.'

## SATURDAY

### 1731 hrs

'Hey, Cam! It's Terry – how are you? You don't want to talk about it? Great – because I don't want to talk about *that* either. Listen, you know how you asked me this morning if there's anything you could bring? Well, there is. Have you still got that enormous punchbowl? Great! Can you bring that along a tad earlier tomorrow? Terrific. And maybe a couple of platters with crackers and cheese because they go so well with punch. With some celery and carrots. And dip. And maybe some kabana as well. And don't forget to clean the punchbowl, only because it's probably dusty – and, oh, of course! Don't forget to bring something to go *in* it as well.'

## SATURDAY

### 1739 hrs

'Hi, Elizabeth, it's your favourite sister here. No, fool – it's Diane. Yes, I know about the lunch – I was there, remember?

No, I'm not ringing to have a chat about that. But I'm guessing you've been trying to get hold of me to ask what you should bring tomorrow? Ah, I thought so – I *know* you wouldn't want to just turn up without anything, would you? Anyway, could you bring some finger-food dessert type stuff? Maybe some little éclairs, or profiteroles, or meringues, or a tray of baby pikelets with some bowls of jam and cream. Or, I tell you what – just bring all of them.'

## SATURDAY

### 1746 hrs

'Hey, Stephen! This is Terry – getting ready for your big date, are you? Well, best of luck. Listen, is it okay if we borrow that green wrought-iron outdoor setting of yours? It's for tomorrow. And is there any chance we could raid that beautiful garden of yours for some flowers? You *will*? Fantastic. Thanks very much – I'll send Nick and Bronte over to fetch them in a minute. Well, say hi to Sven for me and I hope it all comes off. *Stephen!* That's *not* what I meant, but hey – have one for me.'

## SATURDAY

### 2303 hrs

I sigh, and stretch, and snort simultaneously. It's an art I've mastered over many years of dedicated practice. Then I prop myself up on my pillows and stare at the shadows flickering on the far wall. It's *still* raining, and indeed has hardly stopped all day. It's also blowing a gale, with huge breaths of gusty wind whooshing through the trees and battering the ornamental window shutters.

After all the work that went on here this evening, I should be exhausted. But instead I feel all hyped up and sort of agitated. My adrenalin isn't just running, it's *zooming*, and if the state government were able to install interior speed cameras, they'd be raking in a fortune. Well, *more* of a fortune anyway.

But, hell, have we accomplished miracles tonight. My lounge-room has been transformed into a balloon-strewn, streamer-hung, flower-decorated scene of impending celebration. Diane even found all the pink 'It's a girl!' balloons I'd banished to the powder room, and tied them within the clusters of ordinary balloons. The couch has been pushed against one wall, with the armchair at an angle beside it and the coffee table in front. This has allowed for Diane's two fold-up tables to be placed in an L-shape against the opposite wall and draped with Mum's embroidered tablecloths in preparation for the array of delicacies due to arrive on the morrow. And a covered card table has been placed in the corner in expectation of presents.

The round table in my kitchen area has also been draped and decorated, and nearby a mesh playpen has been set up to house the twins. Throughout the two rooms, Diane's spare chairs have been scattered around at appropriate intervals and vases of flowers have been placed on every available surface, and some that weren't available but quickly became so. And we didn't stop there. The covered courtyard has also been attacked and now resembles a magical grotto – with abundant greenery, roses and huge pots of Stephen's maidenhair fern.

And the kitchen is sparkling as well. Which is surprising considering the amount of baking, and mixing, and conjuring that went on in there over the course of the evening. A cheese-cake, sponge-cake and dozens of fairy-cakes. Spicy meatballs and tiny quiches. Boiled eggs with their insides removed and whipped with mayo and chives before being replaced. Crackers with such an array of delicious toppings it beggars belief. The fridge is full to overflowing, and that's without all the dishes Diane and I ordered from various relatives.

As the activity whirled around them, Nick and Bronte just did what they were told with rather stunned expressions. Pick up the crockery, Nick. Whip this cream, Bronte. Go fetch Stephen's flowers, Nick. Sweep out the courtyard, Bronte. Blow up these balloons, the pair of you. I really don't think either of them had any idea about what it entails to hold a party for over one hundred people. However, their pizza did come in handy for dinner while we transformed the unit.

Poor little Sherry was passed from person to person according to whoever was free. Fortunately I made myself available a lot of the time, a situation helped by the fact that Diane is a veritable organisational banshee when she gets the bit between her teeth. I suppose you have to be when you have six children, and four of them are boys. And when her husband arrived and unloaded the goodies he had brought, she barred his escape route and sent him to work on the courtyard grotto. But what a job he did! I never realised David had such a whimsical streak.

The only problem with all these arrangements was that the new semicircular rug looked so ridiculous in the centre of the room without the couch against its straight edge that it had to be moved. And therefore, once again, the bloody stain is centre-stage. But I suppose you can't have everything.

So, with all this activity, by rights I should be exhausted. I should be so tired that the problem is not getting to sleep, but actually waking up in the morning. Instead I sit here, hugging a pillow and staring at a wall. I lift up one hand and, making the peace sign, clench the rest of my fingers together and hold the whole hand side on. Voila – a rabbit! I jiggle my hand along to make the rabbit hop. However, this activity has limited amusement potential after one passes the age of ten, so I soon give up and resume staring at the wall.

The thing is I've got a niggling little feeling in the pit of my stomach that I know why I can't get to sleep. And it has something to do with what I've been pushing to the back of my mind ever since this morning. Perhaps, whether I like it or not, it's time to go there. So I sigh – and then open the cerebral floodgates.

Richard Berry – son of Rose. Well, at least there's one plus: he's already forty-six so if he were going to develop a personality like his mother's, he would have done so by now. But it's a little scary realising I'm attracted to a person who is the spitting image of someone that Rose was *also* attracted to! Nevertheless, I do feel sorry for her. Sorrier, actually, than I feel for Richard. Because I've a sneaky feeling it weighed a lot more on her mind over the years than it did on his. By his own admission he had a happy, contented childhood – with no gaps.

Richard Berry – *Dr* Richard Berry, to be precise. University lecturer. I should have guessed. Anyone who knows what a dork really is has to be involved in academic life.

Richard Berry – brother of Cam. *That* I've got a little more difficulty with. I do believe Cam took the whole revelation a little harder than she let on. I know for a fact, from our many Friday night therapy sessions, that Cam has *always* wanted a brother. And to find out she actually always had one but was never told – well, I suspect that little item is going to fill many Friday nights to come.

Richard Berry – brother of Diane. I think Diane's main stumbling block will be the whole abandonment thing. I don't have the same problem, maybe because I'm outside the blood connection. I don't know. But I appreciate times were different, and Rose would have had it a lot tougher than, for instance, I did when *my* marriage ended. I like to think that once Diane comes to terms with this mother leaving her only child bit, she'll welcome Richard with open arms. If, that is, he *wants* to be welcomed.

Richard Berry – brother of Elizabeth. Who cares?

Richard Berry – father of Eve. Who is she? What's she like? I believe that seventeen year old girls can be the pits – moody, rebellious and argumentative. Just because I struck it lucky with Bronte doesn't mean everyone else does. And what extra baggage does a teenager carry with her when her mother is dead? For that matter, what extra baggage does her *father* carry when her mother is dead?

Richard Berry – love of my life. And that's the real problem – I think I love him, I really do. It's *more* than a big fat crush and maybe I've got to face up to that. I've been with quite a few guys and I've *never* felt like this. The fact he resembles my father is probably incidental, whether I like it or not. All that means is that maybe I've got the same taste in men as my mother – as *well* as Rose Riley.

And the really odd thing is that he seems to bring out all my maternal instincts, and I never thought I *had* any maternal instincts. In fact, I'd have to be the *least* maternal person I know – and that's counting all the men of my acquaintance, as well! But the way he dresses, and the way he struggles to meet your eye, and the way he fumbles his words – I just feel like reaching over, grabbing his hand and saying: 'Never mind, I'm here, I'll help.'

I flop myself down and pull the doona up over my head to plunge myself into darkness. Because the whole thing won't be going anywhere – there's just too much in the way. Bass Strait for starters. And besides, wouldn't it be asking for trouble to start a relationship with someone who is related to people I know quite well? Hasn't Sherry already tied us all together enough without me adding to the mix? Or maybe I just don't want to share him, not with Rose Riley, or Diane, or even Cam.

Or perhaps what I really don't want is to face the fact he's most probably gone by now. Winging his way back to the Apple Isle, because what's to keep him here? He's met all the relatives, even lunched with them, and now it's back to his life. And I don't want him to go. No, what *I* want is to hire a restaurant or something, and just sit with him for, oh – about a week or so. Watching the way his eyes twinkle when he's amused. And talking. I'm *sure* I could get him to open up if I had half the chance. About everything and anything, and maybe nothing at all. Finding out where he's been and where he's going. What's his favourite colour? What does he like to eat? Why does he dress the way he does? Which side of the bed does he prefer? I want information, and I want to soak it up like a sponge, wring it out and then come back for more. No, I don't want to share him and I don't want him to go.

Not at all.

# SUNDAY

*Handy Household Hint No XXX:*

*It doesn't really matter if the grass is greener or not,*
*it still needs to be mown.*

# SUNDAY

## 1445 hrs

'Terry, can you move that way *just* a trifle?'

'Could you please stand over there instead, Teresa?'

'Hey, that's *exactly* where I need to put this Esky, so can you – thanks.'

'Sorry, honey, but would you just –'

I give up. I leave Rose Riley, Diane, my mother and David in complete control of my kitchen and make my escape. As I move away, I spot Nick and Bronte hiding out in the grotto and give them a wave. Bronte frowns quickly and puts her finger up to her lips, gesturing towards the whirl of activity taking place in the kitchen area. I smile acknowledgement and then start picking up a variety of toys and rattles that have been flung out of the playpen in the corner. When I drop the toys back in, the two occupants immediately toss them back out again with screams of delight.

So, after collecting them up once more, I store the toys under the table and give the twins a self-righteous nod. Then, ignoring their shrieks of dismay, I wander into the lounge-room where I fling myself into the armchair. Because there's nothing left to do, except greet the hundred-odd guests in fifteen minutes or so. The place looks great – it's festive, and brimming with food and drink. Even the weather has been kind, with the rain holding off thus far and the gusty winds of last night reduced to mere asthmatic puffs of wheezy air.

And I look great also, if I say so myself. Partly because I've dismissed unrequited love and timid Tasmanians for the duration of the day and partly because I took quite a bit of trouble over my outfit. I am, after all, the mother of the mother of the guest of honour. I'm dressed in a pair of flared black hipsters with a very wide, snug, gold-buckled belt made of the same cottony material, and a three-quarter-sleeved, flesh-pink little cardigan that does not *quite* reach the top of the hipsters. I've pulled my hair back into one of the waterfalls I've been favouring lately and have completed the ensemble with a pair of large gold-hoop earrings. Not bad at all for a . . . grandmother. There! I said it.

The doorbell rings just as I'm congratulating myself on this minor breakthrough, so I get up, smooth down my hipsters and answer the door. It's Cam – or at least I *think* it's Cam. Because, although I recognise the black silk pantsuit, the only identifying facial feature I can see are her eyes. The rest is hidden behind a silky blue scarf she has wrapped around her head and is holding up against the lower half of her face.

'Quick!' She peers around suspiciously and then pushes past me. 'Quick! Up the stairs!'

'Are you being followed?' I ask in a stage whisper as I lean outside and check to see if there is anybody casing the joint. 'Should I be carrying a piece?'

'Don't be stupid,' she hisses, already three steps up the spiral staircase. 'Just come up here, and quickly!'

'You go ahead, Mata Hari,' I say as I shut the door, 'and I'll watch your back.'

But she has already disappeared towards the upper floor so, more than a little curious, I follow. When I get to the landing she is nowhere in sight so I check my bedroom first and there she is, sitting on the side of the bed and still holding the scarf to her face.

'Look what I've done!' she wails as she unwraps the scarf and flings it onto the bed. 'Just look!'

So I do – and do an immediate double-take. Because the entire lower half of her face is red-raw – a throbbing, aching crimson that looks extremely painful. After I get past the initial shock, I walk over to the bed and bend down for a closer examination. And it seems that it's not the *entire* lower half of her face, just all around her chin and the area between her lips and her nose. Sort of like a neat ruby-blotched moustache and matching goatee.

'Hell.' I reach out a tentative finger and then drop it again. 'What *have* you done?'

'Oh god! Oh god!' Cam flops backwards on the bed and puts her hands up to her head. 'Why do these things always happen to me?'

'What things? What happened?'

'You're not going to believe this.' She sits up again and looks at me with disgust. 'Alex took all the kids out so that, just for bloody once, I'd have a few hours to myself. You know, for a bath and stuff. A bit of me-time. Anyway, I get out of the bath and when I'm looking in the mirror, I find a big black hair.'

'Where?' I sit down on the edge of the bed next to her. 'On the mirror?'

'No, on me! And it was *enormous* – this long!' Cam holds out her finger and thumb about three inches apart, and shakes

321

them at me. 'Growing out of my chin! So of course I pulled it out, but then when I looked closer I thought I looked a bit, well – furry. So I hunted around and found Sam's cream for her legs and put that on.'

'What sort of cream?' I ask with foreboding.

'You know, those damn debilitating ones that are supposed to work miracles.'

'Depilating,' I correct absentmindedly, 'they're called depilating creams.'

'Who the hell cares what they're called!' she spits with fury. '*Look* what it did!'

'Did you read the instructions?' I ask slowly, examining the redness and hazarding a guess as to what the answer will be. 'And how long did you leave it on for?'

'That's just it!' Cam starts wailing again. 'I *did* read the instructions – well, sort of. But then I got distracted with other things and before I knew it, I felt this awful burning sensation and remembered I had the damn stuff on, so I washed it straight off – but look! Just *look* at me!'

'I am looking,' I reply, as I try to think what the best course of action might be now. 'You stay here. I'll go and get some cream for it.'

'Just what I need – more cream.'

I leave Cam sitting on the bed, staring miserably at herself in my dressing-table mirror, and run back downstairs. As I pass through the foyer, Bronte is just opening the door to her father, who is neatly dressed in a dark-brown suit and loaded down with alcohol.

'Excellent!' I exclaim heartily. 'Bronte, grab Nick and give your father a hand with the grog. Take it over to David in the kitchen and he'll sort it all out.'

'Hello to you too, Terry,' says Dennis as he looks me up and down. 'And aren't you looking good?'

'Yes, aren't I?' I reply sweetly as I turn into the powder-room and fling open the cabinet where I keep my medicines. After rummaging around for several seconds, I find what I'm looking for and slam the cabinet shut before heading back out. The front door is still open, but this time it's Alex and the three offspring standing on the threshold.

'Hi, Terry!' calls Samantha, leaning around her father. 'How are you?'

'Fine,' I reply shortly as I put my foot on the bottom stair and poise myself for flight. 'See you soon – gotta go.'

'Hey, Terry!' calls Alex, who is hugging a huge glass punch-bowl. 'Have you seen Cam?'

'Yes and she'll be down in a minute.' I run up a couple of steps. 'So just go in and make yourselves comfortable.'

'Hel*lo*, is that my Terry I see?'

I turn back and spot Fergus, looking rather dapper in a pin-stripe suit, strolling in behind Cam's son, Ben. My stomach does an uncomfortable open-pike, double-tuck dive that turns into a bellyflop as it lands on whatever it is that hangs around underneath. While I'm trying to straighten out my internal organs, Fergus walks over to the bottom of the staircase, smiles up in greeting and blows me a kiss.

'Hi! Hi!' I splutter stupidly. 'Gotta go! Back in a minute!'

'Oh. Okay.'

I turn away from the sight of his face falling and run the rest of the way up the stairs. When I get to my bedroom, Cam is still sitting in exactly the same position as she was when I left her. Same dejected slouch, same woebegone expression, same red-raw skin. I unscrew the cap and pass the tube over to her.

'*Lather* it on,' I instruct, 'and let it all soak in. Then lather some more.'

'Okay,' she agrees miserably.

'Trust me – it's magic stuff. And I'll be just a minute.' I back up towards the door. 'By the way, Alex and the kids are here.'

'Hell's bells! Don't let him see me like this!' Cam says, horrified. 'Oh, and what are they wearing? Do they look decent?'

'I'll check.' I make my escape and run back down the stairs, taking them two at a time till I arrive in the foyer with a jump and some fervent thanks for the invention of sports bras.

'Are you auditioning for the circus or something?'

'Pardon?' I look over in surprise and see Maggie, Alex's sister, grinning at me from the doorway. 'Maggie!'

'In the flesh.'

'Just the person I need.' I lean forwards, grab her by the hand and pull her into the house. 'What are you like with make-up?'

'Hah! I am wearing make-up,' she replies crossly, 'so I'm afraid this is as good as it gets.'

'No, no – what are you like at putting make-up on?'

'Ah! Well, I'm all right at it, I suppose.' She looks at our clasped hands with a frown. 'What's this about?'

'You'll see, come with me!'

I rush her up the staircase with some difficulty, mainly because Maggie is not built like someone who frequents aerobic establishments. In fact, she couldn't be much rounder if she tried, and is dressed today in navy slacks and shirt, over which is a loose red vest that only accentuates her circularity. Eventually we arrive back in my bedroom and I wave an arm towards Cam.

'Ta da!'

'Oh dear! Cam – what have you done now?' Maggie lets go of my hand and moves quickly over to the bed, where Cam is now looking not just red-raw, but shiny red-raw.

'A slight miscalculation with some depilating cream,' I explain as I move over to my ensuite. 'But she's put some good stuff on now, and this is where you come in.'

'Hmm, how?' asks Maggie, still grimacing at Cam's face.

'Hang on.' I duck into the ensuite and emerge again with a small wicker basket full of cosmetics. 'See? I need you to make her up.'

'Will it work?' asks Cam hopefully.

'Don't see why not,' I reply, with a tad more optimism than I feel. 'I mean, you'll still look a little pink but at least you'll be presentable.'

'Thank god,' breathes Cam.

'And the cream should've worked by now. Does it still hurt?'

'Actually –' Cam hesitates and feels her chin gingerly '– no! It doesn't!'

'Excellent.' I start backing towards the door again. 'So I'll leave you with it. Is that okay, Maggie?'

'Hmm, no problem,' replies Maggie, who is already starting to go through the make-up basket. 'I'll take care of it.'

I close the door so that nobody can inadvertently stumble across them while Maggie tries to perform a miracle or two. Then I take the stairs two at a time again and land in the foyer with a jump. After all, I'm supposed to be helping down *here* – not helping up there. A couple of dour-looking people I don't know are crowding through the doorway and they look up at me with astonishment as I land. So I bow flamboyantly. But they move away, looking less than amused.

'Well, *I* was impressed,' says my Uncle Laurie, coming in behind them with his hand in that of his wife. 'Good to see you, Terry love.'

'Uncle Laurie! Aunt June!' I smile, genuinely pleased to see my father's brother and his wife. 'You *are* both looking well!'

'Don't sound so surprised,' says Uncle Laurie with a grin. 'And where's your charming mother?'

'I'll take you.' I lead the way through the lounge-room,

which has filled considerably since I was last here. I spot Cam's Aunt Annie leaning in a corner chatting with Harold and a rather plump man who I vaguely recognise as the best man from Rose and Harold's wedding last February. Next to them on the couch are seated the dour-looking couple who preceded us, and a *very* elderly wizened-looking woman is perched on the armchair surveying the rapidly gathering company with disdain. Some of the food has been laid out on the cloth-draped folding tables and there is a group of young people there sampling what is on offer. I continue to the kitchen area and that's where I find Diane and her mother arguing over the best temperature to heat up homemade sausage rolls. My mother, who is standing behind them, spots us as we come in and her face lights up when she sees who I've brought with me.

'Laurie! June! How *wonderful* – come, sit down here and tell me what you've been up to.' She rushes them over to the table, sits them down and starts filling them in on all the facets of her life. I turn to Diane.

'Need any help?'

'Where *have* you been?'

'Don't ask.' I incline my head imperceptibly towards her mother, who is readjusting the stove.

'Oh.'

'Teresa.' Rose straightens up and glances over at me. 'That's a *very* short top you have on, dear. I noticed that before. Aren't you afraid of catching cold?'

'No,' I reply, because that's the *last* thing I'm afraid of.

'I see.' She raises her eyebrows.

Diane starts to tell me what's been happening in my absence. 'Dennis brought the alcohol, and most of the platters have arrived. Oh, and Alex brought Cam's punchbowl and made up a very nice-looking punch. I've put it out in the lounge-room.'

'Non-alcoholic, of course,' adds Rose.

'Of course,' says Diane, rolling her eyes at me. 'So, Terry – I think we may just have pulled it off!'

'Good on us!'

'And I've been meaning to ask you, Teresa, what on earth happened to your carpet?' Rose gestures towards the next room. 'There's a *terribly* unsightly stain!'

'Oh, Mum did that,' says Bronte, passing through with Nick in tow, 'with some red wine.'

'On your brand-new carpet!' says Mum. 'What a shame!'

'Tsk.' Rose closes her eyes briefly, as if in physical pain. 'Perhaps you should confine your drinking to the wet areas in future. If you must drink at all, that is.'

'I must,' I reply truthfully.

'Well, as they say, to each his or her own. Oh, and listen, Teresa –' Rose dismisses my drinking habits as she wipes her hands on a tea-towel '– I'm sure you don't mind but I took it upon myself to invite two more people.'

'What's two more when you've got over a hundred?' I ask rhetorically, glancing at Diane who smiles in sympathy.

'Yes, so I asked my son and his friend.'

'Your son?' I repeat stupidly, my head whipping around to face her as I try to take this in. 'Your *son*?'

'Yes, it has a ring to it, doesn't it?' Rose takes a deep breath and smiles happily. 'My son.'

'Your *son*? You mean – *Richard*?'

'You seem to be having difficulty taking this in, Teresa.' Rose frowns at me. 'Are you on any medication?'

'I wish,' I mutter as I glance around for a saviour. Unexpectedly it arrives in the form of Elizabeth, dressed in *ultra*-skin-tight black leather pants and a loose white v-neck jumper. She sashays slowly over to where we are standing and leans against the island bench, smiling a general greeting.

'Why are you walking strangely?' asks her mother, looking with thin lips at the leather pants. 'Well, Elizabeth?'

'I'd say it's the pants,' comments Diane helpfully as Elizabeth seems incapable of speech. 'I'm stunned she can move at all.'

'She looks like she's had an accident,' says Rose dismissively.

'Thanks, *Diane*!' Elizabeth finds her voice. 'Thanks a bloody lot!'

'Hey, what did *I* do?'

Phillip arrives in the kitchen area with his arms full of dessert platters and gazes with resignation at the scene unfolding before him. I send him a sympathetic smile and make my escape by tugging open the French doors and disappearing into the grotto.

And it's like entering another world. A slightly cooler world, but one that's beautiful nevertheless. It looked great last night, but the extra hour David spent here this morning has sealed the deal. Lush greenery surrounds my white wrought-iron outdoor setting and Stephen's green one. Ivy and long-stemmed roses have been twined around the columns supporting the roof, and copious branches of something dripping with clusters of tiny white buds have been secured to the beams so that it looks like the ceiling is positively cloudy with blossoms. The fountain has been switched on and water bubbles up and then spills into the bowl, which has been filled with white petals. It all looks amazing.

The only things that seem out of place in the little wonderland are the small fan heater that has been placed on top of the barbecue, the super-large Esky squatting in front of it – and the three men lounging comfortably at the green wrought-iron table.

'What do you think?' asks David proudly, waving his hand around his magical paradise. 'Pretty damn good, eh?'

'Fantastic,' I reply admiringly, 'absolutely fantastic!'

'Who would have thought the old bloke had it in him?' asks Alex with a grin.

'Yeah, he should be in interior decorating,' Dennis says before taking a sip of beer.

'Well, you all look like you've made yourselves at home anyway.' I glance at the open beers, the platter of savouries, and the fully loaded Esky. 'Settled in for the duration, have we?'

'Indubitably,' says David, putting his feet up on the Esky and leaning back. 'Mind you, we had to fight for possession.'

'Nick and Bronte,' explains Dennis. 'Just because they were here first!'

'What a cheek!' adds Alex.

I look at them enviously. 'Save a chair for me, okay? I'll be back out as soon as I can.'

'Sure – but it'll cost you.' Dennis leers suggestively at my exposed midriff.

'You can sit near me.' Alex pats the chair next to him. 'Then you'll be safe.'

'I'll hold you to that.' I smile at him and quickly memorise what he is wearing – gunmetal grey suit and black open-necked shirt – so I can assure Cam that at least one of her lot is dressed decently. Then I duck back through the French doors and close them securely behind me to keep the heat inside. Rose is still queen of the kitchen and Harold has now joined her, so everything there is well under control. Elizabeth and Diane have moved away and are deep in conversation. I catch the word 'brother' and 'Richard' and keep walking. The lounge-room is even more crowded than it was earlier so I decide to go upstairs and check on Cam's progress. Halfway up are Ben and Michael, who are sitting on either side of a stair with a Gameboy each and a cable linking the two. I leap nimbly over the cable and take note that Ben is also reasonably dressed in neat black jeans and a patterned shirt.

When I get to the landing, I realise there is noise coming from each of the rooms up here. I open Bronte's room first to see what's going on. There is a crowd of young females and a few young males in various positions on her bed. Some sitting, some lying – but all fully dressed. I spot Sam, Cam's eldest, on the periphery and take a mental note of her flared denim hipsters and black roll-neck before my attention switches to centre-stage and my daughter, who appears to be thoroughly enjoying her moment in the sun. She is reclining on a pile of pillows in the middle of the bed with Sherry draped across her lap while she entertains the crowd with details of her recent labour. They seem to be lapping it up.

'Carry on,' I say needlessly as I shut the door again and open the study door instead.

'Hey, Terry,' says Evan, swivelling around on the chair, 'is this okay?'

'Bronte said we could use the computer,' adds Chris.

'It's fine. Do you know the password?'

'Oh, you don't *need* a password,' says Evan, turning around to the keyboard again. 'All you need to do is press this, and then this – and you're in.'

'Everyone knows that,' adds Chris dismissively.

'Of course,' I agree airily, shutting the door and then opening my own.

'Where have you been?' Maggie looks at me with relief. 'We've got a problem.'

'What?' I ask, moving over to the bed and sitting down beside Cam who, although looking decidedly less red, is still looking miserable. 'What's up?'

'She can't talk.' Maggie throws a tube of foundation into the wicker basket. 'The bottom half of her face's gone numb.'

'You're kidding!'

'Nope.'

'Wow! I knew it was good stuff but – wow!'

'Hmm.' Maggie looks at Cam. 'So what now?'

'Well, it should wear off soon, so I suppose the best bet is for Cam to just stay here until it does. What do you think?'

'I suppose,' Maggie replies slowly while Cam narrows her eyes at me. She looks surprisingly like her mother when she does that, but I don't think I'll share this pearl with her right now.

'Okay, all settled!' I say with a smile. 'Now, would you like a book, Cam? I've got *Gone with the Wind* right here – barely touched.'

'No – I'll stay with her.' Maggie picks up the wicker basket and moves it over to a bedside table. 'You go see to your guests and I'll keep Cam company.'

'You sure?'

'Absolutely.' Maggie smiles at Cam, who is going rather cross-eyed while prodding at her chin. 'After all, I love a captive audience. And I'm sure she's read *Gone with the Wind*, anyway. Who hasn't?'

'Hullahumph,' says Cam, without moving her lips, as she gestures towards her clothing. 'Hureaf?'

'Yes, I've seen them and they're all well-dressed, so I'll leave you guys to it and bring you back some drinks.'

'*Hease!*' Cam says enthusiastically.

I get up off the bed and, after giving them both a sympathetic grin, exit the room again. I head down the stairs, over the Gameboy cable, and come face to face with CJ in the foyer. She is hand-in-hand with a little dark-haired girl of about the same age and both are wearing party dresses, one sky-blue and the other rose-pink, with black stockings and patent leather shoes. Which is a relief, seeing as I just blithely informed her mother that she was looking decent.

'Terry!' CJ greets me with considerably more enthusiasm than usual. 'Hab you got any games for us to play?'

'It's not that sort of party, CJ.'

'No, not *party* games – you know, like proper games?'

'Oh I see.' I point up to the landing at the top of the stairs. 'If you go up there, you'll find a big cupboard and there's some old games of Bronte's in there. Help yourself. And watch out for that cable there!'

The two little girls dance up the stairs and perform a neat synchronised skip over the cable joining the two boys. They continue up in the direction of the landing, and I continue down in the direction of my guests. As I reach the foyer, there's a knock on the door so I open it and a coven of girls, aged twenty-something and dressed entirely in black, crowd in and pass me several gifts. I point up the stairs.

'She's in her room.'

'Cool,' says the coven leader as they troop past me. After watching them ascend the stairs like an upwardly mobile mudslide, I adjust my armful of presents and shut the door. Someone on the other side immediately knocks so I open it again.

'Pat! Trevor! Bob!' I say with surprise as I see my Saturday tennis team.

'Well, don't sound so shocked!' says Pat loudly, putting a silver-wrapped gift on top of the pile in my arms. 'We did get an invite, you know!'

'Of course, of course,' I say quickly to cover my confusion. But I *had* forgotten for a moment that Bronte played in my team for about three seasons until she fell pregnant.

'So where's this baby?' asks Pat, looking around. 'I want to see the reason we don't have a star player anymore.'

'Upstairs – in Bronte's room.' I shut the door and watch them head upstairs. Pat is being a trifle generous when she calls Bronte our star player because Bronte, although she plays a beautiful textbook game of tennis, has all the killer instinct of a dodo bird. If her doubles partners don't take matters into their own hands, they can just about take a nap at the net waiting for her to finish a rally.

Carrying the presents, I walk into the lounge-room and the wizened elderly lady in the armchair hits me hard in the shin with her cane. Right on the bruise I got on Tuesday from the Rollerblade. I whip around and look at her angrily but she just looks implacably back. So, rubbing my shin, I decide she's probably either senile or doesn't realise she just caused me serious injury. I limp over to the card table in the corner and deposit the pile of gifts on top of the rapidly growing heap. Then I turn to Diane, who is replenishing the food tables with an array of delicacies.

'How's it going?'

'Fine. But have you seen Cam?' she asks curiously as she moves a platter of dip and crackers to make room for some savoury vol-au-vents. 'The kids are all here, but I haven't seen her.'

'She's upstairs.' I grin at her wryly. 'And don't ask.'

'Is she okay?' asks Diane with concern.

'She will be,' I say optimistically as we head towards the kitchen.

When we get there, I lean against the island bench while she continues over to the sink, where she dumps her tray. Through the French doors I can see the male bonding group has increased to include Fergus. They seem to be having an excellent time and I wish I could join them. Then I look over towards the other outdoor setting and immediately change my mind. Because there's Elizabeth and Phillip and Joanne – and Richard. My internal organs immediately start playing twister again as he catches sight of me and smiles hesitantly in my general direction. I smile hesitantly back, widening my eyes to make sure I don't blink.

'Well, well, well. Aren't you going to at least say hello?'

I turn around at the sound of this vaguely familiar masculine voice and, after doing an immediate double-take, leap up into his arms and wrap my legs around his midriff.

'*Tom!*'

'In the flesh,' he groans, and staggers backwards. 'Christ! Good to see you're still eating well!'

'Hell!' I jump down before he collapses and stand in front of him, grinning for all I'm worth. 'Where did *you* come from?'

'Not hell, anyway – although sometimes it –'

'America!' says my mother, taking hold of one of Tom's hands and beaming up at him with delight. 'He came from America! Last night!'

'Let me look at you.' I stand back and examine him. My brother and I look quite similar – both blonde and blue-eyed – but he also happens to be one of the few people who make me feel short. He is six foot six in his socks, and with a generous build to match.

'Do I pass muster?' he asks with a distinct American twang.

'Sure do. But how come you're here?' I ask him curiously. 'And did anyone *know* you were coming? Did you know you're getting an American accent? And how long are you staying?'

'One at a time,' says Tom, looking rather pleased with himself. 'I've only been here five minutes – just walked in! And I've got a week before I have to fly out. As to *why* I'm here, I had a meeting coming up in Melbourne in about a month so, when I got Bronte's email, I just pulled a few strings and – well, here we are!'

'We?' queries Mum, looking around apprehensively.

'Oh, did you bring Amy?' I ask, trying to hide my disappointment.

'Nah, she's too busy,' grins Tom. 'So I brought Bonnie instead.'

'*Bonnie!*' screams Mum with delight. 'Where is she?'

'D'ya know what?' Tom frowns as he peers around the room. 'I don't actually know. We walked in and this little blonde tyke came right up and nabbed her. Got no idea where they are now.'

'That'll be CJ,' I comment, remembering the little dark-haired girl in the pink party dress who was holding hands with Cam's daughter. So that was my niece, Bonnie. I can't be blamed for not recognising the child as I haven't seen her in the flesh since she was in a pram.

'Sit down, sit down.' Mum pulls on Tom's hand and guides him over to the table where Uncle Laurie and Aunt June are sitting and beaming. 'Stay here and tell us everything.'

'Thomas, my boy!' booms Uncle Laurie, slapping his nephew on the back. 'Great to see you!'

'Isn't it just,' smiles Aunt June. 'How wonderful for your mother.'

'Ogoodle!' screams an occupant of the playpen in the corner as she sucks in a great deal of the mesh side and then starts to choke.

'Regan!' says Diane, coming over with two bottles full of milk. 'Here, have this instead. And what *have* you two done with all your toys?'

'I'm going to have to leave you guys, but –' I lean forwards and kiss Tom on the top of his head '– it's *great* to see you, and I'll catch up when it's a tad less full-on.'

'No problem, sis.' Tom grins at me before turning his attention to the table where his various relatives are waiting with differing degrees of impatience for his attention. I take a deep breath and smile at his back for a couple of seconds before remembering I'm supposed to be fetching drinks for the duo upstairs. As I turn towards the kitchen, I glance outside again and notice that both Richard *and* Fergus are watching me expressionlessly. I smile at them happily and walk over to lean against the island bench again. Rose, who is arranging parsley garnish on a platter of meatballs, looks up at me cheerfully.

'How lovely for your dear mother.'

'It sure is,' I agree enthusiastically. 'Now, do you know who's acting bartender?'

'I am,' says Harold, tying a floral apron around his generous girth. 'Is that right?'

'Could I have three glasses of champagne then, Harold?'

'Coming up.' He turns to the fridge while Rose continues to shred parsley and smile indulgently at my mother, almost as though she has bestowed this special gift herself. While I'm waiting, I help myself to a handful of nuts from a glass bowl on the bench and shovel them into my mouth.

'So. How are you?'

'Richard!' I spit a large quantity of the nuts straight down the front of his grey jumper. 'Hell! Sorry, so sorry!'

'Ah. It's all right.' He starts wiping down the more masticated nuts that have adhered themselves to the weave of his jumper, so I help him. Our fingers immediately touch and I jump back, feeling like I've been electrocuted. I look up at him in shock, literally, and he looks back with his eyes wide. It suddenly hits me that he has just experienced the exact same electric shock I did. And, as this idea registers, I see the acknowledgement flicker over his face.

'Richard!' Rose discards her parsley in favour of brushing her son down. 'I *swear* that girl's on medication.'

'Here are your drinks, Terry – is that right?'

'Got a minute?' Richard looks at me as Rose continues picking nuts off his jumper. 'Ah, for a talk?'

'No time. Gotta go, back later,' I mutter intelligently as I grab the glasses from Harold and back away. 'Yes . . . talk. Soon.'

'Good.'

I turn away and make my escape just as Rose expands on her theory regarding my medication. After pushing my way through the lounge-room and keeping an eye out for the cane, I reach the foyer with a sigh of relief and lean against a wall to catch my breath. I might not actually *be* on medication but, judging by the way I've been acting lately, I certainly should be. I suddenly get an idea and, shoving some coats aside to place the glasses neatly on the foyer table, weave back through the lounge-room. After checking that Richard has returned to the grotto, I head over to the table where my relatives are sitting and duck down next to Tom.

'Back already?' grins Tom.

'No,' I reply, rather stupidly because I obviously am, 'no, I just wanted to ask you lot a question.'

'What?' says Uncle Laurie curiously.

'See that guy over there?' I gesture through the French doors towards where Richard has returned to the outdoor table. 'No! No! Don't look!'

'Well, how are we supposed to see him then, honey?' asks my mother reasonably.

'I meant don't let him *see* that you're looking. Be sneaky.'

'Okay.' Tom crouches down in his chair and melodramatically peers outside. 'Yep – subject spotted. Now what?'

'Do you mean the man with the black pants and that nice grey jumper?' asks Mum.

'That *is* a nice jumper,' says Aunt June approvingly. 'I wonder where he got it.'

'Yes,' I agree with amazement, forgetting to be surreptitious as I stand up, peer outside and realise that Richard is incredibly well dressed, for him. Today's corduroy pants are a crisp black and the round-necked, loose jumper, which is the same gun-metal grey as Alex's suit, has black sleeves and two thin black lines across the chest. 'Wow!'

'I thought we were supposed to be sneaky,' says Tom with a wry grin.

'Yes – of course.' I duck back down and wait till I've got their full attention again. 'Now *who* do you think he looks like?'

'Looks like?' repeats Mum, as they all peer back outside and squint at Richard.

'I know – Alan Alda!' says Aunt June, putting up her hand as if she is in class. 'Is it Alan Alda?'

'Do you reckon, June?' asks Uncle Laurie. 'Can't quite see it myself.'

'You're kidding!' I stare at them in disbelief. 'You don't see the resemblance?'

'*What* resemblance?' Tom looks at me, puzzled. 'To whom?'

'So it's *not* Alan Alda?' asks Aunt June, disappointed.

'Told you,' Uncle Laurie says smugly. 'Nothing like him.'

'Not bloody Alan Alda!' I stand up and glare at them. 'Dad! That's who! How can you *not* see it?'

'He doesn't look anything like Dad,' says Tom dismissively.

'Honey! He's *nothing* like your father!'

'Not at *all*.' Uncle Laurie frowns at me. 'What's up with you, girl?'

'I think she's on some form of medication,' Rose confides in a stage whisper as she brings over a tray of drinks. 'Hopefully it'll wear off soon.'

I grunt with irritation and turn my back on them all. How can they *not* see the resemblance? When I get back to the foyer I realise the three glasses of wine have been filched, so I kick the wall with annoyance. I don't *want* to go back to the kitchen and ask for more. I lean against the wall again, this time with my arms crossed and looking like a sulky five year old. A sulky five year old who is nearly six foot tall and remarkably well developed for her age. After a few minutes I pull myself together and manoeuvre back through the lounge-room to the island bench in the kitchen.

'Can I have three glasses of champagne, Harold?'

'Certainly,' he says, picking up three flutes with a flourish, 'is that right?'

'I don't think it's advisable to drink so much, Teresa,' comments Rose as she raises her eyebrows at me. '*Especially* when you're taking medication.'

'I am *not* on medication!' I reply crossly. 'I'm just a tad tired, that's all.'

'Ah! Not sleeping well?'

'Not that,' I say, massaging my forehead, 'just getting woken up a lot.'

'Well, that explains it,' says Rose with a nod, 'because broken sleep is simply not the same. In fact, one hour of solid sleep is worth two hours broken – and don't you forget it.'

'I won't,' I answer distractedly as my gaze involuntarily sneaks towards the French doors and the view of the grotto. There seems to have been some seat swapping happening out there. Diane has now joined her husband, while Alex has deserted the alpha males in favour of a seat between Richard and Joanne and appears to be attempting to engage Richard in conversation. Fergus is standing in the garden with his back to everyone, having a cigarette. Harold hands me the champagne so I give him a smile of gratitude and, balancing the glasses carefully, bustle through the lounge-room taking a wide detour around the nasty old woman with the cane. Halfway up the stairs, I step gingerly over the electronic umbilical cord and continue to the landing. CJ and Bonnie have taken up residence here and have spread an old game of Bronte's out all over the floor. I examine it more closely and am hit by a sense of nostalgic déjà vu. Because it was one of Bronte's favourites, a model kit that was all the rage many years ago called 'The invisible woman'. The two little girls have assembled the shell of the woman and are painstakingly fitting in her internal organs.

'Having fun?' I ask as I pass them by.

'Oh yes,' breathes CJ, holding up what looks like a set of shrivelled kidneys, 'this is great!'

'Excellent.' I kick gently at the bedroom door with one foot and wait for it to open. 'Here you go, guys!'

'About time!' says Maggie irritably. 'What on *earth* kept you?'

'Don't ask.' I cross over to the bed and hand a glass to Cam, who looks like she needs it. 'How's it going?'

'Better now,' says Cam slowly, putting her glass down without taking a sip. 'The feeling's coming back but – damn!'

'What?' I ask with concern as she reaches for a tissue from a box on the bed.

'I keep dribbling!' she says as she holds the tissue against her mouth.

'Hmm, at least you can talk,' says Maggie, taking a glass from me and having a sip. 'Oh, I *needed* that!'

'Sorry it took so long, but guess what? My brother's here!'

'Tom?' asks Cam, reaching for another tissue.

'Yes! How fantastic is that?'

'Good for you!'

'Sit with us for a bit,' says Maggie, patting the bed. 'We've just been discussing *Cam's* brother. You know, this Richard.'

'Really?' I stop en route to the door and retrace my steps before putting my glass down on the bedside table and sitting on the edge of the bed. 'Richard, you say?'

'Yes, and what an amazing story!' Maggie leans forwards.

'Cam was just saying that she's not quite sure how to take the whole thing.'

'Right,' says Cam shortly, folding the tissue over. 'But I don't think Terry wants to hear all this.'

'Yes I do.' I nod to give my words added emphasis. 'Really.'

'No you don't. Because you've got a certain bias in this area, don't you? So unless you want to include *your* agenda in the discussion . . .' Cam dabs at her mouth with the tissue as she raises her eyebrows at me. 'Ah, thought not. So let's change the subject.'

'Hmm . . .' Maggie looks at us both questioningly. 'Whatever. Well then, let's talk about what you were telling me earlier, Cam, about uni. How you're feeling a little out of your depth lately.'

'Are you?' I ask her with surprise. '*I* didn't know that!'

'Not so much out of my depth,' Cam replies slowly, 'just sort of a bit overwhelmed.'

'But you're getting good feedback, aren't you?'

'Oh yes.' She scrunches up the tissue and throws it onto a growing pile on the bedside table. 'It's not that. Just that those kids are so focused! And sometimes I stand outside a lecture room and feel a little behind before I even go in.'

'Well,' I reply smartly, 'no *wonder* you can't concentrate.'

'Ha!' snorts Maggie appreciatively as she embarks on a series of guffaws.

'Very funny,' says Cam, reaching for another tissue. 'You can go now.'

'Okay.' I stand up. 'Actually, I'd better anyway – I should be helping downstairs.'

'Why don't we all go?' Maggie looks towards Cam. 'What do you think, hmm? Better now?'

'About as good as I can hope for, I suppose. How do I look?'

'Fantastic!' I exclaim magnanimously. 'I can hardly see *any* redness at all! And if anyone notices, you can always say you've got a rash from your new bearded boyfriend.'

'What new boyfriend?' asks Maggie suspiciously.

'Ignore her.' Cam gets up off the bed. 'Come on then, let's go.'

'Great.' I lead the way out the door and onto the landing, where the invisible woman is becoming more visible by the minute. CJ looks up and smiles at her mother.

'Look, Mummy! A bagina!'

'Very nice, sweetie.' Cam smiles at her daughter over her shoulder as she descends the staircase behind Maggie and me.

'Watch out for the cord,' I warn as I step neatly over the Gameboy link.

'No problem,' says Maggie, following suit.

'Aaaaah!' screams Cam, flying past us and hitting the side of the railing with the top of her head before crumpling in a pile on the curve of the stairs.

'Sorry!' Ben and Michael both jump up and look down at Cam with concern.

'Bloody hell,' says Maggie. 'Are you all right?'

'Oh god,' groans Cam, 'I think I've fractured my skull.'

'Lucky it's not a straight staircase,' I observe calmly, 'or you would have torpedoed all the way into the lounge-room.'

Maggie turns to the two boys. 'Give her a hand into Terry's bedroom, will you, guys?'

We form an awkward procession back up the stairs and into my bedroom, where Cam collapses in an ungainly heap on the bed. She groans, holding a hand to her head and a tissue to her mouth. I fetch a packet of painkillers from the ensuite and, popping two out of the foil, pass them to her with the glass of wine she had deserted earlier.

'Here, take these.'

'Are you okay, Mum?' asks Ben, backing towards the doorway with Michael.

'Well,' I say cheerfully, 'look on the bright side – at least you got out of the bedroom for a minute!'

'God! My head!' Cam pops the tablets in her mouth and takes a gulp of wine, which immediately starts dribbling out one side of her mouth. She rams the tissue against it and sighs miserably.

'Was that *you* crashing down the stairs, Mummy?' asks CJ, looking through the doorway. 'Are you okay?'

'She'll be fine in a minute, CJ,' says Maggie optimistically. 'So off you go and play. You too, boys.'

'Sorry, Mum,' mumbles Ben as he exits the room quickly, pulling Michael with him. CJ hovers around the doorway and looks at her mother.

'Mummy, is that Rudolph man here today?'

'No,' replies her mother with a groan.

'Is he coming?'

'*No!*'

'Oh. Okay.' CJ swings around the doorframe and disappears.

'Who's Rudolph?' asks Maggie, frowning at Cam apprehensively. 'Is he the one with the beard that Terry was talking about?'

'No one!' Cam massages her forehead. 'Oh, my *head*!'

'Hmm.' Maggie drains her glass and passes it over to me. 'Tell you what. Get me another drink and I'll stay with her for a bit. We'll talk – more.'

'Have mine.' I point to the glass I'd left on the bedside table. 'I haven't touched it.'

'Excellent.'

'Well, I'll be off.' I sidle over to the door. 'Come downstairs as soon as you can, Cam. The painkillers should kick in soon.'

'My bloody *head*!'

I open the door and slip outside to the landing. Bonnie looks up at me curiously and I smile down at her although I'm pretty sure she doesn't recognise me – after all, we haven't seen each other for several years. There'll be time enough for introductions later. She's very pretty in a brown sort of way, with dark-brown hair, golden-brown skin and chocolate-brown eyes. Must take after Amy's side of the family. She drops her gaze as CJ passes her a dull red spleen, which is much the same colour as her mother's chin, and they busy themselves positioning it. I run down the stairs and past the boys, who have unhooked their Gameboys, no doubt for safety reasons, and are dangling the cord through the balustrade instead. When I get to the foyer I hear a door open upstairs and then the sound of a multitude of feet stamping down the stairs. I turn to see what's up and then quickly flatten myself against the wall as a veritable tribe of young women, and a couple of young men, tramp past me towards the food tables. They are being led by Bronte, who is holding a sleeping Sherry in her arms.

Pat, Trevor and Bob bring up the rear and smile at me as they pass through into the lounge-room. I follow in their wake and, just as I step into the room, leap nimbly skywards as the cane whistles through the air at shin height. I land neatly and look narrowly across at old Mother Hubbard. But she's still staring expressionlessly into the middle distance. I think I need a sign here to warn unsuspecting guests before I'm sued.

I send one more threatening look towards the old biddy before squeezing my way through the throng around the tables to help myself to something to eat. I've just realised I'm starving. But the only thing I can reach is one of Nick and Bronte's party pies, because the flock of females have spread themselves around the tables two-deep to forage for food. A black-clad, nose-pierced goth next to me snares a couple of

344

meatballs with a cocktail stick and suddenly turns to sniff the air before narrowing her eyes and peering around warily.

'There's fuckin' bad feng shui in this room,' she announces darkly, 'fuckin' bad.'

Well, that's a conversation killer. I grab a couple more party pies and, while nibbling them, walk slowly over to the French doors. Then I take a deep breath and open them quickly before I change my mind.

'Hey, Terry!' calls Alex, who is sitting back at his original table. 'Over here! I saved a seat for you.'

'Thanks.' I shut the doors and head over to their table, where I settle myself down beside him. Diane passes me a glass of champagne and we grin at each other.

'Seems to be going well,' she says happily.

'Thank god,' I agree, taking only a small sip of the champagne because I've decided to cut down on my drinking today. I've a feeling I'm going to need my wits about me, or at least somewhere in the vicinity.

'Hey, have you seen Cam?' asks Alex.

'Don't ask.'

'God, what's she done now?'

'Don't ask.'

'Okay,' he grins. 'As long as it's not serious . . . is it?'

'No.'

'Fine.'

They all launch once more into a discussion of whether Fitzroy should ever have been allowed to merge with Brisbane, and what this meant for the legion of Victorian fans. I lean back and glance casually over towards the other table so that I can tune in on the conversation there.

'So, you see – if you empty your mind, and I mean *totally* drain it –' Joanne looks around her audience zealously '– it's like giving it a thorough clean. You know how if you let your car run low on petrol and then it picks up all the crap from the bottom of the tank? Well, sometimes *it* needs to be flushed as well. And the mind's just the same . . .'

I tune back out and concentrate instead on the people who are listening in to this theory with varying degrees of interest. Richard is watching Joanne politely with a small smile while Phillip is gazing into the distance, his mind obviously on higher things. Next to him, with her brow creased, Elizabeth is nodding every so often and Fergus . . . to my amazement I realise that Fergus is hanging on every word and looking totally enthralled.

'Richard, mate!' David calls across to the other table. 'Come and join us! Actually, why don't you lot shove your table over here and we'll all join forces?'

As everyone agrees to this plan, the other table is carried over and slid into position. Then there is a great deal of chair rearranging and general jostling as everybody gets themselves comfortable. Maggie comes out as this is going on and is greeted all around while she finds herself a seat. Somehow I end up next to Richard, but with Fergus on my other side. Joanne hovers by my chair as if hoping that a spare seat will materialise on this side of the table, so I surreptitiously sidle my chair a trifle closer to Richard.

'What did you think of our little surprise,' she asks me, gesturing with her head towards him. 'Bet you never guessed that!'

'No, I never guessed that,' I agree readily with a quick smile at Richard. 'Not in a million years.'

'I *tried* to give you a clue,' she continues happily. 'Didn't you notice what I was wearing on Tuesday? Brown bottom, green top – it was supposed to represent the family tree. I can't believe nobody picked up on it!'

'Neither can I.'

'And the other thing I needed to tell you, Terry –' Joanne bobs down so that she can impart this without being overheard '– I cast your horoscope this morning and I'm afraid there was a dire prediction for you.'

'Really?'

'Yes. It was quite emphatic that you had to get out of whatever relationship you're in at the moment.' She casts a glance over her shoulder towards Fergus. 'He's *not* right for you and you're probably holding him back from true happiness – oh, and yourself, of course.'

'Seriously?' I pay her a little more attention now because this seems fairly apt advice, given the circumstances. Maybe Cam's right, and I *am* preventing myself from moving forward.

'Absolutely.' She stands up again and then, as no seat has miraculously appeared, wanders over to the other end of the two tables and sits down there. Where she proceeds to chew her fingernails and watch me carefully. And while it's a disconcerting feeling, I really appreciate the fact she is so obviously concerned about my wellbeing.

'And what's happening then?' asks Fergus as he takes a sip of beer and eyes me thoughtfully over the brim. 'Anything I should be knowing?'

'Why do you ask?' I look quickly away from Joanne and towards him.

'Oh, maybe it's just I was seeing you before – with that guy.'

'Don't be ridiculous,' I whisper, so that Richard can't hear. 'I only just met him, for god's sake.'

'Didn't look like that to me.'

'Well, I did. And I'm not talking about this now.' I tilt my head back and stare at the blossoms dripping from the beams. Every so often a gust of wind filters through and they rustle, with the odd white petal floating down to the table.

'Suit yourself,' says Fergus stiffly as he stands, picks up his glass and moves over to a spare seat at the other end of the tables. It happens to be next to Joanne, who nods sagely at me as if her predictions are already starting to unfold. As soon as Fergus vacates his chair, Maggie slips across into it and looks at me curiously.

'What's up?'

'Nothing,' I reply shortly. 'I don't want to talk about it.'

'Hmm, okay.' Maggie regards me. 'Now fill me in, who's this Rudolph? Cam won't tell me.'

'No one!'

'I'll find out, you realise. One way or the other.'

'Oh, Maggie.' I laugh down at her. 'So, anyway, how's Cam?'

'She'll be down in a minute,' Maggie whispers loudly. 'She's just about back to normal. And I *will* find out – about Rudolph.'

'Good.' I glance up towards the house but Cam isn't in sight yet. Instead I observe her mother, who has paused on her way to the kitchen with a plate in her hands. She is gazing pensively at Richard. I glance at him to see if he has noticed, but he seems perfectly oblivious.

'Look,' says Phillip, who is sitting next to Maggie, 'should I be worried?'

'Oh.' I follow his gaze over to the other side of the tables, where Dennis has managed to position himself next to Elizabeth and has his arm reclining casually across the back of her chair. I can tell by his body language, as well as the admiring glances he keeps casting towards her leather-sheathed legs, that he has commenced stalking his prey.

'Hmm,' says Maggie enigmatically.

'That's Dennis,' I inform Phillip. 'My ex-husband – Bronte's father.'

'Oh,' he says with relief, 'that's all right then.'

'No it isn't,' I reply shortly.

'Quite the reverse,' adds Maggie.

'I see,' says Phillip slowly, staring over at his fiancée.

I'm aware of Richard listening with interest to this conversation but I like Phillip, and Dennis has hurt enough people already. I reach out to pick up a cracker off the platter in front of us and, as Richard is doing the exact same thing, our hands inadvertently touch again. The same electric shock. The same silence. The same mutual recognition. I wonder briefly if it would get boring after a while and then decide that, no – it wouldn't.

'Ah well,' sighs Phillip after a few minutes, leaning back and picking up his glass of beer. 'Beth's a big girl. Quite capable of looking after herself and, if she isn't . . .'

'You'd rather know now?' asks Maggie.

'Something like that,' says Phillip, lapsing into silence once more.

Cam chooses that moment to make her entrance, shutting the French doors behind her and grinning at us with a smile that doesn't reach quite as far as usual. She's definitely not looking her best. Pink splotches show faintly through the thick make-up around her mouth and chin, and the lower half of her face looks a little slacker than it normally does. I'm guessing the magic ointment still has some wearing off to do yet. On top of this, literally, are her eyes, which have got the squinty look they always develop whenever she has a bad headache.

'Hi there!' calls Alex, obviously noticing no difference in his beloved as he drags a spare chair over between him and Richard. 'Sit here, Cam. With Diane on my right hand and you on my left hand, I'll be all set!'

'I'll say,' I comment, 'and pretty busy too!'

'Yeah! Leave my wife alone!' says David with an exaggerated frown as everybody chortles appreciatively and Maggie lets out a couple of guffaws. 'Anyone'd think it was Christmas!'

'Not Christmas!' I cry in mock horror, looking from Alex to Cam, who both flush. Which, in Cam's case, is a definite improvement as it turns the rest of her face the same colour as the splotches.

'Drink, Cam?' asks Diane, leaning in front of Alex. 'Champagne? Hey, are you all right? You look a bit – weird.'

'What's new?' asks Elizabeth wittily.

'Yes, please,' says Cam, sending first me and then Elizabeth a filthy look as she sits down.

'Hello,' says Richard politely, half rising until Cam sits, 'Camilla.'

'Oh, Richard!' Cam looks taken aback, as if she had forgotten his existence momentarily. 'Um, have you been introduced to everyone?'

'Of *course* he has,' says Alex. 'We're treating him just like one of the family now.'

'Poor you,' says Cam, smiling rather shyly at her new brother.

'No,' he smiles back, 'not at all.'

The French doors are flung open again and CJ jumps through, looking around with her hands on her hips until she spots her mother.

'Mummy,' she shrieks with fury, 'Ben stole my ut-er-us! And I want it *back*!'

This statement immediately, and understandably, kills the entire conversation around the two tables. Instead, everybody transfers their gaze to the miniature ball of wrath standing by the open doors glowering at us all.

'He *did*! Mummy!' CJ spits out the words. 'I want my ut-er-us back!'

'More trouble than it's worth, kid,' comments David, the first to get his voice back.

'How would *you* know?' asks his wife.

'Um,' says Cam, looking rather confused, 'he stole your *what?*'

'My ut–er–us! I already *said* that! From our game what Terry gabe us!'

'Allow me to explain.' I try to stop grinning before CJ sees. 'I lent the girls an old game of Bronte's. You know, those 'invisible woman' kits that used to be around? Well, they've been putting it together up on the landing. And I'd say that Ben has pinched a piece.'

'Yes! My ut–er–us,' yells CJ.

'Okay, okay,' says Cam crossly. 'I'm coming.'

'I'll come too.' I put my drink down, get up and smooth my hipsters. 'I'd better check on everything. I'll be back in a few minutes.'

I follow Cam, who follows CJ, and we re-enter the house. I shut the French doors behind us and, leaving the other two to track down the missing uterus, go in search of Bronte. This takes quite some time because first I'm stopped by my mother, who wants to introduce me to Bonnie; then I'm stopped by Rose Riley, who wants to know whether Richard has been introduced to everybody; and then I'm stopped by Pat, who wants to know if I'd like a hit next Wednesday seeing as I'll still be on holidays. Finally, I'm stopped by the wizened old sentinel, who narrowly misses my shin and hits a passing goth instead.

Enough is enough. With the help of Cam's Aunt Annie and her middle-aged beau, I confiscate the cane from the elderly lady and store it under one of the folding tables. Then I continue the search for my daughter without fear of being crippled in the process. I find Bronte in the foyer, sitting at the bottom of the staircase with a group of similarly aged persons, who are taking it in turns to hold Sherry.

For the first time, I register what the baby is wearing and

immediately smile with startled pleasure. Because Bronte has used her old christening frock, which I keep tissue-wrapped in a box on the top shelf of my wardrobe. I had thought of offering this gown but imagined that Bronte would find it a tad old-fashioned for what she and Nick were after. But Sherry looks beautiful. All satiny-white, with six-inch-deep lace crisscrossing the hem, and raised white embroidery across the bodice.

'Oh, Bronte,' I breathe as I shake my head slowly. 'She looks wonderful!'

'Mum!' Bronte looks up in surprise. 'Oh, *shit*! It was going to be a surprise!'

'She's beautiful.'

'I'm glad you're pleased.' Bronte smiles at me. 'Like, I thought you would be.'

'Oh, I am. I really am.'

'Ben! Mummy's going to make you gib me back my ut-er-us! *Now!*'

'Benjamin, give CJ back her uterus,' Cam's voice echoes tiredly down the stairwell, 'and do it right now, please.'

Bronte and her friends all look towards the sound of the voice and then back to me with their eyebrows raised.

'Don't ask.' I drag my gaze away from Sherry and look at Bronte. 'Listen, what time is your celebrant getting here?'

Bronte glances at her watch. 'In about fifteen minutes. Why?'

'Just checking that you're organised.'

'Yep. That's why we're all waiting here. Oh, and Mum?'

'Yes?'

Bronte looks at me smugly. 'Did you happen to notice that all the party pies Nick and I got have been eaten, while there's heaps of your fancy stuff left?'

'So?'

'Like, so we weren't that stupid with what we bought then, were we?'

'Whatever.' There isn't really any answer to that so I send Sherry one more smile and then wander back into the lounge-room, where I'm immediately accosted by a grinning Stephen, who is dressed rather flamboyantly in a loose satin bell-sleeved blue shirt and tight black leather pants – almost, but not quite, as tight as Elizabeth's. He is accompanied by a large cactus on legs. With a sinking feeling I recognise the fleshy protuberances and the deformed, carnivorous-looking buds that are waving in my general direction. And, even apart from the fact that it is now on legs, I think it's grown. I step back.

'Um, has it eaten someone?' I ask, looking at the denim trousers and Nike runners sticking out from the base of the pot. 'Was it one of my guests?'

'Ha, ha,' laughs Stephen gaily, 'of course not – you remember Sven, don't you?'

'Certainly,' I exclaim with relief as Sven, the ambulance man, sticks his head around the side of the plant and smiles at me. 'How are you?'

'Not bad. Not bad at all,' he replies, 'but I wouldn't mind depositing this somewhere, that's for sure.'

'But I don't understand – Stephen? I *gave* it to you! Don't you want it?'

'Oh, schnooks!' Stephen shakes his head at me. 'This isn't the one *you* gave me! Of course not! No, no. It's just I thought it was such a little beauty that I scoured the shops till I found another one. It's for Bronte! As a present!'

'For Bronte?' I repeat, staring at the plant dumbfounded.

'Yes, she'll *love* it,' says Stephen emphatically, 'and fancy you thinking it was the one you gave me!'

'Well, it does look exactly the same,' I say slowly, mesmerised by the way the bulbous flowers are swaying backwards and forwards.

'Ha, ha, ha. No, of *course* not!' Stephen grins at me and then looks at the plant, and the smile rapidly slithers off his face. 'By the way – slight delay with your tax return. Is that a problem?'

I shake myself into alertness. 'Not at all, no rush. And come with me, Sven. I'll show you where to put it.'

Resisting the urge to instruct him to fling it out the nearest window, I lead Sven over to the card table where the gifts have all been piled. Sven deposits the plant onto the floor and I bob down to push it in a little closer so it can't present a danger to anybody passing. With it on one side and that old harridan on the other, it'll be like I've provided some sort of macabre party game – a guest quest. And I'm *sure* this is the same plant I gave Stephen. I'd recognise it anywhere. It probably tried to devour some of his friends so he's decided to get rid of it. But one thing's for sure, I'm not letting Bronte take it with her – I'm way too fond of that baby to risk her becoming plant food.

'Come on.' I stand up and turn to Stephen and Sven. 'I'll get you both a drink.'

'Oh, and sorry we're late,' says Stephen with a coy grin as he follows me into the kitchen area. 'We slept in.'

'No problem.' I lean against the island bench. 'What would you like? Beer, wine or champagne – or something non-alcoholic?'

'Champagne for me, and –?' Stephen turns to Sven, who nods. 'Make that two.'

'Two champagnes coming up,' Harold says cheerfully, 'is that right?'

'Would you like something to eat?' Rose, who had been peering out of the kitchen window towards the grotto, turns and picks up a plate, holding it out towards us. 'Fairy-cakes?'

'How *apt,* schnooks!' says Stephen, taking one with evident delight.

'Pardon?' asks Rose with a frown.

'Here, guys.' I grab Stephen by the arm and usher him over to the table before he can explain. 'You remember my mother, don't you, Stephen?'

'Of *course* I do!'

'Well, the others are my brother, Tom, Uncle Laurie, and Aunt June. And everybody – this is my neighbour Stephen and his friend Sven.'

'Pleased to meet you,' says Tom with his American twang as he stands to shake their hands. The others do likewise and, within moments, Stephen and Sven are ensconced at the table and looking happy. Harold brings two glasses of champagne over and deposits them with a smile as he is thanked profusely.

'Oh, and it's Stephen with a "ph", *not* a "v".' Stephen looks around the table.

'Ah,' says Mum with a wise nod, 'of course.'

'And so you're from America?' Stephen turns to my brother. 'Are you over here on holidays?'

'Yes, he is,' Mum answers for him as she takes hold of Tom's hand, 'and I wish he wasn't going back. Those Kleenex Clan over there really worry me.'

'Sherry,' calls Rose from over in the kitchen, 'stop teasing Teresa! You know perfectly well what they're called *and* that Tom's in no danger.'

'What?' I look at my mother in confusion, but she just giggles behind her hand and blushes a bit.

'I had a dream,' says Stephen, with a reminiscent look on his face, 'all about those Klu Klux guys once. Dreadful, absolutely dreadful.'

'It would have been,' says Uncle Laurie, nodding sympathetically.

'Oh, but not as bad as the dream I had the other night!' Stephen looks wide-eyed around at his audience. 'Just let me tell you about *this* one! There I was on a trampoline and . . .'

I exit stage left and Nick almost immediately calls to me.

'Hey, Mil! Come over here and meet my boss from the garage. And his wife.'

'Hello.' I shake hands with a white-haired elderly man and his wife as they nod a polite greeting. Then the man frowns slightly as he peers at me a little more closely.

'Do I know you?' he asks in a gravelly voice. 'You look familiar.'

'I don't think so,' I reply, although I do have a sneaking feeling I've seen him somewhere before.

'You know what it'll be,' says his wife, snapping her fingers, 'you've probably seen each other at Christmas, that's what it'll be! You know, dear, my Joe dresses up as Santa every Christmas for the kids down at the mall.'

'Really?' I smile as I spot Cam walking past in the direction of the French doors. 'Hey, Cam! Come here and listen to this!'

'Hello.' Cam joins the group and is introduced around by Nick.

'And,' I add, after all the handshaking is finished, 'Joe here dresses up as Santa every Christmas for the children down at the mall! Isn't that fantastic?'

'Yep,' says Cam, looking at me with narrowed eyes.

'Twenty-six years now,' says Joe's wife proudly.

'Twenty-six years now,' agrees Joe.

'I think that's wonderful,' I comment, 'and I'm sure Cam does too. She's a sucker for Santa.'

'That's lovely, dear,' enthuses Joe's wife admiringly. 'Too many of you girls think you're beyond the magic of Christmas. It's nice to see someone who still gets into the spirit of things.'

I ignore the look Cam sends me as I leave and head over towards the French doors again. As soon as I open them I notice that Phillip has deserted Maggie in favour of shoving his chair in between Dennis and Elizabeth. Ah, trust! I slide into my seat and pick up my champagne to have a sip.

'All sorted?' asks Richard politely.

'Yes,' I smile at him. 'Bronte, that's my daughter, seems to have everything under control. So – are you enjoying yourself?'

'Actually, yes.' Richard sounds a bit startled as he gazes around the table. 'Nice bunch. Very kind.'

'I'm going to kill you,' Cam hisses in my ear as she passes.

'Gross!' I pat the side of my hair and then examine my fingers fastidiously. 'You're still dribbling!'

'*Really* kill you!' she calls as she sits down between Alex and Richard again.

'You were saying?' I look at Richard with a grin. 'About them being kind?'

'Ah, apart from the homicidal tendencies, that is.'

I look at him, pleasantly surprised he has come out with yet another fairly long sentence. He grins back, focusing somewhere around my left earlobe and then, while I'm watching him, slides his gaze slowly up until we make eye contact. He flushes, but holds the gaze. After a few seconds, I look away and down at my glass instead.

'Hey, Cam,' says Elizabeth sweetly, looking at her sister with a smile. 'I hear you had an interesting experience with a guinea pig the other night.'

'What!' shrieks Cam, looking from Elizabeth to Phillip to me, and then narrowing her eyes threateningly. 'Now, I'm *really* going to kill you!'

'Not fair!' I hold up my hands in mock surrender, glad of the distraction. 'I didn't say anything!'

'What's this?' asks David with interest. 'What's our Cam done now?'

'Beth,' says Phillip, frowning at his beloved, 'come on.'

'Don't tell me she killed it?' Alex looks down at Cam and

shakes his head ruefully. 'Some people shouldn't be allowed to have pets.'

'No, she didn't *kill* it,' says Elizabeth, still smiling across the table at Cam. 'She just thought it was giving birth, that's all.'

'And it wasn't?' asks Maggie, looking puzzled.

'No, it couldn't have been –' Elizabeth pauses as she prepares for the punchline '– because it was a *boy*! Just a little old frustrated boy who was trying to enjoy himself!'

'Then why did you think . . .' Alex, who was looking at Cam curiously, trails off as the rest of the guys start laughing and Maggie rocks the table with a guffaw.

'I don't get it,' says Joanne, frowning.

'It's like this.' Fergus leans over and whispers into her ear. Her eyes widen and then she starts laughing too.

'I don't think it's all *that* funny,' states Diane, looking with sisterly disapproval at Elizabeth. 'So she thought it was a girl, so what?'

'True.' Alex glances down at Cam, who is staring at her sister expressionlessly while she plays with the stem of her champagne flute. 'And it could have been worse. Imagine if she'd decided to assist the birth *manually*!'

This observation breaks up the company once more. David and Fergus double up with laughter while Joanne puzzles that one out and Diane tries not to grin. Elizabeth just smiles serenely at Cam, and Cam looks evenly back. I glance up to see what reaction Richard is having to this fun and frivolity and note that he is watching the three sisters with a small half-smile on his face. It obviously hasn't taken him long to pick up on the vibes.

'Oh lord!' Dennis looks up towards the ceiling. 'In my next life let me come back as Camilla's guinea pig – *please*!'

'To be sure, you wouldn't be saying that if she'd decided on a forceps delivery,' Fergus points out. 'And she'd be having to use her eyebrow pluckers!'

'Well, you pack of idiots, she *didn't* assist the birth,' I say loudly, lying through my teeth, 'and I can vouch for that because *I* was there too. What's more, I thought the same thing she did. So you see, it might sound funny but it's not that stupid a mistake to make.'

'No,' says Cam, flashing me an appreciative grin. 'And let's leave it there, shall we? I now officially hate guinea pigs.'

'They're really called cavies,' instructs Phillip pedantically.

'Don't care what they're called,' replies Cam, taking a careful sip of wine. 'Hate them anyway.'

'Never been one for guinea pigs personally,' says Fergus to Joanne, 'but we were having rabbits one time when I was a youngster. Ah, but they were lovely little fluffy things. Would you like to be hearing the story of our rabbits, then?'

I watch the two of them thoughtfully as Fergus launches into his rabbit story, which I've heard several times. I'm going to have to have a talk with Fergus at some stage – just not now. At least he seems to be enjoying himself talking to Joanne, who can be good company when she leaves all the New Age stuff alone. Today she's wearing a deep-purple pantsuit, so I'm not sure what that means. But if the glow on her face is anything to go by, it means happiness. I must remember to ask her later what's making her so happy.

'That your boyfriend?' asks Richard, looking in the same direction as me.

'Yes,' I answer truthfully as I pick a few white petals out of my champagne.

'Serious?'

'Um . . .' I look at Fergus and chew my lip thoughtfully. 'Um . . .'

'Ah. And the other guy?'

'What other guy?'

'Big guy – blonde.' Richard looks towards the house. 'Inside.'

'*Tom?*' I look at Richard with astonishment. 'He's my brother!'

'Your brother?' Richard smiles and takes a sip of wine. 'Ah, brother.'

'Yes – my brother. He's over from America.' I decide to ask a few questions of my own. 'And what about Joanne?'

'What about her?' Richard looks at me curiously and then raises his eyebrows and grins. 'Ah! You think – we're together?'

'Well, it had crossed my mind,' I say defensively.

'No,' he laughs. 'I mean . . . no!'

'Oh.' I think for a bit. 'But weren't you staying with her?'

'No,' he replies, still smiling. 'Stayed in a motel. Except last night.'

'Last night!' I repeat in a high-pitched voice. 'Last night?'

'Stayed with Rose and Harold,' he explains, the smile sliding off his face. 'Long night.'

'Oh,' I grin with relief, 'so why did you? Stay with Rose, I mean.'

'She asked,' Richard replies simply, examining his fingernails.

'Well, that was nice of you.'

'Yes.'

'Do you know –' I turn around in my chair until I'm facing Richard fully, and then wait patiently until he makes eye contact '– having a conversation with you is like pulling teeth. Is it me? I mean, if you'd rather we not talk, I don't mind. Really.'

'No!' Richard looks aghast. 'No – I want to talk! It's not *you*. It's *me*.'

'You?'

'Yes – see, I'm not very good with this.' He pauses as he looks around the noisy table. 'With all this.'

'Really?' I try to sound astonished at this revelation.

'Yes.' Richard looks glum. 'Never have been.'

'Oh.' I look at his downcast face and am flooded with sympathy. 'Never mind. As long as I know you *want* to talk, that's fine.'

'It *is*?'

'Sure it is,' I smile at him confidently. 'So tell me then, what do you think of your newfound family?'

'You know?'

'I know.'

'Ah.' Richard looks around the table. 'Nice lot. Loud.'

'Overwhelming?'

'Yes.'

'I know how you feel,' I say with a smile as I survey them as well, 'but they really *are* a great bunch. Especially Cam. She's probably my best friend, and she's really good value. When you get to know her. Do you think you will?' I turn to look at him again. 'Get to know her, that is.'

'Don't know.' Richard looks across the table at Cam briefly. 'Maybe.'

'What about Rose?'

'Ah.' He focuses on my right eyebrow and then sighs. 'She wants more than I can give. A lot more.'

'In what way?' I ask with interest, although I suspect I know exactly what he is referring to. 'Do you mean like a mother-son relationship?'

'Yes. Exactly.' Richard slides his gaze down to make eye contact. 'And it's too late. Not that I have any ill feelings towards her. Not at all. Because if she'd taken me with her as a baby, well, I'd probably have been shoved from pillar to post and been the odd one out when she married again. As it was, I had a great childhood. Really great. Spoilt rotten by two bachelor uncles and a grandmother and grandfather who couldn't do enough for me. Grew up thinking I was the centre of the universe.'

'Wow,' I say with surprise, more with regard to his sudden verbosity than to his great childhood.

'But I'm pleased I've met them.' Richard looks around the table again. '*Much* more pleased than I thought I'd be. Just that I've already got a family.'

'Your childhood was that good, was it?'

'Idyllic,' he replies emphatically.

'And I believe you're a doctor now?'

'Doctor of philosophy,' he says with a laugh. 'Big difference. Just a glorified teacher.'

I smile at him and he smiles back. I notice his eyes have started that disconcerting twinkle again, and it sends a surge of warm pleasure through me. But the warm pleasure is quickly followed by warm embarrassment and I glance around the tables to see if anyone has noticed what, to me, seems so evident. However, they all seem intent on their various conversations – except, that is, for Dennis. He is leaning forward in his chair with his chin in one hand and observing me with interest. As our eyes meet, he raises his eyebrows and looks from me to Richard and then back again. I return his gaze evenly and we proceed to engage in one of those staring contests which tacitly acknowledge that whoever drops their gaze first is guilty – of something. I know from experience that I usually win.

'I've just remembered where I know you from!'

I break eye contact with Dennis and look over towards the house, where the elderly gentleman, Nick's boss, is leaning out of the opened French doors. He points at me and grins.

'Monday night. At the picnic grounds. At around eight o'clock. You were asleep in your car, remember?'

'Oh.'

'Knew I'd seen you before,' he says smugly, '*knew* it.'

I watch as he shuts the doors again and disappears inside, no doubt pleased he has solved that little mystery. I quickly look up towards Fergus, who's paused in his ongoing story of the rabbits and is looking at me with surprise. I flush and look away.

'Often fall asleep in your car?' asks Richard curiously.

'Not often.' I rotate my glass slowly to make the wine slop around inside. 'And what were we talking about before? Tasmania, that was it. So, are your family all still there?'

'Grandfather died about fifteen years ago. But my grand-mother's still there. Same house. With my uncles.' Richard smiles and warms to his theme. 'She's ninety-six years old and they're both in their seventies, but she still cooks all their meals, irons their gear, and probably makes their beds! *And* rules the roost!'

'She sounds great,' I grin at him. 'I'd love to meet her.'

'Then do,' Richard says in a low voice as he turns to face me again. 'Come *with* me.'

'Pardon?'

'Sorry.' Richard flushes and fiddles with his glass.

'*What* did you say?' I ask, stunned.

'Nothing. Doesn't matter.'

'Yes it does.'

'No it doesn't. Actually –' Richard unfolds himself and then looks around the table in general '– have to excuse me. People to see before I go.'

Chewing my lip, I watch him drain his wine and then, taking the glass with him, disappear through the French doors. Did he really say he was going? *When* is he going? Surely he wouldn't go without coming out and saying goodbye? Should I *do* something? As soon as Richard gets inside, he is swooped on by Rose. She takes his empty glass and passes it over to Harold for replenishment before starting what looks like an earnest conversation. I *can't* believe they're mother and son.

For starters, Rose barely comes up to his chest and seeing them together just doesn't seem to *fit*. After a few minutes, Rose takes the fresh champagne from Harold and, using her other hand to grasp Richard firmly by the elbow, steers him over to the table where my mother is sitting.

'Did he say what I think he said?' Cam is leaning towards me across Richard's now vacant chair. 'Did he?'

'About him going?' I ask, still staring inside.

'No – *before* that.'

'Well –' I drag my eyes away from Richard and look at Cam '– that depends. What did you think he said?'

'Come with me.'

'That's what I thought too,' I say slowly as I chew my lip some more.

'So?' Cam slips into the empty chair. 'What're you going to do?'

'What do you mean?'

'You know.' She looks at me with exasperation. 'Are you going to or not?'

'Don't be ridiculous,' I say shortly. 'Even if he *really* meant it, how can I?'

'But this is *exactly* what we were talking about on Friday night!' Cam grabs my arm eagerly. 'This is your chance! You know you like him, so be adventurous! And he likes you too, my god – he was even talking in whole sentences to you! So go on – be spontaneous!'

'Hell,' I mutter crossly.

'Hey, Dad!' Nick calls from the French doors. 'Is it raining out there?'

'Not at the moment,' replies his father, looking over to the uncovered part of the terrace, 'but probably soon.'

'Cool. Then can you guys move yourselves? The celebrant's here so we're going to get started in a tick.'

There is an immediate scraping of chairs and tables and everybody extricates themselves, gathers their drinks, and either moves over to one side of the grotto or disappears inside. David climbs onto a table to straighten up a few stray branches while Diane and Alex rearrange the other furniture to make room for more people.

Nick comes outside with the celebrant in tow and I look across at her curiously. She's a formidable-looking female – all planes and angles and power suited. But when she opens her mouth to talk to David, who is now squatting on top of the table, I suddenly understand why Bronte and Nick were so keen on having her. She has the most melodiously sensual voice I've ever heard. Like molten silver. I listen to her for a few minutes simply because it's a beautiful experience, and then decide to head inside. But, just as I step over the threshold, my elbow is grabbed and I'm steered towards the playpen in the corner.

'Teresa,' says Fergus, looking up at me intently, 'what's going on here?'

'I don't know what you're talking about.'

'Yes, you do. Who's the blonde fellow you were canoodling earlier?'

'The *blonde* fellow?' I repeat with bafflement.

'Yes, the blonde fellow. And see here, can't you at least be honest with me? Because I *know* we've been having our problems. To be sure, we have. Why else were you sitting in your car on Monday night and not here with me? So there's things we're needing to talk about, but you need to be telling me – not leaving me in the lurch and treating me like an eejit.'

'I'm not! Well, not much. But what about you, anyway?' I point at him accusingly. 'You made it pretty clear you didn't want to stay here the other night. And you knew I had time off; you could have asked me up to Daylesford with you.'

'And would you have come?'

'Well . . .'

'Exactly.'

'But there *is* no blonde fellow.' I grasp the one thing I'm absolutely certain about. 'You've got it all wrong. But I can't talk now, really I can't. I'll explain it all later.'

'Ah.' Fergus sets his mouth and looks away. 'If that's the way you're wanting it.'

'No, it's not,' I say earnestly, 'you don't understand!'

'Actually, I'm thinking I do.' Fergus looks at me expressionlessly for a second and then, just as I open my mouth again, shakes his head and walks quickly away towards the loungeroom. I watch him go and sigh. I suppose it's pretty ironic that it looks like I'm going to get dumped for all the right reasons, but for the wrong guy. I should go after him and try to explain – but I'll do that later.

Over by the island bench I can see Maggie having a heart to heart with Cam, which is interspersed by some pointing in my direction. I'd say Cam is trying to explain away the Rudolph business without having to admit to decking the halls with Santa on Tuesday. Maggie looks less than convinced.

A sticky little hand grasps my leg firmly and I move away from the playpen as I wipe my pants down. The twin who had tried to snare me waves her fingers menacingly so I move away a bit more.

'Terry!' says Alex, joining me in the corner, 'I need to talk to you.'

'Really?' I ask, still cleaning my pants. 'What about?'

'Two things. The first has more to do with Ben than me but I need your advice. You know how we, that is Ben and I, have been getting on quite well lately?' He pauses while I nod agreement. 'Well, he came up with this rather odd story the other day. Apparently a few months ago he took a video of his mother in the bath – stop grinning. It gets worse, because he sent it to that TV show, *Funniest Home Videos*.'

'Wow!' I straighten up and give him my full attention. 'You're kidding!'

'No, unfortunately I'm not,' says Alex with a sigh. 'Anyway, he showed me this letter they'd sent him about how they were just letting him know not to be concerned that it hadn't been shown. That due to its nature, it was being put with similar videos to be screened on a special show they were running later in the year called *Naughtiest Home Videos*.'

'Bugger!'

'Precisely. So here's my dilemma – do I tell Cam and have Ben never forgive me, or do I keep quiet and have Cam never forgive me? What do you think?'

'I think I'm glad I'm not you,' I reply as I chew my lip thoughtfully, 'but why did Ben tell you in the first place? Maybe that's a sign *he's* having second thoughts?'

'Don't think so.' Alex shakes his head glumly. 'We were doing this swapping secrets thing. His idea. See, I had to tell him a secret and then he told me one, and now we wait six months to see who can, and who can't, be trusted. This was his secret.'

'Damn,' I comment, 'double damn.'

'Is that all you've got to offer?' Alex frowns at me. 'No pearls of wisdom?'

'Actually . . .' I chew my lip a bit more. 'No. You're stuck between the proverbial rock and whatever.'

'Thanks.'

'So what else can I help you with?'

'I'm not sure if it's worth telling you now,' comments Alex. 'You're not exactly proving to be a fount of advice, are you?'

'Ho, ho, ho.' I look at him and smile. 'That's my impression of Santa, you know.'

'Very funny.' Alex grins. 'So you knew it was me, then?'

'Dag,' I reply fondly, 'who doesn't? But I mean, Alex – *Santa Claus*?'

'There's nothing wrong with the jolly old guy,' says Alex, still grinning, 'and all that happened was that we were cleaning out her garage and found the suit. Apparently it'd been used for a playgroup fundraiser years ago. Anyway, one thing led to another and . . .'

'Of course,' I comment sarcastically, 'the first thing anybody thinks of when finding an old Santa suit is to immediately don a pair of antlers and leap into bed. It's only natural.'

'Not when you put it like that,' replies Alex, looking around to make sure we're not being overheard. 'And now to my next problem. See, I've been sounded out at work for a one-year posting to Hong Kong. It's not mandatory, but if I don't take it my promotion chances long-term are nil.'

'Wow! When would you be going?'

'Probably around Christmas.'

'Ah.' I snap my fingers at him. '*That* explains the early festivities!'

'Be serious,' Alex frowns at me, 'because I want Cam to come too. What do you think my chances are?'

'What about the kids?'

'I've thought it all through,' Alex continues. 'Sam'll be just about ready to join the army by then so she could stay here with Diane till she actually leaves. Ben could come with us, and so could CJ. It's only for a year.'

'So why are you telling me all this?' I ask. 'Why not tell Cam?'

'Because I don't want to mention anything to her until it's certain – I don't want to jeopardise what we have.' Alex glances around to make sure his beloved isn't approaching. 'But I want to have an idea of how she'll react. So – how do *you* think she'll react?'

'No idea.'

'Christ, you really aren't helpful, are you?' Alex shakes his head ruefully. 'What the hell do you two talk about on those Friday nights of yours if you can't even give each other any advice?'

'We *can*,' I reply, slightly stung, 'but we don't usually have humdingers like yours. You want me to be honest? Well, I *don't* know. She's always on at me to be more spontaneous, so she might take the plunge – but on the other hand, she's pretty settled at the moment. Then again, she's having some problems at uni, I believe. But, hang on, don't forget that bastard Keith and won't you need his permission? And then there's Ben and his schooling, but she's always wanted to travel – or maybe that's me . . .'

'Thanks, Terry.'

'I haven't finished,' I protest. 'I was just getting started!'

'I noticed,' Alex smiles. 'But I guess I was hoping for something more definite.'

'Then you'll have to tell her, won't you?'

'I suppose.' Alex sighs and takes a gulp of beer.

'Well, I'll leave you with one suggestion.' I fold my arms and attempt to look wise. 'Confucius say man who does not tell sweetheart about rude videotape must take first opportunity to leave the country – alone.'

'Yep,' he smiles, and then sighs again. 'Yep, yep, yep.'

'Alex, you sound like a depressed dog,' says Cam, coming up behind us. 'And what are you two talking about, anyway?'

'Christmas,' I reply promptly. 'I was just telling Alex how you had inside contacts.'

'Ha, ha, ha.'

'No,' I correct her. 'Ho, ho, ho.'

'I'm going to ignore you,' says Cam self-righteously, 'and take the moral high ground.'

'*That's* a good one – coming from someone who satiates rodents in her spare time.' I smile evilly at Cam. 'And now you two will have to excuse me while I check what Bronte's up to.'

A certain methodical thump, thump noise warns me of the approach of the feminine mudslide so I stop by the table to let them pass. En masse, with Bronte and child still in the lead, they surge implacably towards the French doors and then flow out onto the terrace, where they form an indistinguishable blob over by the barbecue. They are followed by the rest of the company, who are being helped along at the rear by Rose Riley.

'Come along, come along,' she says to the stragglers, 'let's not keep the celebrant waiting, shall we?'

'All she needs is a bullwhip,' Cam mutters to me as she and Alex fall into line. Even Chris and Evan have been extricated from the study and, eyeing off the group of females swarming by the barbecue, are moving outside with heightened interest. The two little girls, CJ and Bonnie, flit past me and try to dodge between the adults' knees until Cam pulls them over and makes them walk properly. Next come Pat and the two guys, each holding a full glass of beer, and then Fergus moves past with Joanne and, without even looking in my direction, holds the door open for her. I scan the crowd as it moves slowly past me, and my pulse quickens when I realise I can't see Richard anywhere. Dully I make myself face the fact that it looks like he has gone. Without even saying goodbye.

Just as I come to this conclusion, Alex and Cam reach the French doors and, as he stands back to let her through, I notice Alex give her a surreptitious pat on the butt. Without turning around, she slaps her hand against his, and they let their fingers linger against one another's for a second or two before breaking apart and going outside with innocent looks on their faces. But they aren't fooling anybody – except maybe themselves.

Stephen and Sven have already gone outside, so now Mum and Tom stand up from the table and, taking their glasses, follow Uncle Laurie and Aunt June through to the terrace. And suddenly I'm alone. Except, that is, for the twins – one of whom is fast asleep in a corner of the playpen, while the other looks like she is attempting to chew her way through the mesh to freedom.

'Ooogle,' she says, pointing with a fat, damp finger towards her escape route.

'I agree,' I reply, trying to decide whether to join the service taking place on my terrace or to stay here and think. Of course, I *should* be outside but I can't quite bring myself to it. Instead, I start collecting discarded plates and glasses and take them over to stack neatly by the sink. Through the window I can see the celebrant, standing by the barbecue and talking to the gathered crowd, which spills out from under the covered area and onto the extended terrace. Luckily the rain is still holding off.

'Spare a minute?'

I turn around and there he is – standing by the island bench with a black overcoat draped over one arm and holding a brown overnight bag in the other. I open my mouth to reply, but no words come out.

'Bad time, I know,' Richard says apologetically, 'but I've only got a few minutes. Taxi's on its way.'

'No, fine – that's fine.' I wipe my hands on the tea-towel and glance quickly outside. But the only person paying any attention to us is Cam, who gives me a surreptitious thumbs-up sign and a huge grin.

'Sure?' asks Richard.

'Yes, that's fine,' I repeat, 'come on, let's go outside and then we'll see the taxi when it gets here.'

'Great.'

'Have you said goodbye to everyone?' I inquire as I come out of the kitchen. 'Rose and the girls?'

'Everyone I could find.'

'Good.' I walk around the corner into the lounge-room and there, still sitting on her armchair, is the wizened old dragon, who immediately fastens me with a venomous glare.

'She took my cane!' she shrieks at Richard. 'She took my cane!'

'Really?' asks Richard of me.

'Of course not.' I smile at her sweetly on the way past. 'Poor old thing.'

'I'm reporting you, girlie,' she screams after us, 'just you wait!'

I open the front door and a gust of wind immediately turns my artful waterfall into a geyser, and then slams the door shut behind us. There are cars lined up and down my driveway and all the way up the street. I spot Fergus's distinctive yellow panel van and feel a frisson of guilt gnaw at the excitement that is churning inside – but it can't destroy it. We walk out onto the porch and I lean against the column, shivering. Richard puts his bag down, shakes his overcoat out and drapes it around my shoulders.

'Warmer?' he asks me solicitously.

'Yes thanks.' I smile at him while I breathe in the scent of the coat. 'Much.'

'You're beautiful,' he says simply, shoving his hands deep into his pockets and looking down at me.

'Oh. Um.'

'You know before,' he says, looking up the street towards the corner, 'when I said . . . what I said?'

'Yes.'

'You know what I said then?'

'Yes.'

'I meant it. And wait –' he removes one hand from his pocket and holds it up but still doesn't look at me '– just let me get it over with. See, I'm not good at any of this. Haven't dated since . . . well, for a long time and even then, wasn't my strong suit. But, well, I like you and I think you might like me . . . do you?'

'Yes.'

'Ah, good.' Richard finally looks at me and his eyes start twinkling. 'Incredible, isn't it? Came here thinking I'd find, well, missing jigsaw pieces – and found you. But maybe, well . . . maybe you're the missing jigsaw piece I *really* need. The other ones are decoration, background – *you're* for real. Make sense?'

'Yes.'

'Then come with me.' Richard suddenly puts his hand against the column and leans across me. 'Come with me. I'll cancel the taxi, change my flight and we'll leave later. Spend a week with me and see where it takes us. I've got a meeting tomorrow but the rest of the week off. And Eve – my daughter – well, she's not due till Friday. Meet my grandmother and uncles. I'll show you round – what do you say?'

'To Tasmania?' I say, dumbfounded. 'You want me to come to Tasmania?'

'Yes – come with me.' He looks at me and I realise his eyes aren't twinkling anymore. 'You'll love it. No strings. Just want to get to know you, talk to you. For hours and just . . . explore you. Say yes.'

'But . . .' I think of the million reasons why I can't do what he's suggesting, but find it hard to articulate them. Which is odd because *he* is usually the one who has trouble with words, and yet he's the one who's saying everything just right. While I'm trying to come up with an answer, I hear the sound of an engine and turn around to see a yellow taxi coasting to a halt at the end of the driveway. The driver honks and then, with his engine idling, opens the passenger window and leans across to yell over at us.

'Are you Berry, mate? Any bags?'

'Yes, it's Berry and no – no bags,' calls Richard. 'With you in a minute!'

'Where *are* your bags?' I ask, trying to put off my answer.

'Airport locker,' he replies shortly before leaning even closer. 'Come on, Terry – what do you say?'

'I can't.' I take a deep breath and repeat myself. 'I can't. Sorry.'

'But why? Why not?' Richard lets go of the column and puts a hand on each of my shoulders. 'Don't you *want* to?'

'Of course I want to!' I yell at him in frustration. 'But I can't! I just can't!'

'Come on – how about just a few days, then?' he asks pleadingly. 'Be adventurous!'

'You don't understand!' I feel a well of panic swelling within and swallow to keep it down. 'I've got work! And the baby! She's not even a week old, you know. And there's Bronte – she's staying with me. And I've promised to go to the gym next Tuesday, and I've got tennis on Wednesday. And my brother's just got here from America. And my niece – I don't even *know* her. And then there's the house, and . . .'

'But they can wait! All of them!' Richard looks at me pleadingly. 'You don't understand, this n*ever* happens to me! *Never!*'

'Me neither!'

'So, come on! Give it a shot, give *me* a shot!'

'I can't!' I wail as the taxi driver honks again and then holds his watch up towards the window, pointing at the dial. 'I've got *priorities*, don't you see?'

'Ah. Yes . . . I think I do.'

'Sorry.'

'So it's a no?' asks Richard quietly, looking at me without expression.

'It's a no,' I reply, shaking my head as I look down at the concrete. 'Sorry.'

'And not just to Tasmania, either,' he says slowly. 'It's a no full-stop, isn't it?'

'Um . . .'

'Ah,' he sighs again, and then suddenly he takes one hand off the column and touches my face softly. At the same time, I feel a feather-light kiss on the top of my head that lingers for a few endlessly short moments. Then it's gone, and his hand is gone – and there is an empty, cold feeling where they both had been. He takes a step backwards and I can tell he's giving me a long and searching stare, but I can't look up. I mustn't look up. I won't look up.

I see the brown overnight bag being lifted up off the porch, and I see his shoes moving away, and then I see them walking down the driveway towards the taxi. Then they pass out of my peripheral vision and, to see any more, I'd need to move my head. But I don't. Instead I start listening. And I hear the taxi door opening, and I hear him get in, and I hear the taxi driver asking, 'Where to, mate?' Then I hear the engine being gunned, and I hear the taxi move away from the kerb and down the street until gradually the sound of its engine ceases to be a separate entity as it merges with the rest of the traffic out on the main road.

And while I'm hearing all of this, with my head down staring at the concrete floor of the porch, I'm also hearing a little voice that's screaming so loud I can't believe Richard didn't hear it too. And why he didn't answer it because it's talking to him, after all – saying, screaming, yelling, over and over again: *stay, don't leave, stay, don't leave, stay . . .*

I lift my head up and realise, with surprise, that I'm crying.

So I brush the tears away angrily and then walk quickly down the driveway to stand at the kerb and peer up the street. But he's long gone. Nevertheless, I stand there for some time, staring up at the junction and waiting, just in case a yellow taxi turns back into my street and coasts to a stop in front of me. It starts to rain, slowly at first, with big fat droplets that splash when they hit the road, and then faster and faster until my hair is plastered to my scalp and water drips from my nose. I lick my lips and the rain tastes of salty despair. I wrap my coat around me and suddenly realise that I still have it, and it's Richard's, so I burrow my head into the lapel and start crying again.

After about ten minutes or so, when the crying has turned into sodden hiccups and it is obvious no yellow taxi is returning, I walk slowly back up the driveway and sit down on the porch step under the eaves. The rain increases in intensity until it's cascading in silvery sheets before me, and I can't even see the road anymore. I wipe my face roughly with one sleeve and then bang myself on the forehead several times. Stupid, stupid, *stupid*.

Because this was my chance. My chance to break free, be adventurous, be spontaneous. And my chance to explore a nugget of promise that had been offered to me on a silver platter. Totally unexpected and shining with possibilities, with no strings attached and nothing to lose. All I had to do was reach out and take it, and then spend some time holding it, and peeling it, shedding the layers one by one until, perhaps, the core was revealed. But instead I panicked and threw it away. I wipe my face roughly and then fold my arms across my chest.

And I decide then and there that I've had enough. Because if feeling like *this* is what happens when you play it safe, I've learnt my lesson and learnt it the hard way. But I'm going to take it on board and I *am* going to change. And if I've got to take chances to make changes, then I'm going to take chances. And if I've got to take risks to gain rewards, then I'm going to take risks. Hell, I *deserve* to be happy.

I brush the wet hair off my forehead, then wrap myself more tightly in his coat and look up towards the road. My face is set with determination because this is the end – no more playing it safe. And perhaps I haven't burnt all my bridges after all. Surely he'll be visiting all these newfound relatives again at some stage and even if he doesn't, there's always the postal service, or the internet, or the telephone – maybe even some sort of organised tour of Apple Isle dairies for middle-aged idiots. And Cam's right, I've avoided anything impulsive or daring or adventurous for an awfully long time. No wonder my life has been so . . . continual. No wonder I'm doing the same things I was doing a decade ago, in the same place and with the same people. But no more. Because bit by bit, layer by layer, measure by measure, I'm going to transform myself, my life, my world – and I'm going to do it quickly. In fact, tomorrow will be the first day of the rest of my life and I know just how to begin.

First thing in the morning, I'm making a list.

## ALSO BY ILSA EVANS FROM PAN MACMILLAN

### Spin Cycle

It's Monday morning and this twice-divorced mother of three has locked herself in the laundry to lament the monotony of her life. It just goes to show that you should always be careful what you wish for. Within hours her life is spinning out of control in a flurry of family revelations, friendship crises, work debacles and the inexplicable deaths of her children's pets.

All in the same week that she sacks her therapist. After all, why pay someone to make her feel miserable when her friends and family can do it for free?

### Drip Dry

The twice-divorced mother of three is back. New, improved and stronger than ever – but still struggling to keep her head above water, even in the bath.

And what a week it is in the Riley/Brown/McNeill household. There's one wedding, two babies, three engagements and four birthdays. Then ex-ex-husband Alex's long-awaited return from overseas heralds unexpected results, which in turn heralds the arrival of a most unwanted guest.

Meanwhile, Sam wants to join the armed forces, Ben is setting up embarrassing money-making schemes and CJ's wreaking havoc with sharp fairy wands.

Along the way there's an infectious disease outbreak, a mysterious death in the family, a broken nose, a bruised rump and several bruised egos. Can life get more frenetic than this?